WORMWOOD

J.R. Castor

WORMWOOD
A Novel by J.R. Castor

ISBN (Paperback): 979-8-9990003-1-6
Published by The Black Rose Press
Cover design by: Stone Art
Author website: JRCastor.com

Thanks to my friend Brett and my wife Kim for the years of dedication while distilling Wormwood.

CHAPTER 1

"Thank you for calling, 'Back in the Day', we have ounces of Durban Poison, Green Giant and Purple Microbus for $100 until midnight Friday. Please hold for the next available budtender.," the automated recording placed the man on hold. Tom Stark waited a full five minutes - an eternity for a man of his importance and something he was not accustomed to. He nearly hung up but he had a reason for this call that was more important than his impatience.

A young female voice finally picked up. "Good afternoon, what may I help you with?"

"Do you have an employee by the name of Dan Stone?"

"Yes, hold please. Dan! Phone!" Tom heard her yell across a very busy store based on the din in the background. A clattering and Dan picked up the phone.

"This is Dan."

"Dan, my name is Tom Stark. I am an attorney from Dallas representing the estate of Victor Stone."

"Uh okay. Estate? Uncle Vic died?"

"Well, I am sorry to say, yes he has passed away."

"Ok. I'm sorry to hear that. I didn't know him well. What can I do for you?"

"Dan, I am calling you personally as I am the executor of his will. The reading is Monday."

"Ok. I'm not going to make that. Like I said, I barely knew the guy. And we are slammed at the dispensary I manage," Dan stated.

"Dan, there is a substantial estate and inheritance. Victor has left you the balance of his holdings. It is imperative you are here."

"Hold on, let me go into the office where it is quieter. I can barely hear you. Like I said we are slammed."

Tom listened to more clattering and more noisy unintelligible dialogue of the crowded retail operation. The bang of the office door silenced the competing voices.

"Ok. Now what's this?" Dan asked. "You're saying Vic left me something in his will?"

Tom Stark cleared his throat and said," Dan I understand you were not in recent contact with Victor. He spoke with me before his death and explained his and your situation. Yes, Victor has left the bulk of his estate to you Dan. You will need to be here on Monday to finalize the papers."

"Why me? I haven't seen Vic since my wedding fifteen years ago. Haven't heard a peep."

"Dan, I trust you will be here in Dallas on Monday at 2 pm sharp."

"What did he leave me?"

"Dan, do you need a flight?"

"A flight? No. I'll drive. If I come. But what did Vic leave me. How much?"

"The details are here in Dallas on Monday, Dan. But I can tell you that Victor was a very wealthy man and has left you the balance of his estate. It is a very substantial fortune," Tom said.

Dan paused and considered what this man was telling him. Vic was rich? Dan responded. "Ok. But what are we talking about here? No offense but I am in Denver and Dallas is about 900 miles away. If it's more than like 50k I'll come down. Otherwise just mail me a check."

Tom was growing more irritated by the moment. He paused, took a deep breath and said, "Dan, I understand you were not close to Victor, and this comes as a surprise but snap out of it and listen to me. Victor Stone was one of the wealthiest men in America. Your world is about to change in an incredible fashion," Tom Stark said impatiently. "They do not allow checks this big so I cannot mail it to you. If that answers your question. Now. Pack and get down here by Monday. You are now one of the richest men in America. I can have a plane ticket waiting in Denver."

"No shit. Ok I'll be there Monday. I'll drive."

Tom gave Dan the address of his law office in Dallas Texas.

Dan hung up the phone as the digital bell of the front door of the dispensary chimed. A wild looking woman somewhere around fifty hurried in the door shouting.

"Help me! Help! Help me!"

Dan jogged to the counter to join his young assistant Toni.

Ma'am, what's wrong how can we help you.

The lady was coming unglued. "I drank too much," she cried. "I drank the coffee."

She laid her heavy bosom on the counter. She was sweating profusely. She was wearing a short denim dress very low cut and very revealing in her position on the counter. It was soaked. Wet through and through on her back. Her hair was dripping wet. She looked like she had been caught in a rainstorm.

"The coffee was too much I need to chill out. I'm so fucking nervous. Maybe I'm having a heart attack," she cried.

"What did you drink?" Dan asked.

"I drank the coffee. And I'm so hot."

"Relax, hon it's only coffee. Come sit down. Dan leaped across the counter and helped her over to the lounge area in the dispensary.

"Toni grab her a joint. Indica. Top shelf."

Dan sat her in the zero gravity chair. "Lean back. This will get your feet up over your heart."

Toni arrived with the Green Giant joint guaranteed to drop her into a very mellow coma like condition in about 3 minutes. Dan pulled his lighter out and lit the joint. Drawing deeply he got it burning nicely. "Here smoke on this."

She took the joint with shaking hands. "I can't breathe," she cried.

"Smoke. You'll feel better soon," Dan said. "You just have a caffeine high."

"No, I drink coffee all the time. It's something more like I've been poisoned or something. Or dosed with LSD." She took a long draw on the Green Giant cigarette.

"What's your name, hon?" Dan asked and smiled.

She smiled back. Dan was a very tall handsome man with long blonde hair blue eyes and an athletes build. "Carla." She was calming down. She took another deep draw on the joint.

"Feeling better already I see. This zero gravity chair works every time. We have some people freak a little on this crazy weed. The high can be intense. Haven't ever had a coffee case before today though," he laughed.

Carla smiled and closed her eyes. She left the joint in her mouth and smoked the remainder without removing it from her lips until it was only about a quarter inch from her lips. When she opened her eyes she took a deep breath and smiled at Dan. "Thank you. I feel much better now. That was pretty embarrassing."

"Don't worry at all. That's the best thing about weed. It cures everything," Dan said.

"Well this coffee is the best thing I have ever had."

"Looks like it," Dan laughed.

"No. It cured my cancer. But I had to drink a lot of it. Like 10-12 cups a day," she said.

"Shit, well that would make anyone heat up," Dan said. "That's a lot of caffeine!"

"It's not the caffeine it's the roses. The black roses they put in the coffee," she argued.

Dan raised an eyebrow. "Black roses in the coffee? Ah ok. Well looks like you are feeling better now. I'm glad. Toni can you make sure Carla is feeling well before she leaves?"

Toni said she would and Dan excused himself and went back to the other customers who were stacking up. Another kook raving about that damn Black Lake coffee. Those stores were everywhere and the nutcases were coming out of the woodpile talking about the manna from heaven cure-all coffee. Name it claim it miracles.

Dan's shift ended when the store closed at midnight. The staff broke down the store and locked up the cannabis and money in the vault. Maximum security in a dispensary as all the crooks want to break in and steal the fruit of the plant worth more by weight than gold. Dan left his store keys with his assistant manager and said, "Toni, it's been fun. I hope you get the job. Good luck with the dispensary. I'm going to home to Dallas." Initially, Dan was part of the weed tourism rush, but a one week visit turned into a month which turned into two years. In the words of the immortal Joe Walsh, "It's hard to leave when you can't find the door."

Dan hoped the promise of money was real but either way it was highway time. He had five days to go 900 miles and claim his new life. Simple enough, he didn't have much to pack. The apartment was largely furnished by Amazon; the bed had arrived in a box with the mattress rolled up into a tube, kitchen table and couch were efficiently cut into easily assembled pieces by the same factory in China. TV was a couple hundred dollars from Best Buy; no great loss kicking it and everything else to the curb. "The apartment maintenance can sort this out." Dan had a grow light and a three foot plant in the closet. "Merry Christmas boys have at it," Dan said aloud as he locked his door in the Mile high city for the last time. Two suitcases and his golf clubs went into the trunk of his

Corvette. In the bottom of his golf bag two pounds of Purple Microbus marijuana flower liberated from the stockroom at his store. "Severance pay."

Twenty minutes later Dan arrived at what some hailed as the best view and food in the Mile High City. He celebrated his new lot in life at Brittany Hill, a restaurant perched at the highest point between the city and the foothills. Aside from its world class menu and James Beard award winning chef, the restaurant reputation carried whispers of hauntings. Tales spoke of a spectral couple seen in the tower window— lovers bound by tragedy. The mansion's original owner, guilt-ridden from a scandalous affair, watched his wife leap to her death before hanging himself in the same spot. Now, they lingered, shadows etched into the estate. When Dan heard the tale he smirked — hopefully, his ex- wife wouldn't haunt him when he bought the farm. Either way, he didn't see the spooky couple. Too bad. A missed opportunity in Dans' mind. Dan was celebrating and reacting in his standard fashion; he cheered, got stoned, and got drunk, reveling in the idea of his newfound wealth and the universe finally recognizing the position he believed he deserved all along.

"Drinks are on me, bitches!" Dan shouted, balancing atop a barstool on the crowded patio at Brittany Hill. Below him, Denver spread out in a shimmering tapestry of city lights blurred by the lingering kaleidoscope of smog. He raised his glass high, savoring the buzz of his unexpected windfall as laughter and cheers erupted from his newfound drinking buddies around him.
Dan danced in the bar and made friends fast as he always did. Dan remained impressively athletic at thirty four. At six feet four inches, with long, dirty-blonde hair and bright blue eyes, he exuded an easy charm. His naturally outgoing personality put everyone around him at ease, making each person feel as though they had just found their new best friend.

Dan preferred it this way. The never ending party soaked in booze was the best medicine. The silence always got to him so he avoided it and glossed it over as best he could. The ceaseless voices in his head caused him to wander down too many rabbit holes that were best left unexplored.

He drank and smoked himself into oblivion. He shamelessly flirted with the waitresses in their tight black skirts and white aprons, indulging in the chef's specialties for both lunch and dinner. Dan devoured over a dozen crab cakes, several exceedingly rare grass-fed filet mignons, and an uncountable number of the bartender's signature cocktail, The Colorado Bulldog—a hefty top-shelf White Russian with a splash of Coca-Cola.

It was late and the full moon was high in the dark star filled Colorado sky when Dan decided to head south and 'get a jump' on the long drive.

"Sir, are you ok to drive? Or can I call you a car?"

"Shit kid, I have driven far drunker than this. I can still see out of both eyes," Dan laughed and lovingly ran his hand over the dashboard and gauges in the cockpit of the blood red bullet like car. He slammed the car door, pushed the starter button and let the horses roar to life. "Fuck yes, life is good," he thought. Dan headed for Dallas.

The drive was long. For Dan Stone, anything over two hours on the road felt like a slog, and this 900-mile expedition was sure to be grueling. The stiff sporty ride of the Corvette didn't do much to ease his growing discomfort. The seat was unforgiving after hours of driving, and the monotony of the open road was wearing on him.

He rubbed his temples, his energy fading, and decided some music might help. "Corvette," he said, his voice dry from the mixture of alcohols he'd already consumed. "Find me a station. Something good. Hair metal from the nineties."

The car's sleek dashboard screen blinked to life as the calm, robotic voice of his android driving companion replied, "Searching stations for preferred genres... locating options."

After a few moments of silence, the sound of Warrant's Cherry Pie erupted through the premium speakers.

"Great. Oldies," Dan laughed, leaning back in his seat with a smirk. "When the hell did Mötley Crüe become classic rock? quoting another has-been rock group from two decades later; Bowling for Soup.

"Would you like me to find another station?" the Corvette AI inquired, its tone politely neutral.

Dan waved it off. "Nah, leave it. Let's see how far down this rabbit hole we go."

The car sped down the empty stretch of highway as Warrant transitioned to Sammy Hagar. Dan smirked again but didn't last long before shaking his head. "Alright, Corvette, something less nostalgic, more badass. Got anything?"

The computer paused before responding, "Accessing curated high-energy playlists. Playing now."

Charlie Daniels' The Legend of Wooly Swamp suddenly filled the cabin, the eerie lyrics giving him an unexpected chill. He scowled at the dashboard. "Seriously? Corvette, are you trying to fuck with me?"

"This song has a high-energy tempo. Is it not to your liking?"

"No, it's creepy as hell."

"Understood. Searching for alternatives."

As the car's system scoured the airwaves again, Dan reached behind the passenger seat, fumbling for his backup plan. His hand finally closed around the neck of the bottle he kept stashed there for just such occasions. By the time the voice of the AI cheerfully announced, "No stations available," Dan had already cracked the seal on his bottle of Johnny Walker scotch.

"Guess it's you and me, Johnny," he muttered, taking a swig as the car hummed along the endless road. Nothing like a stiff drink to keep the boredom—and the creeping sleepiness—at bay. He was wishing he had brought Toni along for company and other whatnots.

Through the speakers came Charlie Daniels again.

'There's things out there in the middle them woods will make a strong man die from fright.'

"Corvette. What the Fuck? Turn that shit off and find something else."

The audio attendant did not acknowledge his retort. The haunting lyrics continued.

"Corvette.... Corvette... Mother Fucker!" Dan yelled, pushing the screen and trying to find an off button at the very least. To no avail. Dan angrily slammed on the brakes fishtailing and hitting a patch of pavement slick with sand. The sports car spun 360 degrees and came to a halt at an angle to the road. The radio was silent. The car idled gruffly.

"Jesus Fucking Christ hanging on the fucking cross!" he panted. "That was just about it for you Danny. Fuck." Dan worked to catch his breath and tipped the nearly empty bottle of scotch. Finishing it off. He unbuckled his seat belt and hit the door button. The switchblade doors instantly responded and opened to let the hot humid Colorado air into the cockpit. Dan climbed out and walked around the car coming all the way around and took a leaning seat on the hood. The night was country dark with no moon but with what seemed like one million stars offering no respite to the total pitch-black emptiness.

"Okay Dan, relax. Probably be somewhere soon. You're awake now."

The words to that damn song refused to leave his head, looping endlessly like a haunting refrain. Times like that made Dan wonder if this was how insanity crept in—an unrelenting, gnawing thought pulling someone over the edge.

It was the quiet times that were the worst. They forced him to sit there and listen to his own thoughts, with little or no interruption. The silence gave his mind too much space to wander, to dwell on things best left buried.

He smirked bitterly. That's why I keep my alter egos at bay with weed, booze, and rock and roll.

Ha! It wasn't the healthiest strategy, but it worked—for now.

'Feed him to the alligators.'

Dan had never seen an alligator in Kansas. Probably not there, but if one of those devilish creatures somehow found its way into town, he was sure it would end up near him. Alligators were worse than spiders and snakes in his book. At least with the latter, they'd just poison you or suck your blood. But an alligator? That thing might actually eat you—turn you into an unhappy meal.

Being eaten alive, he thought, might just be the worst way to go.

He shook his head and muttered, "Snap out of it, Dan. Be glad you are in the middle of nowhere Colorado and not in the woolly swamp."

But no matter how much he tried to redirect his thoughts; those haunting lyrics wouldn't stop looping in his brain. Damn Charlie Daniels.

Dan gripped the steering wheel a little tighter and pulled the roaring sportscar to the side of the dark road, edging nearly into the deep grassy drainage ditch lining the country road. He needed some sleep. He was drunk and it was dark. And now these creepy lyrics were working his mind into a frenzy. And with zero cell service out here he only had his burgeoning madness to keep him company. Dan was on the edge of an anxiety attack in the middle of nowhere.

"Rusty mason jars he just dug up out of the sand..."

The words echoed in his mind, sticking to him like glue. Why the hell is this song in my head? he wondered. The quiet was amplifying everything, every unsettling word.

It was like coming down off an acid trip back in college, when his brain was stuck in overdrive, when his crazy thoughts refused to stop no matter how hard he tried to will them away. He thought of that acid trip now a decade and a half in his past and how it had changed his life. And not for the better.

He shut down the powerful engine and sat in silence. He closed his eyes. Just some sleep, he thought.

Dan reflected on that terrible time. That acid trip didn't just change his life—it fractured it, leaving pieces he could never quite put back together. As he squeezed his eyes shut, he tried to think of anything else. The lyrics about the old man being butchered and getting the last laugh played over and over in his mind, like a haunting echo from a speaker lodged inside his skull despite his efforts.

He pictured vividly the fateful night of his bad experience with LSD, no matter how much he wished he could forget—or better yet, go back in time and erase it altogether. It was Dan, Eddie, and Bob, two of his closest friends. They had purchased a few hits of purple pyramid blotter acid from a fellow student's older brother who worked at Chi Chis Mexican restaurant as a waiter. In Dan's tiny two-room apartment in downtown Wichita the three friends tripped on acid.

That was an experience, all right. An experience he'd give anything to undo. They spent the entire day in that living room, too terrified to leave the protective confines of its walls. They watched TV, listened to the stereo, and freaked out over how incredible it was to watch a popcorn bag expand in the microwave. But those mundane fascinations with the eroding psyche were only the beginning.

Dan wanted to wash that memory from the fabric of his existence. He had been closer to Eddie and Bob than anyone else in the world. Yet that day, the things they saw—the things that simply weren't there—altered how he perceived everything.

The Jim Morrison life-sized poster behind his door became a living, breathing thing, darting its eyes from side to side as if plotting something sinister. But it wasn't just Morrison. Across the room hung another piece on an otherwise empty wall, gifted to him by Aunt Margie, Andrew Wyeth's Christina's World, an image that always unsettled Dan in ways he couldn't explain. Tonight, though, it became alive in a way he would never forget.

The woman, Christina, began to stir. Her frail figure on the tawny field seemed to twitch, then jerk unnaturally. Dan's heart pounded as her head turned slowly toward him. The helpless figure was no longer gazing at the distant house—it was staring at him. Her eyes, dark and hollow, bore into his soul, accusing, pleading, warning. She clawed at the earth beneath her, dragging her wasted legs as she began crawling, inching closer to the edge of the frame.

Dan couldn't move. The field in the painting seemed to expand, spilling out of its frame, the golden hues mixing with the muted browns of his apartment floor. He could hear her labored breaths, see the raw determination etched into her face. Her voice scratched at the edge of his mind, low and rasping, but he couldn't make out the words. It felt like a call for help—or a curse -- a sob every few moments.

Suddenly, the figure snapped back into the painting with an unnatural force, the frame trembling slightly as if to remind him it was just an image. But Dan knew better. The hallucination burned itself into his psyche, joining Morrison's mocking grin as fragments of a reality he could no longer trust.

Panting, he looked around the apartment, desperate for something familiar. But everything seemed warped now, as if the objects in his life carried a hidden malice, waiting for their turn to haunt him. The ordinary world was slipping away, and Dan wasn't sure he wanted it back.

And Eddie? Eddie did magic.

Dan didn't know how else to describe it. Eddie's hands moved as if conjuring the air itself, creating patterns and movements that made time seem to warp and flow in unnatural ways.

It was terrifying and mesmerizing, beautiful and grotesque—a kaleidoscope of madness he hadn't asked for but could never quite escape.

At one point Eddie held up a bottle of Three Olives Vodka and told Dan and Bob what they would see in it if they looked real closely into the bottom. And they saw. Dan saw more than he cared to.

"What the hell is it?" Dan asked.

"That is it exactly Dan, it is hell. Inside this bottle is hell and if you stare into the bottom of the bottle, you will see pain and gnashing of teeth...agony worse than any nightmare you have ever experienced and punishment more intense and cruel than the human mind can even imagine. You can see demons and whores of the devil dancing at his feet. The flames you see are real. You are there and you want to go home but your only home is the fiery pits of hell. You will always be trapped in the bottle...a single bottle on the shelf of a mad scientist whose only joy is watching you suffer," Eddie laughed.

"God Damn, shut the fuck up Eddie you're making me freak out. Jerk. Let's have a good trip," Dan stammered his voice training off.

Too late. Dan was there. He could feel everything just like he was there in Eddies nightmarish fantasy world. Dan stammered, "Fucking..." He was beginning to shake all over and heat up. Sweat started to run from his pores. Tears started to run down his face. The acid was doing what it was supposed to do. He was wigging out. A bad trip. LSD can be either very positive or very negative. This was a big negative. Dan could think of nothing other than how badly he wanted this trip to end and how much he wished he hadn't gone down this road. That did not work. He had to ride it out.

He was slipping off the precipice fast. His two friends, Eddie and Bob, had morphed into lifeless monochrome shadows, their outlines flickering like ghosts with the room changing to every color in the spectrum before Dan's dilated eyes.

The room warped and pulsed, colors bleeding into one another like spilled paint on a forgotten canvas. Dan stared at the Jim Morrison poster on the wall, the one he'd passed every day without much thought. Tonight, though, it seemed different. Alive.

A voice from the corner of the room: "Come to hell kid. You wanted to dance with the devil. Here is your big chance." The poster of Jim Morrison was coming alive. His mouth was moving up and down robotically like a paper puppet. His mouth and his eyes. Dan was scared. He could see the strings on his coal black electric guitar shaking with each strum of the music shaking Dan's body with the reverberation.

Dan fell to his knees panting and crawled to the poster on his wall. He reached up to tear it down and silence the image forever.

The smoky blue haze of the poster began to ripple as if caught in a breeze. Jim's piercing eyes, always distant and enigmatic, suddenly locked onto Dan's. His lips moved, though no sound emerged at first. Then, with a low, resonant timbre that seemed to shake the air itself, he spoke.

"You've been looking for me, haven't you, Dan?"

He stared up at the giant likeness of Morrison. Dan blinked, trying to shake the hallucination, but Jim didn't fade. Instead, the image peeled away from the wall, like wet paper curling back from the heat. Morrison stepped out of the poster; his leather-clad figure somehow more vivid than anything else in the dimly lit room.

An engineer boot extended from the picture and the boot heal stomped down the right side of Dan's face smashing into his cheek and nose. The boot was black leather and had a chain wrapped around the ankle. He could smell the leather boot and feel an ice-cold wind that seemed to emit directly from it. He raised a hand to his face and pulled back blood from his battered nose.

The acid was too much for his human brain. He was in the middle of a breakdown.

Dan cried out and cowered in the corner between the door and his poster pressing himself into the carpet, willing himself small and invisible. He looked out to the small apartment living room. He was alone. Eddie and Bob had abandoned him.

Morrison stepped across Dan's body laying prostrate on the floor and slowly walked through the room.

"You think you're the lizard king?" Jim asked, a smirk curling his lips. "You're not even the lizard jester."

Dan struggled to his knees, his breath quickening. He couldn't tell if he was laughing or crying. "What the hell is this?"

Jim spread his arms wide, as if inviting Dan into some cosmic joke he couldn't yet understand. "This is it, man. The great cosmic absurdity. You're caught in the wheel, spinning round and round, thinking you're in control. But you're not. None of us are."

The room around Dan twisted further, the walls bending and melting into one another. The poster, now just a blank white rectangle on the wall, seemed to mock him with its absence. Jim gestured toward the glowing remnants of the popcorn bag lying on the light oak wagon wheel coffee table, its expansion earlier having fascinated them for hours.

"That's you, man. Expanding, contracting, thinking you've got purpose. But what are you, really? Hot air in a plastic shell."

Dan tried to speak, but the words caught in his throat. Morrison leaned in close, his voice dropping to a conspiratorial whisper. "The doors, Dan. You've opened one, but there are so many more. The question is, are you ready to step through? Or are you just going to sit here and melt into the couch?"

Dan looked at the legendary figure before him, larger than life and yet so terrifyingly intimate. The air felt thick, electric. Jim's eyes glowed faintly now, like twin embers burning with some secret knowledge.

"Step through what?" Dan finally managed to choke out.

Jim grinned wide, his teeth sharp and gleaming. He raised his hand and pointed to the door across the room, its edges now flickering with an unnatural golden light.

"That, my friend," Jim said, his voice echoing with a surreal clarity, "is the beginning. Or the end. Depends on your perspective."

"The time has come for you to realize who you are boy. You are one of my finest works of art. I gave you this much time to adapt to the new world surroundings so you can more properly do my work, Jim said sitting down on the couch.

His leather pants creaked as he sat. The chain on his jacket clinked against Dan's retro 1950's green and yellow plaid fabric couch, handmade by Uncle Ira in his downtown Wichita upholstery shop years before.

The room wasn't safe. It shifted constantly, cycling through every color in the spectrum, from fiery reds to icy blues, then bleeding into neon greens and ultraviolet purples. The walls pulsed and warped like a living organism, closing in, then expanding outward as if breathing.

Dan tried to focus, tried to ground himself, but the visuals were relentless, dragging him deeper into the surreal. Jim, impossibly cool, crossed one leg over the other and smirked, his presence a taunting reminder that Dan's grip on reality was gone.

Dan was properly broken by this time and sat in the corner moaning and wheezing. Blood from his damaged nose had formed like a bib down the front of his favorite white, Pink Floyd concert shirt. He could not look away or blank his mind or stop listening to the voice in his head that created this all-too-real seeming person sitting with his feet propped up on his wagon wheel coffee table. Everything about him seemed so real that he began to think it would be illogical to doubt his reality. Real enough. He was beyond words.

"You will soon remember your past lives, my friend," Morrison said, his voice dripping with both menace and allure. "That's the consequence of your journey, one I will savor solving in time. God may claim to be the shepherd of souls, but me?" He leaned closer, his grin revealing teeth that seemed too sharp. "I'm the punisher for those who stray—those who thrive on the darker instincts of humanity. You'll remember it all soon enough: the pain, the blood, the choices that brought you here. But not until you've been fully forged into one of my eternal servants."

Dan's breath caught, but he couldn't move, trapped as though the air itself had thickened around him.

Morrison chuckled darkly, gesturing toward the shadowy corners of the room. "Even your so-called friends, Dan—they're mine too. They might not reach your level of... potential," he said, dragging out the word like a serpent hissing, "but they serve faithfully, in their way."

Dan tried to speak, but his voice came out in gasping croaks.

"Don't worry, son," Morrison continued, his tone mockingly fatherly. "We'll meet again. Not for a while, though. I'll let you doubt all of this first, wrestle with it, fight against it. Denial makes the fall so much sweeter."

Then, without warning, Morrison stood and strode toward Dan. His poster on the wall loomed behind him like a gaping maw. He moved with unnatural grace, his boots silent on the floor. Before Dan could react, Morrison grabbed a handful of his hair, yanking him upward with impossible strength.

Dan's head slammed against the plaster popcorn ceiling, the impact sending flakes cascading down into his hair and onto the rose-colored carpet. Pain shot through his skull, but it was drowned out by the sheer terror of Morrison's laughter—wild, hysterical, and endless.

"You're going to be magnificent," Morrison whispered, his eyes glowing with a cruel, knowing light. Then, with a casual flick of his wrist, he hurled Dan across the room like a ragdoll.

Dan's body collided with the couch, the old springs groaning beneath him as he landed in a heap. Morrison turned back toward the poster, his form beginning to blur and dissolve like smoke caught in reverse.

"I'll see you soon, Dan," his voice echoed, no longer human, but something far more sinister.

With a final step, Morrison melted back into the poster. It hung there on the wall, still and lifeless once more. Dan lay frozen on the couch, his chest heaving, staring at the unassuming image that had just shattered every boundary of reality he thought he understood.

Dan closed his eyes and shook his head. He tried to open his eyes but could not see anything. He saw only spinning dizzying colors, even when he closed his eyes. He leaned forward and threw up in front of him. He thought he was on the couch. And maybe he was. Morrison was gone. He heard nothing, no sound at all. Silence in the room. He tried to relax. He tried to catch his breath.

He slipped into some disturbed kind of sleep then slid further into a hellish nightmare. Dan saw himself as a third-party bystander watching the show. He was in the throes of the acid trip with Bob and Eddie, looking into the bottom of the vodka bottle, but he was out of control. He was jumping around yelling something about blood being all over the floor. The half gallon bottle of Three Olives Vodka was smashed on the coffee table. He stared at the broken bottle. His line of sight shifted and like a dream frame the neck of the broken bottle was sticking out of Bob's mouth. He saw the picture completely then; both of his young friend's throats had been slashed to ribbons with the glass from the bottle. Blood was coming out of the broken bottle neck like a faucet in a maple tree. The room spun and spun. Blackness enveloped Dan, his friends, the apartment. All Dans reality was sucked down into the abyss.

After a time, Dan awoke with the morning sun heating his face and back. Saying a silent prayer to God for allowing him to survive the night Dan pealed his eyes open. Thankful that his memories of the acid trip were finally over, and the nightmare was behind him, just a product of a chemically disturbed psyche. He lifted his head off the floor and noticed his cheap rose-colored shag carpet, recently installed as an upgrade from lime green for his second year of residence, was wet. Dan rubbed sleep from his eyes, turned around and saw his two dead friends leaning against each other, propped up by each other's settling rigor mortis and sitting in a lake of blood. Their throats were cut.

A flash of light and a horn brought Dan back to the confines of his Corvette in his current day. He could hear himself moaning. He was crying. Dan was white knuckle gripping the neck of the bottle of Johnny Walker Scotch. His shaking hands lifted the bottle, and he took a big swig to center himself and wiped the tears from his eyes, adjusting to his surroundings at the side of the road.

"I'm still in the middle of nowhere, somewhere south of the mountain. Snap out of it Dan. You're fucking losing it."

Dan hit the starter, and the car roared to life, its engine echoing through the emptiness around him. The memories clawed their way back into his consciousness—decades old, yet still as sharp and disturbing as the day they had seared into his mind. The acid trip, Eddie's twisted theatrics of hell, and that nightmarish vision of Morrison stepping out of the poster—it was all a delusion. At least, that's what he told himself. But even now, it felt too real to dismiss entirely.

He gripped the wheel tighter, as if the force of his hands could crush the thoughts threatening to surface. Quiet moments like these always betrayed him, squeezing his mind like a vice and milking the dark, unwelcome memories from the shadowed recesses no one should ever explore.

The past was a predator, lurking just behind him, ready to pounce when he was most vulnerable. Dan shook his head, trying to clear the images. "Focus," he muttered to himself, his voice low and strained. "It's all in the past. It's just noise."

The Corvette growled in agreement as Dan hit the gas, the car surging forward, its raw power pulling him away from the silence and toward the unknown.

The miles passed rapidly. Another swig of black label, another joint of the Purple Microbus and the trees became blurry and the scenery irrelevant. Dan could sense he was nearly somewhere civilized. He had a feeling of doom he couldn't explain. He rationalized that it must just be the alone time causing these old anxious memories to bubble to the surface. It had been years since he allowed his mind to recall his old friends. And then there was his ex-wife Becca. Would he see her again now that he was coming back to Dallas? He could feel a sickness threatening in the pit of his stomach. A burning. An awareness like a rat gnawing at his guts.

CHAPTER 2

The next morning Dan watched the sunrise still unnerved by the visions of the night before. Sometime in the night he found a turnoff and passed out in the blackness of the Colorado night. Dan smoked a joint to wake up and clear his head and continue his journey to Dallas and his appointment with Uncle Vic's money.

Victor, his father's older brother, had always been a figure on the periphery of Dan's life. In fact, Dan couldn't recall a single significant conversation with the man.

Growing up, Dan had seen Vic maybe half a dozen times over twice as many years. Twenty years his senior, Vic had always been more of a concept than a presence—a passing conversation at family gatherings about his brilliant uncle inventing new chemicals somewhere in California. The anecdotes were impressive, sure, but distant.

To Dan, Vic had been little more than a name associated with success, a genius chemist whose life bore no resemblance to Dan's own. He never thought to ask questions about Vic, nor did Vic make any effort to bridge the gap.

We're family, Dan thought, but only on paper.

The news of Vic's death didn't exactly stir an emotional reaction in Dan. Indifference, if anything. He stared out at the road ahead, processing the information with little more than a shrug. It was just one more piece of news, one more chapter closing on a life he'd barely registered in the first place.

Vic had always been the family's black sheep, though the reasons were a mystery to Dan. He had lived a quiet, solitary life, shunning the usual ties that kept families connected. As far back as Dan could remember, Vic had never married and rarely reached out to anyone in the extended family. To Dan, he was just another distant relative fading into obscurity—a man who seemed to be quietly counting down the days in some backwoods corner of the country.

Vic was a bit of a family legend as he was rumored to be very wealthy as a result of some new chemical food additives. Yes, Vic had managed to amass a fortune—an incredible fortune--- But more food additives and chemicals to put into our bodies? RFK likely hated this guy, Dan thought.

Life was about choices, he thought—a slight twist, a shift in the wind, and suddenly everything changes. Life really was a game of inches. One splinter in the wrong direction, and the entire story plays out differently. Vic can attest to that.

Dan smirked at the metaphor. It was just like golf. One push too far on his club, and he was in the rough, chasing a ball that wasn't going anywhere good. And so far? His life had been a series of missed putts and overswings. Sure, he was still on the course, but he had spent more time frustrated than winning.

Now, though, things were about to change. Whether it was luck, divine intervention, or plain old coincidence, Vic's fortune was his second chance. Do not screw it up this time, he told himself.

Dan Stone's had no way of knowing what the future held. The curse of man, after all, is to navigate the universe while trapped in the relentless current of time, unable to see what lies ahead or change what is already behind.

Hell, what did Dan really have holding him here in Colorado? Legal weed? A job selling the same weed at the cannabis store? His month to month furnished apartment? Or maybe a couple of girls he saw a few times per week, clinging to the rung just barely above him. Truth be told, he could hardly stand to be in the same room with them. Dan spent most of time off on the golf course, at the bar or on the couch watching tv and smoking weed.

Dan was not completely ice cold—there were still embers of emotional tenderness buried deep within him. Skipping the funeral was not a hard decision; after all, it was not a stipulation in Uncle Vic's will. Funerals were not really his thing anyway—too much posturing, too many forced condolences from people who barely knew the deceased. But the will reading? That was a different matter. He would be there for that.

Vic had orchestrated everything well before his passing, ensuring every detail was in place. It was a smart move, typical of the old man. He had likely figured Dan wouldn't show up unless there was something in it for him, so he made sure to set the wheels in motion while he was still warm. That was Vic for you—calculating, clever, and always one step ahead, even from beyond the grave.

Dan had plans—big ones if everything worked out as he hoped. The money would buy him a place in the woods, maybe a small farm, growing tomatoes, onions, peppers, and, of course, cannabis. Dan had a green thumb and found solace in nurturing life from the soil. Maybe his dream of the self-sustaining life far removed from the chaos of the world would be realized.

Simple logic; he could live there for almost nothing, utilities probably wouldn't cost much, and the taxes were likely dirt cheap in the middle of nowhere. That just left food and a few other odds and ends. Ironically, Dan's lack of ambition had propelled him further in life than if he had been busting his hump climbing the career ladder. Now, he could cruise back to Dallas and cash in. What a crazy old dude. Well, Vic was gone now, and Dan had made out like a bandit—fingers crossed.

`Dan had slept off most of the sickeningly sweet Colorado Bulldogs— concoctions of Kahlua, vodka, cream, and Coke—but they still lingered. He could feel them pounding in his head and taste their syrupy residue in his throat. The weed helped settle his stomach and dull the headache, but it was a temporary fix at best.

A word of advice, he thought avoid the sugar if you plan to knock back more than a few alcoholic drinks—it makes for one hell of a hangover. How many had he had, exactly? Let us just say, plenty. Dan made a mental note to stick to beer and shots on his next bender.

Navigating his old Corvette down the winding mountain road to the main highway, he cranked up the stereo to drown out the wind rushing past his ears. Tom Petty's voice filled the car, crooning about the American dream—specifically, the American girl.

"Take it easy, baby. Make it last all night."

The lyrics carried a bittersweet edge. Another poor bastard, Dan thought, robbed of his life by Big Pharma's drug-pushing empire. "You should have just smoked weed Tom," he said aloud.

Highway time stretched on for a few hours. Dan relaxed in the mountain's majesty rising all around him. The beauty of the landscape gave his mind room to wander, and it did not take long before it drifted to memories of his old preacher. The man had always been trying to set him straight, steering him toward the right path.

"Don't worry about who you were, just who you are," the preacher used to say. "Life is about change. God is about change. He is about rebirth— the new you. The old man is gone, and it is the new man here with us now."

Dan had wanted to take that advice. God knows he did. But putting the past to rest and starting anew was not as easy as it sounded. He figured plenty of people would agree with him on that. It was a nice sentiment, sure, but the truth was, even if he dared to claim some kind of selective amnesia for a clean slate, the man upstairs was not about to let him off the hook. Thanks all the same, but no. At least he could hold onto his self-respect. God would understand that.

A sudden gust of wind snapped him out of his thoughts, jolting the lightweight fiberglass Corvette and causing it to swerve unpredictably. He gripped the wheel tightly, muttering under his breath.

"Wake up, Dan —no time for a dirt nap."

The plan was simple enough: head south on Highway 25 to Amarillo, then cut east toward Dallas. But plans have a way of bending—especially when the universe nudges you off-course. Somewhere outside Colorado

Springs, Dan Stone felt that nudge. He veered off the highway and into the lot of a Black Lake Coffee house. Carla and the coffee induced panic attack. He'd heard the rumors—everyone had. Black Lake wasn't just coffee; it was a phenomenon. There were some claims of mystical healing properties of the strange brew. Some called it a hoax, others whispered about miracles. One rumor claimed the Vatican held a closed-door session about it. Another said Einstein's final, unspoken theory included a crude sketch of the Black Lake logo scribbled on a napkin.

Dan had never gone inside one in person until now. The sign hummed faintly in the sunlight, and the air around it felt charged, like just before a summer storm. A coffee man at heart—though more accustomed to breakroom espresso and a Life Organics cannabis Infused Budder Cup—Dan pushed open the door and stepped inside, curious if the legends were just smoke… or something stronger.

He ordered his usual from the other franchise—a Venti Americano with an extra shot—and indulged in a couple of homemade cake doughnuts. Alongside that, he picked up a few bags of fruit and nuts to keep him fueled for the road ahead. If he was going to be miraculously healed of whatever ailed him he would need some solid nutrition to assist.

While paying, his attention snagged on a tri-fold brochure highlighting the history of the nearby Garden of the Gods, with its breathtaking rock formations and ancient significance. The area had been sacred to various Native American tribes for centuries, including the Apache, Cheyenne, Comanche, Kiowa, Lakota, Pawnee, Shoshone, Ute, and Diegueño.

Dan stood by the window lingered for a while, engrossed in the details, soaking in the history. Before leaving, his eyes wandered to the café's walls, adorned with historical decorations: old sepia-toned photographs of Native Americans and settlers bartering over blankets and supplies. One image caught his eye—a huge white man, deep in negotiation, dwarfing an Indian chief. Dan felt a chill run down his spine.

The photograph, aged and slightly curled at the edges, captured a haunting scene. A tall and imposing white man, his long, silvery-white hair almost glowing against the shadowy backdrop. Beside him, an

Indian chief, held a bundle of items—a trade that seemed innocent at first glance. Dan could not shake the unsettling thought that whatever passed between them had carried far more weight than blankets or trinkets.

Dan stared at the photo, his unease growing with every second. He could swear the eyes of the old man shifted, subtly turning to meet his own. The room felt colder, the air heavier, as if the moment had stretched beyond time. The eyes, lifeless yet piercing, seemed to see straight into him, pulling at some dark corner of his soul. Dan blinked hard, shook his head, and looked again. But the image was still—just a photograph. And yet, he could not escape the feeling that the giant white man in the photo was watching him, even now.

"A deal with the Devil," Dan muttered under his breath, his skin crawling. He turned abruptly and hurried out of the café, the ominous weight of that photograph lingering in his mind.

He quickly jumped into the Corvette and merged back onto the highway, sparking up a joint as he cranked up the stereo. The CD spinning in the player might have been obsolete in the age of internet streaming, but it suited Dan just fine. The greatest hits of Warrant blasted through the speakers: "Cherry Pie," "Uncle Tom's Cabin," "Down Boys," "32 Pennies," and more. Hair metal always worked for him—raw, loud, and unapologetic, just like his life had been lately. The double espresso was quickly taking effect, sharpening his mind to a razor's edge. The rich, bold taste of the coffee lingered on his tongue. Great coffee.

For the moment, he let the unease of the old Quaker and the photograph drift into the recesses of his mind. It could stay there for now. The open road was calling, and Dan answered it with a lead foot and a rebel yell.

Dan felt amazing. Now he understood why everyone was clamoring for Black Lake Coffee. It had to be more than just caffeine—something else was at play. Whatever magic they were working with their beans, it was undeniably effective. As he drove, he recalled an article he had once read, the words coming to him in sharp detail, as if etched in his memory:

"Coffee is a marvel of chemistry, a complex brew containing hundreds of bioactive compounds, including caffeine, theobromine, trigonelline, and chlorogenic acids. These compounds interact in fascinating ways, shaping coffee's flavor, aroma, and physiological effects.

Caffeine, the most celebrated alkaloid, acts as a central nervous system stimulant, but it is far from the whole story. Studies have highlighted lesser-known alkaloids like trigonelline, which contribute to coffee's rich aroma during roasting and exhibit neuroprotective properties that aid memory and cognition. Then there are the chlorogenic acids—powerful antioxidants shown to regulate glucose levels and reduce inflammation.

What is most intriguing is how these compounds work together. Researchers believe the magic of coffee lies in the synergy of its elements—a molecular symphony that enhances alertness, focus, and mood. Coffee's potency, it seems, is as much about the harmony of its ingredients as it is about caffeine alone."

Dan smirked, the words resonating in a way they had not when he'd first read them. Harmony or not, miracles and wonders or not, Black Lake Coffee was now added to the Dan Stone menu.

Dan thought about life, death, the past, and the future, his mind racing as the engine of his Corvette hummed steadily beneath him. He detected a faint ping in the sound—a piston clipping the inside of the head on the left side of the block. The realization came effortlessly, as if his mind were running on overdrive, sharper than ever.

Lost in thought, Dan barely registered the miles ticking away. The scenery blurred, an indistinct smear of earth tones and asphalt. He noticed, faintly, how often he veered slightly from the long white line dividing Highway 25, his hands instinctively correcting the wheel without conscious thought. It was as though his body was on autopilot, leaving his mind free to explore the labyrinth of his thoughts.

At some point he turned onto highway 115 toward the Royal Gorge, he thought, "What the hell, I guess I want to see some natural wonders." He took another turn onto Highway 50 and soon found himself at the entrance to Royal Gorge National Park.

Dan Stone parked in the surprisingly busy and sprawling lot outside a modern glass-and-brass building that stood in stark contrast to the surrounding natural environment. Views of God's splendor being sold for a few bucks just ahead.

He entered the building and immediately sought out the men's room, taking advantage of the facilities while he had the chance. Afterward, he wandered through the multimillion-dollar structure, marveling at its extravagance. A snack bar caught his eye, and he could not resist grabbing a bag of Doritos and a Coke.

Health food, right? he thought with a smirk, popping the tab on his drink.

Dan spotted the colorful brochure rack, a familiar sight in tourist areas, overflowing with pamphlets highlighting dozens of Colorado attractions. Curious and hoping to learn something new, he picked one featuring an inviting headline about adventures awaiting visitors. As he skimmed through it, a few facts caught his eye. It explained that the Royal Gorge, although spanned by a bridge constructed in 1929, had formed naturally over millions of years. The brochure also described how, long after dinosaurs roamed the region, Native American tribes arrived, using the sheltered canyons nearby for hunting and camping. The Ute Indians, specifically, had often spent their winters in the Royal Gorge area, seeking refuge from the heavy snows that blanketed the higher elevations.

"I'm like the Indians getting out of Texas to go to Higher ground," he said aloud. He laughed again.

Dan examined some more old sepia-toned pictures of Indians and settlers in glass display cases, thankful that the old creepy white trader was nowhere to be seen within. He learned about how they built the bridge in 1929 and completed it in just six months. It made him wonder how they could build anything back then that would last. In our age of advanced technology, nothing seems to Dan to last longer than the time it took to pay off whatever trinket the bank financed. "Must be AI figuring out that algorithm," he said to no one.

Dan made his way out to the balcony overlooking the gorge. Peering down, he was taken aback. "Dan almost left a Colorado Bulldog down there. Yep, it is a long way down." He laughed aloud. He yelled at the top of his lungs: "Top of the World Ma!" and laughed some more. A young twentysomething and an old man were on the overlook as well. The elder glared in his direction. "Ah, sorry pops. It's the weed talking'."

Dan walked off and ambled around a bit checking out the local scenery and all the gorge had to offer him. It cost $20 to drive across the bridge and Dan bit the bullet and handed over his dollars to the clerk inside. Finding his Corvette he cautiously drove onto the rickety hundred-year-old structure made from antique wooden planks. A few scenes from bad disaster movies flashed through his mind as he maneuvered his 2000-pound car onto the former "world's highest" suspension bridge.

Dan stopped in the middle of the bridge, stepped out of his car leaving his door open, and walked to the guardrail. Leaning over the side as far as he could and following tradition—like all twelve-year-old boys who never quite grew up—he spat into the river 1053 feet below. Back in the car, he lit his seventh joint of the day and blew smoke into the Colorado air. If Dan had any friends, he could proudly tell them he smoked weed while driving across the tallest bridge in the world.

It was growing late. Dan hit the highway and retraced his route back on Highway 50 to Highway 25 and then onto Highway 87. Stopping in Trinidad, he purchased a few ounces of Northern Lights and grabbed another venti americano with an extra shot of espresso at a Dispensary-Coffee Shop combo floating at seven thousand feet. "Proudly serving Black Lake Coffee."

Driving solidly for six hours through New Mexico and well into Texas, Dan rubbed his bloodshot eyes and concentrated on the big green sign ahead: Welcome to Amarillo. Indeed, it was time to eat. Then, sleep.

CHAPTER 3

Amarillo. "I don't know what you're famous for, but you'll look great in my rearview mirror," Dan laughed to himself. He stretched his right leg and left arm, then his left leg and right arm, elongating his body as much as he could in the driver's seat of the Corvette. Time for a break.

Initially, he had planned to drive straight through to Dallas, but reality got the better of him.

Pulling out his iPhone, Dan scrolled to see what Amarillo had to offer for dinner. The first tourist attraction to pop up was Palo Duro Canyon, often called the "Little Grand Canyon."

"Pass on that," Dan muttered. "One deep rut in the earth is enough for today."

Next on the list was The Big Texan and its infamous 72-ounce steak challenge.

"Yes, please," Dan grinned, his stomach growling at the thought.

He laughed aloud, patting his belly. "Did you hear that?"

It seemed like the perfect place to satisfy his hunger and indulge in a bit of classic roadside Americana. The promise of a giant steak was too good to pass up.

About 30 minutes before the sun dipped below the horizon, Dan veered off I-40 and landed in the parking lot of the famous Big Texan Steak Ranch and Brewery. The gaudy yellow Old West-style facade stood out like a beacon against the fading light, adorned with blue ribbons boasting "Famous for Steaks" and a giant cowboy sign declaring, "The public is welcome—come one, come all." It was unapologetically over-the-top, and it worked.

This was it—the home of the legendary 72-ounce steak challenge. The promise of steak and spectacle was too tempting for Dan Stone to resist.

Dan remembered watching Adam Richman tackle it on Man vs. Food, devouring the massive slab of beef with gusto.

"Figure I'll give it a shoot myself," he said aloud, grinning as he stepped out of his Corvette and made his way to the bright yellow front porch. After all, what wasn't to love about a big, thick, juicy steak?

The glow of the setting sun cast long shadows across the lot as he made his way inside, ready to prove himself—or at least have one hell of a meal trying.

So, Dan took on the restaurant's legendary 72-oz. steak challenge. The rules were simple, in one hour, he must consume the mammoth steak, a shrimp cocktail, a baked potato, a side salad, and a dinner roll. Seated beside him was a fifteen-year-old girl who he did not imagine had a chance in hell, and across from him were an 81-year-old great grandma and her gun-slinging son, Dave, who by day was an accountant. "Bald as an eagle, that one,' Dan laughed. But he might pull out the win with that big gut.

"How would you like it cooked, babe?"

"Rare, please," Dan replied to their young, slightly plump waitress with pigtails and generous proportions. She was cute. And Dan was too long between girlfriends.

Ah, Texas. Her name badge read Suzy.

"How many people have eaten this thing, Suzy?"

"9522 as of last night."

"How many have tried?" Dan smiled.

"About 93,000 Cowboy," Suzy smiled back.

"Damn! Well, the challenge is on I guess!" Dan exclaimed a bit too loudly. Grandma shot him a disapproving glance. "It's on, Dave!" he laughed again.

Dan passed the time people-watching and chatting with his fellow challengers, laughing, and stirring the pot with grandma whenever he saw the chance as they awaited Suzy's return and the arrival of the colossal steaks.

"What's the fastest time anyone's eaten this steak?" Dan asked.

"15 minutes," Suzy replied as she set the massive steak down in front of him. It was more than huge. It was ridiculous. It looked to Dan like it could feed an entire family. The beef was accompanied by a junior football-sized potato, a family size serving bowl of mixed greens, tomatoes, cheese, onions, croutons; a side salad, half a dozen Texas size dinner rolls, and lastly and ironically, a less than shrimpy shrimp cocktail in a green glass goblet. To top it off, Suzy placed Dan's oversized schooner of Rattlesnake IPA beer in front of him, brewed in-house by Big Tex himself.

Dan laughed and threw his arms up over his head reclining over the back of the chair. "Ok, I give up! Suzy, you kicked my ass before I picked up my fork."

Suzy grinned. "Timer has started. Get to eating, Cowboy." She walked away leaving the table to contemplate the food. Dan watched her walk away and she glanced back over her shoulder catching him, smiled and shook her hips a little.
The steak was delicious. Melt in your mouth tender. Juicy. Truly a fantastic slab of Texas grass fed beef. But Dan only managed to enjoy about a quarter of the four-and-a-half-pound steak.

"I should have saved fifty bucks and ordered the filet, Dave! I knew I couldn't eat that much, but hey, when in Rome." Dave was licking his fingers and had made a good dent in the steak and potato but was looking a bit peaked and was not going to last much longer.

Grandma, on the other hand, devoured every last morsel and even had two of their heavy Pecan Porter beers. The lady was a legend. "She'll be dead by morning," Dan laughed at his dark humor again.

When Suzy brought the bill, He signed the credit card slip and left her a generous tip.

"Suzy, where's the best hotel around here?" he asked.

"The Holiday Inn is nice," she replied with a smile. "My sister manages it. I get off at eleven. I could show you the way if you are around in a couple hours. You can give me a ride over."

Yes, please. Again. Local talent. Dan smiled.

"Hell yes, I can wait. Another couple of beers, please, Suzy," he replied with a grin. This night was looking up. Coincidentally, Hank Williams Jr. was singing in the background - "I like to have women I've never had."

So, Dan drank the beer and listened to the country music; old Charlie Daniels, Hank, Merle, David Alan Coe, and some newer stuff with cute little Taylor Swift and the frontman from Staind, Aaron Lewis, now turned country boy. Yeehaw.

Dan was three beers in when he heard Suzy call out, "Well, cowboy, I'm all set."

She had changed from her uniform into a short denim skirt, light blue high-heeled red cowgirl boots, and a nicely fitted white V-neck T-shirt. Makeup. Lipstick. Damn. She looked much better, and she was not bad before.

They exchanged pleasantries, navigated some sexually tense waters, and walked through the now deserted dusty gravel parking lot to Dan's Corvette. He opened her door, and she dropped into the passenger seat. He closed her door admiring her bare legs.

"Hell yes Danny! What the fuck! It is going to be a great night! Dan spoke aloud as he hurried around the back of the car and climbed into the driver's seat.

They sped away from the world's largest steaks house and cruised down Highway 40 with the top down, blonde hair flowing behind from both seats for the ten minutes it took to reach the Holiday Inn Express.

As they pulled into the parking lot of the modest two or three-star hotel, Dan noticed a massive double billboard looming overhead. It featured a towering white cross and, in bold block letters beneath it, the words: "The Cross of Our Lord Jesus Christ Ministries."

"What in the world is that?" Dan asked, leaning forward for a better look.

"That's the giant cross of Groom, Texas," she replied casually, gesturing toward the faint glow of a searchlight in the distance. "They built it a few years back. Biggest cross in Texas. See that beam of light out there? That's it."

Dan squinted, catching the faint outline of the cross against the evening sky. "Well, everything's bigger in Texas, I guess," he said with a smirk, parking the car.

But the image of the cross struck Dan in an unexpected way. He shook his head, trying to clear it, but something about it lingered—unsettling, almost haunting. A giant cross in the middle of nowhere, stark, and alone against the darkening sky, seemed both out of place and profoundly symbolic.

It brought to mind the deep-seated religiosity that seemed to hum beneath the surface of every aspect of the human experience—the weight of morality, the ceaseless struggle against sin, the unyielding pursuit of righteousness. Yet, the thought left a bitter taste in his mouth.

"We're all evil," Dan muttered under his breath, his gaze fixed on the massive cross. "Bad by nature, no matter how hard we try to convince ourselves otherwise."

The words hung in the air, quiet and sharp, as if spoken to no one but himself.

Suzy laughed. "I'm bad, Cowboy." She smiled a devious little grin curling the corners of her mouth upwards. Red lipstick gleaming in the parking lot lights.

The enormity of the cross seemed to mock him, a beacon for salvation that felt impossibly out of reach. He turned away, forcing his focus back to the ordinary—a hotel, a bed, a night to rest. Suzy's hot little body.

"Wow. Amarillo's stepping up in the big leagues," Dan remarked distantly. He parked the Vette between two matching white church vans, each adorned with blue lettering from different churches.

"Oh yeah. God is big out here. Welcome to Texas, Cowboy," she said and leaned over the center console, pulled Dan in close and pulled him back to his reality at the same time.

She has exceptionally soft red, Texas lips. he thought as he smiled. "Thank you."

She laughed and wiped her finger across his lips. "Now that I branded you, I better wipe that lip stick off of you before my sister sees it."

They entered the hotel lobby where Dan met her sister, Stacy. Identical twins. No. Just kidding, Dan thought to himself. Sister was a bit older, protective and a bit disapproving. But all in all, probably a good sibling for wild cat Suzy.

Stacy handed Dan the plastic key card for room 260. "Don't even think about dragging my sister up there," she whispered close to his ear, making sure Suzy could not hear.

"No ma'am, I'll be good," Dan assured her with a wink.

There was a quaint hotel bar nestled at the end of the lobby, and Suzy and Dan settled in comfortably. Apart from Hank the bartender, they were the only two patrons in the place. The only sound coming from the flat screen television mounted to the wall behind the bar.

"Hi Hank," Suzy greeted with a warm smile, gracefully plopping herself on a gray fabric bar stool.

Hank, stereotypically polishing a glass behind the bar, looked up with a friendly grin. "Suzy, what can I get you to drink tonight?"

"We will have two Donald Trumps please," she laughed.

"Donald Trump?" Dan questioned.

Hank chuckled heartily. "It's my creation. You will love it. It is basically sex on the beach, but I top it off with whipped cream and sprinkle it with orange sugar. Get it? For his hair." With a deft hand, he began preparing the drinks.

Oh Hank, Dan thought and laughed.

"So, what brings you to Amarillo, Cowboy?" Suzy asked with a curious smile.

"Cowboy might not fit me all that well," Dan replied.

"Okay, I call everyone cowboy," Suzy chuckled.

"Well then by all means, call me Dan. I like to be different."

"Dan. I like that. So, what brings you to my neck of the woods, Dan?" she inquired.

"Just passing through. On my way to Dallas," he explained.

"Story of my life. Everyone is passing through here except me. So, what's in Dallas?" Suzy asked.

"Uncle died. I'm going to Dallas for the reading of his will," he replied solemnly.

"Oh. I'm sorry," Suzy responded sympathetically.

"Thank you. I didn't know him very well," he admitted.

"Where do you live?" Suzy queried.

"Good question. I have been in Denver for the last year or so. But I live in Dallas. I guess."

"And you didn't know your uncle?" she pressed further.

"Odd I know." he explained with a shrug.

The television cut through their conversation with a sharp alert tone. Onscreen, the image snapped into focus: a news reporter standing before the towering white cross in Groom—the very one they had just been discussing.

A Hispanic female reporter appeared on screen, speaking into a microphone as wind tugged at her blazer.

"We're here in Groom, Texas—home to the world's largest cross. What began last week as a small demonstration has grown into a nationwide vigil against the Black Lake Coffee empire. Christian groups from across the country have made a pilgrimage here, claiming the brew is 'of the devil' and rallying in the name of God."

The reporter turned and held the microphone out to a middle-aged white man in a weathered ball cap and denim jacket. His eyes were wide with conviction.

"You can see it everywhere," he said. "People are being healed—every kind of disease. The blind can see. The crippled walk. Folks with emphysema are breathing like they never smoked a day in their life. It's clearly the work of the Devil."

The reporter blinked, then looked directly into the camera, her brow furrowing.

"Well... that all sounds like good things to me."

"That's the point," the man said, his voice rising with urgency. "It's supposed to look good. That's how the Antichrist comes—through signs and wonders. These are the miracles of the false prophet."

The reporter nodded politely, easing the microphone away. "Okay, well... thank you for your time."

She turned back to the camera, her expression composed but wary.

"And that's what we're seeing here in Groom—thousands of faithful from Christian church groups across the country have gathered and camped out in protest, holding vigil against what they believe is a growing spiritual threat."

Suzy grabbed the remote and hit mute, cutting off the reporter mid-sentence. "Ugh, I'm so sick of that woman," she said, rolling her eyes. "She's been doing special reports nonstop for a week—like ten times a day. Who cares? It's coffee," she laughed.

Hank brought the drinks. "Ha! Donald Trump," he said with a grin and slid the tall, thin glasses across the bar. Bits of orange-topped whipped cream spilled onto the bar top.

"Okay, that's pretty fucking funny, Hank," Dan laughed. "Kind of looks like him."

Hank disappeared like a good bartender, giving us space from the other end of the bar. Suzy and Dan picked up the glasses and clinked them together.

It was clear Suzy was enjoying the evening, her playful demeanor evident in the way she wiped the orange whipped cream from Dan's lips with hers. Leaning in close and sliding almost off the barstool with her skirt riding up, she revealed very sheer panties matching her ruby red lipstick. The suggestive glance she gave him hinted at an invitation for more adventure that night.

"Here's to a long night and a safe trip to faraway places tomorrow," Wild Suzy winked.

"Well, to Dallas. I'm on my way back home, I suppose. I got a little stoned in Denver with their whole legalization of marijuana."

"Married? Girlfriend? Anyone who will come looking for me?" asked Suzy.

"No," Dan laughed. "I'm kind of the eternal bachelor."

"Me too. Bachelorette."

"What, are you nineteen?"

"I'm twenty-three."

"Well, not exactly eternal then," Dan laughed.

"Maybe someday, Cowboy," She smiled and gave him some more of that red lipstick. A lot more. The alcohol in the Donald Trump was loosening her up it appeared. From experience thus far it would not take much. Her sister coughed loudly from her vantage point behind the front desk.

"Hank! Two more of those orange haired devils please," Dan called down the bar ignoring big sister.

He returned to kissing the loose girl with the red panties. More coughing from sister Stacy.

They drank the two presidential drinks. It did not seem like either of would be going anywhere this evening and Dan certainly wasn't planning to drive anywhere until tomorrow came.

After another half an hour and two more Donalds they were both pretty much hammered. Stacy took a break and joined the twosome.

"I told you not to corrupt my sister and here you are," she said sliding into the seat beside Suzy.

Suzy laughed. "Corrupt me? That would be pretty hard. "

"Yes, I know little sis. But I like to think of you as still having some innocence."

Suzy put her hand right on the zipper of Dan's faded threadbare blue jeans. "I'm not innocent."

"Suzy! I can't believe you. You don't even know this dude," Stacy said.

Dan moved her hand onto his thigh. 'Hold on, ladies. Don't get too upset. It's a party. Let's just have a couple more drinks and relax. It has been a hell of a day for me. I started out in Denver when the sun came up and now here I am," he smiled, slurring his words a bit.

"And now you are right here in the middle of nowhere Texas with a couple of sweet young thangs?" Suzy laughed.

"Exactly! Hank! I think we need three President Trumps, please."

"No. No. I'm still on duty. All night," Stacy objected.

"Ah. Then two, please Hank," Dan countered.

"And Suzy will probably fall off her bar stool if you pour any more down her," Stacy said.

"Ok Hank, forget it. I guess we have had enough Republicans for the night."

"Dan spent the last year smoking weed in Denver." Suzy smiled.

"Nice! I told you that in confidence," he feigned offense and smiled a bit too much. Dan was feeling the long arm of the 45th / 47th president's drink.

"No worries. Stacy and Hank don't care."

"Now that is something I can do while I work the night shift," Stacy said.

"Great! Let me grab my bag from the car. I brought along enough with me to get five or ten years in a Texas jail. We better smoke some of it."

"I'll come with you," Suzy said sliding off the bar stool and showing her red panties to Hank, Stacy, God and everyone.

"Jesus, Suzy."

"Don't worry, Mom. we will be right back in." Suzy had to unroll her skirt it had hiked up so high.

Dan and Suzy stumbled out the door, Suzy draping herself on him for pleasure and support. The alcohol had done its job on her hundred and twenty pounds. Dan slid the key into the trunk and pulled out his suitcase. Suzy closed the trunk and jumped up on the back of his Corvette.

"Come here Cowboy Dan," she said grabbing the front of his shirt and pulling him in for a taste of her sweet lips. They stayed locked together for quite some time and were getting pretty carried away in the parking lot. Her legs were spread pressing into his bones on either side as she gripped him hard.

"We better head in and smoke this weed before I can't stop," she said. "Yes, at this point for me it might be hard to walk back in."

"Yes, Hard. She pointed down," and laughed.

"Dan laughed as well as they separated, and Suzy hopped off the trunk. "Okay, let's go in. Shall we smoke up in my room?"

"Stacy won't go for that, but we can smoke in the kitchen and blow the smoke into the exhaust hood over the stove."

"Ah, ok it's a party in the kitchen," he laughed.

They went back inside and followed Hank and Stacy to the small kitchen behind the bar. It was late, and he had not seen any other guests the entire night, so the coast was clear for their midnight snack. Dan unzipped his suitcase and pulled out a small plastic box with the marijuana he had purchased in Thornton a few days before. On the outside of the box was the logo of the weed store, Back in the Day, and the strain, Purple Microbus.

"Check it out, ladies," he grinned, holding up the box. "May I present Purple Microbus, straight from Colorado."

Suzy's eyes widened. "Oh, nice choice! You really loved that Colorado scene."

Stacy chuckled. "Well, I guess we're in for a good night then."

Hank glanced over with interest. "Mind if I join you folks? Been a long shift and a smoke sounds mighty fine right about now."

Dan nodded, offering him the box. "Of course, Hank. Grab a seat. It's about time we all relaxed a bit and anyone who can come up with that crazy Donald Trump drink deserves to get high."

Hank quickly found a spot at the table as Dan set about preparing a joint, the sweet aroma of Purple Microbus filling the air. Soon, the four were gathered around, passing the joint and sharing easy conversation, the kitchen warm and welcoming in the quiet of the Texas night.

They smoked the weed.

Dan said, "This marijuana isn't like it was back in the day, so the store name was a bit of a misnomer. America's nostalgic weed is like David Banner turning into the Incredible Hulk; the same guy is in there somewhere, but the new green guy is a motherfucker," he laughed.

Dan rolled another cannabis cigarette, and they smoked it too. They were all very stoned and happy. Some more conversation and laughter and Stacy and Hank went off to the lobby to sort some papers or something in the office. Suzy and Dan used the opportunity to sneak up to room 260. Sorry, Stacy.

As they quietly ascended the back stairs, hand in hand, stifling giggles, the potent effects of the combined Donald Trumps and Purple Microbus were solidly in play. The hallway was dimly lit, casting long shadows on the faded floral wallpaper. Room 260's door squeaked open easily, and they slipped inside.

"Whoa," Suzy whispered, collapsing onto the bed in a fit of laughter. "This stuff is strong! Dan, I am really fucked up."

Dan flopped down beside her, feeling the room spin gently around him. "Definitely packs a punch," he agreed, his words slightly slurred and his eyes far out of focus.

They spent the next few minutes chatting, laughing, and touching. The walls of the motel room seeming to fold in on themselves from the haze of orange and purple tinted intoxicants. Outside, the night remained still and undisturbed, the only sound the distant hum of a passing car on the lonely Texas highway.

Soon, their laughter gave way to a comfortable silence as they lay side by side, staring at the popcorn ceiling. The soft glow of the bedside lamp cast a warm, surreal glow over everything, and for a moment, it felt like time had slowed to a crawl.

"Hey," Suzy murmured, her voice barely audible in the quiet room. "Thanks for today. It's been... unexpected."

He turned to her, a lazy smile spreading across his face. "Yeah. Unexpected is one way to put it."

She chuckled softly. "I mean it, though. It's been fun."

Dan nodded, feeling a strange warmth in his chest. "Yeah. Fun."

She rolled in his direction and climbed up on top of him like a smooth Texas cowgirl straddling her horse.

She was a lot of fun. A sweet girl. Adventurous. It was very very late. Dan really needed that. What a total freak. Good times, he thought.

And with that, they drifted off into a peaceful, alcohol-marijuana-sex-induced sleep, the events of the day melting away like smoke into the night. Morning closing in on them fast.

Soon, sunlight filtered through the curtains, casting a golden hue over the motel room. Dan woke to find Suzy still asleep beside him, still naked, her hair tousled and a faint content smile on her lips. The bed sheets were laying on the floor, pillows haphazard, memories of the wild night before flooded back, a mixture of laughter, intimacy, and the lingering effects of the alcohol and fine Colorado weed.

Dan slid closer, the warmth of her body still clinging to the sheets. Her sweet perfume lingered in her hair and on the pillow, soft and familiar. He leaned in and pressed a kiss to Suzy's forehead, breathing in her scent one last time before quietly slipping out of bed.

He'd had his share of one-night stands—but Suzy felt a little different. Maybe it was the isolation out here in cow country, a bit of desperation causing her to be extra diligent in her efforts. Maybe she was just a wild ride at the end of a long, strange day. Or maybe it was the fact that she was twenty-three, and Dan was starting to feel time creeping up behind him, whispering reminders he didn't want to hear.

As he gathered his things and prepared to leave, he pictured a black rose on a cream-colored backdrop. He needed a giant cup of Coffee.

With a final glance back at Suzy, he left the motel room, ready to boogie on down the road to Dallas for his uncle's will reading, facing whatever lay ahead with a renewed sense of adventure and a fond memory of a night that would always stand out in his travels with this sweet young horny Texan.

CHAPTER 4

Amarillo was waking up and Dan was on the hunt for some coffee. The hangover and dankover from the sweet Donald Trumps and Purple Microbus left him nauseous and his head in a haze. In his minds eye he could see the clean, angular logo of the Black Lake Coffee storefront. The design was simple, elegant, commanding—a black rose etched into cream. It was a beautiful logo but strange for coffee. But the Black Lake Coffee houses were everywhere so they obviously had their act together. "Growing like a weed," he laughed aloud. He pulled through the drive thru and placed his standard other coffee franchise order; venti with an extra shot, three raw sugars and extra cream.

Dan drank deeply tolerating the hot beverage on his raspy throat. When he entered the highway, he was already feeling better.

Dan squinted out at Amarillo sprawling below—Texas itself was so vast, a sea of endless potential in need of a pilot. Funny, he thought, how he had never noticed it before. The gaps between towns, between lives, felt temporary, like placeholders for billions yet to come. His mind wandered to a population graph he had seen once, the curve shooting skyward like a rocket. Two thousand years ago, at the time of Jesus, the world held only about three hundred million people. Now, over seven billion.

The Industrial Revolution. Global warming. The age of quantum computing. The unnatural assistance of AI accelerating humanity's climb. Dan's thoughts darted, weaving connections at a speed he had never experienced before. It was as if his brain was rewiring itself, new pathways forming tendrils stretching between the right and left hemispheres.

Dan rolled his shoulders back, a new relaxed state. He felt... good. Better than good. His mind hummed, thoughts clear and purposeful. The hangover that should have lingered was gone, replaced by something warm, almost electric, running through his veins. He did not just feel sharp; he felt alive.

"Damn this is good coffee!" he yelled out to the universe.

Dan accelerated and drifted in thought for 250 miles and by late afternoon and Dan was pulling into a welcoming oasis just north of Fort Worth, across from the Texas Motor Speedway. The midday sun was beginning its slow descent, casting a warm orange glow over the landscape as he navigated the final stretch of the long drive. He had taken his time getting here stopping for breakfast and lunch along the way. Smoking quite a few joints of the famed Purple Microbus and reliving the wild night in his mind. The recent memories made for an easy drive. He might have to make his way back to Amarillo sometime soon, he considered.

Dan parked the Corvette under the shade of a sprawling live oak tree that stood sentinel at the hotel's entrance. Stepping out into the hot Texas sun, he stretched his long limbs and looked up into the sun. Removing his black Ray-Ban sunglasses and letting the vitamin D penetrate his eyes all the way through to his brain. Texas. About one hundred miles from the sun. He grabbed his overnight bag from the trunk. The hotel, a modern midrise structure with a touch of Dallas charm, beckoned with its inviting glow of warm lights through large windows. The signage on top proudly declared in red letters "Marriott."

Dragging his suitcase behind him, he entered the lobby, greeted by soft instrumental music and the faint aroma of freshly brewed coffee. The reception desk, polished wood with a marble top, was manned by a young woman with a friendly smile and a badge that read "Emily." Her blue eyes sparkled with warmth as she welcomed Dan to the Champions Circle Marriot.

"Good evening! Checking in?"

Emily's voice was bright and cheerful, carrying the kind of hospitality that Texas was known for. Her blue eyes sparkled as she smiled, her blonde hair pulled back neatly. She wore an ill-fitting white Polo shirt that strained against her ample, unmistakably Texan assets. The fabric was almost translucent, pulled into a threadbare state, as if it had been through one too many laundry cycles.

Ah, Texas—I do love this place, Dan thought with a wry smile, stepping up to the counter.

"Yes, please," Dan replied, grateful for her cheerful demeanor. Emily efficiently processed his reservation, handing him a key card and providing a brief overview of the hotel's amenities. She batted her big blue eyes a time or two. He thanked her and made his way to the elevator, eager to settle into his room and finally relax and take a nice long hot shower.

The hallway leading to his room was softly lit, its carpet plush under his tired feet. Finding his room, he slid the key card into the slot and heard a satisfying click as the door unlocked. Stepping inside, he was greeted by the crisp cleanliness of a well-appointed hotel room. The king-sized bed beckoned with its fresh linens and plump pillows, promising a restful night's sleep.

After freshening up with the much anticipated long hot shower, Dan felt rejuvenated enough to venture downstairs for dinner. The hotel's restaurant, "Lone Star Grill," was warmly lit and exuded a cozy atmosphere with its rustic decor and intimate seating arrangements. Soft chatter and the clinking of glasses filled the air as patrons enjoyed their meals. A bit incongruent, Piano Man was being played on the hotel bar baby grand piano and heartily sung by someone other than Billy Joel. A female someone.

Seated by a window that offered a view of the sunset-drenched Texas landscape, Dan perused the menu. The waitress, a seasoned professional with a warm smile and a not unfortunate look about her, recommended their signature steak: a rare filet mignon with a decadent cherry sauce.

"Rare please. And a bottle of Decoy cabernet sauvignon too please," he said.

As he waited, he took in the ambiance of the restaurant. The walls were adorned with artwork of a distinctly Texas flavor, several with Longhorn cows, the mouthwatering scent of the sizzling steaks, the gentle hum of alcohol fueled conversation, and the soothing backdrop of a bit boisterous piano keys. Dan felt at home in fine hotels and bars. He never met a stranger. The waitress returned with his drink, pouring a generous portion in a bulbous wine glass and placing the bottle on the table.

Moments later, the steak arrived and as promised was prepared perfectly; decidedly rare, seared on the outside and tender within, and adorned with a glistening cherry sauce that added a delightful sweetness.

Dan savored his meal and with the last bite of steak and the final sip of wine to polish off the bottle, he addressed the view of the golf course. He had played this course many times. He would get on in the morning. Tonight, he was feeling the effects of the road, the wine, and two years of Colorado. Mixed in with his fatigue was an undertone of excitement. Although he had spent some time with his ex-wife enjoying the pampered 'good life' it had been some time. The last handful of years were more pedestrian and not to his liking.

Returning to his room, he found solace in the quiet of the night. The soft white feather pillow cradled his head as he slipped into a pleasant deep sleep, his mind and body finally finding some much-needed rest. In the embrace of comfortable silence, under the watchful gaze of the Texas stars through his window, he drifted into a restorative slumber and dreamed of sweet Suzy in Amarillo.

Dan woke refreshed with the golden Texas sun streaming into his room on the fourteenth floor of the Marriott at Champions Circle. The view of the golf course was spectacular from his vantage point, the emerald greens pristine under the morning light. He had Vic's will reading at 2 o'clock today in Frisco but he could definitely squeeze in 18 holes to dust off the cobwebs and still get there in time. It had been weeks since he swung a club. The Colorado winter seemed to last forever. But he had found a gorgeous golf course in the foothills of the Rockies to enjoy a few times.

Reaching for the desk phone, he dialed the concierge. "Dan Stone here in room 1408. Can I get a tee time in about 90 minutes?"

"Sir, let me connect you with the Pro shop, they will certainly be able to accommodate. Please hold."

It had been a while since Dan was in Texas, and he had lost the numbness in his ears that filters out noticeable accents. Everyone sounded very Texan with their slow drawl.

"Pro shop, this is Jake."

"Jake, Dan Stone here. I need a tee time in 90 minutes or so."

"Let me take a look, Mr. Stone. It looks like I have an 8:35. Will you be golfing as a single this morning?"

"Yes, just me."

"Excellent. 8:35, joining Mr. Smith and Mr. Baxter."

"Perfect. See you then, Jake."

Dan hung up and stretched in front of the window, feeling the intense morning heat from the giant sun penetrate his skin. Nothing quite like the Texas sun in June. After a quick shower, shave, and standard morning ablutions, he dressed in black running shorts, a faded red tank top, and his Birkenstock sandals. Ready for breakfast, he returned to the Creekside Cafe, the same in-house restaurant he had noticed earlier.

"Good morning, Sir. May I get you some coffee?" greeted the waitress, her coal black hair and dark eyes catching Dan's attention. A beautiful girl of twenty-something he couldn't help but recall once again why he loved Texas.

"I'll have two eggs, bacon, strawberry crepes, and a large cafe americano with three raw sugars, Tiffany, with extra cream on the side," he replied reading her name badge and throwing her a smile. Breakfast of champions indeed, especially here at the Champions Circle Marriott, he thought, damn, I'm clever.

She returned his smile and bounced off to place his order. Dan spied an electric round logo on the wall with the Black Lake Coffee Rose and the message, "Proudly Served Here." He smirked and nodded.

"Hell yes," he muttered to himself. "These guys are all over Texas. My new best friends."

After breakfast, Dan strolled down to the pro shop, picking up a pair of khaki Nike slacks and a golf shirt adorned with the swirling Champions Course logo. He collected his golf cart and drove it around to the front parking lot where his vintage Corvette awaited. Opening the trunk, he retrieved his well used set of Titleist clubs and comfortable golf shoes. Clothes could be bought anywhere, but clubs and shoes were personal.

Some guys rented or borrowed equipment from the resort, but for Dan, it was not the same. He made it a rule to never leave home without his clubs in the trunk.

Dan felt great. He could feel the strong coffee and energy boost. Smith and Baxter were waiting at the first tee box when Dan arrived. Being a big hitter, Dan confidently took charge and outdrove them on every hole. Smith, although not the most skilled golfer, had a good attitude and graciously picked up his ball whenever he was slowing the threesome down. He seemed like a decent guy, and Dan appreciated his effort to keep up the pace. But nothing mattered every drive was dead straight, every chip landed softly, and every putt rolled true. It was as though he controlled the ball and where it went. He was in the zone. Dan shot the game of his life, just missing a lip out eagle putt settling for birdie on the 18th hole and a fifty-nine.

Smith and Baxter clapped him on the back, congratulating him on a round they would probably tell stories about for years. Dan soaked it in but kept his mind sharp. The reading of his uncle's will was at two o'clock. He needed to shower and change, he'd need to get cracking.'

CHAPTER 5

Dan Stone hustled through the automatic doors of the sleek brass-and-glass building in Frisco, arriving only two minutes early. The polished offices of Stark and Stark loomed ahead, their sharp angles and subtle opulence a stark contrast to the tangled emotions Dan was trying to suppress. He was not prepared for this—not for the will, not for the awkward family reunion, and certainly not for the flood of memories tied to his uncle Victor.

The rush from the Champions Circle Marriott on the edge of the metroplex, eighteen holes and another venti americano on the way had all contributed to Dan being slightly out of breath. His pulse quickened as he stepped into the hushed waiting area. Dan paused and looked toward the room where the meeting was set to begin. "Let's get this over with," he said quietly.

Dan stepped into the conference room, the polished mahogany table stretching out under soft recessed lighting like a runway for whatever drama was about to unfold. Around it sat a mix of familiar and unfamiliar faces—his parents, his uncles, distant cousins, and several strangers in suits who looked like they belonged to lawyers or legacy.

His mother caught his eye first. She gave a small, polite nod—something between warmth and formality. James—Dad—offered a tight smile, then looked away just a second too quickly.

They weren't close. Not lately. But they weren't strangers either. Just people with too much history and too little practice talking about it. More oddity. Grief. No one felt completely 'right' at the end of someone's life.

Dan took a seat without a word, scanning the room as he settled in. His uncles kept their eyes on the table. No one else seemed interested in making attempts at small talk.

Something about it all felt off. The air had a weight to it, like the room itself was holding its breath.

"Will everyone please take their seats?" Tom Stark, the executor of the will, stood at the head of the table. His gray suit was immaculate, his voice firm but measured.

Dan shifted in his chair, sitting a little straighter, bracing himself. He had no real connection to Uncle Vic beyond scattered childhood memories and the occasional passing reference at family gatherings. Still, something told him that whatever was about to unfold would shift the ground beneath him. His life was already in chaos—maybe this would be the break he needed.

At the head of the table stood Tom Stark, Victor's long-time attorney. Composed and precise in a charcoal-gray suit, Stark exuded the kind of quiet authority that required no theatrics. With a subtle wave of his hand, he gestured for everyone to settle.

"Mr. Stone has contracted our offices to disperse his fortune according to his last will and testament," Stark began, his voice clear and firm, resonating through the wood-paneled room.

The space was striking in a slightly dated, corporate kind of way—black granite tiles lining the walls with veins of green cutting through them, polished to a high sheen. The long mahogany table gleamed under recessed lighting, its surface reflecting the tension gathered around it.

"I want to be clear up front," Stark continued, adjusting his glasses, "the total value of the Victor Stone estate is to remain confidential. That stipulation is part of the will and is legally binding."

A few murmurs passed between chairs, but no one dared speak above a whisper. Stark's presence—unassuming in stature, but sharp as a blade—left little room for anything but silence.

The Stone brothers—Vic's surviving siblings—glanced at each other with that announcement. They sat stiffly around the polished mahogany table, their faces a mixture of anticipation, suspicion, and thinly veiled discomfort. Despite the opulence of the setting, with its floor-to-ceiling windows and abstract art adorning the walls, the room felt stifling. It was as though the weight of Vic's empire pressed down on everyone present, an unspoken reminder of just how much was at stake.

"What I'm about to share will no doubt come as a shock—not just to you, but to much of the world," the attorney said, pausing before delivering the blow. "Victor was, in fact, the founder and CEO of Black Lake Coffee."

A collective murmur rippled through the boardroom. The mysterious architect behind the wildly successful—and deeply controversial—Black Lake Coffee Empire was gone. But what left the family reeling, Dan included, wasn't just the loss. It was the staggering truth that Victor Stone—quiet, private, and long estranged—had been behind it all. The same Victor who had left Wichita decades ago, turning his back on their small-town life for reasons no one had ever truly understood.
Dan sat frozen, his mind racing. Black Lake Coffee? His newfound elixir? Everyone knew about Black Lake Coffee. You couldn't throw a rock in Denver without hitting one. How many stores did they have? There must be thousands.

But never—not once—had it crossed his mind that Uncle Vic was behind it. The quiet one. The odd one. The one who'd drifted away from the family decades ago and only showed up now and again.

Now here he was, hearing Victor Stone had built a coffee empire—and kept it completely hidden.

And Dan? Dan was here because he'd planned on life-changing cash. A windfall. A little light at the end of the tunnel. His life had been spiraling lately—this, whatever it turned out to be, had felt like a turning point.

But this? This was bigger than he'd imagined – bigger than anyone could imagine.

The man he barely knew had been sitting on a cash cow—and Dan had been walking right past it for years, clueless. Hell, he could have probably talked Vic into a job.

"Victor," one of the brothers murmured under his breath, his tone a mix of disbelief and envy. "The billionaire..."

"Not just a billionaire," another interjected, his voice low but sharp. "The billionaire. King of coffee. Hell, half the country drinks his stuff every morning. Lines around the damn building half the time."

The whispered comments rippled among them as Tom Stark, the executor, moved to the head of the table. The man exuded authority, his silver hair neatly combed, his tailored suit a symbol of the precision with which he intended to execute this monumental task.

"If everyone can save your questions for the end," Stark announced, his tone cutting through the murmurs.

Dan shifted in his seat, the weight of his uncles' stares settling on him. He could feel the undercurrent of resentment in the room. "Odd birds," he thought.

"Victor Stone," Stark began, his voice steady, "was a man of immense success and vision. His creation of Black Lake Coffee reshaped the industry, turning a single Kansas café into a multi-billion-dollar enterprise with operations spanning most of the United States."

The room hadn't yet recovered from the first revelation when the attorney cleared his throat again, glancing at the second envelope in front of him.

"There's one more matter," he said carefully, his voice shifting. "Victor left explicit instructions for this to be disclosed only after his death. It is a bit of theatrics but that's how Vic wanted it. He asked me to let you all know that he had his reasons for this secrecy."

Dan felt a strange tension in the air. Something electric. He sat up straighter.

The attorney continued, "Daniel... this concerns you directly."

Dan blinked. "Me?"

The attorney nodded. "Victor was not just your uncle. He was your father."

A stunned silence fell over the room. Even the air seemed to stop moving.

"Your adoption by James and Helen was arranged privately. Only Victor and his two brothers knew the truth. It was a secret kept for over three decades."

Dan's pulse thundered in his ears. "That's not possible," he whispered.

But somewhere deep down, something shifted. A puzzle piece he didn't know had been missing suddenly locked into place.

The air seemed to leave the room. Gasps and murmurs broke the fragile silence.

The brothers exchanged glances, their unease growing. Stark glanced briefly at Dan before continuing. "First, to each of Victor's surviving siblings, I bequeath $1 million, along with my gratitude for the roles you have played in my life and the life of my son."

The murmurs began immediately, hushed but unmistakable. A million dollars was generous, but it was a mere fraction of Vic's empire. The brothers leaned forward in their chairs; their attention sharpened as Stark turned the page.

"And now, the bulk of my estate — the entirety of my ownership in Black Lake Coffee Corporation and Stone Industries Incorporated any and all stock in various other companies, the deeds to all properties under my name and all personal assets—shall be left to my son Daniel Stone."

The Stone brothers remained quiet and resolute. It made sense. It was their secret, and this was the end of the years of silence.

Daniel Stone remained seated, stunned into silence.

Son?

He had always sensed that Uncle Vic admired him—but this?

Dan had known he was adopted. The story had always been some vague tale about a college girl back East. He'd never questioned it much. Never needed to. But now?

The sheer magnitude of what had just been handed to him hit like a freight train.

Victor Stone—his uncle, his quiet champion, the founder of Black Lake Coffee—was his father.

His real father.

Dan's breath caught in his throat. The room buzzed with whispers, but he barely heard them. Somewhere, everything inside him had come unmoored.

It was no secret among the Stone brothers that Dan was Vic's son, but it was something they rarely discussed—and never, ever mentioned outside the family. Maybe it was out of respect for Vic's wishes. Maybe it was just easier that way.

Or maybe no one really cared enough to challenge him.

Still, it had always struck James and Robert as strange—how firmly Vic insisted the boy be raised as someone else's son. How he hovered close but never too close, watching from the sidelines like a man haunted by his own decisions.

Dan, for his part, had grown up none the wiser. And now here he was, thirty-four years old, sitting in a boardroom filled with family and lawyers, his world turned inside out.

He looked at James—Dad?—but James couldn't meet his eyes.

Something in Dan's chest twisted.

"Why?" he asked, more to the room than to anyone in particular. "Why would he keep this from me?"

No one answered.

Because no one really knew.

Or if they did, they'd buried it too deep to dig up now.

Tom Stark raised his hand to calm the rising murmur in the room.

"Gentlemen," he said evenly, "this was Victor's decision and his alone. It was well-documented and legally verified. If there are any objections, they can be addressed through the proper legal channels."

The room quieted, but the tension still clung to the air like humidity before a storm.

Stark sighed, his voice firm but measured. "Victor was fully aware of the strange circumstances surrounding Daniel's adoption. He didn't make this decision lightly. He believed in Dan's potential—and saw in him the very traits he valued most: determination, creativity, resilience."

Stark turned toward Dan, offering a brief, almost fatherly nod. "Qualities he saw in his son, Daniel."

Dan sat frozen, his mind reeling. The words landed, but it would take time for their meaning to sink in. His son. Not just a nephew admired from afar—but something deeper, weightier. Intentional.

Questions swirled through Dan's mind—Why keep it a secret? Why now? Why him?

Across the table, James shifted in his chair, eyes low, jaw clenched.

Dan finally spoke, his voice quiet but steady—too steady.

"Did he ever try to tell me?" He turned sharply. "Dad... what the fuck? Why didn't you tell me? I'm thirty-four years old, not some teenager."

His words cut through the room like a blade. James flinched but said nothing.

The silence that followed was deafening. Not awkward—guilty.

James stared at the table, jaw working, but no words came. The man who had raised Dan, coached his little league team, taught him to drive, sat there like a statue—hollowed out by something too old and tangled to name.

Dan leaned back, as if distance might somehow dull the sting. "You let me walk through my whole life not knowing who I really was."

Still, nothing.

Just the hum of the AC and the weight of everything unsaid.

But the silence said enough.

The room fell into a heavy silence, the air thick with a mixture of resentment, disbelief, and something that felt uncomfortably close to acceptance. For Dan, the revelation wasn't about money or legacy—it was about identity.

Victor Stone wasn't just his eccentric, distant uncle. He was his father.

Dan glanced, wide-eyed and incredulous, at the couple he had called Mom and Dad his entire life. He had always known he was adopted—there was never any attempt to hide that. But learning now, in this setting, that he'd been adopted by his own aunt and uncle? That his biological father had stood just across the room at every holiday, every birthday, and never said a word?

It was almost too much to process.

Why didn't they ever pull me aside? he thought. Why now? Why here, with everyone watching?

The silence held like a breath waiting to exhale.

At the head of the long table, Tom Stark, the executor, adjusted his glasses and shuffled the stack of papers before him. The room seemed to tighten as he prepared to continue, the weight of the moment pressing down on everyone like a stone.

The brothers exchanged uneasy glances; their expressions unreadable but charged. None of them said a word.

Dan shifted in his seat. He had been expecting money, .He certainly had not expected this. He was the son rather than the nephew. Now he was the rightful heir.

"Yes," Stark confirmed, his tone unyielding. "Victor was explicit in his wishes."

The tension in the room shifted, thickening with the weight of something unspoken. Dan looked from face to face, noticing the avoidance in the eyes of his uncles, their sudden inability to meet his gaze. He felt like a stray piece of a puzzle no one wanted to fit into place.

And then it hit him. The looks, the avoidance—it was not disbelief. It was guilt.

The pieces began to align in his mind. The way his parents had always deflected questions about his adoption. The strange way his uncles had treated him—never cruel, but never entirely warm. And now this. Black Lake Coffee. A billion-dollar empire, built by his father known to Dan as the uncle he had barely known, his fortune left entirely to him.

"Victor was our client for nearly twenty years, well-known to several partners of this firm, including myself. Victor was my client and my friend. I helped him draft this will over a decade ago and discussed it with him just days before his passing. Victor Stone was of sound mind."

Stark paused, allowing his words to sink in. His gaze shifted deliberately to each of Uncle Vic's four brothers in turn, as if daring them to challenge the legitimacy of the will.

"I have included in the formal filing of the will a notarized copy of my affidavit to that effect should there be any doubt to Victor's ability to elect this option."

The silence in the room grew heavier, the weight of Vic's decision settling over the gathered family like an unwelcome storm cloud.

"Having reviewed and verified the legalities, as the executor of the Victor Edward Stone estate, I hereby confirm Mr. Stone's last will and testament and his decision to bequeath his entire fortune in it's entirety to Daniel James Stone."

The room erupted into muted conversations, buzzing with speculation. Stark cleared his throat once more and shuffled his papers to regain control. When silence fell, he proceeded with the formalities expected on such occasions.

"With that said, we are dismissed. At the front desk will be an envelope for each of you," Stark announced firmly. "Dan, we have some more documents, paperwork, and a few things to go over. If you will remain."

As the family members began to filter out of the room, Stark proceeded to outline the next steps in the estate settlement process, detailing the necessary legal procedures and paperwork that would follow. He addressed questions and concerns raised by some of the more vocal relatives, emphasizing the finality and legality of Uncle Vic's wishes.

Throughout it all, Dan could not help but reflect on Vic's eccentricities and his blunt approach to life, which seemed to carry over even in death. The weight of Vic's fortune now Dan's felt both daunting and liberating despite not knowing the total value.

Dan noticed his mother was crying and his father looked quite disheveled. His father said, "Dan we were forbidden to tell you. We love you. It's important you know that."

Dan merely stared at them.

Tom glanced his way across the table. "Folks please make your way out. I will come out to the waiting area momentarily and answer any individual questions."

Dans adopted parents stood and silently left the conference room. Dan sat back in the same tan leather chair.

"Tom what is the total?"

Tom joined him at the table seated close and leaned forward. "Depends on the day. But ballpark is twenty billion."

Dan just sat there staring for a few minutes hearing the words repeated in his head. "Billion with a B. That is a thousand million twenty dollar bills." Dan let it sink in that he was now one of the wealthiest men in the world.

"Victors investment portfolio is very diverse. Aside from the Black Lake Coffee Empire and numerous chemical companies under Stone Industries, he had positions in all stock markets, futures, and various other investments. Basically, he owns or rather you own little pieces of hundreds of different businesses. He bought high risk and made money. Lots of money," Tom remarked.

"Indeed," Dan muttered, still in disbelief. "That is one metric shit ton of money."

The sheer magnitude of the fortune hit him like a freight train. With that much money, he figured he could own just about anything—or anyone— if he wanted.

Holy Snikeys—I'm rich. Dirty, rotten, filthy, stinking rich—D.R.F.S.R., he thought, the lyrics from Warrant's old 'eighties hairband anthem flashing through his mind. It was surreal, absurd even, and yet undeniably real.

"Dan, Victor did leave you his home in Black Lake, Kansas." It was Victor's sanctuary away from all the craziness of his life. As you can imagine a man with his financial standing and assets is a bit of a target. Now you have that issue too. Twenty billion makes a lot of people illogically angry simply because of your success. It's a lot different from the life you have been living."

"No shit. Tom. Why didn't any of us know that Uncle Vic was so loaded? Hell, he must have been one of the richest guys in America. That is pretty hard to keep quiet." Dan said.

"Yes. He was very low key and virtually unknown by design. All of his transactions have been handled through his corporations and trusts - eventually a bit on automatic pilot. Vic was hands off the last few years for all other companies, completely focused on Black Lake Coffee. He has people in place from the lowest level employee to the CEO in every one of his companies. Not much will change in the day to day unless you want it to."

" Nice. And no - probably don't want to rock the boat. I'm good with just collecting checks. I assume your firm manages everything."

"We provide a large amount of assistance throughout the corporations. I would like you to spend a few days here in Dallas for a complete rundown and of course to inspect the property in Louisianna and Kansas etc. You have an apartment here in Frisco, Texas, and homes in Convent, Louisianna and Black Lake, Kansas."

"Well, I don't want to live in any of those places. My plans involve sandy beaches and bikinis as far as the eye can see, Tom. I'm not my uncle..." Dan stopped himself midsentence. It was taking a lot to wrap his mind around calling Uncle Vic Dad or father or anything that familiar. "I'm not Vic."

"Well Dan, withhold judgement. I imagine the next few weeks will change your mind about a lot of things. You will love Black Lake. You have just over a thousand acres near Lebanon, Kansas. That is where Victor spent most of his time. The lake is beautiful. There is a boat if you like the water. You will love the town. Victor spent a lot of time and energy lifting the town up to a fantastic level. Our partners have had a number of corporate retreats there over the years with Victor."

"Jesus. Well you drive a hard bargain Tom. Ok. I can always buy Florida later," Dan said smiling.

"That's the spirit Dan. Victor got his start in the petro chemical industry and has stipulated that you visit the businesses there in order for you to truly understand the costs of his fortune."

"Great. Ok. New Orleans. When do I leave?"

"We will fly into New Orleans on Friday morning. Then drive to Convent on the west side of town. That's where your house is. You'll meet Sam the chief scientist and the lab is there."

"Lab?"

"Yes, the Black Lake Coffee has special properties. The lab there in convent focuses on those special properties. Trade secret. It's what makes Black Lake Coffee so delicious."

"Yes, I've heard about it and seen it in action even. Crazy cure-all coffee. I saw a person losing their shit just a few days ago."

Tom shrugged and waved his hands like a referee calling the play dead. "Lots of time for a deep dive before you head to New Orleans."

"But for now I need a break," Dan said.

"Yes, let's meet tomorrow morning here at the office. I've been working on a synopsis for you on your holdings and just notes on all the assets. I have a page for you on the Frisco apartment. Actually, it's a condo, only a few blocks from here by the Ford Center. You a Cowboys fan?"

"Who isn't?" Dan laughed.

"Good. You and Jerry Jones have a few projects together. He is a huge coffee drinker. Your condo overlooks the Cowboys practice field."

Plans were made. Signatures were taken. Papers filed. Et Cetera. Tom gave Dan his new condo address and access codes close to the Stone headquarters in Frisco. Dan would settle in and learn all about his new empire over the next several days.

CHAPTER 6

On earth as it is in Heaven,

Matthew 6:10

We serve a merciful, loving, and patient God. His compassion and grace are boundless, extending beyond what humanity can comprehend. Yet even His infinite mercy has its limits. There are moments when justice must prevail when judgment cannot be delayed. Such a moment came during the celestial rebellion, when the war in Heaven reached its devastating climax.

Lucifer, the son of the morning, the brightest and most glorious of all angels, betrayed his Creator. Pride consumed him, and his treachery spread like a contagion, sowing discord, and turning a host of Heaven's own against the Almighty. It was a crime so profound that even God's vast patience was tested.

In the end, there was no other choice. The Creator, in His righteous fury and unshakable resolve, cast Lucifer out, banishing him from Heaven for all eternity. The once-radiant angel fell, stripped of his glory, and with him went those who had followed his path of rebellion. They were consigned to the depths, separated forever from the light they had defied.

It was a moment of finality, a decisive act that reshaped the cosmos. The war was won, but at a cost that echoed through eternity. Even God's mercy could not absolve such betrayal, for justice demanded that rebellion be met with judgment.

The hand of God hurled the fallen angel's ethereal body from the divine dimension to the smoldering pits of hell as punishment for his disrespect and blasphemy. The celestial expulsion of Lucifer was a cataclysmic event that resonated throughout the cosmos. Like a flaming comet streaking across the heavens, the traitor was expelled from heaven, leaving a fiery trail visible from every corner of Earth. The impact of his fall was catastrophic, carving a gaping wound in the earthly realm—a wound that would never heal.

For seven miles in all directions, life perished as the dark spirit's descent sterilized the soil and chilled the environment to bitterness. The crater left behind, nearly a mile wide and descending to the molten core of the Earth, festered with a stagnant, boiling lake ringed by giant wormwood plants and fields of thorny black roses—a stark admonition to steer clear of this accursed place.

As millennia passed, nature tentatively reclaimed the barren land, masking the scar with verdant growth. But God left the rotten spring and the bitter plants as a warning of the evil oozing from that site. A palpable dark power emanated from the spring like a bad taste left after spoiled food. It pulled at the fibers of whatever life was near. If there was a physical place on earth that Satan had a foothold, it was here. It was as though God had allowed Satan this small piece of property as his back porch with the stinking pool of water as his picture window. This was the devil's spring. It was both rancid and beautiful -- and unnerving.

God's people, guided by His protective hand, passed by without a second glance, instinctively avoiding the poisoned waters and their ominous surroundings. A whisper on the wind might attract their attention for a moment but something inside would tell them to keep moving. In fact, most would not even notice the small lake or ever smell the coal-colored roses. God would not allow His people to be contaminated by the evil one.

However, those who embraced darkness and wickedness heard the quiet call of the spring and settled nearby. God was nowhere to be found. In His infinite wisdom, withdrew His divine presence from this unholy place, allowing Satan to exert his dominion more freely over those who dwelt there. The more evil committed in Satan's name, the further God stepped away. His Holy Spirit remained in the shadows offering guidance to His people to seek sanctuary elsewhere. Those who remained eventually succumbed to the darkness. The existence of Black

Lake stood as a profound testament to the mysteries of God's judgment and the consequences of human choices.

A blood thirsty renegade band of Choctaw warriors, shunned by their tribe and drawn to the malevolent power emanating from the cursed waters were the first to establish a village around the dark spring. Initially, the water was too foul to live near, prompting the tribe to settle miles downwind. But each morning the chief would walk to the water and ask his gods to show mercy and allow this water for his people. Eventually the gods answered the persistent chief, allowing him to cast his own lot and that of his people.

"The water must be purified," a whisper on the hot wind emanating from the dark water had instructed. The warrior leader had no issue with his god's commandment. Each morning for the next twelve days, a young female member of the Choctaw band was selected and cast into the scalding water along with her infant child. Their agony and death appeased the dark entity within which responded by cooling the waters to a non-lethal temperature.

The Indian tribe moved close to the water's edge, simplifying their daily lives. The tribe had established their grim dominion over the lake, but the dark spring was never meant to be theirs alone. Its call reached far beyond the tribe, beckoning across the land, summoning others who thrived in the shadow of wickedness.

The tribe flourished for three seasons until an unexpected encounter changed their fate. Welcoming a giant white man named William Joseph Cromwell and his family into their village, enticed by the promise of food and supplies, ended their peaceful existence by the dark waters. Cromwell and his clan were pilgrims traveling east and the first white people the tribe had ever encountered. With long silvery-white hair and a matching full beard, Cromwell stood out starkly against the backdrop of their tribal community.

Initially, the chief's instinct was to eliminate this foreign intruder and seize his beautiful pale skinned wife and daughters as his own. In hindsight, following this impulse would have ensured the tribe's survival through another harsh winter. However, William Joseph proved to be different from others who had come before. He was pleasant and jolly. The chief liked him. The Chief could see the future of his tribe aligning with the clan of the large white man.

Unbeknownst to the chief, Cromwell was drawn to Black Lake like a moth to a flame, inexplicably compelled towards its dark allure. William Joseph was not looking to share the prosperity in this promised land.

The aftermath of the Civil War had left a bitter and fragmented peace, old wounds festering and new divisions rising. In the midst of this turmoil, Cromwell, a man driven by ambition and unyielding conviction, sought escape from the chaos. Born into a Southern family that clung to its old ways like a dying man to his last breath, William Joseph inherited a strict moral code wrapped in hypocrisy and self-interest. The scars of the war carved deeply into his worldview, and with little regard for allegiance to the North or South, he became determined to carve out his own destiny.

His solution was isolation. Away from the poisonous rhetoric and smoldering hatred, he envisioned a sanctuary where he alone could shape the laws, the morality, and the future. Yet the frontier was not the refuge he had hoped for—it was merely another theater of conflict. Each settlement echoed the same debates, the same resentments. So, William Joseph turned to the wilderness, seeking the untouched, the unclaimed, the unknown.

In Colorado, his pilgrimage took a sinister turn. At the Royal Gorge, a towering natural marvel, he made deals that revealed his true nature. One such transaction, memorialized in a photograph Dan Stone would later discover, captured him trading blankets laced with smallpox to a similar tribe desperate for warmth. They also liked the giant white man. He pocketed their meager possessions—pelts, trinkets, and even a cache of venom extracted from rattlesnakes. The venom would later serve his dark purposes, cementing his infamy among those who crossed his path.

William Joseph's journey westward was a calling. Something beyond himself drew him further into the uncharted wild. He spoke of visions—

a black lake surrounded by beautiful dark roses, its waters as deep as the midnight sky. His family dismissed these dreams as the delusions of a fervent preacher with too many sermons in his head. But William Joseph felt the pull of something greater than ambition, stronger than faith.

He knew immediately when he saw the enormous trees, their green canopies stretching like cathedral ceilings. The soil, rich and black, clung to the wagon wheels as if reluctant to let them pass. And there, in the heart of this untouched wilderness, lay the lake. Its surface shimmered like liquid obsidian, encircled by black roses that bloomed with an unnatural vitality. William Joseph fell to his knees, overcome by the sight. This was the promised land he had seen in his dreams—a place of divine providence.

What he could not explain, or refused to, was the gnawing sense of dread that accompanied his arrival. The lake was beautiful, yes, but it was also wrong. Its stillness was too perfect, its water too dark. Yet William Joseph felt no fear. He interpreted the lake as a sign—a gift meant only for him. He named the settlement Black Lake, Kansas, and declared himself its leader.

William Joseph's piety was a thin veil over a heart corrupted by greed and darkness. His dealings with the tribes in Colorado were just the beginning. William Joseph did not seek peace, but power—a place where he could reign unchallenged, free from the constraints of a fractured nation. What awaited him at the edge of the coal-black waters would change the course of history, binding his soul to the lake and the dark forces that called it home.

The tribe welcomed the strange white man with curiosity and warmth, their initial wariness giving way to camaraderie as the evening unfolded. After a lavish feast, where stories were shared around roaring fires, Smith unveiled his gift to the Indian chief: several cases of a strong dark liquor. The gesture was met with enthusiasm, and soon every male member of the camp joined in the revelry, drinking deep into the night. Laughter echoed across the settlement, and as the festivities wound down, each man retired to his teepee with his mate. It had been a night of celebration, leaving the camp in a contented haze.

The strong medicine the old man had shared with his new friends was a concoction of grain alcohol, laudanum, and a few drops of the Arizona black rattlesnake venom generously provided to the victims by a distant cousin from the Diegueno tribe William Joseph had met not long before. The venom is extremely potent and hemotoxic, causing great pain and damage to tissue. Mercifully, the combination placed the men in a dreamless stupor before the acidic venom ate the hole through their stomach lining and joined their blood stream. William Joseph was the only male who lived to see the sunrise over the steaming lake with the black roses. He justified the atrocity with scripture, calling it divine retribution for those who had opposed his path.

The settlers of Black Lake revered him, unaware of the depths of his malice. To them, he was a preacher and a provider, a man of God who had led them to paradise. But William Joseph knew better. He was no shepherd—he was the wolf. And Black Lake was his domain, a place that called to him not from Heaven, but from the deepest pits of Hell.

Some may question God's infinite mercy for allowing Black Lake to persist, yet His reasons remain inscrutable to mortals. This poisoned enclave endured through the ages, its existence an enigma that defied conventional understanding. Over time, it not only survived but thrived, drawing in transient souls who stumbled upon its shores and found themselves ensnared by its peculiar magnetism.

To the casual observer, Black Lake appeared like any other small town, with caring citizens and a semblance of normalcy. Neighbors looked out for each other, and love found its way amidst the quaint houses and serene landscapes. Yet beneath this facade of community and warmth lurked a darkness that permeated its very essence.

At its core, Black Lake was a place where fate often tipped the scales unfavorably. The whispered tales and unspoken fears of its residents bore witness to a history stained by inexplicable tragedies and unanswered questions. Those who dared to stay soon learned that luck was a capricious mistress here, and the flip of fate's coin too frequently landed on tails.

In the shadows cast by the looming pines and reflected in the murky depths of the lake, secrets whispered of ancient pacts and forgotten promises. The black roses that bloomed sporadically along its shores were both a marvel and a warning, their beauty concealing thorns that pricked at the curiosity of those who dared to venture too close.

Black Lake stood as a testament to the paradox of human existence— where light and darkness intermingled, and where the line between good and evil blurred. It beckoned the lost and the curious, offering sanctuary to some and ensnaring others in its inescapable grip. To understand Black Lake was to confront the mysteries that lurked beneath its tranquil surface, where the pulse of the town echoed with the heartbeat of something older, darker, and unfathomable.

CHAPTER 7

Ezra noted the heavy bags under William Joseph's eyes. The color had drained from his old friend's face, his eyes cold.

"I wanted to ask you about the well behind Raymond's store," Ezra said.

"What of it?" William Joseph required in a deep hoarse voice.

"Are you ill my friend?"

"No Ezra," the big man stated. "And if you ever inquire of my private affairs again, I will tear your heart out. Now leave me."

If William Joseph's journey into the darkness had been lacking up to this point it was certainly now complete.

From that point on, the small community was to be radically changed. One by one its members fell victim to the immense power of the evil. Each citizen was to succumb in his own way. The power grew with each spirit it absorbed.

The evil bred until the individual members of Black Lake made up a whole, a complete unit of oneness. An organic unity of evil. The final plan for this culture were known to no man. William Joseph was the leader of this community but not the master. No one fully understood the tasks to be completed but somehow everyone had a good idea what they were.

The people of Black Lake were not given a choice in the matter. Every man, woman, and child became loyal sheep of William Joseph or silently disappeared. As would be expected, the kind of heart refused to accept the bombardment of dark emotions and left town while others simply walked into the hot waters of Black Lake.

On the day the final soul joined the ranks of the living evil, the physical expansion halted as abruptly as it had begun. Forty-seven God fearing individuals had gone to their final resting place.

Within the bounds of the area of darkness, time held no meaning. One day was as the next, as was the last. William Joseph remained as the central paternal head of the town. He was their leader, the Mayor of Black Lake with no opposition as all citizens were loyal servants.

As in a dream, the blur of events during the next several years left no visible marks. The townspeople had become just like the land growing unproductive and stagnant. There was no need. No one aged. No one was ill.

The only break in the monotonous routing was the periodic passerby; sometimes alone, sometimes by the car load. As with everywhere else in the nation at that time in history, people were moving through on their way to somewhere better than where they were. The only difference was the frequency. The dampening field seemed to have some measure of effect on the crowds. It seemed to work as a deterrent to most. The only ones snared in this selectively permeable net were the weak willed, apathetic, and the evil at heart.

Those unaffected who passed through found nothing out of the ordinary or out of place in this dying town, nothing strange even about the fact that they took with them little or no memories of anything which had transpired. This was surely for the best, for if those memories traveled outside the dampening field, madness would surely follow.

The residents became very different people. The orderly chaos of evil was spreading like the black plague. The air, ground, trees, the spot in space, the fabric of the universe had poisoned them all. William Joseph was malignant. His hate spilled to Ezra and the seeds planted themselves solidly in his heart like the fangs of a serpent.

Ezra knew. He could feel the darkness creeping through his soul. In the last several years he had killed for William Joseph, but now he was acting of his own accord for an unseen force. William Joseph was the conductor of a small elite troupe permitted to complete a very important task yet to be revealed. Ezra was important. He had never been important. No one ever even thought he was smart.

Shortly after the confrontation with William Joseph, Ezra found himself standing in front of the fountain in the town square. Although he often relaxed by peering into the fountains strange hypnotic water, today it felt as though some inner plug had been pulled free. His will seemed to drain from him, and he could see in his mind's eye his essence flowing into the dark murky water. He saw himself standing with his head bowed. He was floating above his body looking on like an outsider. He saw the dark water snake upwards into his body. As Ezra was filled, he rejoined his body and could see from his real eyes again. Had he been standing there for hours or days? What did it matter anyway? All of his hopes, dreams, aspirations, and even worries seemed to demand less attention. Less Ezra.

The sensation was both strange and wonderful-- thought with no words -- not exactly feelings either. Instead of actively thinking he found himself being. Yes, that was it. He was Being. It was as though instinctive thought processes had taken over his irrational and useless human methods. This proved to be quite interesting as well as exhilarating to Ezra. Love, hate, passion, lust, rage, all rolled into one, merged into the same. The deeper he stared into the pool the more lost within he became.

Ezra slowly turned and walked down the dirt street of the town still numb from the experience, limbs moving, feeling his strides, arms sliding back and forth against his worn canvas jacket. But he was not in control. Why would he want to be?

After experiencing this distorted time for a while Ezra turned up standing on the whitewashed front porch of his home. As always, this time of year the windows on the first and second floors were open to allow for the cool evening air. The curtains danced in the light breeze. Ezra watched his hand turn the doorknob and push the door inward. His feet carried him into another world within the four walls of his home.

In stark contrast to the bright, dry world outside, the interior of the house was dim and cool, a refuge from the harsh elements. The hardwood floors gleamed, their polish catching faint reflections of light, evidence of a fresh and meticulous cleaning. The air was fragrant with the comforting scents of baked bread and apples, a testament to Clara's quiet industriousness.

A high-backed, cloth-lined chair stood near a small table, atop which rested a large family Bible, its worn pages silently proclaiming truths to anyone who cared to notice. The white wallpaper, patterned with subtle vertical stripes, bore the subtle sheen of recent scrubbing. It was clear that Ezra's wife, Clara, had been hard at work, her touch evident in every polished surface and lingering aroma.

The room spun and stopped with his eyes fixed on the front window. Ezra parted the deep red velvet curtains and relaxed his weight against the glass. The wind picked up and he could feel it against his legs as he strained to see down the street, He could feel William Joseph watching him. He could see him standing in the street laughing with those God damned black roses rocking in the breeze. He was not there. Ezra knew that. Maybe.

"Ezra, how long you going to look out that window?" asked Clara in her thick southern drawl. "Ezra Smith, I am speaking to you. Do you hear me?" her voice grew louder as she grew impatient with her husband.

She touched his shoulder. "You going to---"

Her voice was interrupted by Ezra spinning to his right, knocking her hand off and cracking the windowpane with his opposite elbow. The fire in his eyes warned her of the impending danger.

Clara's always constant smile faded from her face as she watched his large thin weather-beaten hand rise above her.

"Ezra --" Clara started but then noticed the icy glaze that had overtaken her husband's normally placid face. She could no longer see Ezra inside of his brown eyes.

The past memories of Ezra's insane glare and what followed on that miserable day blended perfectly with the present moment. Ezra's tanned, weatherbeaten hand sliced through the still morning air and struck Clara just below the left ear. Her final image on this earth was of the gentle man she had loved a lifetime killing her. She fell like a broken doll of her former being.

Ezra was no longer the man she had known and loved. His journey was complete. And although he was watching the blood flow from Claras now lifeless nose and mouth onto the wooden flood she had worked so hard to polish earlier that morning, he knew somehow that she would be more a part of him now than she had ever been. Afterall, everyone in Black Lake was one.

More evidence of the cancer growing in Black Lake happened on that warm summer morning in 1869. When Ezra struck down his wife, he was committed to the dark life of hate which was to follow. Although William Joseph had trekked the journey to destruction further than Ezra, they were not the only ones to become affected. Raymond Smith, owner of the general store was to show his own depravity, only in a much different fashion.

The sun was just beginning to paint the most eastern horizon copper, soon the sun would rise, brilliantly shining down onto this dark part of the world.

This day, in many respects, was different from any in the brief history of Black Lake. This day was to be the first funeral of a town member.

Clara Smith, struck down in the very prime of her life. A pillar of strength was now gone forever. She left behind her husband Ezra and a town full of mournful relatives. How could they survive without her? In the end, the hate which struck her down would unite them forever.

Raymond Smith rose early in the predawn morning, as was usual. On this fresh summer morning, Raymond awoke easily, which was not so usual.

As he rose from bed, he noted then dismissed a slight difference in his outlook. This pleasant, mild-mannered storekeeper felt the first pangs of anger. Anger which was relatively unknown to him.

As he dressed and ate, Raymond was slightly aware of a shortened temper. The eggs were underdone, the toast overdone, and the milk had soured. How ironic.

Helen Smith ate slowly, limped to the table and sat across from her husband. As always, her hair was pulled back to a tight bun behind her head. Her dress was crisply pressed, her back straight in the chair, Helen always took careful watch of her painstakingly detailed appearance.

"My knee hurts so badly this morning. I was hoping it wouldn't hurt again so," Helen spoke, rubbing her right kneecap.

Raymond sat staring at his plate.

"How do you feel this morning Raymond dear?"

Raymond did not look up. "Why?"

"Oh, you just look like something is bothering you. Are you okay?" Helen asked, still stroking her knee.

"Leave me alone."

Helen knew to change the subject. Raymond usually did not act so short with her, though when he did it was best to just change the subject.

"Don't forget about the funeral this morning. It's so terrible that she had to go so suddenly. I hope Ezra is holding up all right."

"Ezra killed his wife for asking too many questions and continually running her mouth. Unless you wish to temp a similar fate, I would suggest that you leave me be." Raymond spoke in a low, warning tone. Still, he did not look away from his plate.

Struck with the anger of her husband, Helen rose and hurried from the kitchen. Pain or not, she was getting out, and now.

Later that morning the townspeople gathered in front of the rose garden. Everyone was there except Raymond Smith who had other plans for the day.

A thin man dressed in a black tunic was standing atop a small wooden platform holding a large open bible in his outstretched hands. In front of him was his congregation listening intently as he spoke the words to allow Clara to pass into the afterlife.

Behind and looking on was William Joseph Smith, his coal black eyes watching the long black roses sway in the light breeze. At the front of their church stood the recent widower Ezra Smith without a tear and without remorse. The words of the man in black falling on deaf ears. He too watched the black roses rock back and forth.

Black Lake grew like a small weed taking over a large garden. It soon became obvious that William Joseph's family plot had become a small community that had become too large to remain self-contained. The supply of food was merely adequate rather than abundant. The best farmland and business locations had long since been taken. Another town had popped up only a day's ride to the south. New things called automobiles were beginning to surface on the outskirts. Dissatisfaction began to spread through the minds of the citizens like a bizarre illness. William Joseph knew he must act quickly.

"Something must be done," Ezra stated.

"Let me think," the big man returned quickly.

"The people just do not seem to want to stay separated from the outsiders."

"Quiet Ezra. I need to think in peace."

Ezra bowed his head to think alone. He knew the tone his leader had used. He had heard it many times before. William Joseph would decide what should be done. He always did.

"It is done. Leave me and return when I call," he said slowly, opening the front door of his home.

Ezra walked out into the warm spring air. He turned to the giant of a man and looking up asked, "What are we to do?"

"You will understand in the morning my friend."

The town's second in command stepped off the bleached wood porch and walked silently to his own home just next door. He and William Joseph had chosen the most beautiful locations before all of the strangers had arrived. Behind the two cabins were the largest trees Ezra had ever seen. A thick hedge row separated the homes from a large pond that was home to a variety of mammoth fish. It was paradise as far as Ezra was concerned. But the strangers were wandering closer and closer to their neck of the woods. The town was becoming crowded.

The original settlers had understood. They followed William Josephs orders explicitly. The people coming into the area now, however, doubted the leader. Why should they blindly follow and assume he was the most competent? They did not recognize William Joseph as the chosen one. There had been talk of setting up free elections to determine who should lead Black Lake. People were calling him a doddering old fool whose time had passed. Thoughts of the democratic process filled the minds of the strangers and were bleeding into the thoughts of all but a few of the most loyal. The faithful.

A few hours before William Joseph had called Ezra to his cabin, Jacob a young man still dedicated to the old ways approached William Joseph and told him of a plot to take his life. Jacob named the men he overheard at the stable as Martin Ames and Carl Becker. William knew the men. They were responsible for striking the first match that sparked disillusionment. The flames grew rapidly and soon filled too many hearts for William Joseph to merely overlook their actions. He had given an order to a man in town. Ames and Becker had publicly defied him. No. These two traitors would be dealt with severely.

That night Ezra awoke from a very strange dream. Cold sweat ran from his face and his nightshirt clung to his thin frame. "How odd," he said aloud and climbed out of his bed. Stumbling across the dark room to his kitchen table. Ezra pulled out an old wooden chair and sat down hard. "Amazing," he spoke aloud once again. The vision had been an instructional session for the plan William Joseph had devised. He knew the dream was to be followed to the letter. His leader, his friend, had come to him that night directly into his mind.

A dinner was to be prepared for the entire town. A celebration to dedicate a large statue to honor William Joseph and declare him their eternal leader. Ezra had been told the statue was in his own outbuilding behind his house. Ezra pulled on his boots and put his coat over his nightshirt. "Clara," he bellowed across the room.

There was no answer. The sound of his unnecessarily loud voice shocked Ezra back to the reality that Clara was no more.

There was to be a celebration dinner for the town. Food must be prepared. He would enlist the help of the faithful. Only women he knew to be loyal to William Joseph and Black Lake. The dinner was at noon.

The door slammed as Ezra set out on his task. It was nearly dawn. If he were to get help and have the food prepared on time he would have to get moving. He had a lot to do.

Ezra walked to the shed between the great trees and his home. He knew such a thing was not possible but obeyed the orders from his friend and leader despite his reservations. He pulled the heavy wooden doors open to reveal an eight-foot likeness of William Joseph. The statue seemed to be made of solid iron, smoothly finished with a satiny black texture. "Incredible," he gasped. Never before had he seen such workmanship. The attention to detail was amazing. If he had stumbled across the statue, he would have done a double take thinking it was actually his leader.

It took Ezra more than an hour to harness his horse to the wagon and manipulate the iron monster into the bed and drive to the town square. The statue was to stand between the lake and the field of black roses forming a perfect triangle.

Ezra took his time placing the statue in position. In the dream he had watched the sun rise behind it and had to recall the perfect angle. Around the base he placed the largest stones he could find and loaded them in the wagon. He installed the final block just as the sun snuck over the horizon.

"William Joseph," Ezra said quietly as he knocked on the cabin door. "William Joseph."

"Yes Ezra. I see you have done as I asked. Is the town awake?"

"They are just rising. Jacob and his brothers pulled as many tables as they could find to the street. The ladies have prepared the feast. The finest of everything has been chosen."

"Good. Seat Carl and Martin and their families at the same table. Place them close to the front. Close to me. Spread this on their plates before they are served." William Joseph handed a small jar filled with clear liquid the same consistency as water.

"It will be done," Ezra stated.

Children ran through the streets laughing and screaming while they entertained each other. This was the perfect spring day for a town party. The sun was shining brightly. Small white clouds drifted aimlessly through the clear blue sky. Not a care in the world was considered by the citizens of Black Lake. Everyone in town loved the statue or claimed to. Carl and Martin raved.

"It is fantastic, Ezra! How long have you been planning this incredible honor?"

"Absolutely beautiful, Ezra. Who did you find to create this masterpiece?"

They will get theirs, Ezra thought.

A pretty blonde girl of twenty years led Carl, his wife Emily, and their three children to the table Martin, Sue and their infant son were already seated. Soon everyone had a chair and a place to eat and listen.

"Fine people of Black Lake," Ezra began. "We have gathered here today to pay tribute to our great founder and distinguished leader of our town.

Many years ago, this fine man led a small group of settlers across some very rough territory to arrive here in our little corner of paradise. After a great deal of work spanning several years, we had a town, and we had a home. Thanks to him. I think it only fitting after years of dedication and service that we show our appreciation in any way possible. As you can see, we have a beautiful new statue to grace our town and honor our founder for his outstanding leadership. I give you the guest of honor, Mr. William Joseph Smith."

As William Joseph stood, Carl and Martin exchanged glances. They could say nothing against him under the circumstances. Each realized there would be a better time and place to object to his leadership. Tomorrow was another day. Tomorrow they would stick a knife in the old coot and drop him into the lake with that stupid statue. They both cheered louder than anyone else in the square so William Joseph would be feeling good and satisfied with their loyalty.

"Thank you, my friends. I have been through a great deal with a great many of you. I offer my services to this town as long as it will have me. Please enjoy your meal," he said raising his wine glass high over his head. "A toast to Black Lake." The towns people raised their wine glasses. "To Black Lake."

"To William Joseph," Ezra called out.

"To William Joseph," they repeated.

The ringing of glasses filled the air. Then Ezra shouted, "Long live William!" The townspeople erupted in more cheers and applause and emptied their glasses of the strong red wine.

The young ladies in charge of seating led each family to the serving table in turn where William Joseph was carving meat from a large roasted pig. Carl and Martin were first to the table. William Joseph pushed a long fork into the hind quarters and sliced a large piece of meat from the bone. "Carl. Good to see you," he said placing the pork on his tainted plate. Martin, this piece has your name on it," he said stabbing another large shank and dropping it on his plate as well. Soon all the people of Black

Lake had heaping plates of pork, pheasant, fried potatoes, biscuits with sawmill gravy and thick slices of hot apple pie.

As the towns people ate William Joseph stood. "Once again, thank you for attending and remaining loyal to our way of life. From this point forward no others will be allowed to settle in our community. we are Black Lake."

There was a slight hesitation in the reaction of some of the citizens, but it was not noticed over the cheering majority. Ezra, however, noted who did not respond to their leaders' words immediately.

The feast was soon over. The people of Black Lake returned to their homes. Carl and Martin and their families retired early unusually exhausted. The children were put to bed as soon as they walked in their doors. The two traitors thought, nearly at the same moment, "Just a little nap, that's all I need. Then I will be good as new." The eight members of the disloyal families were buried in a community grave in the middle of the garden of black roses. As the months passed the town thinned substantially. Those who did not wish to obey the laws and reflect the thoughts of William Joseph left town or silently disappeared during the night.

The remaining loyal members of Black Lake evolved.

CHAPTER 8

As time passed and humanity evolved, the seasons of existence shifted, much like the Earth itself. A long winter of hibernation was giving way to the inevitable change that follows—a stirring of renewal, of transformation. Humanity had reached a point where its growth and its failings had intertwined to form something altogether different. And as man changed, as the Earth groaned under the weight of time, so too did God's perspective on His creation.

God thoughts are veiled in mystery, His plans woven in ways one can only glimpse through the consequences they leave behind. He moves according to His will, His purposes often beyond the grasp of mortal understanding.

The time had come for change. Something new, something profound, was stirring within the fabric of existence. What had been was no longer sufficient. The world demanded it. Humanity demanded it.

And so, change came. It swept through creation, subtle at first but growing, unstoppable, reshaping everything in its path. For better or worse, the old order was fading, and the new had begun to take its place. What that change would bring, only time—and the will of God—would reveal.

Change was coming to the Earth herself. Black Lake is the Alpha of this story and is the Omega as well. When Satan was cast from the heavens, God's wrath opened up a festering hole in the earth affecting all who tread near. But this was no ordinary wound on the Earth. The scar was sour and soft, bitter and acrid, coated with bile and stinking of infection. Truly an ulcer; a malignant cancer had penetrated the Earth's skin as a contagion for the life blood of our planet.

Over time the walls of the lesion, the long deep sides of the Black Lake began to crumble and ooze into the steaming water falling to the bottom and into the Pit. The fabric of the Earth being exposed each new day was tender new flesh quickly becoming irritated and dissolving into the maw of the black lake. The spear of the Choctaw Indian Chief, had it survived would have been one hundred feet offshore on the day Dan Stone inherited ground zero.

The cancer that had been contained for millennia was awakened by Dan Stone's imminent arrival—now stirred with purpose. This Cancer was sentient. Malevolent. Ancient. And it was moving—at last permitted to walk the earth for its season.

CHAPTER 9

Victor Stone was nothing short of a prodigy. Born and raised in Wichita, Kansas, Vic exhibited brilliance from an early age. By the time most kids were thinking about prom, Vic had already graduated from high school and secured an internship at Vulcan Chemical. At the same time, he enrolled in Wichita State University, pursuing a degree in organic chemistry.

Vic did not just excel—he obliterated every academic expectation. He earned his bachelor's and master's degrees in organic chemistry before his 20th birthday, a feat that had professors and scholars alike hailing him as a savant. Words like brilliant and genius became synonymous with his name, and he soon found himself on the national radar as one of the country's brightest young minds.

But Vic did not stop there. Hungry for more, he set his sights on the Massachusetts Institute of Technology. By twenty-two, he had not only earned a double PhD in chemistry and materials science but also an MBA, cementing his place as an intellectual powerhouse.

It was during his time at MIT that he met Betty Smith. Betty, a vivacious and intelligent woman, seemed to be the perfect complement to Vic's calculated brilliance. They quickly moved in together, and not long after, Betty became pregnant.

Vic secured a prestigious position at California Institute of Technology, where he would begin working on groundbreaking projects in applied chemistry. Betty stayed behind in Massachusetts temporarily, preparing for the child they were expecting.

But tragedy struck.

A car accident claimed Betty's life weeks before she was to give birth. Her twins were born prematurely but healthy. In the chaos following Betty's death, her extended family made the decision to place the babies for adoption.

Vic was not kin nor in touch with any of Betty's family. Vic was unaware of Betty's death, and did not find out about her passing—or the adoption of his children—for nearly a year. He had been angry and bitter assuming Betty had simply ghosted him and moved on for whatever reason. Vic was absorbed in his demanding new role at Caltech and pushed the entire relationship from his mind.

When the news reached him, it shattered him. Through a frantic search, Vic discovered that one of the twins, Dan, had ended up in an orphanage in Massachusetts. And through a bureaucratic error in hospital paperwork the other twin was deleted from their records and never was discovered. Heartbroken and guilt-ridden, Vic knew he could not stand by and let his child be passed around the foster system. As a single man with a career that demanded every ounce of his time, he also knew he was not the best choice to raise a child.

Vic made an extraordinary decision: he facilitated Dan's adoption by his brother and sister-in-law in Wichita. They were married, stable, and firmly rooted in the city Vic had left behind. He believed they could provide Dan with the home and family he could not.

But the adoption came with conditions. Dan's existence would be a family secret, hidden from everyone outside their immediate circle. It was Vic's way of protecting his son, while also ensuring that he could focus on the monumental plans he had for his future.

Even so, the knowledge of Dan's existence shaped Vic's life in profound and unexpected ways. It became a driving force behind his relentless ambition—a reason to amass the resources and influence that might one day help him reconnect with his son, or at least ensure Dan had the best opportunities in life.

The burden of that secret, however, never left him. It followed him as he built his empire, a quiet shadow behind every decision he made. It was not just guilt—it was a sense of responsibility, a need to prove that he was worthy of the sacrifices he'd made, and to leave behind a legacy that would matter.

What Vic did not know—what no one told him—was that Dan had a twin brother, Lucas, who had been adopted by a family in Pennsylvania. The records from the hospital had been muddled, and Vic's search for information never uncovered Lucas's existence.

Lucas grew up in a small Pennsylvania town, raised by a kind but reserved couple who gave him a quiet, stable upbringing. Though Lucas never knew about Dan or Vic, he often felt a strange sense of incompleteness, as if some vital connection in his life was missing.

Unbeknownst to Vic, his legacy now stretched beyond what he could comprehend—hidden in the life of a second son he never knew existed.

***

Victor Stone rarely visited Wichita, but he always kept track of Dan. Despite their distance, he never stopped caring about the boy he had secretly placed with his brother. Dan was family, his blood, his son.

Vic followed Dan's college experience closely. In fact he had arranged for the tuition payments. Dan was brilliant just like Vic. High school was simple. Grades were B's and C's as usual for the most gifted. College was going fast like it did for Vic. On paper Dan was in his third year of college after only completing one year. It came easily. He was a young man with promise—a hint of the prodigy he had imagined. One evening, Vic came into town and quietly slipped into a restaurant where Dan was meeting his girlfriend Becca. From the corner of the room, Vic observed.

What Vic saw wasn't what he'd hoped for. Dan was relaxed, laughing, and clearly in love. The young man before him didn't resemble the driven, disciplined student of life Vic had envisioned. There was no hunger in his eyes, no fire—only comfort. Contentment.

It bothered Vic more than he cared to admit. Dan looked like someone drifting—caught in the gravity of youth, not propelled by the force needed to shape a future. He wasn't carving out his place in the world. He was floating through it.

Yes, he was advancing in academia, but that wasn't enough. Dan needed to be a hard driver. Relentless. Ruthless. He needed to go after the gold—and take it. But, Dan would grow out of it, surely, Vic reasoned. The reckless arrogance of youth was temporary, he told himself. But the truth was, Vic drove away with a pit in his stomach. What of the brilliance? The potential? The distraction of this woman he was with was unsettling.

Victor left the restaurant without saying a word. He would check in again. Have a heart to heart with Dan. Maybe even tell him the truth. Unveil that Victor was indeed his biological father and explain to his Vic's reasoning for keeping it a secret all these years.

Northbound on the highway, Vic was lost in thought, unable to shake his fear that the woman would distract Dan and yet the excitement for the future of his scion was palpable. He drove for hours, his thoughts spiraling. Two hundred miles later, he found himself in Lebanon, Kansas. It was late, and the full moon cast an eerie glow on the empty country roads. Vic turned down one wrong road after another, the labyrinth of gravel and dirt making him feel even more lost—both literally and figuratively.

Then, in the exact center of the continental United States, he saw the lights of a town.

He followed the glow and entered a small, quiet place with a sign reading Black Lake, Kansas. It was unlike anything he had seen before—a quaint, almost forgotten town, tucked away from the world. Vic parked his car and wandered into a local bar. The sign on the wall outside said "The Strings."

Bob, the gruff yet friendly bartender, welcomed Vic like an old friend. They chatted about the town, its history, and its peculiarities. Bob told him about the mystical black lake just beyond the town limits, a place shrouded in mystery and local legend.

Intrigued, Vic could not resist. Vic stumbled out of the bar, sobered by the cool night air. The streets were empty, the quiet broken only by the occasional rustle of wind through the trees. His head was cloudy, and he was physically exhausted, but something he could not explain drew him toward the lake.

The drive was a blur of moonlit dirt roads and twisted shadows. The headlights of his truck struggled to pierce through the suffocating black mist that seemed to spill out from the lake itself. Light from his headlights disappeared into the haze, swallowed whole by the unnatural black fog. He slowed to a crawl, cautiously moving to keep from finding the lake the hard way. The fog thickened the closer he got, heavy and dense, clinging to his windshield like smoke from a burning tire plant.

An intense gust of wind shook his truck from side to side and provided a moment of clarity. He had arrived. Black lake was hauntingly beautiful, its surface shimmering under the moonlight. Surrounding it were fields of black roses, their long stems swaying gently in the night breeze. Vic had never seen anything like them. He stepped closer, drawn in by their otherworldly allure, and felt the heat emanating from the water's edge. Tentatively, he reached down to touch it, and the sensation was electric burning, almost alive.

But the beautiful black flowers were seductive. The roses emitted a pheromone-like scent drawing him in - he had to smell one up close he had to feel it in his hand and touch it like a lover's caress. He needed to do it. He could not help himself. He leaned in and put his nose nearly inside the petals of the beautiful flower. Inhaling the aroma deeply. It was a strong scent, a mixture of floral and savory. A human scent like sex and roses, he mused. And then it bit him. Or stung him. He was not sure which. But it was inside his nose. Like a needle.

Vic jerked back coughing and howling with pain. He blew out his nose to clear his nasal passage. He fell to his knees, dizzy. He saw the hot water. He did not care how hot it was, he needed the rose out of his nose. Kneeling at the water's edge Vic stuck his hands into the burning water and cupping the near boiling liquid stuck his injured nose into his palms washing his face and nose as best he could. Actually, snorting some water into his nostrils to cleanse the passageway. Another two handfuls of water. Strangely, he could not feel the burning sensation of the hot water. It soothed him. His nose felt better. No, he felt better. In fact, he felt fantastic. Vic sat back on his heels. He felt incredible. He felt alive. He reached forward and scooped more water out. Not burning. He splashed it on his face. He drank. Then he drank more deeply. The water was pure, clean, and delicious. It tasted like the rose smelled. He knew the roses and the water were one. He knew a lot about the beautiful black roses, the water in the ink-colored lake, and the town of Black Lake. It was not possible, but Vic felt his knowledge and intelligence rise.

Vic pulled off his clothes and walked into the lake. He felt exhilarated. He was not ill, but he felt healed. Vic laid back on the water's edge. The thick black mist had settled on the water, and he could see the full moon and a sky full of stars. The environment seemed to pulse with energy, a feeling Vic could not ignore. It was not just a lake—it was something more.

At the time, Vic was not the wealthy man he would later become. At 45, he was successful, with a solid job and several patents to his name. He was comfortable, yes, but not rich. Retirement was not in the cards for him, nor would he have wanted it to be. He was driven, ambitious, always looking for the next challenge.

Black Lake felt like a challenge. It felt like destiny. That night, Vic fell in love with the black roses and the dark waters. He dressed and drove away with the seeds of an idea forming in his mind—seeds that would one day grow into something far bigger than he could have imagined.

Vic drove back into town. Black Lake. He drove up and down the streets. What can this town do for him, he wondered. Could he live here? He went back to the bar.

"Bob, the lake was fantastic!" Vic exclaimed as he burst through the bar's creaking door, his voice echoing through the room. Heads turned toward him, and the lively hum of conversation abruptly stopped. The bar was crowded now, alive with the smell of spilled beer and cigarette smoke, but the energy shifted the moment Vic spoke. It was nearly midnight, and something about the air felt off.

A giant of a man turned slowly to face Vic. He had ghost-white hair that fell in unruly waves past his shoulders, a long black coat that hung from his broad frame, and skin so deeply lined it looked like cracked leather. But it was his eyes that stopped Vic cold—coal black, bottomless, and as unyielding as the dark waters of Black Lake.

"Bob isn't here," the man said, his voice low and gravelly, with a hint of menace. He did not move closer but didn't have to. His presence filled the room like a thundercloud.

Goosebumps prickled up Vic's spine as the man's gaze bore into him. He was not just large—he was enormous, nearly seven feet tall and easily four hundred pounds, by Vic's quick estimation. And there was a meanness in his expression, a cold disdain that made the hairs on the back of Vic's neck stand up.

"Sounds like you've been out to the lake," the man said, his tone deliberate, each word landing like the toll of a bell.

Vic hesitated; his initial burst of excitement now dampened by the weight of the man's stare. The bar remained deathly silent, the other patrons watching the exchange as if caught in a spell.

"I... uh, yeah," Vic stammered, trying to gather himself. "I just came from there. It is—well, it's unlike anything I've ever seen."

The man's frown deepened, his coal-black eyes narrowing. "And what did you see?" he asked, his voice carrying a challenge, as though the answer mattered more than Vic realized.

The silence in the bar grew heavier, and Vic felt the weight of every gaze on him. This was not the warm, curious reception he'd had earlier with Bob. This was something else entirely—something darker, something that crawled under his skin and clutched at his breath.

"I saw the lake. I saw the roses. I saw the power," Vic breathed, his voice trembling as his eyes locked onto the towering figure before him.

The giant of a man tilted his head, his coal-black eyes unblinking as they bore into Vic's soul. A slow nod. A knowing look. "Yes," he rumbled, his voice like a distant storm. "Yes, you did, didn't you."

He is the one we have been waiting for William.

Time seemed to stand still as they stared at one another, Vic trapped in a vision of shimmering, scalding waters and blooming black roses. The big man remained motionless, head tilted and eyes distant as though listening to whispers that only he could hear, his expression unreadable. Finally, after what felt like an eternity, he spoke again, his voice laden with an authority that seemed to echo through the room.

"My name is William Joseph Cromwell," he said, his words deliberate and final. He extended his hand, his shadow seeming to stretch over Vic like a shroud. "Welcome to Black Lake, Victor."

# # #

Vic left the bar in the early hours of the morning, stumbling into the cool night air after far too much alcohol. His thoughts were muddled, his head spinning, but something—something inexplicable—compelled him to return to the lake.

The drive was a blur, the moonlight illuminating winding dirt roads as he navigated back to the mysterious black lake. He parked his car on the edge of the water, its shimmering achromatic surface eerily calm under the pale glow of dawn. His gaze was drawn to a broken-down cabin perched precariously near the lake's edge. The structure looked like it had not been inhabited in decades, but it didn't matter. He was not planning to go inside.

Vic sat on the cabin's rickety porch, staring out at the lake as if hypnotized. Exhaustion eventually overtook him, and he dozed off, though his dreams were anything but restful.

In his sleep, he dreamed of the water. It was not serene or calming—it was alive, almost predatory. He saw sirens rising from the depths, their hauntingly beautiful faces calling to him with songs he could not resist. Their ethereal voices promised him everything he had ever desired— power, knowledge, immortality. But just as they reached for him, their eyes turned black, and they pulled him into the dark abyss of the lake. He woke with a start, gasping for air, his heart pounding like a drum.

The first light of dawn was breaking over the horizon, and the lake looked different now. The water shimmered faintly, and steam rose in ghostly tendrils from the surface. Vic's thirst was insatiable, and before he could second-guess himself, he walked to the edge of the lake and found the source of the heat—a small spring bubbling up through the rocks.

He cupped his hands and drank deeply from the hot water, the strange metallic tang sharp on his tongue. Instantly, he felt a surge of energy coursing through his veins. The lingering fog of alcohol vanished, replaced by a clarity he had not felt in years. He felt fantastic, invigorated, as though his very cells had been charged with new life. A call to destiny -- far too fast for his conscious mind to grasp or even acknowledge.

Vic knelt by the spring, his chemist's mind racing. There was something in the water — something extraordinary. He pulled an empty Ozark water bottle from his car, dumped its contents onto the ground, and carefully filled it with the bubbling spring water.

Standing there, bottle in hand, he stared back at the lake. He did not know what he'd just discovered, but he knew one thing for certain: this wasn't the last time he'd visit Black Lake. Whatever secrets it held, he intended to uncover them all.

Vic pointed his car south and got moving. He intended to get to his lab and analyze the water. What was in it? He wanted to have another drink. Maybe just a small one from the bottle. He had sixteen ounces he surely would not need it all to test it adequately. As he drove, he thought about his life as a chemist. His PhD was in inorganic chemistry, but he had enough botany classes to get at least a master's degree. If he could find a company who focused on botanicals or a nutritional company, he could work for them; leave Cargill Chemical and move somewhere where exploring the water in Black Lake would make sense. Vulcan Chemical in Wichita was always there. He could move back to Wichita and work there. Better yet he could sell his four patents and have a nest egg to do his own thing. Yes. He could then work full time on the water. The miles passed quickly.

Vic's burgeoning excitement carried him all the way back to Wichita on a cloud of anticipation. The strange energy he felt after drinking from the spring seemed to fuel him, both physically and mentally. His mind raced with possibilities as he replayed the events of the night—his discovery of the hot spring, the mesmerizing black lake, and the unshakable feeling that he had stumbled upon something extraordinary.

For the first time in years, Vic felt alive. Not just alive but driven—more driven than he had ever been, even during his early days as a chemist chasing patents and breakthroughs. The water had done something to him; he could feel it in his bones, his blood, even in the clarity of his thoughts.

By the time he crossed the Sedgwick County line, his mind was already working in overdrive. What is in that water? What makes it different? Is it chemical, biological, something else entirely? He envisioned himself back in the lab, running tests, isolating compounds, uncovering whatever hidden properties gave it such power.

The closer he got to Wichita, the more focused his excitement became. He knew this was not just a personal discovery—it was something bigger, something that could change everything. He would need to keep it quiet, at least until he knew more. But one thing was certain: the mysteries of Black Lake were not going to stay hidden for long.

Vic arrived in Wichita with a sense of purpose he had not felt in years. Whatever awaited him in the lab, whatever answers he might uncover, he knew this discovery could be the key to everything.

Vic pulled his car into the parking lot of the Wichita Marriot. The high-rise hotel was iconic in East Wichita. He hurried in and requested a suite on the top floor. A northern exposure please. He wanted a view. Maybe he could see Black Lake or at least the steam from the beautiful ebony water. It would be in the air towards the north. He was sure of that.

Vic's excitement was not just fleeting—it was transforming into action. Once he was settled in his hotel room in Wichita, Vic made a phone call to his employer and quit his job. He had back pay for vacations he never took for the last ten years of employment. 30 weeks. He called his landlord and told him he had moved out of state. He broke his lease. Yes. He understood. Send him the bill. There was nothing there in California he needed or wanted. He told the landlord to have it all hauled off and let him know the charges. Okay, that was done. He was now homeless.

He fished a business card from his wallet. It belonged to a broker who had been pestering him for months to sell his chemical patents. The broker had claimed there was a buyer already lined up, eager to acquire Vic's intellectual property.

Without hesitation, Vic dialed the number. When the broker picked up, Vic's tone was brisk and decisive. "Sell all four patents," he said, leaving no room for negotiation.

That evening, Vic went downstairs to the hotel bar and grill for dinner. He barely tasted the meal as he waited for the broker to call back. Halfway through dessert, his phone buzzed.

"We've got an offer," the broker said. "Eleven million for all four."

Vic did not even flinch. "Counter at twenty-five," he replied, as though the figure were a foregone conclusion.

Another call came in just as he was finishing his drink. The buyer agreed to the terms: $25 million. The deal was done.

Vic hung up, a satisfied smile on his face. But he was not done making moves. He called the real estate office in Black Lake, the one he had found while driving through the town and familiarizing himself with its quiet streets.

"Yes," the agent told him, "There is a house for sale. And there is a large parcel of land just south of the lake that stretches all the way to town. It even has an old cabin on it."

"Perfect," Vic said.

Within five days, Vic was a full-fledged resident of Black Lake.

CHAPTER 10

 Saint John's Monastery began its ascent amidst the rolling, lush green hills of the Scottish Highlands in the autumn of 1517, a mere week after Martin Luther defiantly affixed his Ninety-Five Thesis to the door of the castle church in Wittenberg, Germany. This bold act reverberated across Europe, sparking a tumultuous period of religious upheaval and reform.

Construction of the monastery progressed steadily over the decades that followed, a testament to the unwavering dedication of its builders and patrons amidst the swirling currents of religious and political change. The monks toiled with a steadfast resolve, their hands shaping stone and timber into a sanctuary of prayer and contemplation. The Isle of Skye is not famous for its hard wood trees. The original monks carried nearly all of the wood from the distant area of the clan McLeod.

By January of 1587, Saint John's Monastery stood complete, its spires reaching towards the heavens just days before the tragic execution of Mary Queen of Scots in the grand hall of Fotheringham Castle. The monastery, nestled amidst serene landscapes and steeped in centuries of spiritual devotion, would soon bear witness to its own share of trials and tribulations, as history continued to unfold beyond its tranquil walls.

Erected upon an improbable peak amidst the rugged Black Cuillin mountains, a few miles distant from modern-day Portree on the Isle of Skye, the abbey's ornate design stood as a testament to God's boundless mercy and grace. Legend held that the construction of such a marvel was beyond mortal capability; indeed, the belief persisted that divine intervention was the only plausible explanation. Various semi-plausible theories emerged over time, each attempting to rationalize the abbey's existence, but all fell short in capturing the true essence of God's hand in its creation.

Amidst the swirling mists of myth and reality, the abbey appeared like a structural twin to Glasgow Cathedral, rising majestically against the backdrop of the Scottish Highlands. Its intricate stonework and towering spires seemed to defy the very laws of nature, inspiring awe and reverence in all who beheld its splendor. Whether viewed through the lens of faith or reason, the abbey on the impossible peak remained a beacon of divine mystery and human aspiration, a testament to the enduring power of belief and the transcendent beauty of God's providence.

Crafted from the nearly black phaneritic gabbro stones extracted from the peaks and upper reaches of the Cuillin mountains, the abbey struck visitors with an immediate sense of foreboding upon their first sight of its dull, obsidian-colored structure. As they drew nearer, that initial apprehension deepened like a thorn embedded in the mind. The walls, composed of these dark stones, displayed an unsettling uniformity, lacking any discernible seams that might hint at mortal craftsmanship.

The edges of doorways and windows were meticulously cut, sharp and precise, lending the abbey an almost unnaturally crisp appearance against the rugged backdrop of the mountainous terrain. Its austere beauty, draped in the shadow of myth and mystery, stood as a testament to the skill and dedication of those who had labored to raise it in such a formidable location.

To behold the black church was to confront both its tangible solidity and its intangible aura of enigma, evoking a primal reverence and a whispered awareness of forces beyond mortal understanding.

Through the years, the natural darkness of its construction material and the harsh environment of the Isle of Skye worked in tandem to shelter the monks of the monastery from malevolent forces. Situated amidst the rugged landscape of the Cuillin mountains, where high winds and persistent rain were commonplace, the monastery often found itself enveloped in a natural cloak of low-hanging clouds.

This atmospheric combination, characterized by perpetual gloom and an almost constant shroud of mist, created a formidable barrier against the intrusion of evil spirits and mystical malevolence. The monastery's sturdy walls, crafted from the dark phaneritic gabbro stones indigenous to the region, seemed to absorb the ambient darkness of their surroundings, further fortifying its protective aura.

For the monks who dwelled within its sanctified confines, this natural defense offered not only physical shelter but also spiritual solace. It reinforced their faith in the divine providence that had guided the construction of their sanctuary amidst such challenging conditions. Amidst the tempestuous elements and the stark beauty of the Isle of Skye, the monastery stood as a bastion of light against the encroaching shadows, a beacon of hope and resilience in a world fraught with unseen dangers.

Survival and God's will have elevated St. John's to prominence as a globally renowned center for scholarly pursuits in modern times. Situated in a sparsely populated region that is effectively removed from mainstream civilization, the abbey's protected walls offer an ideal environment for students dedicated to religious research. The tranquil surroundings and solitude of the abbey grounds provide a conducive atmosphere for deep contemplation and focused study.

Residents of the abbey often indulge in long walks amidst the brisk, damp air that characterizes the Isle of Skye. Despite its northern latitude, the island benefits from unusual warm winds that mitigate the harshness of its climate. The weather, heavily influenced by wind direction, exhibits distinct patterns: North and East winds tend to bring dry conditions, while South and West winds typically bring moisture, resulting in rapid and sometimes dramatic changes in weather conditions. These swift transformations mirror the breathtaking scenery that surrounds the abbey, adding a dynamic element to life on the island.

For students and scholars committed to their academic pursuits and spiritual growth, St. John's Monastery on the Isle of Skye offers not only intellectual stimulation but also a serene refuge amidst the untamed beauty of nature. It stands as a beacon of learning and contemplation, anchored in centuries-old traditions yet open to the transformative possibilities of modern inquiry and discovery.

###

Lone Pine, Pennsylvania was a small town with less than five hundred people set deep into the hills north of Pittsburgh. The year Father Lucas Fisher was born was significant to the members of this town for several reasons. In April of that year, the town changed its name from Twin Pines to Lone Pine immediately following a severe electrical storm that eliminated one half of the town's namesake. In July the small town was ravaged by a particularly deadly strain of measles which claimed the life of thirty-nine residents. There were only a dozen or so families that were not trimmed in population.

Lucas's natural mother was killed in a three-car pile-up on interstate seventy. He and his twin brother Daniel were then swept into the government system. Max Carson was the mayor of Lone Pine and received a call from his sister from another mother Grace who bore the responsibility for finding Lucas a home. Although technically not by the book and a violation of the employee handbook, Grace could not bear to think of this little baby fresh from the hospital lost in the public domain.

And from a far too personal standpoint Max wanted a real family to take care of the child. Max and Grace knew what orphanages were like. They both had bad memories of the hole in which they grew up and Max personally knew the bad things that could happen to a boy after lights out. No god damned way was he going to let some poor little kid cling to his pillow every night, cursing the darkness and praying for the morning light. He recalled how fast he ran out those doors when he turned eighteen. This wasn't the first time he had thought of the Maude Parkers Home for children over the last twenty years, He and Grace had stayed in close contact helping the children stuck there as often as possible. Max closed his eyes and thanked God for making him forget some of the bad times and using him to rescue the kids when he could. He knew there was a better place for the kid. Anywhere.

"Father Bagby," Max called from the doorway of the town's only church.

"Max. Good to see you," he answered extending his wrinkled right hand. "I need a favor. There is a boy that needs a home. A baby, actually."

"I might just know a couple that would love to have him. They are an older couple but, they would love the boy as their own," he answered.

"As long as they want him, I can get it through the proper channels, Father."

"Oh, we want him," the old man smiled.

And it was done. Father Richard Bagby and his wife Helen dreamed of being parents. They were nearly sixty years old and never had any children of their own. Mrs. Bagby was forced to have a hysterectomy early in her twenties due to medical complications following a third trimester miscarriage. Modem medicine would have solved the problem less radically and handled the procedure on an outpatient basis-- probably before lunch. However, medicine in the 1960's was relatively primitive and doctors were butchers by no fault of their own. The resulting procedure resulted in Helen's carved up insides despite their best efforts to be helpful and eliminating any chance for Richard and Helen to have a biological son or daughter of their own.

Now through the grace of God their new son born into their household and was christened Lucas James Bagby with the help and insistence of Helen's sister Martha. For years Martha had kept a maid on staff primarily because her maid was married to an extremely handsome flirtatious man by the name of Lucas. Luke affectionately. Martha was a large woman with very unfortunate looks, and rather mean. Maybe due to any or all of those attributes she never married. But Martha was very shrewd, very rich, and very convincing. Martha was certain the name Lucas would fit any new baby boy who would surely grow up to be just as handsome as her unrequited love. And he had the same shiny black hair and glimmering blue eyes. She was right, the name did seem to fit the boy.

"Happy birthday, Lucas," Richard said to him across their bacon and eggs.

"Thanks, Dad."

"I have a surprise for you. The church needs an altar boy, and it can be you if you would like."

He did like. He had wanted to be an altar boy for the last five years but, his dad said he had to wait until he was fourteen. Lucas was surprised. He was twelve today and his father usually meant exactly what he said. This time, however, his father had given in very early and told him it was because he was extremely mature for his age. This made Lucas even more excited about his new job. He was going to be the best altar boy ever.

For five years Lucas assisted his father. The community loved the father-son arrangement and attendance was never better. Lucas seemed to exude Gods light, and no Sunday went by without someone remarking at how beautiful the boy was. Richard's confidence grew at the same time and powerful sermons erupted from that small country church. The congregation grew tremendously as word spread of the young boy and the old priest. Dozens of people drove in from Washington and the surrounding area. A few were coming from Pittsburg and one young couple drove the forty miles in from Wheeling West Virginia each Sunday. Religiously. It was an excellent opportunity for the Episcopal faith to bring the message of God to those previously unreachable.

"It's time you had some formal seminary training, Lucas. The church is willing to pay for you to attend if you would like."

"Of course I would. But can you manage here without me?"

"The Lord will provide, Lucas. There are others in the world that need you more than our little town... and me," he trailed off and turned away slightly to move attention away from the unfamiliar wetness in his eyes. Maybe you can come back after seminary. I'm getting pretty old."

"I will make you and Mama proud of me."

"We already are son. The Lord smiled on us every day since you arrived," he said hugging his son and hiding the tears that now streamed down his worn cheeks behind Lucas's shoulder. The Lord had allowed his life to be complete by adding Lucas to his life. How could he possibly hold him here when he knew in his heart that great things were coming his way?

Lucas excelled in all of his seminary classes. In his final year he was awarded the Denton Smiley Award for Excellence and was the class Valedictorian. When he applied for further education in languages at St. John's, he was accepted immediately. The week before he left, he received the news of his father's death.

Lucas returned to Lone Pine, now struggling with inner conflict. More than anything he wanted to attend the mysterious school in Scottland. What then of the parishioners who paid for his education to this point? He had a responsibility to the people of his father's church. His church. The town had been more than simply good to Lucas, it had been his home, his confidant, his supporter. He prayed on this problem before and after his fathers' funeral. Finally, he realized he must stay on at least until a replacement was found.

"Mother. I am going to the school in Scotland as soon as I can find another priest for the town. I think I know a young man who may like the opportunity to have his own church who attended seminary with me."

"How long is the program, Lucas?"

"It lasts as long as I wish to stay."

"Are you coming back?"

"I can't be sure. I want to learn all the ancient languages, Mother."

"That could take the rest of your life. Can you not study here in the states?"

"St. John's is the most highly respected school in the world. If I am going to study, I should go there. Most do not even get the chance to turn them down. I studied very hard to get this opportunity."

"Of course. I am sorry. I just wanted you to be around. I have not seen you for a few years, " she laughed.

But Lucas knew the laughter was just a cheap replacement for the tears that wanted to run down her cheeks. She was a very tough woman. It could not have been easy living with a man as dedicated to serving God as Richard Bagby. He often overlooked the little things that were not related to his worship. Lucas knew his mother was scared.

"I missed you too, Mama. But I have to go where God wants me to go. I have a purpose in living. I have to find it. I will come back for Christmas every year and I'll call."

The new preacher was named Paul Little. He arrived before Thanksgiving and Lucas left a few weeks after Christmas. Paul had attended seminary with him and was a very effective speaker. He promised to look after Helen.

###

Lucas only felt truly alive perched above a thousand feet and on slippery rocks. Challenging Death always entered his conscious mind. Capital D: conjuring the mental imagery of the black cloaked supernatural entity complete with the sweeping scythe. Lucas made a blasphemous habit of imagining the swinging blade narrowly missing his chalked hands or feet as he passed from one precarious rock wall to another. Not every time but most of his life was dependent on making the right move, the hooded specter would be flying just above and behind him anticipating his misstep and rapid descent to the base of the mountain. An odd obsession but, Lucas considered his personification of Death a talisman of sorts.

And today he was living his life. Before calling home to the states to let the family know he arrived in Scottland safely. Before checking in at the seminary. Before any other activities to get settled in on the Isle of Sky. Lucas was on the Cuillin.

This would not have surprised anyone who had spoken with Lucas more than a few times. Lucas made no bones about being a passionate driven climber. His selection of St. John's at the base of the most challenging rock climbing in the world was not happenstance. The Black Cuillen wasn't the tallest in the world but depending on the time of the year was the most treacherous. Lucas planned on making at least one major climb per month as long as he was called to stay on the island.

On the flight over Lucas read The Reverend A.B. Scott's 1918 book The Pictish Nation, its People and its Church. Dry but it helped him pass the time and there were some interesting passages with excellent trivia to fill his mind and inject strategically in conversation. Secondary to Lucas was the thesis of the book focused of course on the religious nature of the Scotts. Primary in his thoughts were the 9th century Viking origins and the ancient names for Scotland. According to the good Reverend Scott, the early Basque seafarers from the north of Spain, as well as Greek shipmasters navigated around the British Isles and referred to them as Alba or Albion meaning "white." Lucas was gifted with close to a photographic memory but only on topics which interested him greatly. He had heard of his ability to recall only interesting or emotionally charged memories referred to as a flashbulb memory. Oddly, The Reverend Scott had made a deep indention on Lucas' grey matter with his writings on the cold desolate land. From that point forward for the remainder of his life Lucas would refer to his time in Scottland as his years in The Kingdom of Alba.

Jamming with his right foot and left shoulder Lucas gripped a small flake of rock and pulled himself up over the final ledge where he sat and caught his breath. The air was cold and damp and exhilarating. The sun was getting low, and he would need to hustle to make it back to his rented Land Rover.

Getting to his feet, precariously balanced at the peak of his climb and looking out over the hills in the distance he strained to see the North Sea, the Norwegian Sea, and the North Atlantic. Well, he could almost see the water. He could see the horizon and somewhere in the distance, in the three general directions were the bodies of water.

Good enough for the first day. Not bad. Not a bad day at all Luke, he thought smiling broadly through his three-day beard and soaking in the view one last time. Lucas was now ready to begin studying in earnest the Word of the Lord his God.

"Let's go Reaper. Let's get off this mountain," Lucas spoke aloud.

"Until we meet again."

# # #

Lucas was every bit as successful in graduate studies as he had been in his prior education. He was brilliant, talented, and gifted. He brought more to the school than anyone had previously. In less than five years the church considered Lucas fluent in Aramaic, Hebrew, Greek and Latin as any of his instructors. He accepted a position researching ancient documents and worked diligently at that task until his mother died. A short leave of absence was permitted, and he flew home. He delivered the eulogy for his mother, sold the home he grew up in to Paul who had decided to set up permanent residence with Amy Change, a kindergarten teacher in the small adjacent town of Amity, and returned to the monastery. This was his home now.

And he settled in and became a leader in his home. Time passed. Months turned into years which turned into a decade. Lucas was the youngest priest in the order at thirty-three. He was content with his life. But now something was wrong. He felt a twitch; an itch. He was being called.

###

Lately, Lucas's nights were filled with nightmares—visions of a future too dark to comprehend, all centered around a man named Dan Stone. In his dream, Lucas found himself in the monastery's garden, yet it was unrecognizable. The roses, once pale and serene, were now black, their thorny stems writhing as though imbued with malevolent life. A fierce wind tore through the garden, forcing the flowers to bow toward an unseen power. On the towering stone wall of the monastery, horrifying scenes played out—glimpses of an ordinary man's life, destruction, and despair. Lucas could feel the weight of it all, a crushing dread that whispered a terrible truth: this man, Dan Stone, was tied to a future Lucas was destined to confront.

The haunting conversation of Lucas and the elder priest Father Moray echoed above the storm.

"Lucas, help him," the elder priest beseeched. "His intentions are not his own. He is being led to hell by the dark one."

"Yes. There is only one answer. He must die. Pray for his guidance and his death. Death will save his soul," Lucas breathed.

"He has sinned so much, Lucas. The blackness that smothers his soul can be seen creeping out of his body. He is far too burdened to enter Heaven."

"With God, all things are possible," Lucas countered, though his own faith wavered in the face of such darkness.

The dream unfolded and brilliant light penetrated the storm—too pure, too perfect. Golden clouds. A voice like silk and sunlight.

"Lucas Fisher. Robert Moray," it said warmly. "His champions of a dying cause."

They stood paralyzed in the vision, unable to move, their hearts pounding.

"You have been chosen," the voice continued, sweet as honey. "Chosen to chase after what is already lost."

The brightness around them trembled—like glass just beginning to fracture.

"If you accept this cup your God offers, you will surely die."

The voice deepened now, losing its luster. The light warped, twisting into something jagged and wrong. The dark clouds and stagnant wind returning.

"Dan Stone is mine," the voice hissed, stripped of all beauty. "He has served me in ways your kind cannot fathom. His soul is sealed. His heart is branded."

The last of the golden light shattered into blackness, leaving only the voice, echoing.

"You cannot save him. You cannot save yourselves."

The shadow engulfed the wall, now massive and pulsating, as if it were alive. The roses bent and shriveled under its presence. A cold, wet wind tore through the garden, and Lucas instinctively recoiled. The shadow spoke, its voice an amalgamation of growls and whispers, reverberating through the space.

"You cannot hope to pull his soul from my grasp."

Lucas wanted to scream, to rebuke the creature, but he was frozen, powerless to move or speak.

"You think you can beat me at my own game, Lucas Fisher? Fool. You do not have the faith," the shadow hissed. "You listen to the lies your God whispers and accept them blindly. But here is some truth: I killed your mother and father."

The words tore at his heart. He stared into the dark emptiness of the devil's face blurred from a mere outline of blackness to substance. The sockets where eyes would have been stared back and he could see the light oak caskets he bought for each of his parents.

"Look into my eyes Lucas. Want to see Mom and Dad?"

The shadow's form twisted, and the lids of the coffins flipped open. Inside, his adoptive parents mangled bodies lay motionless, their faces contorted in pain. Blood soaked the white satin linings, pooling beneath their broken forms.

Lucas screamed and slapped the heels of his hands against his eyes. "Stop it!" he croaked.

"Lucas, we're proud of you," his father's voice rasped, drawing his gaze back to the horrific scene. His father struggled to sit up, blood leaking from a gaping wound across his abdomen.

"Do what you have to do, son. Do not worry about your mother and me."

"Dad? My God, what happened?" Lucas stammered, his voice cracking.

"Lucas, help us," his mother whimpered, her face battered and bruised. Her torn dress hung in shreds, revealing more evidence of torment.

The shadow laughed, a guttural, bone-chilling sound. "You will have to excuse her appearance, Lucas. My minions get a little carried away when they welcome new female guests."

"Lies!" Lucas shouted, his voice breaking with anguish. "My parents were dedicated Christians. Children of God. The Lord would never let you possess their souls!"

Deep booming laughter filled the air as the winds increased to an arctic gale freezing Lucas's dream body to the core of his soul. "You silly, naïve, child," the Devil cooed. "Have you never heard of Job, young Lucas? In all of your diligent book reading? I am certain that you have. I take anyone I want. I torture anyone I want. He is powerless against me. Surely you know enough by now with all your pathetic studying to know that the Earth is mine", he mocked. "Now, if you will excuse me, I have to go stick pins in your mothers' eye."

"You will not win," he whispered through clenched teeth.

The shadow leaned closer, its voice dropping to a cruel whisper. "Oh, Lucas. I already have."

Lucas screamed as the image dissolved into darkness. The echoes of his mother's cries and the shadow's laughter faded, replaced by the sound of his own voice shouting in the cold monastery room.

"Father Fisher! Father Fisher! Wake up!"

A young student burst into his quarters, grabbing his shoulders and shaking him hard. Lucas jolted upright, gasping for air, his whole body trembling. The thin, frayed sheet clung to him, soaked with sweat—and worse. He reeked of fear, something primal and raw.

Lucas's lungs ached; his nose burned. He could smell it—sharp and acrid, like sulfur, like a spent match still smoldering. The stench of evil had seeped into his dimension, leaving a residue the dream could not contain.

"It's all right, Don. I'm all right. Thank you," Lucas managed, catching his breath. His voice was raw, shaky. "Just a nightmare."

###

Lucas turned towards the familiar voice of his most learned instructor and friend. Both men wore the traditional full-length black tunic and white collar. The monks of Saint John's were said to have started this tradition. The vows of poverty accepted by each member of the order included the avoidance of proud clothing and Father Robert Moray went strictly by the ancient books. At Saint John's the Bible was the inspired word of God for use by His faithful and the monastical laws were there to ease interpretation and establish order. This was the man who first helped Lucas to understand that his learning would only be interrupted by death. "There will always be more information to assimilate. More translations to read. More writings to decipher." Lucas' bailiwick was interpretation of the ancient languages. The ease with which he learned was another gift of God that could not easily be explained by man. But it was still Father Moray who gave him his daily dose of knowledge. Father

Morays back was twisted from years of studying Gods word each day seated in the same slat wooden chair. His joints were plagued with arthritis and his hearing was nearly gone but, his vision was perfect and his mind as sharp as a tack. "The Lord takes only the things I do not need, Lucas. When I have read all I can read and my mind grows weary, I will know He is calling me home," he would say on occasion. Lucas loved the old man.

"Yes?" he answered as he turned, the comers of his mouth curling into the beginnings of a smile.

"I must speak with you, Lucas." The old man placed his small, wrinkled hand upon his shoulder gently.

"Certainly, Father."

"I have been having very disturbing dreams lately. In fact, I believe I have had the same dream each night for more than a week," the small man stated.

Lucas paled. His smile was quickly placed far back into his mind. Lucas rarely showed any sort of emotion and the words he had just heard were less than pleasant. Dreams. Father Moray had instructed him on his first day at the monastery to head the instructions and warnings the Lord presented in dreams. He believed that man is at his most attentive when asleep. Lucas recalled his dreams almost as often as he bubbled with emotion. He always respected and listened to his ageing teacher but, until a few weeks ago, had never given much credence to his dream philosophies.

"What kind of dream, Father? He asked dreading the answer and already telling himself he was crazy for even considering what had passed through his mind.

"A very strange and unnerving dream. A dream about you and a man. Come upstairs with me so we can discuss it, Lucas."

Lucas followed the man up the stairs. The stairway hugged the outside wall and was as everything else deep black stone and wide enough for three or four large men to walk side by side. Just the same Lucas could feel the walls closing in and smothering the air from his lungs. Lucas began to perspire as he followed his nearly crippled mentor up the sixty-six stairs. His mouth was very dry. Lucas had a dream the night before that had ended his sleep at two o'clock and troubled him all day. In fact, he had the very same dream the night before that as well. And the night before. And the night before. Father Roberts' lectures about divine inspiration and prophecy echoed in his mind. He knew it was possible but, why would the Holy Spirit choose to make use of him so directly? Neither of the two men spoke until the heavy wooden door to Father Roberts' study was closed. The long walk up the stairs gave Lucas a great deal of time to think about the dream he had the nights before. This was a dream he would never be able to forget. He knew God was speaking. In his heart he knew but his mind was still denying this fact.

"Forgive me, Lucas, but the nights have been very long of late and the days even longer," he said sitting down feebly in a dark oversized willow chair with blood red velvet cushions. It was his favorite chair. The chair his mentor had instructed from for fifty years, and his mentor before him. It was the cherished seat held by the leader crafted by the founding monks centuries before. Lucas hoped to be awarded this position someday if it was God's will for him to lead.

"What was the dream?" Lucas asked, still standing.

Father Moray looked thoughtful for several moments. He looked up and into the fiery blue eyes of his young pupil and then back down to the empty black stone floor once again. Finally, he said, "The beginning of the apocalypse."

A white pasty image passed quickly over the young priests long narrow face. In the distance he heard himself groan as he clawed for the arms of the less stately chair directly behind him. Pulling in oxygen as quickly as possible, Lucas tried to regain his composure. It would not do to allow himself to fall apart in front of the man he respected most in this world. No, it would not do at all. He shook his head violently and ran his quivering fingers through his long black hair.

"Lucas...are you all right? Do you need some water? Here let me get you a cup of water," the old feeble priest said lifting himself from his chair.

"No. No, I will be fine. I just...felt a little faint. It must have been the walk up all those stairs. I haven't had a chance to eat yet this morning."

Father Robert found his seat once again. "Well, if you are certain you are all right..."

"Quite."

"My dream, Lucas."

"Yes, please tell me about it," he said wringing his large, calloused hands. One would think a priest stationed on this remote little island would have very small pale hands with delicate palms; Hands that exercised only in the confines of a book. Lucas Fisher was a dedicated scholar of Gods' word, but he was also fanatical about his fitness. A large part of his decision to seek an appointment here at St. John's was influenced by the Black Cullin mountains and his desire to surpass the summit speed climbing record. Lucas spent his free time hill running and scaling the majestic black mountain walls. His hands certainly took a brutal punishment either clinging to the slick black rocks or burning with the dry nylon ropes. Lucas relished the tingling in his hands he felt daily as he worked at his Real job studying the word and searching for new clues never before released to humanity.

"It was, to say the least, very disturbing. I was standing in the courtyard below the chapel window with you. It was high noon, and the sun was very hot. That in itself was strange considering our weather here. But I could actually feel the sun scorching my skin through my tunic. You were pointing towards the wall as if to instruct me or lead me through some kind of puzzle." He paused and looked up from his desk.

Lucas had grown even more pale, and tears were running from his eyes.

"...and you were crying ... you looked much as you do now, Lucas. Tell me..."

"Can you remember what I was saying to you in the dream, Father?"

"No, I cannot. I have tried each morning. I can see you saying the words, but I just can't seem to recall the sounds."

"Father, you must remember. It means a great deal."

"I can almost recall the words but, they are just hidden from me. The Lord is speaking but He has not been ready to reveal this to me. You were pointing at the wall as scenes flashed across it. There was a man," Father Robert ended abruptly.

"Listen to the words that have been haunting me in my dreams, Father."

"Lucas, what are saying?"

"I too have been dreaming of this man."

The old man was silent for more than a minute. He stared at the cross centered on the worn leather cover of his bible. He traced the raised image of his faith with his small, wrinkled index finger. Finally, he said, "We both have been given similar visions. We must determine the meaning. What has been troubling you, Lucas? What do you see?"

"Listen to what I told you in my dream, Father Moray: 'This man is the scourge of humanity. He is the antithesis of all good men. He is the one we have been warned against since the dawn of time, Robert. Remember his face forever. Pray for his guidance and his death," Lucas spoke.

"Yes. Yes, that was what you said to me in my vision. Lucas, you also had this dream?"

"Yes. For nearly a week I have seen the image of this man in my nightmares," he managed to spit the words out. His mouth could not possibly get any drier. His tongue stuck to the roof of his mouth as he tried to swallow. "Perhaps, I do need that water, Father," Lucas said walking to the wide stone windowsill where a silver tray and crystal water pitcher beckoned.

"You must go to help him. It may not be definite. He must make the choice of his own free will and you can guide him. You must pull him back, Lucas. It is God's desire that not even one soul should parish. He is not beyond the redemptive powers of our almighty Lord."

"I do not even know who he is, Father. He could be anywhere. How could I change his mind even if l did find him?" Lucas argued. Lucas did not want this task. This challenge. This responsibility. "Father, surely this cannot be something God is intending for me to undertake."

"The Lord will provide you with all you need. He will direct you. He is calling you. I feel that there is much at stake, Lucas. You must succeed. Leave immediately."

Lucas left the study without saying another word. What was left to say? He knew what the dreams had meant before he ever spoke with Father Moray. He may be skeptical of some of the things his old mentor believes about dreams but, he is not an idiot. His teacher having the exact same recurring dreams had secured some sort of message. Lucas locked the door to his room without turning on the light. He made his way past the sparse furnishings to the small altar he had set up in the corner. There was only one way Lucas knew to find the answers. He prayed on his knees for twelve hours without realizing the passage of time.

The calling was not to be ignored. It was a knowing like a rat in a box tied to his gut. It was unbearable. He would leave to find Dan Stone today, or he would surely go insane.

CHAPTER 11

Victor never made it back to his lab in Wichita. The bottle of lake water he had brought with him was enough to keep him enthralled. Each day, he sipped a small amount, savoring the energy and vitality it seemed to provide. On the fifth day, with the bottle nearly empty, Vic found himself back at the lake, filling several five-gallon jugs with the bubbling hot water.

The cabin might have been run-down, and the land rugged, but to Vic, it was paradise. He did not see decay—he saw potential. He signed the papers, wrote a check and he was home. But Black Lake was not just his new home; it was the start of something far bigger than he'd ever imagined.

Vic made Black Lake his home, fully committing to the charm and mystery of the town. One of his first major decisions was to purchase the building that housed The Strings, the small, rundown bar he had first wandered into upon his arrival.

The place had potential, but Vic envisioned something far grander. He partnered with Bob, the bartender and the town's unofficial storyteller, to brainstorm ideas for a redesign. Bob's passion for old movies aligned with Vic's own experiences at the Plaza Hotel in New York, where he had spent countless evenings at the legendary Oak Room. Together, they decided to rename the bar The Oak Bar in homage to the Plaza's iconic space, a nod to timeless elegance with a touch of Black Lake's unique charm.

Vic spared no expense. The renovation was nothing short of a masterpiece, blending warm, polished wood, deep leather seating, and antique brass fixtures. Rich oak panels adorned the walls, and a long, gleaming bar stretched across the room, reminiscent of the classic speakeasies of the 1920s. The lighting was soft and inviting, casting a golden glow that made every patron feel like they had stepped into another era.

Above the bar, on the second floor, Vic created a master suite that doubled as his home and office. It was both luxurious and functional, with sweeping views of the town and, in the distance, the shimmering black lake that had captivated him from the start.

To bring the vision to life, Vic assembled a crew of skilled workmen, paying them handsomely to ensure the job was done quickly and to perfection. What would have taken months under normal circumstances was completed in weeks, a testament to Vic's drive and financial resources.

But that was not all. Vic wanted The Oak Bar to be more than just a place to drink—it was going to be an experience, a curiosity that no one could resist. Drawing inspiration from brewpubs with their gleaming tanks and visible brewing systems, Vic installed a custom-designed tap system unlike anything anyone had ever seen.

Behind a glass wall, prominently displayed for all to see, was a massive 1,000-gallon tank. Its polished steel surface gleamed under soft ambient lighting, giving it an almost futuristic presence. The taps at the bar were not labeled with typical beer or cocktail options. Instead, they were labeled simply: Ice Cold, Room Temperature, and Scalding Hot.

The secret, of course, lay in what the tank held. Vic filled it with water from Black Lake.

It wasn't just a gimmick to Vic—it was part of his experiment. He wanted to see how the townspeople would react to the water, even if they didn't know its origin. He was curious if they would notice the subtle effects he had felt: the vitality, the energy, the spark of something almost indescribable.

When the doors to The Oak Bar finally reopened, it was no longer just a literal watering hole—it was a destination. Townsfolk marveled at the transformation, and Vic found himself at the center of Black Lake's community, his once-solitary life now intertwined with the people and the place he had unexpectedly come to call home.

Patrons marveled at the innovation, often ordering drinks straight from the mysterious taps just to be part of the novelty. Bob loved telling exaggerated tales about the origins of the water, weaving local lore into his descriptions that blurred the line between myth and reality.

The glass wall, the glowing tank, and the unique taps became the centerpiece of The Oak Bar, drawing in both locals and visitors who were eager to experience what Vic had created. Unbeknownst to them, every sip they took was another step in Vic's unfolding experiment—a silent test of the power of Black Lake.

Everyone in town stopped by daily to grab a quick cup of Vic's water. A single sip left them instantly refreshed, rejuvenated, and ready to tackle their day. The townsfolk buzzed with newfound energy. They worked harder, thought faster, and seemed sharper overall. There were rumors of coughs disappearing, arthritis being cured, cancer being eradicated. Vic watched with quiet satisfaction as his experiment unfolded before his eyes. He had proof of concept: the water was incredible.
Vic had turned a natural resource into a cash cow, capitalizing on what seemed like an inexhaustible supply of free water. But this wasn't just any water—it was Black Lake water, rich with properties no one fully understood yet impossible to ignore. The results spoke for themselves: patrons claimed to feel invigorated, sharper, and even healthier after a single cup. Word spread quickly, and demand surged.

To meet the growing appetite, Vic expanded The Oak Bar's menu, adding coffee and tea brewed exclusively with the enigmatic lake water. Hot or iced, plain or flavored, every drink carried its signature taste and the rumored "magic" of Black Lake. The offerings became the bar's cornerstone, drawing crowds from nearby towns and beyond.

But Vic knew he couldn't let the secret out. The water was the lifeblood of his burgeoning empire, and he took extreme measures to safeguard it. Purchasing a stainless-steel milk truck, he began siphoning the lake himself, transporting the liquid gold under the cover of darkness. It was a one-man operation, ensuring no one else could uncover the source of his success.

The secrecy only added to the mystique, and Black Lake Coffee was born from those humble beginnings—a brand that would soon grow far beyond the small town, becoming synonymous with excellence and an almost supernatural allure. Yet, Vic understood the price of the lake's bounty, even if he never spoke of it. The secret came with a weight, one he carried alone.

Then he got creative, adding 13 flavors for the ice-cold water: cherry, pineapple, bubblegum, butterscotch, and, of course, plain unflavored Black Lake water. Ice cubes were crafted from the room-temperature Black Lake water, and mixed drinks were made with the same. Crushed ice in nonalcoholic margaritas and daiquiris. Every opportunity to incorporate the magical water into recipes was seized, turning the bar into a hub of innovation and attraction.
The supply side was fantastic, endless Free water!

But Vic wasn't content to keep his success confined to Black Lake. Recognizing the potential, he expanded his business into Lebanon and the neighboring small towns. The new stores were simple, focused exclusively on selling coffee, tea, and flavored ice water. He branded the chain Black Lake Coffee; each location featuring the signature water tank and tap system that had become synonymous with the brand.

Vic's operation was expanding faster than he had anticipated. A second water truck had already joined the fleet, and a third wasn't far behind. He hired a couple of local guys Bob trusted, good men who didn't ask questions, to manage the growing delivery schedule. But even with their help, Vic realized the logistical strain would only worsen as demand continued to skyrocket. He needed a better, more efficient plan—and above all, a way to keep the lake's secret.

One evening, after closing the bar, Vic wandered out into the stillness of Black Lake's town square. The statue of William Joseph Smith loomed large under the faint glow of the streetlights. At its base, the old wishing well shimmered faintly, its surface reflecting the dark skies. Vic sat on the edge, deep in thought, when it hit him—the water. The wishing well, fed by an underground spring, had to be connected to the lake. A natural fissure must have been feeding it for decades, perhaps even since the town's founding.

Vic knew this could solve everything.

Late one night, under a moonless sky, Vic gathered Bob and the two water delivery boys for a covert mission. Armed with shovels, tools, and a map of the town's underground infrastructure, the group set to work. They dug carefully near the side of the wishing well closest to the bar, tunneling a narrow canal. By dawn, they had laid a four-inch stainless steel pipe that connected the wishing well to the bar's vats.

The operation was seamless. The water from the well now flowed directly into the bar, filling the massive tanks with the same unearthly liquid Vic had been hauling from the lake. No one in town would suspect a thing—the well remained as picturesque as ever, with townsfolk still tossing coins into its depths, unaware of its new purpose.

For Vic, it was a masterstroke of ingenuity and secrecy. The direct pipeline eliminated the need for additional trucks, streamlined his operations, and allowed him to focus on growing the business further. The lake's secret was secure—for now.

Vic's operation was hitting its stride, and he wasted no time scaling up. He added several large water storage tanks in the far back of the building where the water trucks parked for the night. Each evening, the trucks would simply pull in and refill from the tanks, eliminating the need for clandestine late-night runs to the lake. By morning, they were ready to set off on their delivery routes, efficient and professional.

Always a shrewd marketer, Vic had the trucks vinyl-wrapped with a sleek cream-colored graphic, featuring the Black Lake Coffee logo emblazoned boldly on each side. The trucks became mobile advertisements, their pristine design turning heads wherever they went. Business boomed as the brand gained visibility, and Vic's vision of empire-building seemed well within reach.

Recognizing the need for more infrastructure, Vic purchased the building adjacent to The Oak Bar. He gutted the interior, transforming it into a sleek, modern warehouse with bays for additional trucks and a space to accommodate a growing workforce. The renovation was seamless, blending the new facility with the rustic charm of the town's aesthetic.

The days of secret midnight runs were over. Vic's operation was now a legitimate powerhouse, expanding with every passing week. Yet, despite the streamlined processes and outward professionalism, the secret of Black Lake's water remained known only to Vic and a select few. As the trucks rolled out each morning, carrying their precious cargo to coffee shops far and wide,

Vic couldn't shake the feeling that he was riding a wave of something far larger—and darker—than he had ever imagined. The thought lingered at the edges of his mind like a shadow that refused to be illuminated. Yet, Vic was nothing if not pragmatic. That was a worry for another day. Today was about expansion. More stores. More coffee. More people drinking the miracle water and thriving.

The numbers didn't lie—profits were soaring, testimonials were flooding in, and the brand's reach was spreading like wildfire. People spoke of newfound energy, clarity, and even improved health, all credited to the "secret" behind Black Lake Coffee. Vic basked in their gratitude, knowing full well that the secret wasn't in the roasting process or some exotic blend of beans. It was the water—the dark, enigmatic water of Black Lake.

Vic's vision was clear: Black Lake Coffee would become a household name, synonymous with vitality and success. He mapped out new territories, eyeing key cities where he could plant the brand's roots. Each new store was a beacon of hope, a sanctuary for those seeking something extraordinary in their morning brew.

But in the quiet hours, when the last truck had returned and the town was still, Vic would sometimes find himself staring at the tanks, the faint hum of the pipes carrying the lake's essence into his empire. He'd think about the lake, the roses, and the whispers of something ancient.

Expansion was the goal—but at what cost? Something was in the water, but what was it? Vic could not quite shake the unease creeping into his thoughts, like the faint hum of the pipes carrying the lake's essence into his growing empire. He felt good most of the time—better than good, in fact—but the nightmares had started. Fragmented, vivid, and disturbingly real, they left him disoriented and drenched in sweat. Was it the water? Was it the price for harnessing something so potent, so celestial?

Vic stared at the tanks in the stillness of the night, their reflective surfaces gleaming under dim overhead lights. He wanted to believe the water was a gift, a miracle bestowed upon him to share with the world. But the edges of his dreams whispered otherwise. They whispered of chains, fire, and the black roses swaying as if alive.

He rubbed his temples, trying to shake off the lingering images. "It's nothing," he muttered to himself, a mantra he repeated more often these days. For now, he pushed the thought aside. There was work to be done. Expansion could not wait for nightmares, no matter how unsettling. The empire was not going to build itself.

As demand grew, so did Vic's ambition. He opened Black Lake Coffee stores in Wichita, Kansas City, Oklahoma City, Tulsa, and Dallas. Dozens of trucks were transporting water from Black Lake, transporting it in brand new gleaming stainless-steel tanks to his expanding network of stores across the region.

The brand exploded in popularity. Customers loved the refreshing taste of the water and the unique concept behind it, and they could not get enough of the energy boost they felt after drinking it. Black Lake Coffee became a business on fire, with lines out the door and growing interest from investors.

Vic had turned the mystical waters of Black Lake into a phenomenon, proving that his small-town discovery was not just special—it was a revolution in the making. Vic had opened one hundred stores before the end of the first year in business.

Vic grew Black Lake Coffee into a billion-dollar enterprise, a juggernaut fueled by the seemingly magical properties of the lake's water. But Vic was not just in it for the money. He saw Black Lake as his home, his sanctuary, and he poured his newfound wealth back into the town, reshaping it into a vision of perfection.

He paved every street, replacing the old dirt roads with smooth cobblestone walkways that invited leisurely strolls. Nearly every building in town was renovated, their weathered facades transformed into charming storefronts and homes. Vic embraced the concept of a small, quaint cityscape from a bygone romantic era—where life moved at a slower pace, evening walks were a ritual, and neighbors gathered in the square to share stories and laughter.

At the heart of his revitalization efforts was the creation of a park, a lush green oasis in the center of town. Winding paths led to a picturesque gazebo surrounded by manicured gardens and benches where people could sit and enjoy the scenery.

In the middle of the park, towering over the square, stood a massive statue of William Joseph. The dark, ominous figure was in stark contrast to the idyllic beauty of the town Vic had crafted. Its presence was both a curiosity and a mystery, as William Joseph's history remained shrouded in local lore. The statue's imposing form loomed over the square, a reminder of something deeper, something darker—an unsettling counterpoint to the otherwise peaceful atmosphere.

The townspeople marveled at the transformation. Black Lake had become a beacon of community, a picturesque destination that drew tourists and admirers from miles around. Vic, for all his ambition and eccentricities, had turned a forgotten town into a thriving, magical place. But the shadow of the statue and the secrets of the lake lingered, casting a subtle unease over the idyllic landscape Vic had built.

Vic wanted to expand the water globally. Vic knew distribution would be the obvious problem. He needed to know what was in the water, He needed to synthesize the compounds within, so he did not have to ship tankers of water. Vic made some calls and hired a head-hunting firm to find him a group of scientists to analyze the water. They returned Dr. Sam Reynolds in New Orleans working for Koch Methanol. Vic could have simply hired Sam, but he needed a lab. He could build it or buy it. He opted to buy the Methanol plant from the Koch brothers in Wichita. Vic drove to Wichita and flew to New Orleans. He and Sam collaborated beautifully. Important work was being done.

The Koch brothers liked the profit they made selling out to Vic and offered him several other operations close in proximity to the Methanol plant. Vic purchased them too. Vic could feel it if it was a good buy. A voice in his head. The more water he drank the faster his brain worked. It seemed to fuel his intuition. He struck gold every time he purchased a company. Vic would buy a fledgling company near bankruptcy for pennies on the dollar and it would strike oil. He would sell off a dog and the buyer would pay twice its value. He was Midas.

Word got out that Vic was a buyer. He acquired oil and gas, chemical, and petro chemical operations from ExxonMobil, Total, Chevron, and Koch, Stone Industries became the largest oil holding company in North America. Vic credited all his success to the water in Black Lake. But its influence went far beyond mere energy or focus—it carried a mystical quality, as if something or someone were guiding his every move. He would look at a deal and know—without doubt—whether it would bring him fortune or failure. It was an inexplicable certainty, a clarity that felt divine.

To charismatics, it would have been called the Holy Spirit—an active, empowering force that moved within a person, granting supernatural gifts like prophecy, healing, or extraordinary wisdom. A manifestation of divine presence, energetic and undeniable, working through individuals to accomplish something greater than themselves.

For Vic, it felt as though he had another voice in his head, one he could consult. A presence speaking directly to his mind, offering insights, solutions, and assurance. It was not just intuition—it was as if God Himself was in his mind, walking with him, showing him the way. This connection, this partnership, drove Vic's decisions, fueled his ambition, and solidified his belief that Black Lake's water was more than a resource—it was a divine gift.

A gift with teeth, it seemed. The nightmares continued, each more vivid and terrifying than the last. Vic found himself trapped in recurring dreams, floating in the middle of the black lake, its scalding waters searing his skin. Too far from shore, the burning agony became unbearable. He would wake up drenched in sweat, screaming, his body aching as though the dream had been real.

But it did not stop there. Each time he fell back asleep, the nightmare resumed, as if in a loop, pulling him deeper into the lake's torment. The water seemed alive, vibrating with malice, as if it had its own consciousness. Just before the pain overwhelmed him completely— before he could feel his sanity slipping—a dark, guttural laugh erupted, echoing through the lake and reverberating through his very bones. It was an evil that felt ancient and primal, shaking him to his core.

Vic began to dread the nights, fearing the dreams that came as relentlessly as the sunrise. Yet, even as the nightmares tore at him, he could not shake his belief in the water's power—or its cost.

Now that the water had been distributed widely through his Black Lake Coffee empire, stories were pouring in—too many to ignore.

People were talking. The anecdotes were not just about feeling rejuvenated or sharper; they were about miraculous, inexplicable healing. Cancer patients declared themselves cured, their scans suddenly clear. Chronic conditions like emphysema and asthma disappeared as if they had never existed. Even the flu, COVID, and other once-dreaded maladies were reported to vanish after consuming the water.

At first, the world dismissed the stories as coincidence or exaggeration. "A placebo effect," they said. Skeptics scoffed, dismissing it as another health craze with no real science behind it. But the stories did not stop. In fact, they grew louder and more impossible to ignore. Videos of people recounting their miraculous recoveries went viral. News outlets began running pieces on the phenomenon, initially with cautious curiosity but quickly with mounting excitement.

Doctors and scientists started paying attention, trying to find explanations for the unexplainable. How could so many incurable ailments vanish seemingly overnight? The skepticism gave way to cautious optimism, then to outright astonishment.

The public's reaction was electric—and chaotic. People were excited, but excitement quickly turned to desperation. Crowds formed outside Black Lake Coffee locations, lines snaking around blocks as people clamored to get their hands on the water. Social media exploded with stories, theories, and pleas for more information. Everyone wanted the water.

The small town of Black Lake became a focal point of global attention, and Vic found himself at the center of it all. What had once been his quiet experiment had turned into a phenomenon that the world could not get enough of—and couldn't explain.

And then there was the Church.

One might think that the Church, faced with such an extraordinary gift, would fall to its knees in gratitude, thanking God for His infinite mercy in providing a miraculous wellspring of healing and renewal. Surely, they would see this as divine providence, a modern-day fountain of life to heal the suffering and restore hope to the faithful.

But the reaction was far more complex. While some religious leaders praised the water as a miracle and a sign of God's favor, others viewed it with suspicion, even fear. Sermons were preached both exalting the water as a blessing and condemning it as a temptation—something too good to be true. The Church, fractured in its response, found itself at a crossroads.

Was this truly God's gift? Or was it something darker, something unnatural, something humanity was not meant to wield? Some called it a miracle, but others whispered that it was a test, a warning, or even a deception.

The Vatican issued a statement urging caution, calling for investigations into the water's origins and properties. Smaller congregations split down the middle, some flocking to Black Lake with jars and bottles in hand, while others denounced the water as heretical, unclean, or a trick of the devil.

And yet, the miracles were undeniable. Congregants who had been terminally ill were healed. Priests with failing health suddenly stood straighter and stronger. Even skeptics within the Church were forced to confront the evidence.

The tension grew. Should the Church embrace the water as a divine miracle or resist it as a challenge to faith? The debate raged as Black Lake became not just a phenomenon but a battleground for belief, science, and the mysteries of life itself.

Vic stayed focused on the business, throwing himself into expansion plans with an almost manic intensity. His time was increasingly spent in New Orleans, working closely with Sam and the lab full of scientists who were desperate to crack the chemical code of the Black Lake elixir. The pressure was mounting—venture capitalists were chomping at the bit, eager to fund global operations. There was talk of opening Black Lake Coffee locations in Europe, Asia, Australia—everywhere. The world was ready, and so was Vic, if only they could make the water portable.

The lab was close, tantalizingly so. Sam and his team had broken the lake water down into its constituent parts, but the deeper they dug, the stranger the results became. Each analysis revealed compounds and elements that did not align with anything in known science. Some defied even theoretical chemistry, as if they were from another world entirely. Vic's obsession deepened as the possibilities unfolded.

Finally, the breakthrough came. After countless experiments, the scientists discovered the key to replicating the water's properties. The solution was astonishingly simple yet deeply unsettling: a 10,000-to-1 ratio of distilled water to Black Lake water. When mixed, the Black Lake water "converted" the entire batch. It was not dilution—it was domination. The original water seemed to absorb the neutral distilled water, taking it over like a cancer consuming its host.

The only difference was that the newly synthesized water was slightly off—it appeared cloudier and darker, its consistency just a touch thicker, denser than normal water. Sam noticed it immediately, pointing it out with scientific curiosity, but Vic dismissed it with a wave of his hand.

"No matter," Vic said with a grin. "It'll be filtered through coffee beans, steeped in tea, or blended into drinks. No one will even know it's water."

In fact, the darker, denser quality turned out to be a bonus, helping mask its true origin. It added a richness to the beverages that customers would rave about—a "fuller body," as coffee enthusiasts might put it. The oddity of its appearance became an unspoken feature, rather than a flaw, ensuring the secret of its origin stayed safely hidden behind the façade of premium blends and specialty drinks.

The slightly opaque texture served another purpose, one Vic quietly acknowledged to himself. It helped obscure the unsettling reality that this was no ordinary water—it was a force, a living entity of sorts, now made portable and ready to be unleashed on the world.

The implications were staggering. With just a fraction of the lake's supply, they could create an endless stream of the elixir. For Vic, it was a triumph beyond his wildest dreams, the answer to global expansion and unfathomable riches. Yet, in the back of his mind, a shadow lingered—a gnawing sense that they had unleashed something far more powerful, and far more dangerous, than they could control.

Sleep became the enemy, and he avoided it at all costs, succumbing only when his body could no longer resist. Even then, he tried to trick himself—sleeping lightly during the day, napping in short bursts—but nothing worked. The nightmares found him no matter what, seeping into his restless moments like a malevolent tide.

As time wore on, the dreams escalated. The black lake became a recurring setting, but its torments grew more elaborate and grotesque.

On the worst nights, when exhaustion claimed him entirely, Vic found himself trapped, unable to wake no matter how desperately he willed it. The lake's scalding waters would peel the skin from his body in long, agonizing strips, leaving raw muscle exposed to the air.

In the especially horrific dreams, his blood would be drawn out, pulled from his veins by the lake's dark, insatiable power. It was as if the black water had transformed into a living succubus, draining him completely, milking him dry until only bones remained. The sensation was so visceral, so real, that Vic would awaken screaming, clutching his arms and legs, half-expecting to find himself flayed to the bone.

Each nightmare took a toll. His once-robust demeanor became gaunt, his face etched with exhaustion and fear. Yet, through it all, Vic pressed on, driven by an unstoppable force. He could not abandon the water. Could not stop the expansion. Could not let go of the belief that what he was doing mattered—no matter the cost.

Armed with the breakthrough knowledge that a single 5-gallon bottle of Black Lake water could transform 50,000 gallons of ordinary coffee; Vic wasted no time. He placed an order for 100,000 lab-grade, smooth brown glass 5-gallon bottles, each meticulously vinyl-wrapped to match the branding on his fleet of delivery trucks. These bottles would soon be the lifeblood of more than 3,000 stores across North America.

Vic's expansion efforts shifted into hyperdrive. The demand for Black Lake Coffee was skyrocketing, and the investors, now fully aware of its explosive potential, eagerly signed contracts to bring the elixir-infused brew to all corners of the globe. Europe, Asia, South America, Africa, and Australia all clamored for their share of the miracle coffee.

Within months, Vic had orchestrated a global coffee empire. Over 10,000 stores on six continents served millions of customers daily, all unknowingly consuming the enigmatic brew from Black Lake. What had begun as a simple concept had become an unstoppable force, powered by a substance that seemed to defy the natural order.

Vic stood at the helm of this worldwide phenomenon, the mastermind behind a product that was changing lives, invigorating minds, and raising questions about its mysterious source. Yet, even as the accolades and profits poured in, he could not shake the creeping unease—this wasn't just coffee anymore. It was something far more powerful, far more dangerous, and it was everywhere.

CHAPTER 12

At exactly 8:00 a.m., the Gulfstream's engines roared to life, their deep-throated hum vibrating through the cabin as Tom and Dan settled into their leather seats. Outside, the Addison Airport runway shimmered under the pale morning sun, the air still cool but beginning to warm with the promise of a Texas spring day.

The jet taxied smoothly to the runway threshold, guided by ground control with effortless precision. A moment of stillness passed. Then the engines throttled forward, and the aircraft surged ahead, pressing them gently into their seats. The nose lifted, the earth fell away beneath them, and in seconds they were airborne—climbing into a clear blue sky streaked with high cirrus clouds.

Dallas faded behind them as the city gave way to patchwork fields and winding rivers. The hum of ascent smoothed into the steady rhythm of cruise. Tom glanced over at Dan, who was already staring out the window, lost in thought.

They were headed southeast, toward Reserve, Louisiana—toward the edge of something deeper. Something that had already begun.

The pilot came on the load speaker; hardly necessary since he was 12 feet ahead of them but likely better than kicking the cockpit door open and yelling back.

"Ladies and Gentlemen welcome to Dan Stone's private jet. I am your Captain Mike Smith. My co Pilot is Stan Gable. Your flight attendants are Carrie and Heather. The flight from Addison Airport in Texas to Port of South Louisiana Executive Regional Airport in Reserve, Louisiana is approximately 1 hour and 30 minutes in his Gulfstream G650. The Distance is roughly 450 nautical miles at our cruising Speed of approximately 516 knots or Mach 0.85. Our actual flight time may vary slightly based on weather, flight routing, and air traffic control, but I am estimating 1 hour 25 minutes. Please do not hesitate to ask Carrie or Heather for anything your hearts desire. Captain out.

Carrie brought Dan a double shot of Jack Black with an Anchor Steam craft beer to chase it down. That was all it took—within minutes, Dan was out cold.

The next thing he knew, they were on the ground in Reserve, taxiing toward the terminal or the FBO—the fixed-base operator where private jets unload passengers in comfort and discretion.

"Well, there you are," Tom laughed. "Smooth flight, huh?"

Dan rubbed his eyes, still shaking off the fog of sleep. "Guess so. Looks like I needed it."

Carrie lowered the air stairs with a metallic clunk, the warm Louisiana air already creeping into the cabin as the door opened.

Tom had his laptop secured and in it's leather satchel, strap over his shoulder and led the way to the exit door where Carrie stood smiling. Dan followed. No gear.

"Thank you for flying today Mr. Stone," she smiled.

"Thank you, Carrie. I'll see you again and will plan on staying conscious on the next flight," Dan laughed.

On the runway was a long black stretch limo. Tom and Dan dropped into the back.

"Dan, let's get settled at the Stone Plantation just west of Convent. We can review the itinerary while we drive and I can fill you in on all the holdings here in New Orleans we will visit," Tom said.

As they rode through Reserve in the black SUV, Tom pointed out one facility after another, his voice steady and matter-of-fact.

"That's Stone Industries #1—old plastics facility, now mostly storage. #2 is a refinery we picked up last year. #3 is the distribution hub for Louisiana and the Gulf. #4 handles solvents. #5 is our export terminal."

Dan stared out the window as the endless maze of pipes, tanks, and security fencing passed by, each site more industrial than the last.

"#6 is a blending operation. #7 and #8 are R&D and water treatment. #9, small-scale hydrogen testing. And #10—Koch-Stone Methanol #1," Tom said, nodding as they drove past a chainlink gate and guard booth," Tom pointed to the right. "Not the most creative names, but hey."

Dan gave a tired grin. "Straight to the point."

"This is where Sam's set up—running trials in the lab. You'll want to see what he's working on. You can do that tomorrow. "I have to jet to New York tonight. But, I'll get you settled in and intro you to the staff.

"Quite an industrial operation around here" Dan remarked.

"It's a money machine. Good place to visit—if you have to," Tom said. "New Orleans has Bourbon Street, the French Quarter, chicory coffee, and beignets. Beyond that? Billions in oil and chemical plants," he added, shaking his head. "Vic kept a house here because of all this."

"Well I think we can move the lab anywhere else. So far my vote is Carrie and another double Jack," Dan replied.

"Victor kept it separate so no one knew what was the real foundation for the Black Lake Coffee recipe. He figured no one would come snooping around a methanol plant in the middle of all this toxic wasteland," Tom said.

"Yes, he was right there. I don't even want to come snooping around here," Dan laughed dryly.

The limo slowed to a stop in front of a towering wrought iron gate, intricately adorned with a tangle of black roses—each one crafted from gleaming steel. Long, sharp thorns jutted from their stems, catching the light like blades. On either side, a ten-foot-high stone wall stretched for nearly a mile in both directions, shielding everything beyond from view.

With a soft mechanical hum, the gate opened. The black limo eased forward, gliding up the long, winding road that led to Dan's estate in Convent.

Tom glanced out the window. "Vic called it The Hollow. Don't ask me why. Said it sounded better than The Fortress. Victor was pretty high on security and obviously kept to himself."

They continued for nearly a quarter mile along a blacktop road lined with ancient live oaks, their massive branches arching overhead and trailing Spanish moss in soft, ghostly curtains. The drive led to a grand plantation-style mansion, its columns and wraparound porch echoing the old estates that once dotted the Louisiana River Road.

When the car stopped, Tom climbed out without a word and disappeared inside. Dan lingered a moment longer, retrieving his luggage from the trunk—a brand-new Louis Vuitton Horizon 55 roller, the iconic monogram gleaming in the afternoon light. It was packed with fresh clothes and gear from the high-end men's shops Tom had marched him through earlier that week. The leather still smelled crisp—like money and reinvention. The new and improved Dan Stone.

Dan stepped out of the car slowly, taking in the façade.

"Well," he said, "this is definitely not a shotgun shack."

Tom laughed. "Welcome to your inheritance."

They entered through the grand front doors, stepping into a vast foyer where the air was cool and faintly scented with orange oil. Warm dark wood floors contrasted with the winding staircase with balustrades of cold steel black roses. Gilded mirrors. The silence pressed in like velvet.

"This is just the front third," Tom said, leading the way. "There's a west wing with guest rooms, an east wing with the library, and Victor's suite is upstairs at the end of the hall. Take your pick—his room has been cleaned etcetera but largely how he left it."

Dan dropped his travel bag in the master bedroom. "Looks great. Good view."

"Yes, view of the pool and garden. Two hundred acres stretch into the swamp lands. Watch for alligators," Tom laughed.

"Alligators. Ok. I'll stay in the house," Dan said.

They toured in silence for nearly an hour. Dan took it in slowly—the museum-like sitting rooms, the cavernous study, the industrial kitchen with gleaming black marble counters. Along the hallway walls, a striking collection of Japanese and Southeast Asian art hung in careful symmetry: Edo-period ink scrolls, minimalist woodblock prints, gilded temple relics, and carved jade figures displayed in inset niches. It wasn't loud or flashy—it was curated. Intentional. Like everything else Vic had left behind.

Eventually, they ended up in the kitchen, where Tom pulled two cold brews from the oversized fridge.

"The refrigerator is always stocked with good stuff. Abita brewery is local and conscientious. Victor was discussing providing a water supply for these guys."

Before Dan could respond, a shadow filled the doorway.

The man who stepped into the kitchen was enormous—six-foot-five, matching Dan in inches but dwarfing him in girth, built like a brick wall. Muscles beneath a tailored black polo shirt with a silver embossed rose on the left chest strained with every movement. His jaw was square, his skin olive-toned, and his presence was quiet but commanding, like a loaded gun left casually on the table.

Tom turned. "Dan, meet Jerome."

The man nodded and extended his hand. "Mr. Stone, it's my pleasure."

"He ran the house for Victor," Tom continued. "Chef extraordinaire, bodyguard, driver, whatever you need here in New Orleans. He's got hands like sledgehammers and the mind of a chess player. You're in good hands."

Jerome's voice was deep, calm, and perfectly controlled. "Mr. Stone. I served Mr. Stone for the last decade. He trusted me with his life. I intend to honor that trust with yours."

Dan, still blinking at the sheer size of him, extended his hand. "Appreciate it. That's a hell of a résumé."

Jerome shook Dan's hand and smiled, "Whatever you need—I'm at your service."

Tom handed Dan a thick folder. "This is everything you need on the ten properties. Stone Industries #1 through #10. Maps, contacts, Vic's personal notes. Read up if you feel like working."

Dan flipped the folder open. "This is your idea of preliminary?"

"Think of it as a light appetizer," Tom smirked. "Tomorrow, Jerome can take you on the grand tour of the various facilities actually go inside and get the full flavor if you like."

Dan looked at Jerome again. "Okay, looks like I'm in good hands then."

Tom clapped him on the shoulder. "You are. Now get some rest, settle in and I will be back in a couple days."

And with that, he turned and left.

Dan stood in the kitchen, the silence folding in around him once again. He glanced at Jerome. "What's for dinner?"

The faintest glint sparked in Jerome's eye. "I make a mean étouffée, sir."

"When in New Orleans I suppose," Dan laughed."

Jerome went to work gathering ingredients while Dan went to explore the house.

Another turn, then another—and Dan found himself standing at the threshold of a vast, temperature-controlled garage. The polished concrete floor reflected overhead LEDs like a mirror, and the air smelled faintly of rubber, motor oil, and wealth.

Lined up in precise rows were more than twenty vehicles—an immaculate collection of performance, prestige, and pure indulgence.

"Damn," Dan muttered, stepping in slowly. "Vic enjoyed his money, I guess."

A candy-apple red Ferrari 812, a Lamborghini Aventador in matte graphite, a Porsche 911 GT3 RS, two Mercedes G-Wagens, and something unmistakably armored and military-looking in the back corner. On the far end sat a Bugatti Chiron, deep black with blood-red trim, as still and serious as a coiled predator.

"A fucking Bugatti," Dan said, grinning now. "Damn right, Vic."

He walked among them slowly, hand trailing along the curves of a McLaren, the silence humming with restrained horsepower. Each vehicle seemed untouched—detailed, fueled, and ready, like everything else Vic had left behind. Not abandoned. Preserved. As if he'd planned for someone to take the wheel.

Dan let out a low whistle. "What the hell have I walked into?"

He turned back toward the main house, the scent of roux now floating faintly through the air, pulling him back to the promise of Jerome's étouffée and a night full of questions.

Dinner was fantastic—every bit as decadent as promised.

Dan and Jerome shared a ridiculously large, family-style spread of New Orleans staples: smoky boudin, shrimp and grits, crawfish étouffée, and blackened catfish over dirty rice. Warm cornbread. Cold coleslaw. Two massive Hurricanes sat sweating on the table beside them, refilled more than once.

Dan leaned back, full and a little buzzed, picking at the last of the sausage.

"Jerome, how well did you know Vic? Ten years with him, you said—had to come with some insight."

Jerome wiped his mouth with a cloth napkin and set it neatly on the table.

"Vic was a great man. Truly. He played the part, sure—money, toys, the jet-set life—but underneath it all, he was grounded. He really did have the interests of mankind in his head."

Dan raised a brow. "Yeah, I saw the Bugatti and the multi-million-dollar sports car collection. Could've fed a lot of starving Africans."

Jerome smiled but didn't take the bait. "Vic had a lot of cash, no doubt. And he loved what he loved. But he also carried the weight of things. He spoke often about fixing what had been ignored."

Dan tilted his glass, swirling the last of his Hurricane. "Cryptic. What kind of things?"

Jerome's expression shifted slightly—something more cautious settling behind his eyes.

"Like the broken systems. The ones no one talks about anymore. Water. Energy. Food. The human machine and everything connected to it. He believed something fundamental was failing, and he wanted to be ahead of it."

Dan studied him, unsure if this was philosophical small talk or the beginning of something deeper.

"Sounds a little messianic."

"Maybe," Jerome said, his voice even. "Or maybe he just saw the edge before everyone else."

Dan leaned back, absorbing that.

"You buy into all that?"

Jerome met his gaze directly. "I buy into the man. And I've seen things, Mr. Stone. Things that don't fit the normal story."

Dan didn't reply right away. Somewhere in the house, the HVAC kicked on with a low hum.

Finally, Dan exhaled and said, "Well... now I'm definitely not sleeping."

Jerome gave a slow smile. "The house is new construction—no ghosts here."

Dan laughed. "Good to know." He paused, swirling the last of his drink. "Tell me something... Did Vic have anyone else? No offense—I can see you two were close. But maybe... a woman? Someone important?"

Jerome leaned back slightly, folding his thick hands on the table.

"One. A young woman named Stephanie. Smart. Quiet. Worked with him closely at the lab. They were close, but... complicated. I believe she's still there—probably this week."

Dan nodded slowly. "Yeah. The lab. I need to get over there."

"Say the word," Jerome said, "and we'll load up and go. In the daylight."

Dan chuckled. "Couple days. I just want to relax. Maybe play some golf. To be honest, I'm not used to this jet-set life. I like to play golf and smoke weed. That's about as deep as I go. Saving the world? I don't know if I'm up to it."

Jerome looked at him, calm and unblinking.

"You are," he said. "Vic knew it. You're the man for the job."

Dan raised an eyebrow. "Yeah?"

Jerome gave a slow nod. "You're the fruit of his loins, after all."

Dan blinked, then burst out laughing. "Jesus. You just made that sound so Biblical."

Jerome allowed the corner of his mouth to twitch upward. "It's a sacred mess we're in, Mr. Stone."

Dan blinked, then forced a smile. "Jesus. So Biblical."

Jerome allowed the corner of his mouth to twitch upward. "It's a sacred mess we're in, Mr. Stone."

Dan tilted his head. "Sacred?"

Jerome met his eyes, steady. "In the way that anything world-changing is. Dangerous. Uncomfortable. But necessary."

Dan didn't respond right away. He just stared down into the dark remnants of his Hurricane, suddenly unsure if he was in over his head— or just finally standing in the right water.

After far too many of Jerome's hurricanes, Dan retired to the master bedroom.

"Well, you're drunk, Danny boy," he spoke aloud. His own voice sounded strange as it echoed off the walls and ceiling of the empty cavernous bedroom. The feelings that accompanied the echo were unsettling. He knew he was alone. And he felt exactly that. He was trying to get used to this new whirlwind life. Maybe he should sober up; get off the bottle. He recalled trying that before when his ex Becca walked out the door.

When you drove her away.

Dan knew the score. He had fallen off the wagon and pulled her unwillingly behind him to break his fall. But the ground was even harder with Becca underneath him. She hopped to her feet and said, "So long sucker" and walked out the door. And good old Danny boy just silently crept into the waiting bottle. For weeks the world was distorted and out of focus. He thought about what he did, what he lost and who she was with. Oh, he knew. Yes, indeed he did. She was with that fucking creep from the country club. That rich bastard was probably screwing the bolts out of his big brass bed and Becca was helping him hold the wrench.

But Dan did not act. He drank himself into oblivion, passed out, came to, vomited, etcetera. And then started over. Second verse same as the first. But then a registered letter came from the estate of Victor Stone and life returned. A new chance with no work to be done and new people who did not know what a total fuck up he was. Hey if you don't like who you are change your life he remembered saying. But now Dan was thinking of her again. Constantly. Obsessively. But who could blame him? His thoughts and dreams of a new life filled with wine, women and song could include Becca. Now. But, Becca could be twenty miles away or twenty billion light years away with no difference. He could not fathom she would want to get back with him. But now he was a billionaire. That should do it. Dan fell onto the oversized king bed Vic had slept in probably a week ago? Who knew? His head spun from the alcohol as sleep overtook him. Dreams came harshly. A fitful sleep filled with memories of Becca.

CHAPTER 13

"You are drunk. You are always drunk. Every single time we leave the house you have to get wasted and make a total fool of yourself and me. How embarrassing. I am sick of it. Just fucking sick to death of it."

Becca went on about what a terrible husband Dan was while he tried to concentrate on anything else. Anything at all besides this tiresome lecture.

Blah blah blah. Always an argument. Every time they went to a party it ended like this. Her friends would tell the proper stories, comment on the country club tennis instructor, talk about old furniture or tired old clothing designers, or something else equally trivial. Everyone around them would hang on every syllable agreeing mindlessly and waiting for their turn at bat. The shit was the same in every single conversation. And she wondered why Dan got hammered. It was either booze or setting himself on fire in one of their well decorated bathrooms.

"No matter where we go you embarrass me. One of these days I'm going to let you see how you act by setting up a hidden camera. Maybe I should film you with my iPhone so you can see what a total..."

Dan blocked out his wife's derogation. He could tell you damn near word for word anyhow. It was a repeat performance of the last party which, by the way was a rerun of last month's episode. So, Dan got drunk. Big deal. That's what you're supposed to do at parties isn't it? That's what makes them a party and not a seminar or a lecture or some other boring event.

"...kick your ass out. Now I guess you'll go home and pass out cold as a rock. You are a real jerk, Dan Stone. Well forget it."

Dan did not want to fight with her. A slight argument was all right, but a full-fledged fight was just not a good thing. Dan always tried to control his temper but usually failed. Dan did not want to get mad. He had had too much alcohol that night to lose his temper and say things you can't unsay. Like Becca always did. Dan was sure she loved him but some of those vile things simply can't be forgotten.

"It's time you grew up and started acting like a man-- like a mature professional man. You are not that eighteen-year-old kid anymore."

Dan was beginning to lose that distinct ability one has to separate emotions. When Dan went past the tipping point every feeling just blurred into one big cacophony of hurtful epithet. Dan was getting angry and unable to block the sound from entering his ears and penetrating his brain. The words crowded through the passageway and slipped into the covering of his eardrum. First slowly and then more rapidly. Now Dan was hearing her. Now his attention was focused on all the various words she was using to insult him: asshole, stupid, jerk, loser, idiot, joker, funny guy, drunk, bum, failure --

"Shut up," Dan said quietly with a last-ditch effort to maintain his stability.

"Oh, now you show some backbone? After all night of swimming around in the bottle?"

"Fuck you." Dan said quietly and walked to the door of her best friend Sues' bedroom.

"Fuck you then, Dan Stone," she said to his back.

The door was wide open and Becca grabbed the edge and slung it closed catching Dan on the side of his face and head with the edge of the door. Dan touched his eyebrow and felt an immediate bump grow beneath his fingers. He felt the warm sticky blood on his fingers. Becca had split his head open with the damn door.

Dan turned and saw the eyes of thirty some couples fall onto the spectacle. Sue, the owner, and operator of the social party of the season hurried forward.

"You need to leave, Dan," she said quietly. Sue had seen this activity play out before and it never got better from this point.

"I am, Sue. Sorry about this," Dan said. "We were discussing an emotional issue." Dan turned towards the crowded room. "I'm very sorry to interrupt your party. Please excuse us," Dan said as he walked toward the front door.

Dan found himself on the front porch of Sues home in the Vickridge development in East Wichita, coatless, keyless, and cashless. "Shit," he said aloud. He didn't He jogged up the long driveway out the tall open iron gates. Three miles or so to their home, light wet snow, brisk wind. Lots of fun.

Two blocks flew by. The third block his lungs were burning. The fourth kicked him square in the gut. Dan stopped and puked up a quantity of the Bootle's Gin and soda from Marions open bar. Dan started walking with his thumb out praying for a miracle.

His mind traveled back in time. Rebecca B. Dillon. Five feet and five inches of high-class female. Dan married her less than a year before and after living with her for a year before that. Her parents supported her, and Dan took advantage of their generosity and did nothing. Dan really loved her more than he loved her money. More than she would ever know. They had a great time together and fell deeply in love in a matter of weeks. Dan just could not seem to keep himself in line. She was so pretty, so outgoing, so loving -- shit. Dan was scared to death about losing her. Any man from New York to LA would be a fool for passing her by. Heads turned no matter where they went or who they were with. Dan was paranoia; constantly worried about her safety. There was a rapist around every corner. A car coming with her name on it. But, most of all there was a bus ticket taking her to wherever Dan wasn't. And Dan couldn't blame her. Dan wasn't exactly a driven businessman. He wasn't a secure provider. He wanted to be. He just couldn't come up with the right idea and he couldn't bring himself to simply get a mindless job. But he had plans. He had ideas. Just not the right one yet. But he was trying and for now Dan was sure he would come home to a note on the refrigerator or get a text on his phone:

Dear Dan - Sorry for ruining your life. Signed you know who.

But it never came. Dan knew there was no chance in hell of hanging onto such a fantastic catch-- his line was bound to break. But she loved him. She swore she would never leave him.

But, deep down Dan knew she would not be able to stay with an ordinary guy like him. Maybe it was manifest destiny. Dan calling his own future out. He didn't know. But, he knew she was slipping away. It was getting worse. Now she was simply pushing him too hard.

No one picked Dan up for a mile or so but then a beautiful soul saw him suffering and pulled onto the shoulder in front of him. They likely didn't know Dan was a failure of a man who's wife was kicking his ass on the daily - not exactly the type of guy you would want to sit in the passenger seat on a cold dark winters night. But they did a quick tap on the horn and the passenger window came down, signaling to run up and come in out of the snow.

"Climb in Dan," Jenny yelled to him.

Dan opened the door of the dark blue BMW z4 convertible and dropped in.

"Thank God. I thought I would just high tail it out of there before she really got rolling, Jenny."

Leggy little legs contained in deep red Christmas velvet pants. Tight sweater pulling threads over her ample surgically augmented chest. 420cc of silicone in each Dan estimated. Jenny was one of Becca's tennis friends from Crestview Country Club; Husband was a dentist if Dan recalled correctly.

"Well, thanks for leaving and sparing us all. But you'll freeze to death out here. It has to be ten degrees. I brought your coat. I'll drop you at your house," Jenny offered sympathetically.

"Thank you. I thought I would end up walking the whole way. It is pretty brutal out here. I didn't think that through." Dan laughed as he slipped his heavy down coat on. "You are a true lifesaver," Dan said slamming the door and blowing warmth into his hands.

"Becca would kill me if she knew I picked you up," she said hesitantly.

"Well, Becca has her demons. Thank you so much for thinking of me I think I might have actually frozen to death in another minute -- and no worries, it's our secret," he laughed.

She smiled and relaxed a bit. "Oh Dan," she sighed.

"Turn left on Stafford -- couple more blocks -- it's the tan stone ranch with the circle drive and all the white Christmas lights."

"Your brain frozen? I know where you live."

"Yes, it is," Dan laughed again. "Sorry. I guess you have been there."

She pulled into the portico immediately in front of Dan's front door. "Can I come in for a drink?"

"Drink?" Dan hesitated. "Of course, come on in Jenny."

"Great. I really don't want to go back and talk with Becca and I do not want to just go home and do nothing tonight, it's only ten thirty. Besides, you need one too."

Shit. Dan this can't end well. Be careful. Maybe she just wants a drink ... Bullshit.

"Ok come on in."

Jenny shut off her BMW and she followed Dan to the big double doors. He entered his code into the keypad beside the door and they went inside.

"Okay Jenny, home sweet home. What would you like from the bar?"

"How about a rum and coke?"

"Coming right up. Make yourself at home. TV remote is on the coffee table."

"So, is Becca staying at Sue's for the night?"

That's not a good sign, Dan, Kick her ass out.

"Probably. She was pissed. I think she will stay there tonight and cuss me." Dan laughed. "She usually does when she goes on a tirade like this. But you never know."

"Well, I hope she does. I would hate for her to walk in and catch me consorting with the enemy," Jenny laughed.

"Enemy?" Dan handed her the drink. "I don't think I am exactly that." Dan sat down on the couch beside her.

"You're right, Dan. I'm sorry. I didn't mean it like that." She tipped the glass and drank the strong liquor down.

"That's ok. I get it. We certainly are having a rough patch lately. You two probably have had all kinds of conversations on the tennis court. And here it sounds like," Dan sighed.

"Well she doesn't seem to be a happy person," Jenny said.

Dan raised an eyebrow. "Really?"

"Well there are just a lot of our friends who are divorced or getting divorced or cheating on their husbands."

Oops she said it. This was skittering downhill on ice.

"Okay," Dan took a long drink of his own 11-year-old Bacardi and coke. The conversation was uncomfortable not only because Jenny was an incredibly beautiful and sexy woman but because she had discussed Dan with Becca apparently on numerous occasions. Becca was unhappy. In fact Becca was unhappy with Dan. Dan took another long drink. Jenny did the same.

Jenny set her glass on the coffee table and slid over close to Dan. Taking his glass from his hand she set it beside her own. She then turned and pushed her risqué mouth onto Dan's. It was warm and inviting. Jenny was nice and kind and beautiful. Dan hesitated and was lost in her kiss. It had been a while since someone actually wanted him.

Jenny and Dan did a damn crazy thing and he prayed to God Becca actually did stay away this night.

# # #

Oh shit, was Dan's first thought when he woke the next morning.

While Dan slept off those heavy rum and cokes, he had a dream about Becca coming home. Dan had just barely shoved Jenny out the back door when Becca slipped into bed beside him.

"I forgive you Honey," she cooed.

Dan could see Jenny's red panties hanging on the top of the antique American walnut rocking chair on the other side of the room. A cold hand sealed itself around his jugular and his breathing became shallow.

"I love you, Dan."

Don't look over there! Please God!

"I know you were just drunk. You didn't mean it."

"I'm sorry, Becca."

In the way you can do in dreams, Dan could see her behind him as she rotated her head and spotted the little red Victoria's secret panties her friend Jenny had left behind. Her eyes got big. "Who the fuck was here, Dan? Not getting enough from me? First thing you do when I turn my back is fuck someone else? In our bed, Dan?"

And so, in the dream world it all started again. She is kicking his ass, and he bent over and took it. Dan wanted to tell her how sorry he was, that he didn't mean to cheat on her; that it just happened. Dan wanted to tell her that it was not his fault that Jenny was also needing a hug- probably. That she was simply fulfilling some crazy fantasy of fucking her friends husband. Tell her that it will be okay after she forgets about it. Honesty is the best policy. No. Dan wanted to tell her to shut the fuck up.

She kept going. She rolled up all of the arguments, all of the lectures, all of the preachings of the sermon that never ends into one loathsome diatribe of Becca. Here in his own private dreamland where anything can happen -- good or bad --- she droned on and on and delivered her final speech. And Dan snapped.

Dan was dreaming and Dan knew it. Dan was dreaming so Dan could do anything Dan wanted to with absolutely no repercussions. How liberating. It was time Becca closed her big mouth. Time to play this out pretend. Tell Becca to get the fuck out of his life.

But Dan didn't do it not even in dreamland. Not even in the one place on earth that didn't really matter. A place where there were no repercussions. Dan could not do that to Becca even in a dream.. Dan simply got out of bed and floated out of the bedroom and through their well apportioned home. The front door opened in front of him and Dan saw Jenny's convertible still parked under their portico. Dan awoke with a start.

"What the Hell?" Dan said aloud and sat up in bed. His head was pulsating with alcohol. The hangover was as bad as ever. What in the world had Dan done? What was her name? Dan's head was cloudy. Jenny. That was it. Jenny was gone. Dan flipped over quickly in bed. No panties on the rocker. Thank God. Dan relaxed back on his pillow. The night had been everything a depressed, drunk, cheating husband could have hoped for with his wifes tennis buddy. Shit.

How was Dan going to patch things up with Becca? What a jerk, he thought. Dan walked to the kitchen and got an ice pack and a cold orange Gatorade. He drank half of it in standing front of the refrigerator. Dan opened the cabinet and poured a few inches of Tito's vodka into the Gatorade. Hair of the Dog. He'd be good as new in a few.

# # #

The shoe dropped just a week later. Jenny couldn't hold it in. She told her husband the dentist. Dentist called Becca. Shit.

"Get the Fuck out!" she screamed.

"You fucking son of a bitch!"

"Get out motherfucker!" she screamed while the tears flew from her mouth and face. She stood up and began pushing and striking him. Herding him toward the door. Her face was smeared with her eyeliner and tears.

"Let me explain, Babe," Dan said." Let me…" Dan hesitated. "There is a perfectly…"

"Fuck you!"

"Honey, please."

"Don't say 'Honey' to me you fucker. She ripped the heavy wooden door open and pushed him through.

"Please Becca." The door slammed into him striking his shoulder and ringing off his left ear. Dan yelled in pain.

"Forget it," Dan thought. "She's better off without me."

Ok. Goodbye Becca," Dan called through the closed door.

And the next thing you know, they were divorced. Dan received a settlement of $250,000 to sign away any possible claims to any family money. Dan played a lot of golf for the next ten years until it was gone. Then Dan found himself in Denver, Colorado, perched in the haze of a city that seemed to mirror his state of mind. He was smoking himself to death, joints and cigarettes alternately hanging from his lips, as if each exhale might purge the guilt, the anger, the self-loathing that had taken root inside him. It was a sacrifice and a penance, or so he told himself. Each drag was an offering to the gods of regret, each plume of smoke a prayer for some kind of release. Too many years clinging to the fragments of a life that had once been good, a life he had somehow managed to poison, turning everything bright into shadows.

But then, out of nowhere, Vic died. The news came like a lifeline, dragging Dan from his self-imposed purgatory. One day he was sitting in his car outside a bar, thinking about how to avoid the next day, and the next, and the next. The next thing he knew, he was staring at the edge of an unexpected inheritance, an unimaginable fortune—and a past from which he'd been running.

CHAPTER 14

According to the map Jerome had forged, Dan was to go from Convent Louisiana to Pelican. There Dan would find the Country Club, where Victor was an icon and relaxed quite often. "Who knew Vic was a golfer?" Dan said aloud.

Dan's petrochemical fortune and the majority of his holdings were in and around Convent and Vacherie in St. James parish. Before getting through the massive steel gate, Dan paused and dug out a joint from his bag to ponder his circumstances. He pulled up the internet on his iPhone to see a few more details on the excursion. Big Easy Magazine came up first with Cancer Alley: They don't call it Cancer Alley for nothing.

Dan clicked on the hyperlink to read all about this hell hole: Roughly between Baton Rouge and New Orleans, the banks of the river are home to some of the highest concentrations of such facilities. Known as "cancer alley," this area includes Iberville, St. James, St. John the Baptist and East and West Baton Rouge Parishes. In just Saint James Parish, home to about 22,000 people, three new chemical plants are currently in the planning stages: a Formosa ethane cracker that would include multiple production plants and a natural gas plant (the "sunshine project"), a Wanhua plant 250 acres in size that would manufacture the base ingredient of polyurethane, and a South Louisiana Methanol plant 1500 acres in size.

Jerome had worked up a detailed color map of the area, generously slathered with post it notes referencing the 10 Stone facilities and a number of sites to see. The map was covered with a dozen or so neatly placed notes around the edges, allowing Dan to consult the map while simultaneously taking in bits of local lore. Each one was concise and engaging, perfectly tailored to Dan's scattered yet curious mind.

Jerome was clearly on top of his game. The home was immaculately organized, a shrine to efficiency, with "a place for everything and everything in its place," as the saying goes. It made Dan smirk; unsure if it was Vic or Jerome who crafted it with such precision.

First things first, I need food; a gator sandwich, he thought as his stomach growled. "You hear that?" he said aloud.

Dan picked up the top printout, noticing a bright yellow post it note stuck to it that read: "Pelican Point Country Club. You're a member. Just off I-10."

He grinned and spoke the directions into the Mercedes G wagon's navigator. Instantly, a full-color map popped up on the console, and the route materialized before him. His exit was coming up fast.

After making a few quick turns and following the navigator's play-by-play AI generated verbal directions, Dan soon found himself at the entrance of the golf course. The sprawling greens beyond the gate were just what he needed to unwind.

He pulled in, spotting the unmistakable pro shop surrounded by golf carts in the circular drive. A little further in, another entrance proudly announced the 19th Hole Restaurant in bold lettering.

"Food, then golf," Dan muttered to himself with a satisfied grin as he parked. He was not in a hurry; this was shaping up to be a perfect stop.

Dan stepped into the establishment — the bar and grill attached to the golf course was quiet at 3 p.m., nearly deserted. Behind the bar stood a brunette in her mid-twenties, dressed in a sleeveless black silk top and skin-tight black leggings—or yoga pants, tights, whatever they were called. High heels, too. Not exactly standard clubhouse attire. She was striking—pretty face, great figure—and gave him a look that was equal parts curiosity and amusement as he approached. "Just one today?"

"Yes, just me. Lauri," Dan said reading her name tag.

"Right this way, Sir."

Dan was seated looking at the golf course and a large whitewater fountain shooting twenty feet in the air and settling into a mote surrounding the island green of the 18th hole. Lauri left the menu and walked back to the front greeter's station. Dan eyed the menu and Lauri quickly returned.

"I will have a beer. Looks like Abita is your local brew from the menu?"

"It is," she smiled. "We stock all their styles as they are just down the road. I highly recommend their Purple Haze, it is a raspberry lager, but not too fruity or if you like an IPA their Alpha Gator."

"Ha! funny. Okay I will go with the Gator and a Catfish Po Boy and fries, Lauri."

"She smiled and disappeared."

Dan punched up the internet on his iPhone to pass the time and investigate this cancer alley more thoroughly.

St. Tammany county: Northshore of Lake Pontchartrain, long considered the summer getaway of New Orleans elite. The tradition of summering began during the 1800's as an escape from the disease and yellow fever epidemics that plagued the city.

Didn't that sound lovely? Dan was afoot in the largest cancer cluster in north America as well as a mosquito haven plagued with yellow fever in distant history. "Ug."

Lauri returned with the beer in a frosty glass, condensation dripping from the side. "The humidity is hell here and that is a fact. But this beer will make it all better," she smiled.

"Dan Stone," he said extending his hand.

Lauri wiped her hand on a small black towel she had belted around her waist and took Dans hand. Dan held it fast and shook it firmly, giving a tug at the end. And smiled broadly. Lauri smiled and pulled out the chair opposite and sat down. "So, who are you my friend" she asked leaning forward on her hands perched on her elbows.

"I'm Dan, just a guy passing through taking a look around and seeing what this burg has to offer," he smiled.

"Ah, a tourist, huh. But who are you really? I looked you up and your member number is 'one'," she laughed.

"Hm. Okay you got me. I understand I am a member by relation to my father Vic Stone. I imagine it's a corporate membership. Vic just passed and he handed me the membership in his will."

"Oh, I'm sorry," Lauri responded. "We heard of Victor's death. .He spent a lot of time here. Excellent scratch golfer, by the way."

"You knew him?"

"Well no. He came in and had a few beers sometimes after golf, but I never really knew him more than that. Great tipper. Ah, but I'm sorry for your loss."

"No, no. It's fine. I didn't even know him really. It's actually all a bit baffling and a bit of a whirlwind as well. But, I am just looking to relax a bit here at Pelican."

A distant digital bell rang. "Let me grab your food," Lauri jumped up and hurried off. Dan watched her go. A sweet girl; inquisitive. Maybe flirting with him. Most likely though just working for the tip and he was the only one in the bar, he thought. Lauri came right back carrying another two beers in the bottles and his plate complete with a large steaming sandwich with a red plastic sword stuck in each half of the baguette and piled high with Cajun spiced French fries.

Lauri sat and popped the tops of the purple haze Abita. "Figured you would want to try this one since I'm joining you," She laughed. "It's my break. They don't really care if I have a beer anyway. Especially with you Mr. Stone."

Dan smiled too. "I make it a rule to never pass up the company of a beautiful woman when it's offered."

Lauri slid Dan's beer and held hers high in the middle of the table. "To your father."

Dan toasted by clicking the dripping cold beer bottle with hers. "Thank you, Lauri. I appreciate that."

Lauri took a long drink of her Purple Haze. "Funny you should ask what's my story she stated."

"Please share. I'll eat and you regale me with your tale. I am famished," Dan smiled and dug into his fries and Po Boy while Lauri began.

"Well, here I am in Gonzales, Louisiana, working at the country club," she said with a shrug and a smile. "I was on my way to New Orleans and stopped in for a bite... ended up staying. It's part of a country club exchange through Argis Golf—I used to work with them back in Dallas."

She paused, then added, "Well, technically I was at Lantana Golf Club, out in Flower Mound. But close enough to Dallas."

Her voice was easy, unpretentious, the kind of rhythm that came from someone used to talking to strangers.

"Grew up there—family-friendly suburb, lived there my whole life. Single, if you're wondering." She smiled, unbothered. "Decided I needed a new view. Something with a little more humidity and a lot fewer expectations. That was six months ago."

Dan had finished his fries and three-fourths of his sandwich. He took a long drink and polished off the last of his Gator IPA. "Very nice to meet you, Lauri. I have lived in Dallas as well for most of my adult life. I guess that length of time is about ten years longer than you have roamed the earth."

"Subtle she laughed. "I'm 27."

"Perfect." Dan laughed. I'm 34."

"So, are you going back to Dallas? Can I get a ride?" she laughed.

"Not feeling it here huh?"

"No. I will be moving back to Dallas pretty soon. I have a 6-month lease on an apartment here in town and my six months are up. This is a good job. The people are nice but it's too industrial here. Go any further south you'll see what I mean. This is paradise where you're at now. Are you going to play golf? It's a great course."

"I am," Dan said. "Figured I'd play eighteen—maybe thirty-six if I'm feeling ambitious. I need to get some rest."

"Rest, huh?" Lauri laughed, giving him a playful look.

"Well, I like active relaxation. Golf centers me."

She tilted her head, intrigued. "Well, I'm off all night. After your round, give me a call—I'll show you around."

She picked up his phone from the counter without asking, typed in her info, and handed it back.

Dan grinned. "Okay, great. Why don't I pick you up at seven? We'll find some dinner."

"Done. I'll text you the address—it's those apartments right there, overlooking the 9th green."

Dan gave a casual salute as he turned to leave. "See you tonight."

He found the pro shop easily, grabbed a sleeve of balls and an iced Black Lake Coffee from the cooler near the door, then headed out toward the first tee—feeling lighter than he had in days.

Dan showered at the club after his round, tossing his towel over the bench in the locker room, still shaking his head at the scorecard. He'd only played eighteen—plans with Lauri had kept him from chasing thirty-six—but somehow, even playing casual, he'd shot a 59. Again.

He wasn't even sure how it was happening. His swing felt relaxed, almost automatic. The putts dropped like they were magnetically attracted to the hole. Everything just... worked.

The iced Black Lake Coffee he grabbed on the first tee hummed in his bloodstream the entire round. It wasn't adrenaline. It wasn't caffeine. It was something else entirely.

\###

Dan opened the passenger door of the G-Wagon, and Lauri climbed in, settling into the soft tan leather seat. She leaned back and crossed her bare ankles, glancing over at him with a relaxed smile.

They went for food at Don's Seafood, settling into a cozy booth beneath low-hung lights and the hum of local chatter. They started with chargrilled oysters, Don's signature dish—smoky, rich, and sizzling in their shells. Then came crawfish, piled high on butcher paper, their fingers dripping with spice and butter as they cracked shells and laughed through the mess.

Conversation flowed easily—unforced and unfiltered. Then came the Hurricanes, Dan's new standby. Sweet, strong, and deceptively smooth. One turned into three which turned into too many without either of them noticing.

Halfway through their fourth round, Lauri leaned forward, her eyes steady.

"I'm not typically this forward, Dan," she said. "But I get a feeling sometimes. A sixth sense. You want me to be here. You need me."

Dan laughed, caught off guard. "I do?"

"Yes."

He grinned. "Well, when you're right, you're right. I do want you here. I could use a beautiful companion while I'm in New Orleans. Someone who knows the area... and loves oysters and beer."

Lauri laughed, brushing a strand of hair behind her ear.

"I'll be here a week or two," Dan continued. "I really don't know yet. I've got a house in Convent, and I'm checking out Vic's businesses while I'm here. You'd be the perfect tour guide."

She smiled. "Okay. I'll show you around. But just a warning—I don't know that much about the area."

"Perfect," Dan said, raising his glass. "We'll just drive around blind and enjoy each other's company." "Well... I know a few things," Lauri said, her smile widening. "And the rest? We'll figure out. Shall we go explore some more?"

Dan leaned back and laughed. "Actually, I'm pretty hammered. I should probably sober up a little."

"Responsible and charming," she teased.

"How about we grab a coffee and take a stroll?" he suggested.

They ordered two Irish coffees, which didn't exactly help their blood alcohol levels—but the base was Black Lake Coffee, strong enough to jolt their minds back into sharpness even as the whiskey warmed their veins.

CHAPTER 15

Dan woke early, feeling sharper than he had in days.

He picked up Lauri at her apartment just after sunrise, the Bugatti Chiron rumbling like a restrained predator in the parking lot. She laughed when she saw it, shaking her head but climbing in without hesitation.

Before they left, Jerome had briefed Dan further—catching him up on logistics, contacts, and what to expect. Jerome had also understood, without needing to ask, that Dan had met a woman and would once again be operating on his own.

Professional as ever, Jerome made a few quiet calls, ensuring the right people knew Dan was coming.

They stopped at the Black Lake Coffee House on the edge of town, grabbing bags of hot beignets dusted with powdered sugar and double espressos with chicory—the old Southern staple given a new intensity by Black Lake's brewing process.

The day was just beginning, and Dan had the wheel, the girl, and a mission humming in the air. Dan hit the gas, and before he knew it, they were surrounded by smokestacks and the thick haze of oil smog. The stretch between Pelican Point and Lake Pontchartrain was a jarring mix of greenspace and industrial sprawl.

Giant cylindrical oil tanks loomed on the horizon, pipelines snaked through fields like metallic veins, and industrial yards sprawled across the landscape. Then, out of nowhere, clusters of half a dozen houses would appear, stubbornly planted amidst the chaos.

"What are these people thinking?" Dan muttered, shaking his head. The stark reality hit him—Cancer Alley. A nickname well-earned for this stretch of Louisiana.

"You don't make your home at the dump," he thought, his grip tightening on the wheel as he accelerated past another cluster of homes, the juxtaposition of industry and domesticity unsettling. It was a reminder of how people endured in the shadow of the unimaginable. Maybe he should invest in a u-haul franchise and help these people get the fuck out here, he mused.

As Dan drove into Convent proper, the scenery shifted to a surreal mix of fields of green, industrial yards, and rows of shotgun shacks. The mighty Mississippi carved its way through the middle of the town, a lifeline running through a place that felt abandoned to its fate. The air hung heavy, carrying the unmistakable tang of oil and something far worse.

"This isn't a very nice town," Lauri said, her nose crinkling as she stared out the window.

"Yeah, a bit rundown," Dan replied, glancing at the rust-streaked industrial buildings. "And it smells like oil."

"Everything smells like oil or something worse around here," she frowned, folding her arms.

Dan tapped the steering wheel, as if to distract himself from the oppressive atmosphere. "My guy sent me some things to check out. In that briefcase under your feet."

Lauri glanced down. The Bugati was not exactly roomy, its tight quarters making the briefcase feel larger than it was. She reached down, pulling out the expensive leather case and placing it on her lap. The brass locks glinted faintly in the dim light as she snapped them open.

"What's inside?" Lauri asked, her curiosity momentarily eclipsing the bleak surroundings.

"Mostly paperwork," Dan replied casually.

"And weed," she laughed, pulling out a large Ziplock bag filled with Purple Microbus marijuana from the neatly packed briefcase.

Dan chuckled. "That's prescription med. But there should be a document in there with notes on places to see. My guy sent it."

"Your guy, huh?" she teased.

"Well, I guess my butler," he clarified, smirking.

Lauri dug further into the briefcase and pulled out a folded printout. "Ok, here's a map of Convent with a bunch of red X's... and a post it." She read it aloud: "'Dan, in Convent, LA, find Burton Road. You own most of it.'"

Dan nodded, taking a moment to process the information before speaking into the Bugati's voice assistant system. "Bugati: Route Guidance to Convent, Louisiana, Burton Road."

The android voice of the car's navigation system responded immediately. "Starting route guidance to Burton Road, Convent, Louisiana." A detailed digital map popped up on the console's screen, the route clearly highlighted.

Dan grinned, easing back into his seat as he followed the directions. "Looks like we've got a destination," he said, glancing at Lauri.

"Great," she replied, still examining the map. "Let's see what your empire looks like." Lauri smiled and kicked off her high heels. She put her bare feet and fire engine red polished toes up on the dashboard.

Dan smiled at her. She was a very unusual girl. In his experience women were vapid and interested in things that didn't matter much to him. Laurie was interesting and intelligent, very comfortable in her skin, cute, sweet, and a bit brazen. Sexy as hell. He liked her.

After going north on 44 and crossing the Sunshine Bridge and back down 18 and a few turns down the sad, neglected streets on the other side of the river, Dan finally found Burton Road and gunned it. The Bugati roared forward, its tires kicking up dust as they left the small town's rundown core behind.

For miles, the landscape barely changed—on either side of the road were rows upon rows of giant cylindrical oil tanks. White and corroded with rust, the massive vessels stood in stark contrast to the surrounding green, their industrial sprawl stretching as far as the eye could see.

Eventually, the road came to an abrupt end, and looming ahead was a massive refinery. Smoke billowed from its towering stacks, a gray plume that smeared the horizon. The air was thick with the acrid stench of chemicals and oil.

Behind a barbed-wire fence stood a gatehouse with a guard shack. A weathered metal sign hung on the chain-link fence, its bold black letters reading:

STONE INDUSTRIES — KEEP OUT

Dan slowed the car to a crawl, eyes fixed on the sign as the weight of what he'd inherited began to settle in. It left a bad taste in his mouth. This place—whatever it was—stood in stark contrast to the clean life he'd built around golf courses, easy women, and cannabis dispensaries.

A far cry, indeed.

"Well," Lauri said, breaking the silence, "guess we found your empire."

"Yeah," Dan muttered, his voice tinged with disbelief. "This is something all right. I guess we know why this area stinks."

"Well, you are some kind of rich, Dan Stone. There must have been one thousand tanks filled with oil I would guess," she smiled despite the stench penetrating the car.

"Yes. I am. But this is a nasty way to get it. Yuck."

Well, Vic had made his choices obviously and hadn't cared about the industrial wasteland he helped to create here in New Orleans. I won't be staying long here in this hell hole, Dan thought. Dan hit the gas and spun the car around, the sports car's tires screeching as he left the industrial sprawl behind. Within minutes, they were back on Highway 18, heading south.

The road seemed rural at first glance, but on either side stood six-foot fences topped with razor-sharp concertina wire. Periodic gates broke the monotony, each marked by three-foot signs titled NOTICE in bold red letters, followed by paragraphs of dense legal jargon. Adjacent to those were larger signs that read:

AUTHORIZED PERSONNEL ONLY
ALL VISITORS MUST CHECK IN AT THE OFFICE

It was as if the entire stretch of road existed as a fortress for industry.

As they continued, the scenery shifted slightly. Ahead, a small, quaint stone church came into view—St. James Catholic Church—its white steeple surrounded by a green pasture that looked out of place against the industrial backdrop. Directly opposite the church, rows of raised crypts in a cemetery jutted from the earth, the style unmistakably local to Louisiana, designed to combat the waterlogged soil.

But even here, industry cast its shadow. The cemetery's backdrop was a sea of oil storage cylinders, stretching into the distance. Just past the cemetery, a small, nondescript sign appeared, pointing down a narrow road:

EXXONMOBIL PIPELINE — STONE INDUSTRIES FIELD 3245

"Well, that's something," Lauri said, her voice dripping with irony.

Dan smirked but said nothing, his eyes flicking between the sign and the endless industrial sprawl. It was clear that every inch of this land had been claimed by either death or oil. But this land was clearly the possession of Dan Stone. And it makes money. Lots of money. Hell, that's what made Vic so rich. The world runs on chemicals and petroleum fuel.

"Well, I'm no tree hugger," Dan said "But this is disgusting. Seems the air is getting worse as we go. My nose is burning sniffing these fumes. I can't wait to get out of here and back to the hotel."

They continued south on Highway 18 in silence for the next half hour, the surreal landscape stretching endlessly ahead. Tens of thousands of oil tanks dotted the fields to their right, systematically placed every few hundred feet. To their left, modest frame houses stood in stark contrast to the industrial sprawl, occasionally giving way to stretches of barbed wire fences and signs declaring:

KEEP OUT — STONE INDUSTRIES FIELD XXXX

The uneasy juxtaposition lingered until Lauri finally broke the silence. She had been sifting through the briefcase, examining the printouts, maps, and photos Jerome had left for Dan.

"Here's another map," she said, holding up a printout with a yellow post it notes attached. "'Dan, find St. 5160 Emma Street in St. James. You own that stretch of road between Highway 18 and 3127 and basically everything you can see from there,'" she read aloud. Then she picked up another note. "'Find the Koch Methanol Plant.---Tom. '"

Dan snorted. "Nice, fucking methanol. I watched a show on Discovery once—place in Texas, maybe Louisiana. Whole town got sick. Dogs wouldn't drink the water. The mayor's kid went blind."

"Who is Tom?"

"Ah. Yeah that makes sense, I thought Jerome was a bit too prepared. Tom is my attorney who dropped me here. He is the brains behind all this stuff here I guess."

A few minutes later, they pulled up in front of a sprawling industrial yard. In the distance stood a giant red brick building, partially obscured by a vast parking area, a guardhouse, and a chain-link gate topped with concertina wire. A series of signs plastered the fence:

NOTICE — AUTHORIZED PERSONNEL ONLY
STOP
KOCH METHANOL — STONE INDUSTRIES

"Well let's have a look." He pulled up the guard booth where an old black man with thick glasses, a blue polo shirt logoed with Stone Industries, and a name tag that said Jacob emerged.

"Help you?"

Dan leaned out of the window, his voice calm but confident. "Yeah, I'm Dan Stone. I'm guessing this is one of mine." Dan handed his Texas drivers license to the guard.

Jacob raised an eyebrow, his gaze shifting between the Bugati and Dan and the ID, after a moment, his expression softened slightly. "Oh," he said, drawing out the word as if processing the revelation. "Well, Mr. Stone... What can I do for you?"

"Let me in and tell whoever's in charge I'm here and want to meet," Dan replied casually, as if it were the most natural request in the world.

Jacob blinked, momentarily incredulous. His eyes narrowed slightly as he studied Dan, then he gave a small nod. "I'll call the boss in the office. Jerome told me you were comin'," he said, before disappearing into the guard shack, the door shutting behind him.

Dan leaned back in his seat, glancing at Lauri, who was still thumbing through the briefcase. "Let's see what the big boys have to say about the new boss showing up," he smiled, "Guess Jerome ruined my surprise," his fingers drumming lightly on the steering wheel as he waited. It will be good to check out what father Vic had been doing here in this shithole of a town, he thought.

After fifteen minutes an enclosed electric golf cart appeared traveling down the long entrance driveway towards the guard shack and the visitors. Two men in khaki chinos and red polo shirts approached the gatehouse. They entered the small structure and came out of the door opposite the Bugati.

"Hello Mr. Stone. We spoke with Jerome who said you would be coming today. We are happy to escort you into the building. Please come through the gate and ride with us." Jacob pushed the button, and the gate rolled open for Dan to pass. Dan parked immediately inside the fenced area, One of the men motioned toward the cart as Dan stepped out.

"Mr. Stone, Ms...." the man began, his gaze shifting to Lauri as she climbed out beside Dan.

"Just Lauri," she replied with a polite smile.

The men nodded, one of them sliding into the driver's seat of the cart while the other took the passenger side. Dan and Lauri climbed into the back, and the cart whirred to life, carrying them across the yard toward the imposing three-story brick building in the distance.

The cold, industrial exterior of the Koch-Stone operations building loomed larger as they traveled closer, its stark design emphasizing function over form. Smoke billowed from the nearby stacks, darkening the horizon, while the rhythmic clank of heavy machinery reverberated through the air.

Surrounding the methane refinery were more of the giant white oil vessels scattered across the landscape, their corroded surfaces contrasting with newer, gleaming ones that held the gas, Dan assumed. The sheer scale of the operation was staggering.

He adjusted his sunglasses, squinting slightly against the haze, taking it all in with a mix of awe and disbelief, undertones of natural gas slightly burning his nose.

"Quite the operation," Lauri murmured, breaking the silence as the cart approached the main entrance.

The golf cart approached the imposing building, and a large roll-up door opened with a mechanical hum, allowing the cart to glide inside. They entered a long, windowless hallway with pristine white walls and a gleaming black floor that reflected the overhead fluorescent lights. The cart finally came to a stop in front of a heavy, dull-gray steel door.

The driver turned to Dan and said, "Here we are, Mr. Stone. Doug Ramsey is our chief around here. He'll meet with you."

He hopped out of the cart, punched a passcode into a panel beside the steel door, and pushed it open. Holding the door for them, he gestured for Dan and Lauri to follow.

They stepped into a small, utilitarian waiting room with a glass partition on one wall. Four simple chairs lined the room, and another steel door stood across from them.

Behind the glass sat a woman in her mid-fifties with coal-black hair and features that suggested Japanese descent. She smiled warmly as they entered.

"Mr. Ramsey is expecting you, Mr. Stone. I'll take you right in," she said, her tone professional yet welcoming.

With a buzz, the second steel door unlocked. Dan pulled it open, and they stepped into a cream-colored hallway with soft tan carpeting that muffled their footsteps. There was a smell of vanilla in the air. It was a warm welcoming environment in stark contrast to the industrial world they had just passed through, the quiet interior almost unsettling after the din outside.

# # #

"Dan Stone, it's great to meet you!" Doug Ramsey exclaimed, bounding forward with an energy that bordered on anxiousness. "Plant manager, chief cook, and bottle washer," he added with a laugh.

Doug was tall and rail-thin, a middle-aged man in a white short-sleeve shirt with black-rimmed glasses perched on his nose. His pocket protector was stocked with four black pens, and his salt-and-pepper hair was slicked back with just a touch too much oil. He practically radiated enthusiasm as he extended his hand.

Dan and Lauri each had their right hands vigorously pumped up and down at least half a dozen times in greeting.

"Really great to meet you," Doug said, beaming. "Can I get you something? Water? Coke? Dr. Pepper? Maybe some food? We've got a great cafeteria here."

"No, we're fine, Doug, but thank you," Dan replied, managing a polite smile.

"Please come into my office and have a seat. We can talk."

Dan and Lauri followed Doug into a large room with a shining twelve-foot dark wood conference table, bare and a small wooden desk in the corner cluttered with paperwork. They sat at the conference table.

"Well Dan I am sorry for your loss."

"Thank you, Doug, we weren't really close. So, I didn't know Vic had officed here. I kind of figured he was more city rat than the country mouse."

"Ha, Ok yes Vic was in and out a lot, but he seemed at home here."

"Why? Dan asked. What was Vic doing at a methanol plant in this... area. It is a bit nasty here, no offense."

"Well, I know Vic was working closely with Sam on something. But, neither of them discussed the particulars with me. Sam is our head of biological research. Dr, Sam Reynolds."

"Ok. Well Tom sent me here for a reason, I assume. Is Sam around here today?

"He is. I will let him know you are here, and he can meet with you." Doug nodded quickly, clearly eager to please. "Well, I imagine you want to see Vic's office. You can all meet there. Follow me—it is just down the hall."

He gestured enthusiastically, leading the way with a bounce in his step.

Doug opened the doors back to the hallway. The golf cart was gone so they were on foot. Doug led the way past a few more nondescript grey metal doors closer to the heart of the facility. Lauri clung close to Dan, her heels clicking against the polished concrete floors as they were escorted down an eerily quiet corridor.

"This is it," Doug said, gesturing toward another unassuming steel door with a keycard panel. "Vic's office." Doug handed him a key card.

Dan swiped the access card, and the door clicked open. The room inside was both minimalist and clinical, with cold steel furniture matching the color of the door and a faint chemical smell lingering in the air. There were several doors off this first anteroom.

Lauri walked over to a glass cabinet filled with lab equipment. "This doesn't look like your average office," she said, her voice tinged with unease.

"It wasn't," Doug interjected. "This is where Vic worked on more private items. The kind of work that didn't make it into the quarterly reports."

One of the interior doors opened and a young man in a lab coat entered the room. Walking towards the group he extended his hand. "Mr. Stone. I am Sam Reynolds."

Sam was medium height, weigh and description. Thirty. Brown hair. Glasses.

Doug excused himself and left the group alone.

"Sam it's good to meet you. But we don't want to take up much of your time. Vic's attorney. Well now my attorney Tom Stark wanted me to stop by and apparently see Vic's operations here."

"Yes. Tom called me and asked me to give you the rundown," Sam said. "Please follow me." Sam walked back through the same door from which he entered.

Lauri and Dan glanced at each other before following Sam through the door he had entered moments earlier. They stepped through an air curtain into a larger, more elaborate laboratory. The air carried a faint sterile scent, and the walls gleamed with stainless steel. A long table dominated the center of the room, covered in glass beakers, centrifuge tubes, and various instruments that looked far too advanced for standard methanol plant operations.

Large monitors displayed streams of data, graphs, and molecular structures. On one screen, a time-lapse animation of human cells dividing played repeatedly. Another screen showed what appeared to be the chemical breakdown of a compound labeled EX-47, its sequence flickering in glowing green text.

"This is where Vic spent most of his time," Sam explained, gesturing to the lab. "He was obsessed with Black Lake, for good reason."

"What was he working on?"

"We are isolating the compounds in the roses and water of Black Lake."

"I guess you found something interesting," Dan said.

"World changing," Sam responded.

"Well I'm all ears."

"The compounds seem to slow the aging process. But more importantly they fundamentally alter how cells degrade and regenerate."

Dan glanced up from staring at the screens. "And you helped him with this?"

Sam nodded. "I worked closely with Vic as his lead biochemist. I am actually a botanist. But my PhD is dual. Vic had a brilliant mind, but... let's just say he drove the limits most wouldn't dare, and he hired me to bridge the gap between science and science fiction I suppose. He believed the compounds we discovered could change everything—

eliminate disease, extend life indefinitely. He was already seeing results on himself."

Lauri raised an eyebrow, glancing around. "On himself? The risks -- It is crazy. I think it is cliché—mad scientist and all."

Sam chuckled softly, shaking his head. "Vic did not see himself that way. He thought he was a visionary. The problem is visionaries do not always think about the cost."

"And he's dead," Dan said flatly, folding his arms. "Is this what killed him?"

Sam raised his hands defensively. "Hold on now. I do not want to scare you all. This is not some Frankenstein concoction. It is a supplement we are working on. All-natural. Extracted from the flower."

Dan raised an eyebrow, "Sorry to be the bearer of bad news, but plants can kill you, Sam. If I recall correctly, Socrates was sentenced to death a few thousand years ago. Killed by drinking poison hemlock distilled into his tea."

Sam paused, his face showing a hint of discomfort. "Strange that you would reference that particular historical event. Perhaps you are closer to your father than you think. Vic —he often quoted Socrates final words."

Lauri tilted her head, intrigued. "What words?"

Sam hesitated before reciting in a low voice: 'Even if I drink this poison... My body will be destroyed, but by destruction of my body, I am not going to be destroyed.'

Dan let out a low grunt, his expression darkening. "Well, that is just great. So, Vic fancied himself a billionaire-philosopher-chemist? What was he trying to prove—immortality through wild unbridled experimentation?"

Sam exhaled slowly, crossing his arms. "He believed this flower held the key to something profound. Not just a longer life, but a better one. But whether that's what killed him..." He trailed off, glancing at the formula glowing on the screen.

Dan 's gaze hardened. "What was this flower?"

Sam gestured toward the notes on the desk. "It was something unique. Vic called it Nigram Rosa, The black rose.

"We call it Wormwood around here," Sam said, his tone dropping slightly as he gestured toward the notes. "When we isolated some of its compounds, we discovered hundreds of chemicals—many of which we have never seen before. It's like nothing else. But we have managed to identify a few with the highest concentrations."

He moved to a nearby monitor, bringing up a chemical diagram. "For starters, there's a unique form of geraniol, similar to what you'd find in the oil of run-of-the-mill roses, but with molecular variations we can't explain. Then there's alkaloid compounds we see in the opium poppy. Alkaloids morphine, codeine, thebaine, noscapine, and papaverine, though this strain has altered binding properties we have never encountered in any natural poppy."

Sam tapped another line on the screen. "And here—alpha-pinene, a volatile oil you would usually associate with juniper. But this one? Its structure is more complex, almost as if it's been biologically engineered."

Dan frowned, leaning closer to the screen. "So, you are saying this isn't just a regular rose? It is... engineered?"

Sam shook his head. "Not engineered—at least not by anything we can understand. This is entirely natural, as far as we have evaluated. But its properties do not align with anything else in botany or biochemistry. It is as if it is... alien to the ecosystem."

Lauri raised an eyebrow. "Alien, huh? That is comforting."

Sam exhaled, clearly choosing his words carefully. "What I mean is, it is unique. And its effects? Well, those were what had Vic so convinced it was the key to something extraordinary."

"This flower is a combination of hundreds of flowers, it seems," Sam explained, his voice tinged with both excitement and frustration. "It's like everything was dumped into a pot and somehow generated a completely new breed. But here's the kicker—we're finding entirely new chemicals. Even elements we don't have on the periodic chart. Maybe a hundred so far. Compounds that don't exist anywhere else on this planet, as far as we know."

He gestured toward a stack of notes and data charts. "Vic was planning to unveil the findings once we reached a stopping point, but the problem is... we keep finding new compounds. Every time we think we have cataloged it all, something else shows up. It is truly incredible."

Dan leaned back in his chair; arms crossed. "Okay, so let me summarize. Vic finds a flower on his property in Black Lake, Kansas—some exceedingly rare, mixed-up species with potential medicinal properties. He thinks it's the ultimate super elixir, and you guys are busy dissecting it to figure out what makes it so special. Along the way, you discover a bunch of new chemicals. Sounds like Vic was looking to cash in big time."

Sam shook his head. "Not exactly. Vic wasn't in it for the money. He was more philanthropic than capitalistic."

Dan smirked, raising an eyebrow. "Sam, the guy had billions. That's pretty capitalistic by anyone's stretch."

Sam hesitated, his lips pressing into a thin line before responding. "Fair point. But Vic's vision went beyond money. He thought this flower had the potential to change the world. He believed it could eliminate suffering, extend life, maybe even cure disease. Vic had enough money not to care about simply getting more. This was his legacy. All of our legacies. Your legacy."

Dan pondered what Sam was saying, narrowing his eyes slightly. "You seem to use compound, chemical, and element interchangeably. Have you actually proven anything earth-shattering here, or is this just a new recipe for a flower flavor we haven't seen? Don't get me wrong—it's enticing to think about the fountain of youth."

Sam smiled faintly, as if he'd expected the question. "Fair point. Let me clarify. A chemical refers to any substance with a defined composition, which can include both elements and compounds. An element is a basic building block of matter—it's pure and consists of only one type of atom.

"A compound, on the other hand, is a substance made up of two or more different elements chemically bonded together. Even if we discover an entirely new element, the moment it bonds with another to create a unique substance, that substance becomes a compound.

"Essentially," he continued, his voice more animated, "a compound is a type of chemical made from multiple elements working together in a specific ratio or structure. What's groundbreaking here is not just the compounds we're finding, but the possibility of entirely new elements contributing to them. That would shift this from being interesting to a florist to recasting parts of the periodic table."

Lauri raised an eyebrow. "So, you're saying this flower isn't just rare— it's rewriting science?"

Sam nodded. "Exactly. It's like finding a recipe for something you didn't know could exist. The implications could be enormous—for medicine, biology, and even chemistry itself."

Dan leaned back, crossing his arms. "Well, that's a bit more exciting than an exotic bouquet."

Dan leaned forward, resting his elbows on the sleek metal table as Sam continued to outline the findings from the enigmatic flower. Despite the scientific jargon and the clear excitement in Sam's tone, Dan couldn't shake the growing unease creeping up his spine. This wasn't just a quaint story about some mysterious plant—this was something far more profound, and possibly dangerous. But high risk yield high rewards.

"This all sounds incredible, Sam. So now what? Where are you at and how can I assist in carrying on your mission," Dan asked, instantly making the decision to roll the dice again and carry on Vic's legacy, come what may.

Have you been to Black Lake, Sam?"

"Yes, a number of times. The Lake is fantastic. The roses are like nothing I have ever seen."

"Well, get ready to head back up there as we are doubling down," Dan smiled.

As Sam pulled up more data, charts, and even microscopic images of the flower's cellular structure, Lauri chimed in with questions about potential applications. Sam answered eagerly, his enthusiasm barely contained, but Dan was only half-listening. His gaze drifted back to the notes labeled "Project Black Lake" spread across the desk. The words "experimental trials," "unprecedented synthesis," and "long-term physiological effects" stood out, each carrying a weight that seemed impossible to ignore.

"Sam," Dan interrupted, breaking the rhythm of the conversation, "how much did Vic really know about this stuff?"

Sam hesitated, his eyes darting between Dan and the notes. "Your father wasn't just a businessman, Mr. Stone. He was a chemist by training—a brilliant one. His work in the chemical industry made him a fortune, but his curiosity always drove him further. When he found this flower, it became an obsession. This dwarfs anything he ever accomplished. From a humanist perspective the opportunity to be responsible for changing life as we know it. Redefining medicine. Potentially eradicating all diseases. From a monetary perspective, Vic created a company with patentable discoveries propelling the value to multi trillions. Maybe the most important company in history. How much did he know? I'm not sure we know much other than some of what the flower can do. But, he was sure it could do so much more."

Dan stared at Sam. Silence for a full minute as Dan pondered the pros and cons. Then Dan laughed, "Seems like a no brainer here. Dan Stone. Trillionaire. I like it."

# # #

Dan and Lauri left the methanol plant and headed back toward the Pelican Point Country Club area, where Lauri's apartment was conveniently located. The day had dragged on, and both were starving, but Lauri insisted on stopping by her apartment first to freshen up.

Her place was on the ground floor of a well-maintained complex called Pelican Ridge Apartments, a modest but charming unit overlooking the 13th green of the club's golf course. It was not extravagant, but it was cozy, with a hint of style that felt very much like Lauri.

They walked in, and Dan immediately found the couch, sinking into it with a sigh. The soft cushions offered welcome relief after a long day. Lauri tossed her keys on the counter and gestured toward the kitchen.

Make yourself at home," she said, flashing him a grin. "Grab a beer from the fridge. I think I still have your favorite—raspberry Abita or whatever that was you loved at the bar."

Dan smirked. "Raspberry beer. What can I say? I'm a man of refined tastes."

Lauri laughed as she disappeared down the hallway toward her room. "I'm going to take a quick shower... get the oil and gas off me," she called over her shoulder, her voice light and teasing.

Dan chuckled, stretching out on the couch and staring at the ceiling for a moment before standing to investigate the fridge. He opened it and smirked as he pulled out a bottle.

"Purple Haze," he muttered, taking a closer look. "Oddly close to Purple Microbus," he added with a grin, recalling the strain of Colorado cannabis he had been smoking earlier. He took a sip of the beer, the tangy sweetness refreshing him. "I could use a joint," he said to himself. Luckily, he had one tucked in his shirt pocket.

As he lit the joint and exhaled a thin stream of smoke, he heard the water running from Lauri's shower. Curious but cautious, he wandered toward the bathroom, making a mental note that the door was slightly ajar. Without crossing the threshold, he called through the opening.

"Hey Lauri, mind if I smoke a joint in here?"

Her voice came light and unconcerned over the sound of running water. "Go ahead!"

Dan chuckled to himself as he took another drag, glad she approved of his choice. Feeling emboldened, he decided to push his luck. "You want some?"

There was a momentary pause, and then the water shut off.

"Come in, Dan," Lauri called.

Dan's heart skipped a beat. Now that is what Dan wanted to hear. He stepped into the steamy bathroom, his joint still burning.

Lauri stood with the shower door open, air drying in a relaxed, confident manner. She caught his gaze and smiled, her expression casual and inviting. "Thank you," she said, her tone warm. "I'd love some."

Dan extended the joint toward her, his grin widening. This day just keeps getting better.

The happy twosome headed to dinner about an hour later, their hunger finally catching up with them. Lauri, eager to share her local favorites, took Dan to Don's Seafood House, a classic spot known for its authentic Cajun flavors. The lively atmosphere, combined with heaping plates of gumbo, crawfish étouffée, and blackened catfish, made for a perfect end to a long day.

After dinner, they found their way back to Dan's home in Convent, full and content, yet still energized by the budding connection between them. On the way they stopped at a Black Lake Coffee house and Dan purchased them each a venti Americano with three raw sugars and extra cream. It was the best coffee they had ever tasted; the brew even sweeter with the knowledge of the hidden black rose formula. Lauri and Dan recounted the day with Jerome. Time stood still as they planned the next days adventures until very late in the night before moving to the bedroom and sharing their excitement in other ways.

Dan and Laurie spent all their time together, falling into an easy rhythm, splitting their time between the Pelican Point Club, Lauri's cozy apartment overlooking the 13th green, and Dan's Convent mansion.

Many hours were spent at the lab with Sam, uncovering the secrets of the Black Lake elixir. The more Dan learned, the deeper he sank his teeth into the mystery, like a hungry wolf tearing into fresh prey. It wasn't just curiosity driving him—it was something more primal, an insatiable appetite for the possibility of power, influence, and wealth. The word trillion kept bouncing around in his mind, haunting him with its limitless potential. Money breeds power.

Between lab visits, Dan found himself at the Black Lake Coffee house focused on the all-consuming allure of what the elixir could mean for his future.

Eventually, though, it was time to go. The pull of Black Lake was irresistible, and Dan knew he needed to see it for himself. Dan and Laurie discussed it one evening over drinks by the swimming pool, seated on the gazebo overlooking Dan's acreage behind his home. Lauri needed to return to Dallas before joining him in Black Lake. The plan was for Lauri to visit with her parents, tie up some loose ends and head north where they'd meet up in a few weeks.

"You've got things to do," Lauri said, her voice soft but supportive. "And so do I. But this isn't goodbye, okay? Just... a pause."

Dan nodded, though he felt the weight of leaving her behind. "Black Lake isn't going anywhere. Neither am I. I'll see you soon." Dan would miss her. It had been a long long time since he had spent good times with a beautiful intelligent woman. In fact he had actively avoided connections like this since his divorce. Dan wondered if he could keep it together and build anything long term with Lauri. The last two weeks had been great. Better than great, fantastic. Time would tell. Lauri would head back to Dallas, and Dan would begin the next chapter of his journey—to Black Lake and whatever secrets it held.

CHAPTER 16

Dan hit the button for Tom who answered quickly. "Tom, I am on the way to Black Lake. I really didn't know Louisianna was such a shit pit. I'm going to head to out."

"Victor assumed you would want to go to the Lake House after you saw what was there in New Orleans. Now you know where your money came from. But, there is more to learn. A lot more."

"Well money is green, right. But this is some kind of soul darkening activity here. These people are getting cooked from the inside out with all this shit here."

Tom ignored his complaint. "When you're done there go to New Orleans International Airport and follow the signs for Executive Air. It is the last exit before leaving the airport there. Your plane is on standby and will get you to Wichita this afternoon. It's time to go home to Black Lake, Dan." Tom hung up.

Crazy old coot, Dan thought. Dan now owned all this smog he was breathing in. That did not make this any sweeter. Dan told the Corvette Z06 navigation to plot a course to New Orleans airport and got a displayed map with blow-by-blow instructions in three seconds. Fuck post it notes Tom, he thought.

He glanced at Lauri, sitting in the passenger seat, her eyes scanning his face for something unsaid as they drove to the airport. He smiled softly, a touch of warmth creeping into his expression. Her hand rested on his leg. Dan lightened the mood; "We need to find a good spa and juice bar to decontaminate after this New Orleans mess. The smog is worse than LA," he laughed a bit uncomfortably.

Entering the lower lever and following the signs for private aircraft departures he pulled to the curb close to the double doors. "Well here it is, baby," he said, his voice low and intimate, like he was letting her in on a secret. "Come to Kansas when you get your thing taken care of in Dallas."

Lauri tilted her head, her lips curving into a faint smile as she looked at him. They kissed. "Don't worry," she said, her voice carrying that playful edge he had grown fond of.

Dan hit the button to pop the trunk and stepped out of the car. The sound of his footsteps echoed briefly as he walked to the back, pulling out his clubs and bag. He hesitated for just a second, glancing back at her through the open car door.

"Take care Lauri," he added with a wink, "and drive safely."

Lauri leaned out the window, her hand resting lightly on the doorframe. "Don't miss me too much, Dan. I'll see you in a couple weeks."

He chuckled, slinging the bag over his shoulder as he turned toward the flight area. Dan looked back and lifted his iPhone up in the air, signaling to Lauri that they would be talking soon. He smiled.

The automatic doors slid open, and the cool air hit him as he stepped inside. Behind him, the sleek car and the woman leaning against it were a reminder of the kind of connection he kept himself from —but maybe this time, he wouldn't run so far. Could he do it? Should he? Becca had done a number on him or he on her. Dan wasn't sure he deserved to get close to anyone again.

"Good afternoon, sir," a valet met him just inside the doors and took his bags.

"Dan Stone, here"

"Yes, sir we have been expecting you. Your plane is ready and waiting. Right this way."

They walked through a relatively nondescript lobby area and into a hanger with a half dozen aircraft. A twenty something female dressed in a tennis skirt and sleeveless red top greeted them. The valet handed him off.

"Good afternoon Mr. Stone, watch your step climbing in please." She motioned and directed Dan to the stairs built into the drop-down door of the small jet. He walked up the four steps and found a seat midway back. He was the lone passenger, so he had his pick. Dan sat.

"Would you like a drink while we taxi? I understand you are in a hurry," she said. "My name is Carrie, and I will be attending to you from here to Wichita's Jabara Airport."

Dan's head was spinning; still a bit buzzed from the weed, quite a bit unnerved by being the owner of the harbinger of death for too many souls in Louisiana, melancholy from the departure from Lauri, and excited to be jumping a private jet in thirty minutes flat. "Yes, Carrie. How about a cold beer and a few fingers of bourbon? Neat no ice." The last thing he wanted was to drink the fucking water from Lake Pontchartrain.

"Yes, Sir." Carrie disappeared.

Dan closed his eyes and reflected and dozed off for a minute or two. The plane started to move, and he started awake. Carrie set the booze on the tray table in front of him.

Dan slammed the whiskey as the small jet plane started to taxi and they were in the air fast and hard a few minutes into his first beer; an Abita Alpha Gator of course. "Goodbye Laurie. Until we meet again," he said aloud.

"Carrie, bring along that bottle of bourbon please and another cold one."

She did and they flew.

The music oozing from the surround sound speakers of the gulf stream began playing Hank singing: I need to get whiskey bent and hell bound. How ironic. Or maybe not.

CHAPTER 17

On another airport in a faraway land Lucas's adventure was also beginning. Father Robert drove Lucas to the only airstrip on the island without speaking. He too had the dream. His own personal nightmares were unleashed in his dream and the effects were nearly the same. Each man knew what was at stake and what Lucas must do. The silence was broken as the car pulled into the small airport parking lot.

"Lucas." The old man spoke tenderly for the first time since they had met. "Yes, Father?"

"God be with you, my son. God help you in this mission of mercy."

"Thank you. I know He will."

"Lucas. The dream last night..."

"Perhaps it is better not to rehash it, Father."

"You are right," he said as Lucas stepped out onto the cracked concrete.

Seldom were repairs made to anything but the aircraft. There was little traffic in this section of the country and expenses were whittled to the bare bones as often as possible. The airport nearly closed half a dozen times in as many years. Lucas would ride in four different planes before arriving in Wichita, Kansas.

"But Lucas please keep in mind that Satan is the father of lies. His power comes from deception and temptation. Jesus Christ died on the cross as the final sacrifice. Satan answers to God. God protects the faithful in Christ. Your parents are in Heaven. Your dreams are merely illusions to weaken your defenses. Remember that Faith is a choice. You have the power to make the choice always, Lucas."

"Yes, Father. I know. And thank you. God bless you, my friend."

The door slammed and Lucas walked toward the entrance. Robert listened to the choppy sound of a single engine that could be heard through the windows. He could hear the growl of Satan speaking to him in his nightmare. The words haunted him.

You won't have Lucas to protect you now old man. When you sleep next, I will be waiting.

"God help you," the old man whispered. Father Robert would meet his young protege again in the mansion of the living God. Robert looked forward to the sweet embrace of death that would come later this night at the end of an old rope he had taken from the gardeners shed early that morning. No, he would not be meeting the devil again.

The plane was a tiny twin engine Cessna that was sadly in need of remodeling. The seat cushions were a mass of small cuts and tears. Each seat had at least one larger gash from which dark green cotton matting oozed. There were two others on the plane. Lucas selected the seat closest to the window. If he were going to die in an airplane crash, at least he would have a good view on the way down. The smaller the aircraft, the less Lucas enjoyed the flight. He hated the rough and tumble rides, the big monsters, the 747's or DC-IO's, were more like riding in a train or a flying bus. Lucas knew where he was going. God had placed it in his mind. Black Lake, Kansas, USA. He knew the town. He knew the address. He knew Dan Stone. His schedule consisted of this flight to Edinburgh, a 727 to London, a 747 to Chicago with a short stop at JFK in New York, and the last leg getting him into Wichita late afternoon. He could tolerate the trip if he lived past this first flight. He decided to close his eyes until it was over.

"Hello, Lucas," a deep pleasant voice whispered.

Lucas opened his eyes to see who had spoken his name. In the seat beside him was a tall thin man with light olive skin and jet-black hair pulled straight back from his face. He wore a razor thin mustache and a smooth pointed goatee and looked to be a very handsome forty years old.

"Hello. How did you know who I was?'' Lucas asked. "Surely you remember me. Last night? Ah how soon they forget."

Lucas realized he was speaking with the evil one. A familiar tightening of his stomach gripped him. But he was awake. Was he awake? Lucas looked around the small airplane. He could smell the faint scent of jet fuel. He could feel the bouncy rise and fall of the small prop plane. No. He was awake. He was sure of it.

"What is it you want, Satan?" Lucas stammered.

"Why, I want to talk you into abandoning this nonsensical quest. What else?"

"I am not going to do that. God is sending me on this mission. Now go away." Lucas closed his eyes again hoping he would fade out of this nightmare or get back to sleep, he wasn't sure which.

"You can't wake up, Luke. You cannot wake until I say you can. In fact, I may keep you asleep for a few thousand years. By the time you wake up your flesh will have rotted off your bones."

"Liar. Go away. My savior Jesus Christ protects me."

"I will. After you listen to what I have to say," he bargained.

Lucas knew he was dreaming. But what were the rules in this game? The last few weeks had shattered any image of the reality he had formerly known was real. "Fine. Speak your piece, Satan."

"Simply that the man you seek is not one of yours. He is one of mine. Always has been. You are not welcome to interfere with my dealings with one of my servants," he smiled.

"He is searching for God."

"Ha!" he boomed. "Dan Stone has never even given God a second thought. His entire life has been given to satisfying the flesh."

"He still is in need of God's help. You cannot merely stake claim to a child of God."

"Dan Stone was born a sinner. He grew up sinning. And he continues to sin."

"Man is imperfect. God allows for that. If Dan wants help, God will give it to him. I am Dan 's guide to the Lord and I will not betray him or refuse my God."

"You will see then. Dan does not want your help. His soul has been permeated with the evil he has done. He will serve me forever."

"If l can help him I will. God has instructed me to go to him and He is who you must deal with. I am only his instrument."

"You cannot compete with me. You are a mortal. A human. And I am the all-knowing supernatural ruler of the earth. I am god of this land. I will not allow you to interfere."

"You are a fallen angel. A traitorous servant of the only true God. A sick twisted demon powerless before the living God. I am not afraid of you, Satan. The Lord protects what is His. As I said, this is between you and God. Now, since you have said what you insisted on saying, be gone."

The pleasant voice had steadily grown more ferocious. The light olive skin had turned to a dark maroon. Whiffs of steam floated up from his nostrils and from the corners of his eyes.

"Careful Priest. I have dominion over this realm. I will smash this little plane on the rocky hills below us ending your fantastic journey to save this rotten apple."

"I am in the hand of God. I am following his command to go to Dan Stone."

"Lucas Fisher. You will surely die if you attempt to pull this meat from the lion's mouth. He is evil and is rightfully mine," he growled. "You cannot take this soul to Heaven. It is much too heavily burdened."

"All the burden can be released if Dan accepts God and asks for forgiveness."

"I have dedicated a great deal of my time facilitating these circumstances. I will make certain you die in helping this man if nothing else."

"I too am going to Heaven."

"So were your parents but I have them in my workshop."

"Liar. You have demons that look like their earthly bodies. Their souls are in Heaven with my God. Your lies are useless. I gain my protection and comfort from the blood of the lamb Jesus Christ." Lucas spoke the words but his fear was just below the surface. He was wavering. The father of lies certainly knew which buttons to push.

"Well then you can tell mommy and daddy all about that when you come down here yourself," Satan laughed. "I steal all the souls I want, Luke. And everyone screams down here. I guarantee that I will snatch you from your God's grasp before He even knows what happened. I warn you again and for the last time, go back to the monastery, put your face back in the book, and forget this evil fellow."

Lucas awoke abruptly as the small plane dropped onto the runway, bounced a few times, and turned sharply to make its way to the main airport building. The nightmares seemed to begin as soon as he drifted off to sleep. Sleep is supposed to be a time for the brain to rest. This conscious dreaming was taking its toll on his psyche. He made a mental note to stay wide awake for the duration of the flights. He made it to London where it was raining. He boarded the 747 for New York, sat down and fell asleep before takeoff. It was raining when the 747 landed at John F. Kennedy Airport in New York. Lucas had slept his way across the Atlantic with no nightmares to the best of his knowledge. It was his best sleep in months.

Wichita was dark and stank of the exhaust of far too many automobiles. Luke was not used to the strong sweet smells of the inner city. The odor was not foreign to Lucas, He often took the bus into New York City from the college with fellow students. But that was many years ago now.

"What can I do for you?" the salesman at Trusty Ed's used cars asked over his red and white striped tie.

Lucas decided to find and buy a cheap car rather than renting from the airport because he had no idea how long God would require him to be here in America. How long would it take to change Dan's mind, to rescue him, to pull him from the jaws of the wolf? No way could he sign an open ended contract.

"I need a car. Cheap yet dependable," Lucas answered. The bus did not run through the town he needed. In fact, the young man at the bus terminal had not even heard of Black Lake Kansas.

"Got the perfect one friend. This caddy over here only has seventy thousand actual -- sell it to you for nine."

"Too much. Way too much. What about that one?" Lucas asked motioning to a beat-up primer gray Chevy Nova.

"That one runs perfect. It's an oldie but a goodie. 1975. Does the quarter mile in 12 seconds. Two thousand."

"I only have one thousand for a car."

"That one will outlast all of us. Fifteen hundred."

Lucas pulled out his wallet and counted out ten of his twenty one hundred dollar bills. He had obtained two thousand dollars from the monastery and could always call for more to be wired if necessary, but Lucas knew to be frugal. The more money he spent the less that could be used to accomplish Gods missions elsewhere.

"One thousand cash. Take it or leave it. I see another good car across the street."

"Sold."

Lucas pulled the map from the papers he had collected from the airport travel boards. Black Lake was nowhere to be found. He drove north. Almost everything was north. He found 35 and drove across Wichita. He continued north as it became Park City and the Newton. He had to stop. Exhaustion was setting in. He stopped and found an inexpensive looking motel with no name other than the neon sign that read 'vacancy.'

He crawled out of the car and slammed the heavy steel door. Yes, an oldie but a goodie. He walked into the hotel which matched the age of his new car and waited for the attendant. It was nearly ten o'clock. After a few minutes Lucas rang the small silver bell on the counter. A stooped shouldered white-haired wisp of a man came from a narrow wooden door behind the counter and squinted at him through small round bi-focal that had slid too far down his nose.

"I'm comin'. You impatient kids are all the same. You think I'm out choppin' wood in the middle of the night?" he snapped.

"Sorry. I didn't see you back there," Lucas answered slightly taken aback. Monks were rarely rude, and he was out of condition to the American personality.

"What do you want?"

"A room. Small and cheap."

"Don't got no cheap rooms. This is a tourist town, son. Forty bucks."

"I can't afford that I'm a priest visiting this county and have very little money."

"A priest, huh? Never seen any soldier of God drive a supped up hot rod before."

"It was cheap."

"You can sleep on a cot in the backroom for twenty," he offered.

"That will be fine," Lucas answered. "Have you ever heard of Black Lake?"

"Yes sir. But I wouldn't go there if I was you. The people there aren't too friendly. And they don't take to religious types too much."

"Where is it?"

"Ninety minutes north. Turn west at Mabel's Cafe. Fifteen minutes and you'll be right in the middle of it."

"Thanks. It's not on the map."

"That's because of your boss, I suspect. Hey Father, let me tell you about this hornets' nest you wantin' to put your hands in," he said leaning over the smooth plastic counter and lowering his voice to a strong grainy whisper. "That town ain't fit to go to. You bein' a man of God is going to know that right off the air there is rotten."

"Like smog?"

"Like cancer," the old man hissed. "The town is Satan's own. It's his church. It ain't like nothin' you ever seen."

"The whole town can't be bad. Not all the people," Lucas Said.

"There ain't a soul in that place ain't piss poor."

"Well I am looking for a particular man. I need to find Dan Stone."

"Never heard of him. None of those demons come out of the nest. Word has it they can't even if they wanted to."

"You ever been there?"

"Lord no! The fly don't go looking for the web. I ain't no idiot."

"Well, I'm going to go out and get my suitcase," Lucas said dropping the subject.

"If I were you, I'd jump in that hotrod and run your ass right out of this state. If you lookin' for one his boys, he knows it. He'll be lookin' for you."

Lucas walked out the door without saying another word. The old man was certainly spooked over that town. He wondered what else local legend held. He sat in his car for several moments before carrying his suitcase back inside. Lucas walked past the counter and through the small doorway. The room was only about eight feet by eight feet, had a too short ceiling, and uniform dirty white paint on all surfaces. The old man was seated in an old black rocking chair with chipping paint puffing on a beautiful, burled root pipe. The canvas army cot Lucas was to sleep on was only a few feet away. He dropped his suitcase at the foot and sat down in the middle.

"I gotta fess up. I lied to you preacher. I went to Black Lake once. But it was forty- five, fifty years ago. I'll never go back though. Not never." He shoved a thick wrinkled finger into the smoking tobacco. "I saw enough to last me."

Lucas pulled his old, ragged plaid suitcase onto the cot and pulled the zipper around. The sweet smell of the pipe triggered the urge for nicotine. Early in seminary he started smoking Kool Kings during bible study. The members of the group would smoke three packs an evening, four, if the subject were particularly fascinating. "What can possibly be that horrible? Did they run you out?"

"Nope. Not the people. The town. The land is alive," the old man answered as he flipped open a well-worn silver Zippo lighter.

"I don't get it. How can a town scare you?" Lucas asked, leaning into the open flame. "Thanks," he said drawing deeply on the cigarette. In Scotland he was forced to smoke Russian Black. They were pretty good but, nothing quite compared to good old American Kool as far as he was concerned.

"You know when you get there. It has a personality. The people are cold and stare at the strangers. And the air seems real close. Kinda heavy."

"What made you go to that town?"

"Curious. I had to see what everybody was warnin' me against. I was a kid. Knew of nothin' that scared me on this earth." The old man leaned forward and lowered his voice once again as though someone were listening just outside the window. "I'm going to level with you, preacher. I pissed my pants runnin' out of there. And I lost a good friend that day," he said pausing and staring directly into the younger man's eyes. "Me and Bill Thompson went in there to look for a little girl that had disappeared from her home a few miles from here. Nobody expected to find her with all the shit that goes on in this world, but we found her. She was dead. Slashed across the throat with a straight razor," he paused again and puffed on the pipe. "Bill ran into the woods screamin'. I tried to hold him back and shut him up but ain't nothin' that could of helped him. He went plum crazy seein' that poor girl."

Lucas cleared his throat as the grotesque images of his parents flashed through his mind. "I went in after him and found him lying in the mud. His mouth was moving but no sound would come out. Then he yelled, 'Run!' I grabbed him by the shoulders and shook him. He started sucking in nothin' like a fish layin' on the shore. Then he died. Scared to death." The inn keeper sat silently in his chair for some time. The room had an unpleasant air about it. The night was as quiet as a tomb. Then the old man barely whispered. "And I didn't look back as I run out a there."

"They ever catch the little girl's killer?'

"Nope. Her body was gone when we went back. So was Bills. And everybody thought I was lying'. I never been back since."

The two men sat in silence smoking their chosen vice. At two o'clock the old man stood up and shuffled off to bed without speaking. Lucas laid on the cot smoking and thinking about the strange things he had learned for another hour before sleep insisted. He dreamed.

He was kneeling before a gigantic cross. The wood was rotten, amassed with giant bore holes. Wormwood. An endless field of black roses surrounded him frozen in place despite the cold wind that blew his hair. Beside him were the bodies of the little girl, Bill, his parents, and several others he could not recognize. He could feel the warm tears running across his ice-cold cheeks. A thick nauseating laughter shook the earth. "We're waiting for you, Lucas. Mommy needs you."

He snapped awake hearing himself gasp. He could smell the rich aroma of sausage frying and hear the grease popping in the skillet. It was six a.m., and the inn keeper was already awake. Lucas swung his legs out of bed vowing not to sleep again. Fishing a Kool out of the pack he reflected on all the dreams he had had to date. There were forces working on him that he could not even fathom. "God help me through this mission," he breathed as he forced himself to his feet.

"Thought you'd like a little food in your stomach before you got on the road, preacher. You got a tough job to do."

Lucas sat down at the table quietly.

"Coffee?"

"Please."

"I was thinking, we never really introduced ourselves. I'm Red Baxter," he said turning an egg over.

"Luke Fisher."

"Good to know you, Luke. You can forget about the twenty for the bed. My gift." "Thank you, Red."

He placed a steaming cup in front of the frazzled looking priest. He desperately needed a shower and a shave. "Cream?"

"No thanks. Black is just fine."

Red slid a plate in front of him and sat down hard in the old wooden chair opposite Lucas as he dropped his own plate on the table. The sausage and eggs were perfectly cooked, the result of decades of routine.

"You pass back through here stop in," the old man said swallowing a mouth full. "I'll be bringing a friend."

"You do that, boy. You do that."

As Lucas roared out of the gravel driveway, he saw an unusually large man wearing a black felt hat and old-fashioned black suit. The white-haired gentleman smiled broadly as he slowly waved his hand. His face resembled that of a cherub and his body that of a eunuch. Lucas pulled the car up beside him and rolled down the passenger window.

"You need a ride somewhere, Mister?" he asked.

"Much obliged," the strange looking man said falling into the seat beside him.

The large man took up two thirds of the bench seat and his belly was only a few inches away from the dashboard. Lucas thought his voice was far too deep for his face and noticed that every other tooth had rotted out of his mouth. The man was unpleasant looking and smelled like a musty cellar.

"Where you heading?" Lucas asked him.

"Black Lake." A cold damp hand pushed his testicles close to his body. Coincidence was beginning to be too narrow to explain anything that happened. Several moments passed before he responded.

"I am going there myself," he said finally and depressed the accelerator.

"I know. My name is William Joseph Smith."

"What are you saying?" Lucas asked suspiciously.

"A friend of mine warned me that you were coming."

Luke slammed on the brakes fishtailing the rear of the car. "Get out!" he yelled.

The big man opened the door and stepped outside. The dream like laughter echoed in the damp morning air. Leaning his big head in the open door he said, "You can't beat me at my own game, Lucas. Dan Stone is mine. You fuck with me Priest and I'll bury you face down in the shithouse." He smiled, laughed and slammed the door.

Lucas was shaking. He swallowed hard and closed his eyes remembering who he was and what he was doing. "Dan Stone is leaving with me. Whatever it takes," Lucas quietly said. He punched the accelerator kicking small rocks and dust over the large man's feet and legs. He could see him standing in the same position in the rear-view mirror for over a mile. Four words reverberated inside his head:

Dan Stone is mine.

CHAPTER 18

"Dear Lord, forgive the sins of this man because he is ignorant. If you allow me to help, I can pull him back to Your ways. I know he was born in sin, but he can still be a servant of God. In Jesus' name I pray. Amen."

The hours had grown longer in the last few weeks. After Lucas left the monastery, he grew ever more certain of the permanence of this journey. He realized that this mission was probably the most important thing he could ever accomplish on earth and was proud to serve his God in this manner. But there is always the human flaw to overcome, fear. Despite his acceptance of the duty and his certainty of the afterlife, he was afraid to come face to face with all that is evil. Questions raced through his mind at any given moment with little or no warning. Was his faith strong enough to endure? Why was he chosen? Death? Death. There was the real question. What can one expect after death. According to his religious beliefs he was to look for eternal bliss, peace and tranquility. But what if he was wrong? What if he was on a quest conjured by the misfiring of mutated neurons? What if his life had been spent chasing a dream? A story created to instill hope in the masses during severe oppression. He would die and simply be extinguished like the spark of a brittle wooden kitchen match plunged into a glass of ice-cold tap water. The end. But that was not what he believed. He was a Christian and believed in what the Lord had set forth in the Bible. After his life was over, he would be taken to heaven to be judged for his sins.

Faith is a choice, Lucas. The words of Father Moray echoed in his mind.

Life was not over, only altered significantly. This was his firm belief, but the little voice in his head kept asking 'what if...'

Some people would say it is a sin to question the teachings of the Bible. Lucas was not certain in this area. He only knew that he would answer God as best he could on his judgment day and beg Him for forgiveness for his foolish human ways.

Lucas rose from the dusty worn carpet that covered the creaking wooden floor of the hotel room. His knees were covered with callouses and he was accustomed to long hours of kneeling. Nevertheless, there was a distinct numbness in his muscles and a steady ache in the joints. Lucas had been worrying about Dan 's fate for several weeks. He had not figured out exactly how he was to help this man, but he knew the Lord would show him the way in due time. Lucas was the Lord's tool and would wait patiently to be used as intended.

As he slipped between the highly starched sheets of the Lucky 7 Inn a cold chill crept up from his toes and stiffened the fine transparent hairs on the back of his neck. A feeling of intense fear crawled across him and sat on his chest like a cold lead block. He had heard a voice whisper in the dark. He huddled beneath the thin green blanket as the red and yellow neon shifted in the night air. Again, he heard:

I'll get you too, Lucas. Prepare yourself. I look forward to drinking in your screams.

CHAPTER 19

The gulf stream landed in Black Lake and Dan was somewhere between pretty drunk and outright hammered. As he staggered off the plane, he couldn't resist grabbing Carrie's ass on the way out, eliciting a mix of a grin an eyeroll and a knowing smirk from her as she tolerated her new billionaire boss's lasciviousness. In Dan's other hand, he clutched a half-empty bottle of Black Label Jack, his makeshift companion for the flight.

The blinding lights of the tarmac hit him, and he squinted as another handler approached, this one tall and neatly dressed, holding a set of car keys. The man guided him toward his waiting ride.

Dan stopped mid-step, his jaw dropping slightly as he laid eyes on the gleaming red Lamborghini parked a few feet away. Its sleek curves and aggressive design screamed power and indulgence.

"Now that," Dan slurred with a grin, "is what I call a proper welcome."

The handler opened the door for him with a polite nod, unfazed by Dan's state. As he slid into the driver's seat, the intoxicating scent of leather and luxury surrounded him. With a satisfied smirk, Dan muttered to himself, "Let's see what this baby can do."

"I love sexy fucking Italians," Dan laughed aloud. "Guess a step up from the old, ragged corvette." Which was officially abandoned in Dallas and a second less ragged one now temporarily in the hands of the Lauri in New Orleans. "I'm sure she will enjoy the car," he thought.

Dan struggled to figure out how to close the scissor doors on his new Lambo.

"Sir, you home is one mile straight up this road. This is your landing strip. The key fob opens the gate and the staff in the house will greet you. Drive safely."

"Carrie! Come with me! I'm lost with out you!" Dan yelled slurring the words such that he was likely the only one who understood. Dan laughed aloud. He pushed the button and the drivers door slid down and closed him in.

Dan gunned it and flew down the one lane road lined on either side with large black light poles with a set of three yellow white globes atop. Seeing the cabin he pulled the Lamborghini up to a gnarled oak tree and shut the engines down.

"I can drive drunk if I want to!" Dan laughed.

His uncle's cabin—or rather his fathers cabin – or rather Dan's cabin was more than a little dilapidated. It was a complete wreck. Could this be the right address? It was the end of the road. Must be right.

The shutters hung off broken windows, the glass jagged and missing in places. The front door wasn't even on its hinges, just propped against a termite-eaten frame that looked like it might collapse if the wind blew the wrong way. This wasn't just a fixer-upper—it was the kind of place no sane person would want to call home.

Dan sat in the car, staring at the shack with growing incredulity as the sun rose over the dark lake. He was drunk, stoned, exhausted, and in no mood to deal with a shack deep in the wilds that looked like it housed more critters than humans. No way could he sleep in there and absolutely no way could he bring Lauri here.

"From the frying pan into the fire?" he muttered, running a hand through his hair. "And what the fuck is Tom Stark trying to pull with this?"

As if on cue, something dropped out of the tree overhead and landed on the hood of the car with a loud bang.

Dan jumped, his heart nearly leaping out of his chest, as a pair of glowing eyes stared directly into his. The creature hissed loudly, baring every one of its sharp, gleaming teeth.

Dan froze for a moment, his brain scrambling to process the scene, before regaining his composure. It was just a raccoon—albeit a particularly large one. The scrappy, dog-sized varmint glared at him with an attitude that suggested it could probably take him in a fight. If Dan had to guess, it was the toughest raccoon this side of the Bronx—and likely rabid to boot.

He debated honking the horn to scare it off, but the little demon seemed to lose interest on its own. The raccoon gave him one last dismissive look before hopping off the hood and skittering away into the shadows.

Dan let out a long breath, shaking his head. "Great," he muttered. "Even the wildlife think I look like shit after that drive."

Seated in the cool confines of the low-slung Lamborghini Dan could see hundreds of the infamous coal black long-stemmed roses. He hit the button, and the driver's door opened upward with a smooth, mechanical hum. He reached into his bag, pulling out a perfectly rolled joint—a little gift from Lauri after their most recent intimate escapade. Lauri had a natural gift and rolled up a few dozen as a care package, to remember her by she had said. But, how could Dan forget her, Lauri was beautiful, sexy and clever. Maybe the best thing to happen to him since Becca. Fuck. Maybe he should forget her. Maybe he should avoid another woman he could maybe love as much as Becca. Dan worked to quiet his mind and dismiss the encroaching thoughts as he lit the fat cigarette. The familiar aroma of cannabis wafted through the air baptizing his new surroundings with his own flower. His angst settling with each long draw on the joint.

Stretching and reaching high into the air, he walked around the front of the car and could see the enormity of the Black Lake.

The sight stopped him in his tracks. The lake was mesmerizing, its glassy surface reflecting like a mirror of ink. The black roses were not merely by the cabin, there were fields of the long-stemmed black roses everywhere, their dark petals shimmering like velvet in the sun. It was hauntingly beautiful, a surreal blend of natural wonder and foreboding mystery.

The lake stretched endlessly, its darkness complemented by the impenetrable barrier of roses that hugged the shoreline. The dark blooms seemed almost spectral in the moonlight.

Dan walked toward the cabin, his steps slowing as he took in the details of the structure. The wraparound porch creaked under his boots, its weathered boards buckling in places. As he turned the corner, the side of the cabin came into view, revealing an unsettling detail—the cabin seemed to merge with the landscape in an almost unnatural way.

The black roses, with their long, vine-like stems, extended right up to the side of the cabin, their dark petals brushing against the aged wooden walls. They twisted and tangled, disappearing into the lake as if they were part of it, their thorny vines creating an impenetrable barrier.

It was as though the roses had claimed the cabin, wrapping it in a tight embrace, cutting it off from the rest of the world. Even the narrow path from the porch to the water seemed precarious, the roses crowding it on either side as if reluctant to give any ground.

Dan stopped at the edge of the porch, staring at the scene before him. The water was still and eerily dark, the roses reflecting faintly on its surface like a mirage. It wasn't just nature—it felt deliberate, as if something had grown here with purpose. There were no other plants. No grasses. No weeds. No competing foliage.

He exhaled sharply, the joint in his hand smoldering as he took another drag. What the hell kind of place is this? he wondered, the weight of the silence around him pressing down like a physical force.

Dan took a long drag from the joint, the smoke curling lazily into the air as he exhaled. This place... he thought, a chill running down his spine. It was both captivating and unsettling, a place that felt like it was truly magical. He could understand why his uncle spent so much time here. The lake was awe inspiring with its hidden secrets lying just beneath the surface and protected by the invasive flowers.

Dan walked down the path to the water's edge to see the dark water up close. He knelt. He wanted to touch the water. No. He needed to. He was compelled. Dan reached his right hand into the water.

"Jesus!" Dan yelled. The water was scalding hot. Nearly boiling hot. Dan could not pull his hand free. He jerked at his arm, but his hand would not come out of the water burning his flesh. "Fuck!" he yelled again. Dan threw himself backwards landing on his back in a heap on top of thorny black roses which cut into his back and neck.

"Jesus Fucking Christ!" he yelled gain and rolled out onto the path. Dan reached up and plucked a one-inch-long thorn from the back of his neck. The back of his left hand was bleeding from another thorn which sliced him. He put his free hand also injured from the burning black water to his neck and drew back a palm full of blood.

Dan hurried back to the Lambo and popped the trunk for the first aid kit that came with the luxury vehicle. He stripped off this blue chambray shirt now covered in his blood and wiped off more blood. He grabbed the scotch and taking a long pull on the bottle to steel himself he poured a dose onto the shirt and wiped off his neck and back. He poured a generous dose onto his burnt right hand and the gash on his left hand. He dabbed at the deep puncture wounds on his neck and back. The bleeding subsided and with blood still smeared across his skin despite his best efforts, Dan dressed his wounds. He unzipped his suitcase and pulled out a clean black golf shirt with the Flatiron Golf logo embroidered on the chest, and carefully slipped it on. He tipped the bottle high and drank the remainder of the scotch.

Standing outside the car, his breath ragged, he turned toward the cabin, its weathered silhouette framed by an eerie dark glow of the lake, the sweet acrid smell of the black roses filled the air.

"What the hell Vic" Dan yelled at the cabin. There was no answer.

CHAPTER 20

Dan decided to get to the Black Lake city limits proper and nurse his wounds. Navigating the rumbling sports car down the country road and driving far in excess of the speed limit, the town appeared behind the trees after only a few moments, and it was more than Dan thought it should be. It was not the crumbling backwater he had expected. Instead, it had the charm of an old movie set—the kind you would see in romantic films, with warm, inviting storefronts and small sitting parks adorned with wooden benches.

In fact, Dan thought, it might very well have been the model for all those picturesque towns from 1950s cinema. He half-expected to see Audrey Hepburn and George Peppard strolling arm in arm through the park, or maybe Gene Kelly whistling a cheerful tune to celebrate the morning.

The town had a brightness to it, a sense of nostalgia that felt almost surreal, especially after the stark, unsettling atmosphere of the cabin. The contrast was striking, as if the two places belonged to entirely different worlds.

Dan eased back in his seat, his fingers drumming on the steering wheel. Quite the difference, he thought, letting his eyes wander across the quaint little town that lay before him.

As he rolled through town, a sign caught his eye, marking City Hall as the last building on the right. Next to it stood something unexpected—a bar that looked like it had stepped straight out of a classic Hitchcock film.

Its polished oak façade gleamed in the sunlight, the kind of craftsmanship that whispered of another era. Above the heavy wooden doors hung an intricately carved sign that read The Oak Bar, its lettering elegant and understated, a far cry from the neon monstrosities you'd find in modern dives.

The large windows were framed with dark wood trim, giving a glimpse of the dimly lit interior, where gleaming brass fixtures, leather booths, and a long, polished bar beckoned like a scene straight out of North by Northwest.

Dan could not help but smirk as he pulled over. Now this... this is more my style, he thought. Hitchcock would approve.

He stepped out of the car, running a hand through his hair and the bandages on his neck he headed toward the bar, half expecting to see Truman Capote nursing a scotch on the rocks inside. He needed some better first aid from the cuts from those damned black roses and certainly needed some booze.

"Two birds with one stone," he laughed at his cleverness, pulling the car to a stop in front of the bar. "What else could a man ask for?"

The name above the entrance read The Oak Bar, spelled out in letters crafted from the hardwood on a shining black background. It really was like a blast from the past.

Dan recalled the old movie North By Northwest, a memorable scene took place in the Oak Bar, where Cary Grant got kidnapped, but then quickly escaped through the Fifty-ninth Street entrance. No he thought, it was the Oak Room but close enough.

I am in the twilight zone. Dan mused, shaking his head as he climbed out of the car. A strong scent of flowers wafted toward him, and for a moment, he debated whether going in was a good idea or if he should high tail it back to Wichita. No that's all he needed was to get back in touch with his psyche for another two hour road trip.

Dan went in. The bar was a was a grand, elegant space with a German Renaissance style with highly polished light oak walls, Bavarian castle frescoes, Faux wine casks in the woodwork, and a rose-laden chandelier with a barmaid holding a stein. The faint scent of fine bourbon oozing from the very fabric of the warm surrounds, a near replica of the famous New York Bar in the Plaza Hotel.

"Yes sir, what can I do for you this morning?" the old man behind the bar asked, bar cloth in hand. The gentleman wore wire rim gold tone glasses, a stiff white collared shirt and a blue and red paisley bow tie.

"Double Jack Black," Dan said, still shaken from the experience at the lake. He needed a few stiff ones.

"Kind of early for that hard a drink isn't it, young man?" he asked as he poured a three-ounce dose into a small crystal highball glass.

"Nectar of the gods and all old man," he smirked at his quick wit.

Dan could see the bartender start to change his mind about being friendly, so he said, "Breakfast of champions," and grinned before gulping down the spirit with one swift, very practiced motion.

"A lot of good that kind of nutrient will do you mister Stone." The old man turned away and began wiping off the counter with his dish cloth moving rhythmically from one place to another.

"You know me I guess," Dan said. Or of me anyway.

"Can't miss you. And we knew you were coming. You can have some real food if you want, the kitchen is open. I was just going to have some eggs and bacon. You're welcome to join me. We don't get a lot of new faces around here."

"Appreciate that. Thanks a lot," Dan said extending his right hand. "Dan Stone is my name. But you already knew that."

The old man glanced up and eyed Dan's outstretched hand. "Yes," he said. "You are the spitting image of your father. He would order the same breakfast you just did and sit with me at that table right over there. I would say three times a week for the last few years. I would usually convince him to eat some real food rather than drink his breakfast. It's a shame he died so suddenly."

"So, you knew my father. I only spoke to him a few times and I was his heir apparent. Go figure?"

"I am Bob Parker. I own this place and was maybe your father's best and only true friend. Your father had his reasons. He talked about you quite often. A lot closer to the end. Especially what was to be done when you arrived." He looked into Dan's eyes sternly then added, "I've got a lot to tell you and a letter he wanted you to have as well."

"Did he know he was going to die? I thought he died unexpectedly," Dan said feeling a little uneasy.

"Nothing was ever unexpected to Vic. I might as well be the one to tell you before some nut gives you some half-truth. Dan, your father was a very special man."

"What exactly do you mean, Bob?"

"I'll be back in a minute. I'm going to get our breakfasts from the kitchen."

"Wait. Hit me again with that Jack Daniels. I need to fuel up. And where is the men's room so I can wash this blood off my hand?"

Bob eyed him warily. "I've got something to help with those wounds. I'll get the food and then I can give you a hand. You been out to the Lake I guess."

"I have. But what does that have to do with it?"

"Looks like a burn and I can see the roses got you. I have something better than alcohol for you to fix you right up."

Bob took Dan's glass and turned towards the mirrored wall and the counter behind him. Holding the small crystal glass under a gleaming brass spigot with ice-cold in silver letters above the tap, he filled it up. Then, picking up the bottle of Jack Daniels Black he topped it off. "Try this."

Dan took the near frozen concoction from the bartender with a smirk. "Water with a splash of whiskey. Thanks Bob."

Bob smiled and disappeared into the kitchen.

Dan took a moment to look around. The place had a quiet elegance that felt timeless, like stepping back into a distant golden age.

Dan took a sip of the cold beverage. It was sweet, floral but like licorice too. He could barely taste the Jack Daniels Whiskey. He drank it down. It was delicious and the cold numbed his throat. "Strange," he said aloud.

The bar itself stretched long and polished, its oak surface gleaming under the soft, golden light of antique sconces. Brass fixtures lined the edges, catching the glow, while a row of high-backed leather stools invited patrons to linger. Behind the bar, a mirrored wall reflected shelves filled with top-shelf liquor, each bottle sparkling like a trophy.

The room was cozy yet refined, with light oak wood panels and low, leather booths tucked into the corners, offering just the right amount of privacy. Framed black-and-white photos adorned the walls—snapshots of smiling patrons from decades past, a nod to the bar's storied history.

The faint hum of jazz played softly in the background, adding to the old-world charm. A few locals sat scattered throughout the space, nursing their drinks and talking in hushed tones, their conversations blending seamlessly with the quiet ambiance.

Dan leaned casually against the bar, taking it all in. Classy place, he thought, his fingers tapping idly on the oak surface. Not what I was expecting in a town like this.

He glanced around again, noticing a distinguished older man in the corner sipping from a cup of coffee, and a younger couple laughing softly in one of the booths.

Dan strolled along the walls; his curiosity piqued by the black-and-white photos framed in dark wood. Each one told a story, a snapshot of moments frozen in time. There were scenes of parties, glasses raised in cheer, and camaraderie captured in warm smiles.

His steps slowed as his eyes settled on one photo in particular. There was his father, Vic Stone, standing near the center of the frame, a drink in hand and his trademark wry smile lighting up his face. Surrounding him were others—a towering man with white hair, women in 1980's party dresses swirling around the room, and a figure Dan guessed was Bob, the bartender, in his younger days, sporting a neatly pressed vest and a confident grin.

Each image seemed to mark a holiday or celebration: Christmas wreaths in one, champagne glasses in another, and a giant Thanksgiving feast in yet another. The bar had clearly been a gathering place, a cornerstone of the community.

Dan could not help but linger, his fingers brushing against the edge of one frame. Vic looked at home here, he thought. Maybe this place warranted withheld judgment until he could really soak it in. If his estranged father loved it here maybe a home could be calling to Dan too.

Bob's voice broke the moment. "See something familiar?"

Dan turned back toward the bar, his lips curling into a half-smile. "Yeah," he said. "My… father. Looks like he was a regular around here."

Bob nodded, and set down two plates heaped with scrambled eggs, hashbrowns, two biscuits covered in white sausage gravy and topped with four slices of thick bacon.

"Victor Stone, we are going to miss him. Always knew how to throw a party. This place has not been the same without him."

Dan nodded slowly, the gravity of those photos settling over him. Vic lived a life in this little town in nowhere Kansas, he marveled.

Bob reached over the bar and grabbed a pot of coffee from the Bunn coffee warmer and two mugs. Walking around the bar he motioned to the nearest booth.

They sat in the dark leather booth warmly lit by an overhead handblown droplight. The aroma of the coffee warmed Dan's senses and prepared his stomach for what was to come. The two men tore into their plates like ravenous animals.

"Delicious Bob," Dan said wiping his mouth with the white linen napkin.

Dan finished his coffee, and Bob poured him another cup.

"Salud Bob. You sure know how to throw a breakfast."

Bob said, "How is your hand?"

Dan hadn't thought about his wounds. "Well actually they don't hurt anymore," Dan said focusing his attention back on his hand and neck.

"Yes, Bob said.

Dan pulled back the bandage on his left hand and there was dried blood but no mark. No indication there had been a gash. He looked at his right hand. No burn. "What the Fuck?" He exclaimed aloud.

Bob stared into Dan's eyes. "That's the water Dan."

Dan stood and walked to the men's room bewildered. How could this be? When in privacy of the washroom Dan pulled off his shirt and touched his neck. He twisted around to see his back where the sharp knife-like thorns pierced his back and side. He withdrew a soft paper napkin from the ornate container on the granite counter and turned on the polished brass faucet to dampen the cloth with the HOT water. Dan wiped each of the spots of the wounds which were no longer there. He cleaned his dried blood from his frame. His hands were clean.

Dan returned to the bar. "Bob, I do not know what to say here. I was pretty cut up. My hand was at least second degree burns maybe third. And now nothing." Dan stretched his hands out and wiggled his fingers. Laughing he exclaimed, "Nothing!"

Bob hesitated and looked at Dan's smiling face. "I know it is amazing, Dan, but there is more to it. You need to settle in. Your father's office is just upstairs. See what all he left for you to deal with and judge for yourself. I will always be here for you to talk to just like I was for Vic when he came into town. That is my job."

"Ah. Yes, the cabin out there at the lake is a disaster. Glad there are better accommodations."

Bob laughed. "The cabin? Yes, Vic left it there like a memorial. The house is about a half mile up the road. Through the trees. You cannot really see it from the road."

Dan just stared ahead realizing he still had not reached his destination. "Nice. Tom is some character. Why he didn't tell me that I don't know," he said aloud.

"Yes. Tom." Bob took the empty plates behind the bar and set them on a large tray on the dark walnut backbar. He looked into the mirror, through bottles of Johnny Walker and Old Grand Dad and caught Dan's eyes. "Be careful Dan."

Dan just sat there, staring at Bob's back as the bartender busied himself behind the bar, arranging bottles and wiping down the counter.

The possibilities are endless. No wonder Vic was obsessed, Dan thought, rubbing the polished oak under his hand.

Bob handed Dan a digital card key. "The Elevator is around the corner. It is the dark walnut door at the end of the hallway. Vic's... or rather your offices are upstairs."

CHAPTER 21

Dan walked down the dimly lit hallway, his footsteps clicking faintly against the polished red oak floors. Bob's instructions had been clear, but the hallway seemed to stretch endlessly, each panel blending into the next with meticulous craftsmanship. At last, he spotted the faint outline of the hidden elevator door. The dark walnut panels were seamless, almost indistinguishable from the surrounding walls, save for the small card reader beside them.

He slid the card key Bob had given him into the reader. For a moment, nothing happened, and Dan wondered if he had done it wrong. Then, a soft chime broke the silence, and the hidden elevator doors slid open with a near-silent whoosh.

Inside, the elevator was as understatedly luxurious as the rest of the building. Polished brass accents glinted subtly, and the walls were paneled in walnut, inlaid with delicate ebony trim. A single button marked 2nd Floor waited for him. He pressed it, and the elevator began its smooth ascent.

The doors opened to a corridor with soaring ceilings and a cool, almost sterile air. The marble floor beneath his shoes gleamed in the muted light, and faint traces of leather, aged wood, and something floral lingered in the atmosphere. Ahead of him stood a set of large double doors, slightly ajar. Beyond, Dan glimpsed the faint shimmer of something polished and refined.

He pushed the doors open and froze. The office was nothing short of breathtaking. It was a huge room maybe fifty by one hundred, the top floor of this building made as a loft, its walls and furniture crafted from rich walnut and oak, accented with intricate mother of pearl and ebony inlays. The high ceiling, at least fifteen feet above, adorned with shining embossed copper tiles, gave the space an almost cathedral-like presence. The glossy black floor, reflecting the light from brass sconces and the faint glow of a desk lamp.

The decor spoke volumes about Vic's taste and uncompromising embrace of the finest of all. Safari accents were scattered throughout the room—mounted antique rifles, polished silver and gold fixtures, and a few taxidermy pieces that seemed almost alive. In the corner a massive hot tub was covered with a black leather top, its sides made of shining silver metal. At the end of the room there was a wall of floor to ceiling windows. A black leather armchair sat behind a massive oak desk in front of the glass, cluttered with neatly arranged papers, business documents, and a sleek laptop.

Dan's gaze shifted to one of the side walls, where framed plans for a sprawling building lined the space. The detailed blueprints, encased in sleek exotic wood frames, showcased a vision of grandeur—arched windows, towering spires, and intricate stonework that seemed ripped from a bygone era. Photos of the house under construction were arranged below the plans, capturing its imposing silhouette against the backdrop of Black Lake. Positioned to overlook the water, the structure exuded a gothic elegance, both mesmerizing and ominous.

He moved further down the polished walnut wall and stopped in front of another display. Dozens of groundbreaking photos for Vic's coffee shops were meticulously arranged, each marking a milestone in his empire's expansion.

In one image, Vic stood at the center of a crowd, a golden shovel in hand and a wide grin on his face. The signs behind him read "Black Lake Coffee" in bold, sophisticated lettering. Other photos featured cheerful ribbon-cuttings, smiling employees, and bustling storefronts. The transformation from a simple idea to a nationwide phenomenon was clear, and the pride in Vic's face was unmistakable.

Dan lingered on one particular photo—Vic sitting casually in a Black Lake Coffee shop, a steaming cup in hand. The tank of lake water, visible through the glass wall behind him, gleamed like liquid obsidian. It wasn't just about coffee, Dan realized. The water was the foundation of everything.

"Damn, Vic," Dan muttered, running a hand through his long blonde hair.

Dan looked around the long ornate room. It was a hardscape of stone, wood and metal, the warm woods and leathers offsetting the cold of the other elements. The lights were dim, the furnishings impeccable. A cold chill was in the air or maybe just in Dan. He shivered.

Dan pulled out his phone and scrolled for Lauri's number. Maybe he needed Lauri here. Maybe he at least needed to hear her voice. This all seemed so surreal. Lauri was a real flesh and blood. It would be nice to connect back to some solid reality.

"Hey," he said when she answered.

"Long time no hear mister."

"Sorry. I was getting my feet under me here."

"Thought you forgot about me."

"Well it's been what forty eight hours?"

"Two long lonely days on the road," she laughed.

"Well you're not going to believe this."

Try me," Lauri replied, her tone teasing.

"A crazy ornate safari office that I am sitting in right now, plans for a mansion my father built—right on the lake. Huge, gothic, and honestly... very impressive. I cannot believe I missed it last night."

"Missed it?"

"Ya," Dan laughed. "I slept in the car. The cabin Vic had was just a run down marker on the edge of the lake. Turns out this crazy house was just beyond the trees where I couldn't see it."

"That's hilarious. But, the house sounds like your excentric billionaire father," Laurie said. "Find anything else?"

Dan walked toward the desk, his attention shifting to the laptop. Beside it, a yellow Post-it note caught his eye, the login credentials scrawled on it.

"Nice. Not too secure, Vic," Dan muttered, peeling the note off. He powered on the laptop, curiosity taking over as the screen blinked to life. A desktop filled with folders, files, and cryptic labels appeared.

He leaned back in the chair, "His laptop. I am going to check it out."

"Ok. You miss me?" Laurie teased.

"I do. Where are you?"

"My parents' house in Dallas."

"Already?"

Laurie laughed. "I didn't even go get my stuff. I just abandoned it and hit the highway from the airport. Your Corvette is very fast. And next thing you know I am back in my old bedroom. In bed. And completely naked."

Dan laughed. "You are something else. You know I am trapped in this town all alone. But, I'm glad you made it home and left that cesspool in the rearview. You'll live longer."

"Now you really miss me," Laurie said with a playful laugh.

"You should come here and I won't have to," Dan said.

"I will. I'm going to spend a couple days with my folks and then head up," she replied.

"Ok. I will call you later. Don't do anything to yourself in that bed I wouldn't do."

"hmmmm, bye Dan see you soon." Lauri said and disconnected.

A twinge of the past pinched him a little. Dan refocused his attention on the laptop. He felt better. Lauri was a new addition to his life and certainly a bright spot in an otherwise rather dismal recent past; twenty billion dollars not included. The screen glowed in the dimly lit office, casting faint reflections on the black marble floor. His fingers hovered over the trackpad as he scanned the desktop, each folder labeled cryptically—"Project BL," "Eternal," "Financials," and one simply marked "Journal."

Curiosity gnawed at him. He opened the "Journal" folder first, expecting a dry recount of business dealings or a log of day-to-day activities. Instead, a series of entries appeared, each dated and titled. The first entry of the long list caught his eye dated fifteen years prior: "Discovery at Black Lake."

Dan clicked it, and a document loaded with handwriting digitized into text.

"The water is unlike anything I've ever encountered. Not just its properties, but its energy. I feel it... coursing through me. I know this will be the breakthrough of my life. But is it truly mine to use? Or something more—something ancient and untouchable?"

Dan raised an eyebrow.

He scrolled down towards the bottom of the list and selected another cryptic title of "Compound Omega." This entry contained data tables, chemical breakdowns, and highlighted passages referencing results of some kind of experiment. The accompanying notes detailed the compound's effects on cellular regeneration and immune response.

"Early tests indicate unparalleled healing properties. Cancerous cells eradicated within hours. Subjects report increased vitality, improved cognition. A modern miracle—but not without side effects..."

Dan sat back in his chair, his pulse quickening. Sam hadn't mentioned any of this. A cure for cancer? What side effects? Well maybe burning alive. Vic was taking it to the limits for sure. Sam needed to be here. Every day was just more questions.

Dan stood and looked out the windows lining the wall behind the desk. Green pastures of Kansas in the distance. A giant bright white concrete warehouse was set back from the street behind the Oak Bar building, an oversized monument sign with the familiar Black Rose logo and Stone Industries proudly displayed marked the territory. Small tanker trucks were running in and out of the gate their cabs wrapped in the Black Lake Coffee signature cream color, black roses on the doors and pasted to the sides of the gleaming silver tanks. A monster operation.

CHAPTER 22

Dan drove back to the Black Lake, deep in thought; pensive as the cabin came into view. But instead of stopping, he pressed onward per Bob's instructions, following a narrow path through a break in the trees. The road ahead quickly turned into a tunnel of encroaching brambles, their thorny vines scraping the sides of the Lamborghini like nature itself warning him to turn back. The further he drove, the denser the vegetation became, nearly swallowing the road entirely.

And then, as if by magic, the brambles gave way. The trees parted like welcoming arms, revealing a towering wrought iron gate adorned with intricate designs—black roses entwined around an elaborate "S" crest in the center. Beyond the gate, a pristine paved driveway stretched ahead, winding gently uphill through perfectly manicured grounds. On either side of the driveway, miniature black roses lined the path—delicate, almost innocent replicas of their larger, more menacing counterparts. Their perfect, fragile petals seemed to pulse with a dark vitality, as if mocking the softness they pretended to embody, hinting at something far more sinister beneath their surface beauty.

Dan hit the remote on the key fob he retrieved from Vic's office, and the gates creaked open, the sound echoing ominously in the still air.

As he ascended, the house came into view, rising like a dark cathedral against the horizon. It was massive, almost transcendent, with gothic spires and arches reaching skyward. The façade was a blend of polished black stone and dark wood, its textures creating a visual symphony of elegance and foreboding. Large bay windows glinted like eyes in the dying light, and a grand staircase curved toward the entrance, flanked by two gargoyle statues that seemed to watch his every move.

"God damn. Nice work Dad," Dan laughed aloud.

Dan pulled the car to a stop in front of the house, his tires crunching softly against the smooth cobblestone drive. He stepped out, taking in the enormity of the estate. The air was cooler here, tinged with the faint sweet, spiced aroma of roses from the black flowerbeds surrounding the house. In the distance, the lake shimmered faintly, its surface reflecting the blood-red hues of the setting sun.

The large double doors, carved from huge slabs of pure black ebony, each panel etched with dozens of giant roses. A pair of heavy brass knockers gleamed in the dim light. Dan hesitated for a moment, then placed a hand on one of the knockers, its coolness biting against his palm. He pulled his hand back and laughed out loud. No way was he knocking so Vic could emerge from the abyss.

As he stood there, dwarfed by the house's grandeur, a strange blend of awe and unease settled over Dan. He pulled the oversized skeleton key from Vic's desk and slid it into the lock. It turned with a heavy click, a fresh mechanism made to feel centuries old, smooth and deliberate beneath his hand.

With his left hand, he pressed the latch mechanism. His right hand went instinctively to the door to give it a push—fingers splayed across the thick wooden surface.

The pain hit instantly.

The wood was white-hot—scalding, like the boiling lake water. Dan yanked his hand back with a startled shout. A patch of skin from his palm clung to the door, sizzling slightly on contact.

He staggered backward, cradling his hand, eyes wide with shock. A raw burn bloomed across his palm.

"Jesus!"

This was not just a house. It was something else. Something alive.

Dan quickly turned and descended the stone steps, the presence of the house looming large behind him like a wolf. He could almost feel it grinning an evil grin. He got back in his car cradling his hand, pushing it against his shirt. The pain was searing, excruciating, relentless. He looked down at his hand. The palm was a mess of raw blood red, broken blisters. The edges of the remaining skin were blackened, flesh peeled back and cauterized where he tore his hand away from contact with the door. He could see veins and capillaries pulsating, the blood pushed to the surface beneath the freshly exposed skin lost on the red hot door. "Fucking Vic. What the fuck!" he moaned.

"Fucking Vic," he moaned through clenched teeth. "What the fuck!"

Dan popped the trunk and climbed out, wincing as he found the first aid kit from earlier that day. Kneeling beside the car, he fumbled with the tube of antibiotic cream, finally managing to squeeze the contents of it across his blistered palm.

The instant it touched his skin, he swore he could hear it sizzle. The cold ointment seared against the raw flesh—pain and relief twisted into one sharp sensation.

Clumsily, he tore open a packet of gauze, wrapping it around his hand in slow, shaky passes. The fabric stuck in places, catching on torn skin, electrifying him in pain each time. When it was done, he sat back, breathing hard, leaning against the still warm rear tire of the Lamborghini, staring at the house.

"Another day. I can't take any more of this shit today," Dan said aloud. "What the hell is this."

After a few minutes Dan arose and climbed back in the car with plans to sleep in the office and get some more of that water for his hand. And get drunk, always the best medicine, he thought.

Dan hit the gas and the giant engine roared to life careening Dan past the iron entrance gate, the glistening black roses, the dark waters of the lake and back into the small sleepy town of Black Lake, Kansas.

CHAPTER 23

Satan, the leader or dictator of devils, is the opposite, not of God, but of Michael.

~ C. S. Lewis

The days first light slipped through the golden windowpane of the Archangel Michael's meticulously organized office. As had always been his practice he required order. Michael's nature really commanded a desire for a lack of chaos. His home was impeccably decorated in a minimalist fashion but incredible by any measure. The polished deep black floors upon close inspection were actually millions of tiny black pearls. The walls were shining sheets of hammered silver. The ceiling stretched to eternity emitting heaven's light. Money was no object. In fact, everything around him was breathed into existence.

The archangel prepared for another busy day of war. The gruesome siege was relentless. In heaven as on earth the war with Satan and his demons has never ceased since the dawn of man's time. Practically speaking man is either mostly good or mostly bad and rarely influences the scales. But on occasion and more so of late as the Day draws closer and closer a teetering soul becomes the primary focus of all things supernatural. This day another critically important creature hung in the balance with the resulting battles charted to perhaps become the most important yet.

"Michael," his assistant spoke softly, closing his eyes and exhaling slowly and quietly.

"Yes, Ezekiel. I am all right. I was just considering this situation. Dan Stone has reached the crossroad of his life. Satan knows it and is pulling out all the stops to possess him. All the while this young man seems oblivious to his own actions and the poisoning of his soul. Today he will make the decision of his life. We must make sure the young man Lucas reaches him in time."

Although God has allowed both man and angel to know that good triumphs over evil in the end, He has withheld the details. Perhaps the details are truly in flux. Strangely all the players in this masquerade have an instinctive glimmer that the ultimate destiny can be altered. God's angels have the difficult job of protecting man from Satan and his wicked henchmen. War erupts when Satan tries to take control of a man who has not refused the saving grace of Jesus Christ. The fight for that soul is more vicious and intense than any battle ever waged on earth. Immortals not bound by space, time, or dimension cannot die and never tire. The battles drag on and on; never ending. Overlapping. Merging together. Difficult or impossible to comprehend how the heavenly interacts with the earthly. How the timeless interface with the creatures blessed or cursed by time.

Throughout history God has always allowed his angels to prevail but Michael knew the time was drawing near that God would permit Satan his victory, to gain his foothold and produce his heir. The enduring Good wins out but with all things in creation connected the victory is not free. Although the notion of putting an end to Satan for all eternity was appealing the agony that man would suffer would torment heaven.

Michael prayed that this man Dan Stone would choose God. If he refused Michael and the angelic realm would be rendered powerless. And then God help us all. He beseeched God to allow His angels to emerge victorious from the field of battle. "God be with Your warriors on this most important day," he prayed. "And God be with Dan Stone."

CHAPTER 24

Dan drove past the imposing iron statue—likely the town's founder—standing sentinel in the center of the old stone wishing well at the center of town. The silhouette stretched long and distorted in the fading light. Dusk had settled over Black Lake, casting a muted orange glow across the deserted streets as the first streetlights flickered to life. He couldn't take any more surprises tonight. The house could wait. The office, at least, felt familiar. Maybe he'd read a few more entries from Vic's journal. Maybe even sleep.

As Dan approached his building, he saw a crowd gathered around the entrance, spilling out from inside the Oak Bar. A warm yellow glow poured from the windows, and the air was filled with the hum of laughter and conversation. He slowed as he passed, glancing at the faces turned toward him. Dozens of eyes followed the car, and Dan offered a polite smile and a wave with his gauze covered hand. But those who saw him didn't wave back—they simply stared, their expressions flat and unreadable.

Standing in the center of the doorway, half-framed by the glowing bar light, was a towering man with a mane of snow-white hair. He stared directly at Dan, his face unmoving, a scowl without tension or effort—like stone. As Dan drove past, the man's gaze tracked him, never blinking.

A chill ran up Dan's legs, goosebumps rising from his calves to his thighs, then crawling all the way to the back of his neck. He didn't look back.

Dan decided to loop around and drive past the warehouse he'd noticed behind the building. As he turned the corner and approached, he got a clear view of the rear side of his own building—the one that housed the Oak Bar and his office. From this angle, he could see the floor-to-ceiling glass wall behind his desk on the second floor, glowing faintly in the dusk. Below it, on the ground level, were a series of commercial roll-up glass doors revealing a huge garage that occupied the entire back half of the building. Pulling up to the doors Dan parked and climbed out of the car.

"Well Vic you built some kind of something here," he spoke aloud.

Beside the glass doors was a windowless steel door, painted the same soft cream as the trucks and storefronts, adorned with the Black Lake Coffee logo. Dan tried the handle—it turned easily but the door did not budge. Dan peered through the flawlessly clean glass of the oversized door.

The floor was a gleaming expanse of polished cream-colored concrete, perfectly matching the door, the trucks, the coffee houses. In the center of the room, a massive black rose had been painted with stunning precision.

"You certainly had a flair for presentation."

He walked back to the Lamborghini and leaned against it juggling his keys with his left hand, his righ hand still aching from the burn. Dan had a thought and pushed the button on the key fob he used for the gate at his home and the doors began to slide upwards. Dan waited and pulled the car in parking immediately to the right of the giant black rose.

In the far corner, a flight of black iron stairs rose to a matching cream-colored door on the upper level. Dan climbed slowly, the echo of each footstep sharp against the sterile silence.

Halfway up, he paused and glanced back. The vast room below was silent, pristine—almost surgical. Aside from the polished floor and the painted rose, three massive stainless steel tanks dominated the space, polished to a mirror finish, the kind you'd find in a high-end brewery or dairy plant. He didn't need a label to know—they were filled with water. Black Lake water —silent, still, and undisturbed, as if they'd been waiting forever for Dan to arrive.

Dan continued to the top of the stairs and entered his office. The door was unlocked. The automatic lighting illuminated the giant room as he stepped across the threshold and his foot hit the sparkling black marble.

Dan seated himself behind the oversized wooden desk like a captain taking his place at the helm of a ship. He looked down at his hand and the mixture of antibiotic cream and lymphatic fluid from this raw wound seeping through the gauze.

His smartphone buzzed. Lauri's beautiful face lit up the screen.

"Well, hello there, Lauri. I was just thinking about you."

"How are you doing up there, Dan? Miss me?"

"I do. And I'm doing... well, I guess. Lots of strange things. And strange people."

"I'm planning to drive up this weekend."

"That sounds great. I think I can survive another three days."

"Did you go see the house?"

Dan hesitated and said, "I did. It's fantastic—phenomenal, actually. Incredible. I just... haven't made it inside yet."

"What? Why not?"

"It's hard to explain. But I will before you get here. I'll have the bed turned down and everything."

"Easy, boy. We've still got a few days."

"Ha! Yes, indeed. And hey—drive safe, okay? It's the real boonies after you hit Wichita. It almost drove me off the edge. No lights, just white lines of the broken highway."

"Oh, I bet," she said with a smile in her voice. "I'll be careful."

"Good. I need you here in one piece."

"You'll get me—whole, rested, and ready."

Dan disconnected with a smile and walked to the hot tub at the opposite end of the room intent on submerging his wound. A bit of a creepy feeling passed through him as the tub would undoubtedly be filled with Black Lake Water and Vic surely would have par boiled himself within on a number of occasions. Dan removed the gauze from his hand.

Well, when in Rome. Here goes. Should heal me up, he thought.

Dan pulled the cover back. To his surprise there was no a blast of steam from the near boiling tub of lake water as expected but a thin coating of ice on the surface.
"What the hell?"

Plumes of frozen vapor wafted up from the crystal clear sheet of ice. Dan tapped on the ice with the back of his blistered hand and an electric chill surged through his knuckles, shooting up his arm and striking the base of his skull—right where his spine met the bone. He jerked his hand back instinctively, clutching his neck and doubling over as though slapped with a giant invisible hand. It was like a frozen bolt of electricity that didn't exactly hurt but left his arm and in fact the entire right side of his body strangely numb.

He straightened slowly as the cold sensation faded, rubbing the atlas joint at the top of his neck. His eyes returned to the surface of the tub, now cracked where his knuckles had struck. The cold vapors rising from the shattered ice were smoking a blue white. Dan focused and blinked the tears from his eyes. So... not a hot tub.

Dan flexed and relaxed his hand a few times. It was no longer cold from knocking on the ice. It was also no longer burned from pushing on the red hot front door of his house.

CHAPTER 25

The next morning Dan stood at the bar's entrance, watching as a sleek convoy of black SUVs rolled into Black Lake. The sight was a stark contrast to the town's quaint streets, a modern disruption that seemed to mirror the shift in Dan's own life. He adjusted his jacket as the lead vehicle pulled to a stop in front of The Oak Bar.

Tom Stark stepped out first, his presence commanding even in the relaxed air of Black Lake. His suit was immaculate, a sharp black that seemed to absorb the sunlight. Behind him, a small team of assistants emerged, each carrying briefcases, tablets, or stacks of papers. Eight females and two males all dressed in black slacks and white button down shirts.

"Dan!" Tom called, a wide smile on his face as he extended a hand. "Finally, here in person. Welcome to the heart of the empire."

Dan took his hand, shaking it firmly but still feeling the unease of being the newcomer. "Good to see you, Tom. Guess it's about time I got the real grand tour rather than just stumbling around this place."

Tom's grin widened. "You've inherited something truly special. Vic built a hell of a legacy. Happy to show you what you're working with and sorry for the delay. There was a lot to sew up after Vic's death."

"Well, glad you came up here --- New Orleans was eye opening and this place is strange but nice," Dan said.

Bob stepped out of the bar, giving a subtle nod toward Tom before retreating inside. Dan caught the unspoken respect there, a hint of history between Bob and Vic's right-hand in-town man. It added another layer to the mystery of this place.

They started at The Oak Bar, where Tom highlighted the hidden systems, Vic had put in place. The tap lines connected to the vats of Black Lake water, the discreet filtration system, and the space's dual function as both a bar and a central hub for the coffee operation.

"This place is where it all began," Tom said, gesturing toward the sleek black taps gleaming under the bar's subdued lighting. "The water comes straight from the lake—purified, of course. It's the soul of everything Vic built. You could almost call it an artesian well pure and delicious, endless, damn near perfect. Just don't get tangled up in those roses." He chuckled, but there was an edge to his laughter that didn't quite reach his eyes.

Dan nodded, recalling the wounds from the coal black flowers, his mind racing with questions he didn't yet know how to ask. Instead, he followed Tom to the office upstairs, where Vic's meticulous planning was on full display.

Tom walked him through the logistics, outlining the network of warehouses, the fleet of delivery trucks, and the sheer volume of operations Vic had managed from this seemingly quiet town.

"Your father had a vision," Tom said, sliding a folder across the desk toward Dan. "He built this from nothing, and he left it all to you. Now it's your turn."

The tour continued to the new warehouse Vic built across the alley behind the Oak Bar, where rows of gleaming trucks stood ready to deliver coffee and water across the region. Workers moved efficiently, their pace suggesting a well-oiled machine.

"This is incredible. Vic had it all together here in Black Lake. Why was Sam in New Orleans?" Dan asked.

"The lab was there and Sam and the team were already solidly in place when Vic bought the company. And well, Black Lake is pretty private and can get under your skin let's say. Vic wanted to keep Sam some distance from some of the people here in Black Lake," Tom said.
"Ok, I can see that it makes sense to keep him a bit neutral. He said he had been here a number of times but nothing long term. I told him to pack and come up again. I think I will drag his ass up here for an extended period and put the research into hyperdrive."

"Well let's think on that. For now let's grab some coffee and relax in the bar before we make our way to the lake," Tom suggested, his tone light but with the usual sharpness that came from years of commanding attention. "I am guessing we could all use a bit of rejuvenation. And I know just the beverage for it." He laughed, the sound echoing softly against the polished wood and marble surfaces of The Oak Bar.

Bob, ever the consummate bartender, moved swiftly behind the counter. In minutes, he served up steaming Americanos, frothy Lattes, and spiced Chai Teas to the group. Each drink was made with the mystical Black Lake water, its properties lending the beverages an almost addictive smoothness.

Dan sipped his Americano, the taste sharp and revitalizing. The caffeine hit was real, but there was something else, a feeling of clarity, like the fog in his mind was lifting. He glanced around the bar, watching the others take their first sips.

The group settled into the plush leather seats scattered around the bar, the room filling with the buzz of conversation. It was a swirling, chaotic symphony of voices—assistants trading notes, Tom cracking dry jokes, Bob chiming in with his laid-back humor. The chatter ebbed and flowed in a way that might have overwhelmed anyone stepping into it cold. Yet, somehow, Dan felt entirely in tune with it.

Every word, every thought, every intention—they all seemed crystal clear to him, as though he were sitting in the middle of a carefully orchestrated meeting where everyone's contributions were synchronized. But that wasn't right. It wasn't possible. It was just noise, wasn't it?

And yet, it wasn't. Dan wasn't just following the conversation—he knew what everyone was thinking, feeling, saying, even before they finished speaking. He could hear the red headed girl Stephanie thinking about getting another cup of coffee but she was pining away for it like a deep nearly painful craving fighting with herself. He heard Mike thinking about a recipe for a boozy coffee drink and wondering if he could make it in New York as a bartender. He heard Tom saying a prayer of sorts, but it was more a jumbled mix of gibberish and an undertone of dark disturbed emotion. The realization hit him like a jolt of electricity, a clarity that was too sharp, too precise. It was exhilarating. And terrifying.

His head swam as the room around him seemed to shift, the voices blending into a strange, harmonious rhythm. Something about it felt right, almost euphoric, as though he'd tapped into a hidden channel connecting them all. But beneath that euphoric hum was a deep unease, a sense that whatever was happening wasn't natural.

Dan rubbed his temples, trying to steady himself. It had to be the coffee? Ultimately the water he figured. Or was this just what Black Lake did to a person? He forced a smile, lifting his cup in a silent toast to no one in particular, hoping no one noticed how off-balance he felt.

Dan froze, his cup hovering midair. The synchronized motion of the group was uncanny, their raised cups a mirror image of his own. It wasn't just their timing—it was the way they turned toward him as one, their eyes shimmering with a knowing intensity, their smiles frozen and unnaturally wide. A chill snaked up both legs all the way up to his chin, and his lips moved involuntarily, as if controlled by an unseen force.

"To Black Lake," Dan said, his voice blending seamlessly with the chorus of the others.

The words echoed through the room like a chant, their collective tone strangely resonant, as though it came from somewhere deeper than their throats. The moment hung in the air, oppressive and surreal. Dan's pulse quickened as his gaze darted from face to face, searching for some sign of normalcy, some clue that this was just a strange coincidence.

But their expressions didn't waver. The gleam in their eyes didn't fade. They were watching him, waiting, expectant.

Dan forced a sip of his coffee, hoping to steady his nerves. The rich, dark brew burned slightly as it slid down his throat, a stark contrast to the icy dread coiling in his stomach. Whatever was happening, he knew he'd just crossed some invisible threshold—he could not unsee the healing power of the water nor unfeel the unusual thoughts that had flown into his mind. He had seen some of the unimaginable power in action and that there was no turning back

Soon, the group began to filter out of the bar, their chatter and laughter echoing faintly in the quiet stillness of the late afternoon. Tom signaled to the assistants, and they gathered their belongings, making their way toward the waiting fleet of sleek black Suburban's idling outside. The vehicles gleamed under the gray sky, their tinted windows reflecting the shadowy outlines of the towering trees.

Dan lingered for a moment, watching the group file into the SUVs with practiced precision. Tom, ever the leader, gave Dan a knowing nod before stepping into the lead vehicle. "You'll want to see this, Dan," he called out, his voice carrying an edge of anticipation. "Ride with me. I'll have one of the guys bring your car to the house later."

Dan took a deep breath, steeling himself for whatever lay ahead, and climbed into the passenger seat of the second Suburban. The convoy moved smoothly down the narrow road, weaving through the thick forest that surrounded the town. The further they went, the denser the trees became, their gnarled branches intertwining like skeletal fingers reaching across the sky.

The lake came into view suddenly, as if the forest itself had parted to reveal it. The dark water glistened like black glass, framed by the eerie blooms of the coal-colored roses that thrived impossibly close to the shore. The convoy took a hard right before the main gate of the house and after a few hundred yards stopped near a cluster of guest houses nestled in a clearing on the far side of the lake. Dan was amazed he hadn't seen them before, but they were obscured by more trees, brambles, and black roses. The houses were modern yet rustic, their cedar exteriors blending harmoniously with the surrounding wilderness. Beyond them, the imposing silhouette of the main house loomed in the distance, its gothic spires barely visible through the trees.

As the group stepped out of the Suburban's, the air seemed to shift— heavier, charged with an unspoken tension. The assistants moved briskly, unloading suitcases and equipment, while Tom clapped Dan on the shoulder. "Welcome to the heart of Black Lake," he said, gesturing toward the sprawling scene before them.

Dan nodded ignoring Tom and the group and not planning on telling a story about that morning and his charred hand and his rapid egress back to the relative safety of his fractionally familiar office. He would keep that to himself. His gaze was fixed on the lake. Still unlike anything he had ever seen—beautiful and haunting, its surface impossibly still, as if holding its breath. He couldn't explain why, but something about it pulled at him, whispering to a part of himself he didn't quite understand.

"Get settled," Tom said, breaking the moment. "We've got a long day tomorrow. But I'll be along in an hour and we can have some dinner. Chef John is already in your kitchen whipping it up."

Dan tore his eyes away from the lake and followed the others toward the guest houses, his thoughts swirling with questions he was not ready to ask. Not yet.

"And this," Tom said as they stepped onto the porch of the first guest house, pointing towards the lake and leading Dan toward a small trail that wound through the trees, "is the core of it all."

The path opened to the edge of the lake, its dark waters shimmering under the afternoon light. The black roses framed the shoreline, their sharp thorns glinting ominously. Dan stood there, silent, as the reality of what he had inherited began to sink in.

Tom watched him closely. "This lake—this water—is the key. It is what makes Black Lake Coffee what it is. Vic understood its power, its potential. That is why he stayed here. Why he built all of this."

Dan finally tore his gaze from the lake, his expression unreadable. "And now it's mine," he said, a mixture of emotions coursing through his mind; joy, fear, regret. He wasn't sure exactly what to think.

Tom clapped him on the shoulder again, a rare moment of levity breaking the tension. "Damn right it is. Let's get you settled in properly."

As they walked back, Tom pointed toward the cluster of guest houses "That is where my team and I will stay for the night. You have the main house to yourself for now, except for the kitchen staff and the maids and security but they steer clear most of the time. After the crew gets settled into the guest house trust me, Dan—you'll be seeing a lot of us."

Dan nodded absently, his thoughts drifting back to the lake and the first time he'd attempted set foot in the house. He moved in a daze, staggering toward his own fantastical palace, haunted by the memory of the bar— and the unsettling synchronicity of the assistants who had mirrored his every gesture with uncanny precision. Black Lake wasn't just a town, and it wasn't just a business. It was something far stranger, something vast and unknowable. There were secrets here, layered and shifting, as treacherous as quicksand—and Dan could feel himself sinking deeper with every step.

CHAPTER 26

Dan walked to the house and climbed the two dozen granite steps leading to the imposing gothic entrance for the second time. Today the house seemed to radiate light despite the setting sun and the ebony stones used in its construction. It exuded an almost preternatural glow, as if it were alive, pulsing with an eerie energy; "Pure uranium 238," Dan muttered to himself with a dark chuckle as he crossed the covered loggia just outside the massive double doors.

He hesitated as he reached towards the door and quickly pushed and withdrew his hand. It was cool to the touch unlike his first visit. He push opened the heavy oak doors, and the sheer scale of the interior stole his breath. The space he entered could hardly be called a mere living room; it was more akin to a grand ballroom, vast and cavernous, with polished black stone floors that reflected the fiery glow of the setting sun streaming through tall, arched windows. The cathedral ceiling soared high above, its intricate wooden beams crossing like the ribs of some ancient, massive creature.

Dan moved through the stone-walled room, his footsteps echoing faintly, and reached a staircase that spiraled upward, crafted from the same black stone that dominated the entire building. Its balustrade was wrought iron, fashioned into elaborate patterns of roses and thorns.

"A castle," Dan thought as he began his ascent, running his hand along the cold iron. "That's what this is." Each step echoed in the silence, amplifying the sense of being in a place that was more than a home— something closer to a monument, a fortress, or perhaps even a mausoleum.

Dan found the master bedroom at the end of the corridor, its entrance marked by a heavy wooden door that was a masterpiece in itself. The door was intricately hand-carved, adorned with dozens of painted black roses and their thorny stems. The thorns, crafted from dark, razor-sharp metal, protruded slightly, catching the dim light and casting sinister shadows. It was as much a warning as an invitation—beautiful, intricate, and undeniably ominous.

He pushed the door open and stepped into the room, his boots clicking softly on the black stone floor. The interior carried the same gothic elegance as the rest of the house. Black stone walls were softened by dark, richly woven tapestries depicting scenes of roses intertwined with serpents and cryptic symbols he didn't recognize. The only hint of color came from deep crimson accents within the tapestries, adding a touch of blood-like vibrancy to the otherwise monochrome space.

At the center of the room stood a giant, elevated California King bed, its base carved from ebony wood and its headboard towering high, etched with more black roses. The bed itself was four feet off the ground, its imposing height making it feel like a throne. It was draped in a thick, black silk bedspread embroidered with shimmering black roses that seemed almost alive, their intricate petals catching the faintest glimmers of light. The bed was piled with a mountain of down pillows, their silken cases gleaming faintly like polished obsidian.

The room exuded power, mystery, and unease in equal measure. Dan ran his hand over the edge of the bedspread, marveling at the craftsmanship, and then let his gaze wander over the rest of the chamber. It wasn't just a bedroom—it was a statement, a sanctuary, and a shadowed fortress all at once.

Dominating one side of the room was a massive black stone fireplace, its mantle and surround mirroring the intricate craftsmanship of the bedroom door. The same delicate black roses were carved into the mantle's edge, their stems twisting and curling into sharp, dark thorns that seemed to creep outward as if alive. The roses were painted with a faint metallic sheen, catching the flickering firelight and giving them a numinous glow.

The fireplace itself was hewn from the same black stone as the rest of the house, its polished surface glistening like volcanic glass. Above the mantle, a large tapestry hung, depicting an ancient, shadowy forest encircling a lake that seemed to glimmer with an unnatural darkness. The imagery felt oddly familiar to Dan, though he couldn't place why.

The hearth, was four by four certainly wide enough to hold a blaze large enough to heat the entire room, was lined with iron and fitted with heavy, ornate grates. Embers crackled softly, casting dancing shadows across the walls and ceiling, filling the room with a warmth that seemed at odds with the gothic chill of its surroundings.

Dan stepped closer to the fireplace, warming himself from the chill in the night air and the cold emanating from the very pores of his father's dark manor. His gaze was drawn to the mantle. It was as much a focal point as the bed, its craftsmanship exuding the same ominous elegance. The roses carved into the stone seemed to almost pulse in the flickering light, their beauty offset by the sinister sharpness of their thorns. It was a hearth fit for a king—or a dark ruler.

Dan found the ensuite and stripped off his clothes. He needed this shower to wash the heaviness of the long day away. The shower appeared to be carved seamlessly from the same black stone as the rest of the house, its smooth surfaces glistening faintly under the soft light. It was less a traditional shower and more like a cave—a cavernous, open space with no doors, where the steam swirled freely into the room.

Heat lamps glowed from above, their warmth enveloping the space as Dan stepped in. The scalding hot water cascaded down in torrents; the spray imbued with a faint shimmer that made him suspect its source. He was certain this water came straight from the lake. The intense heat felt almost alive, soaking into his skin and seeping into his bones, as if trying to consume him whole.

In each corner of the shower, subtle carvings of roses emerged from the stone, their intricate petals and razor-sharp thorns blending harmoniously with the natural elegance of the design. Shelves carved into the walls held soap and shampoo, their scents identical to the dark, intoxicating aroma of the black roses encircling the lake. The fragrance filled the chamber, clinging to the steam and creating an atmosphere that was equal parts luxurious and unsettling.

It wasn't just a shower—it was an experience, a baptism in the essence of Black Lake itself.

Thick crimson bath towels had been neatly folded and set on the vanity, their luxurious texture hinting at the attentiveness of the manor's unseen staff, who seemed to anticipate and cater to his every need. Dan stepped into the adjoining closet; a cavernous space lined with tailored clothing. His gaze settled on a pair of sleek black Adidas warm-ups and matching Nike running shoes—both his size, both exactly to his taste. How they knew, he didn't bother questioning. It was as if the house itself had been designed with him in mind.

Dressed and refreshed, Dan descended the long stone staircase. The cold surface of the steps contrasted with the warmth radiating from the grand chandeliers above, and he paused at the top to take in the view. Thirty feet below, the ballroom stretched out in all its imposing majesty, an echo of centuries-old elegance brought to life by the polished stone floor and soaring ceilings.

He continued down, his footsteps faintly echoing in the vast space, and made his way to the kitchen. The aroma of freshly roasted meat drew him in as he entered the expansive culinary hub. Chef John, a stocky man in a pristine white uniform, was flanked by two sous chefs as they worked in precise synchronization, their movements fluid and purposeful. The chef was just pulling a massive prime rib from the oven onto the enormous kitchen island, its golden crust crackling faintly in the open air.

"Sir," Chef John acknowledged with a nod, his tone formal but respectful. The sous chefs glanced in Dan's direction before returning to their tasks, focused on garnishing the dish with fresh herbs and preparing the accompanying sides.

Dan nodded in return but said nothing, the tantalizing scent enough to momentarily silence any thought. He moved on, passing through the kitchen and into the dining room—a room as grand as any in the house. The long, polished table sat beneath an ornate chandelier, its cascading crystals refracting the light into delicate rainbows that danced across the dark walls. Heavy drapes framed the windows, and tapestries depicting hunting scenes hung on the walls, adding a medieval gravitas to the space.

The dining room was another masterpiece of design and decadence, a room built to entertain the elite. A far cry from the rickety Chinese kitchen table purchased from Amazon furnishing his North Denver apartment, only a month before.

Dan sank into the massive black leather couch, its surface adorned with intricate embroidery of black roses, the thorns subtly raised as though warning of their sharpness. The couch faced the grand black stone fireplace, its roaring flames casting a golden glow over the room, making the shadows of the carved roses on the mantle dance ominously.

Opposite him stood a matching sofa, equally grand and equally adorned. Between them, a coffee table unlike anything Dan had ever seen dominated the space—a solid block of crystal, six feet long, four feet wide, and two feet thick. Within its depths, ripples seemed to shift, frozen in a mimicry of flowing water. As the firelight refracted through it, the effect was almost hypnotic, as though the table held the essence of a restless lake within its transparent heart.

Dan stared at the crystal, lost in thought. It was beautiful but unsettling, much like everything else about this place.

Dan's thoughts were interrupted by the din of a crowd coming in the front door and noisily parading through the ballroom finding their way to the grand dining room. Obviously, they had been here before. Four of the female assistants crowded onto the couches opposite Dan while the other four assistants went to the bar and began helping themselves to the well-stocked bar. Comfortable. Tom came straight to Dan smiling broadly, obviously overjoyed to be in Black Lake and in the presence of the heir to Victor's fortune. Tom was eager to get Dan acclimatized to his new lavish lifestyle.

"Dan, this is great!" Tom smacked him on the shoulder giving it a squeeze at the end. "I can't wait to tell you about your father and the plans he had. He was a very detailed, driven man who knew you would slide in perfectly to lead the Black Lake expansion.

"Expansion?" Dan raised his eyebrows. Looked pretty expanded already to Dan.

"Dan, right!" Tom laughed, tapping Dan's arm. "See what I did there? Hey, let's get a drink. Mike! Pour us a couple of Manhattans!" he called across the room. "Mike here used to be a bartender in the Big Apple— one of those cocktail joints where they toss bottles around like a circus act." Tom let out an exaggerated laugh, his voice booming as he jogged to the black stone bar adorned with intricate rose carvings on the far side of the fireplace.

"Coming right up, Boss," Mike said, spinning a fifth of bourbon across his palm like a well-balanced torpedo, head-high, while clinking a couple of glasses together in his left hand.

Dan followed Tom over a bit incredulously. A party had erupted. The girls on the couch were animated, chatting, laughing in a sea of flipping hair. Drinks had miraculously appeared in their hands. Coats had been scuttled. The boys at the bar were mixing drinks like talented pros striving to outdo one another. Chef John and his team had dropped gleaming trays of hors d'oeuvres — bite-sized delicacies that looked almost too good to eat.

Dan glanced at Tom, who was now gesturing wildly at the twin bartenders, his laughter filling the space like it belonged there. A grin tugged at Dan's lips. "Tom," he thought to himself, "I'm really going to like this guy."

The party continued as everyone imbibed in the top shelf alcohol compliments of Vic or Dan now actually. The assistants were lively and relaxed, cute and fun, laughing easily. Tom was the consummate host working the crowd and keeping the glasses full and smiles bright. Dan snuck off-- he needed a joint to top off this celebration of life.

Sliding around the edge of the dining room, leaving the cacophony behind, Dan found the grand staircase and began his ascent—step after step—until he reached the quiet sanctuary of his bedroom.

Once inside, he went straight to the bedside drawer, pulling it open with a sense of purpose. There they were a handful of Lauris carefully rolled joints waiting for him. Too bad she is in Dallas and not here with me. Yet. Guess it's time to meet the assistants, he thought placing the weed in his pullover hoodie front pocket, a mischievous grin breaking across his face. "Let's really get this party started," he chuckled to himself as he hurried back to the lively gathering below.

When Dan returned, dinner had been served magnificently on the grand dining table. A pristine white cloth draped over the black stone surface, its stark contrast complementing the largely ebony interior of his new home. The spread was lavish: prime rib, mashed potatoes dripping with butter, an array of colorful vegetables, fresh rolls, and salads of every kind. It was a feast fit for royalty.

Dan took it all in, nodding appreciatively. "Hell of a spread," he thought, as the others began to seat themselves. With a quiet confidence, he strode to the head of the table—the place of honor—and settled in, feeling the weight of his new role settle around him like a mantle.

CHAPTER 27

Dan woke with his head buzzing, the weight of the late night still reverberating like a gong. Too many Manhattans. Anything in those but alcohol? He doubted it, though he did recall a few maraschino cherries making an appearance—several with their stems tied into knots courtesy of Stephanie, the redhead with oversized... assets.

"Lovely night," he muttered, rubbing his temples. It was a minor miracle he'd managed to make it upstairs and into his bed alone. His bleary eyes flicked to the heavy door with its carved roses and imposing dark metal thorns guarding the entrance to the bedroom. "Thanks for keeping me pure," he chuckled to himself, his laugh raspy and dry.

Dan squinted at the sunrise blazing over the inky black lake, the water catching the light in mesmerizing ripples. The coal-colored roses surrounding the shore shimmered like polished onyx, their dark beauty almost fantastical. But what caught his attention wasn't the view—it was the sight of nine figures sprinting across the property.

Tom led the pack, running hard. The others followed in unison, moving with an eerie synchronicity that made Dan's breath hitch. This wasn't the leisurely jog of suburbanites sweating out last night's booze; this was a race—no, a bolt, charged with a primal intensity. "What the ever-living fuck," he said shaking his head.

Dan showered, smoked a bowl of Colorados finest from his glass bong, and dressed in his now signature black Adidas warm up suit and Nikes. Down to the kitchen. Chef John had his venti americano three raw sugars and extra cream. Blueberry bagels and butter. A spread aside from that like a breakfast buffet at the Four Seasons. "Well, what the hell," Dan said aloud. Good coffee.

The red head Stephani came into the kitchen. Not breathing hard and not sweating despite the maniacal sprints around the lake. "Hello Dan. Good morning sleepyhead," she smiled.

"Yes, looks sunny and beautiful out there. That was some running."

"Yes, she laughed. Tom likes to exercise the troops. He keeps us in shape. That man is a machine."

"I guess so. Well, hey I'm on my way to the office. Just let Tom know I will see you all there."

"Can I ride with you?"

Dan thought for a minute. And then another minute. "Well, I like to wake up a bit slower than you do, I think. Maybe I'll just see you there."

"Come on. After last night I think everyone is going to be fine with it. Tom certainly won't care," she laughed.

"After last night?"

"Well, I did let you sleep while I got out of bed and went for the run. I guess I should have awakened you differently," she smiled.

Dan just smiled. "Ok. We will ride in together."

Dan had no recollection of getting up to his room. He could recall a few empty bottles and now that he focused in, he recalled a girl or two had lost her shirt and was dancing on the crystal glass coffee table. Oh yes, and there was Stephanie. He did recall his head in the crook of her neck struggling to see the gleaming chandelier through her thick deep auburn hair. The last he could recollect there were three joints being passed around the table like a cannabis merry go round. Okay. It was a party and likely he knew these folks a lot better than he thought. Oops.

But the Black Lake Coffee was kicking in, and Dan didn't care. He felt invincible, the caffeine sharpening his senses and silencing any lingering doubts. He was the boss now—the heir apparent. Of course, all the women wanted him, and all the men wanted to be him. Big Dan Stone, ruler of the roost, sitting at the top of the world with his empire at his feet. A smirk tugged at the corners of his mouth. Life wasn't just good; it was practically scripted. Okay baby let's show these stiffs what Dan can do.

They each grabbed another to go cup of Dan's Black Lake Coffee and headed for the garage. They walked down the stairs into the huge garage where the Lamborghini and one of the black suburbans were parked. Dan hit the button on the key fob and both doors scissored up.

He held her hand as she lowered into the passenger seat. Dan dropped into the driver's seat both doors sliding silently down and into place. The Lambo roared and he backed out.

He reached over and grabbed her by the hair, his hand tightening just enough to make her breath catch and pulled her towards him and kissed her hard—an electrified moment of passion and control. The engine roared to life, a symphony of power and rebellion, as the car shot forward, leaving everything and everyone else in their wake.

Dan pulled to the back of the Oak Bar building and hit the button on the key fob. The large double glass garage doors slid up and out of the way. Dan pulled the car in and he and Stephanie exited the sports car. Walking across the shop area to the entry door to the Oak Bar and Dan said, "Stephanie, what is your goal for the day? Tom brought a lot of you along."

"Tom said we're here to help you settle in—and maybe show you how much fun this place can be," she said, her smile teasing but not entirely innocent.

"Ok. What do you think so far?"

"Well, I think we are having a great time and it's only going to get better. Your father always had a great time when we would come up. He really cut loose and relaxed. I think that was the only time he did."

"I never really knew him."

"He spoke of you," Stephanie said softly. "He regretted not being closer." He planned to get in contact with you before-- well before he passed."

The Oak Bar was eerily quiet, the only sounds the faint hum of the taps and the echo of Dan's steps across the polished stone floor.

"Did he?" Dan asked, his tone caught between bitterness and curiosity. "Would've been nice to know. Life's been... dull. Could've used the challenge."

It was early. Bob was nowhere to be found. Dan and Stephanie dropped their bags on the bar.

"Well boring is over, Dan." she smiled. Let's get a drink to wake up."

Dan walked to the other side of the polished oak counter. "What are you having?"

"Just cold water, please."

Dan grabbed a glass and placed it under the "Ice Cold" tap, filling her glass. The water sparkled and immediately frosted the outside of the glass.

"Damn, that's cold," Dan said, watching frost creep over the glass, his fingers tingling against the icy surface. Flashbacks to the Cold Tub momentarily drifted through his grey matter.

"Yes, Vic had us find a very specialized solution for all of the Black Lake stores. Ice Cold is 33 degrees. Real Hot is 210 degrees."

"Damn near Freezing and boiling," Dan shook his head. "Why did he care?"
"The Lake swings from 210 to 33," Stephanie said, her voice dropping as if sharing a secret.

"What? The lake gets to 210 degrees?"

"It swings wildly depending. Boiling one day, freezing the next," she said, pausing as if weighing her words. "Vic never did figure out why."

"Mike, Zack, Kim, and Zoey are all scientists," Stephanie said. "They're constantly bringing in samples, running tests—mostly focused on New Orleans."

"Sam. Yeah, I met him and his crew in Convent," Dan replied. "These four—are they here on his behalf?"

She hesitated, her eyes drifting toward the window. "The lake's... complicated. More than you might think. Sam's juggling a lot, and they handle the fieldwork."

Dan leaned forward slightly. "Funny—I didn't see them in New Orleans."

Stephanie didn't answer right away. Her silence said more than she intended.

"They were probably here... or in Dallas," she said quickly. "They run back and forth like—"

She stopped herself.

Dan raised an eyebrow. "Like what?"

Stephanie forced a smile. "Like ants. Always moving. Always... collecting."

He watched her carefully. Her tone was too casual. And that second glance toward the hallway—too rehearsed.

"They're not just collecting samples, are they?" he asked.

She looked down. "It's better if Sam explains. It's... sensitive."

"I don't want Sam. Or Tom. I'm asking you—now spill it."

Stephanie hesitated, fingers tightening around her coffee cup.

"Data. Samples. Environmental readings. Movement patterns. That sort of thing."

She exhaled slowly, her voice quieter now, eyes flicking toward the hallway again as if someone might be listening.

"There are anomalies," she said. "Readings that don't match any known environmental pattern. Biological shifts. Mutations. The lake's affecting people—affecting us—in ways we don't understand. Sam's trying to stay ahead of it, but..."

"But what?"

Her voice dropped to a whisper.

"But I think we're already behind."

They sat quietly and drank. Stephanie with the ice-cold Black Lake water and Dan with his third venti americano. They were interrupted by the group pouring in the front doors of the Oak Bar.

Tom led the way pushing the vestibule door open and calling out, "Good Morning! Dan. Stephanie. You two are the talk of the town. Well, the talk in the SUVs anyway," he laughed.

Dan looked at Tom and the group of assistants all grinning with a knowing smile. Dan glanced at Stephanie who sat up straight, put her hands on her hips and pushed out her chest. "We should be," she laughed.

Tom laughed and clapped Dan on the shoulder. "Like father like son," his voice boomed and echoed off the polished wood and stone hardscapes in the bar.

Dan tilted his head, raised his eyebrows quizzically and glanced from Tom to Stephanie who offered a small, knowing smile and a shrug, leaving him to puzzle it out.

Mike jumped around the bar. "Who wants some of Black Lake's finest?" Apparently, everyone—including Dan.

CHAPTER 28

The day unfolded as a relentless barrage of information. Dan was immersed in the world of Black Lake Coffee and the vast holdings of Stone Industries. Dan had been given the Cliffs Notes version in Toms office and a minimalist version of Sam's work. Now it was a crash course in family legacy, history, chemistry, botany, geology, and, of course, coffee. Tom and the assistants each delivered polished presentations, each lasting 30 to 45 minutes, diving deep into their respective areas of expertise.

The group drank Black Lake Coffee like it was lake water—cup after cup, no breaks, no food. The caffeine-fueled drive was palpable, an almost manic determination to absorb every detail and leave nothing unexplored. Dan couldn't help but marvel at the energy in the room. It wasn't just a lesson—it was a battle to conquer the knowledge and emerge victorious.

Dan returned to his home. The business associates went to the guesthouse and Dan went to his bedroom for some well earned peace and quiet. The day had been full of conversation and non stop planning.

"Lauri. What are you up to?"

"Hi Dan."

"Just Hi Dan? How badly do you miss me?"

"Text me the address and directions sexy. I'm heading your way tomorrow and I will show you in person."

"Hell yes. That's a day early at least. Directions coming at you right now. And turn left at the big oak tree and the shitty cabin."

"Okay. Yes, I can't wait any more. I need some of that patented Dan Stone lovin',"
 Lauri laughed.

More small talk and some flirtatiousness. Great anticipation and some goodbyes and drive safes. Dan stood and stretched his long arms towards the ceiling. He had a smile that had not been familiar to him for a long, long, time.

Back to business and get these people out of here. The plan was to meet in the dining room at 7pm.

Dan took a shower and smoked a joint and fell asleep on the massive king-sized bed. When he awoke it was 10pm. He went downstairs and the colleagues had gone back to the guest houses. Chef John and his crew were cleaning up the dinner dishes.

"Mr. Stone would you like some dinner? We have plenty remaining. In fact, we are preparing to eat ourselves," motioning to the island kitchen covered with the food from dinner.

"Yes, please. I fell asleep. I will just make a plate."

"The others left about 30 minutes ago. They took a few bottles with them. I think their party is just starting. They planned on swimming if you want to join them."

Dan raised his eyebrows and took his food to eat on the couch by the fire. The food was delicious. Salmon steaks with a beurre blanc, some kind of potato dish with asparagus and a small bowl of caviar and naan bread.

"Swimming. What the fuck. That water is boiling hot and full of thorn bushes," he pondered.

Dan finished eating and headed for the guest houses. He walked across the acre side yard. and through the trees. Then he saw them. Sure enough all of the staff members were in the water up to their necks floating in the darkness about ten feet offshore.

They were screaming—high-pitched, guttural cries of pain that carried over the still water. Giant boils marred their blood-red faces and hands as they thrashed to stay afloat.

"Jesus Christ," Dan yelled, running toward the shoreline. "Get out of there!"

Most ignored him, their cries unrelenting. But then Stephanie and Tom turned to him at the same time, their voices oddly synchronized. "Come in, Dan! The water's great!" Stephanie's laughter twisted into a shriek of pain mid-sentence.

Dan froze, the grotesque scene gripping him in horror. Tom swam toward shore, his burned skin glistening in the faint light.

"Dan," Tom gasped as he reached the edge. "Thank God you're here. We got stuck out there." He turned back to the others. "Ladies and gentlemen, come to shore!"

The six women and two men obeyed, swimming sluggishly to the bank and dragging themselves onto land. Dan stared in shock as they staggered toward him, completely nude, their bodies beet red, covered in angry welts and blisters from the scalding water.

"Go get some coffee," Tom instructed, his voice calm, almost detached.

The group moved wordlessly toward the guesthouse, their burned and battered bodies shuffling in eerie silence. When the last figure disappeared inside, Tom turned to Dan.

"Okay," Tom said, raising his hands in a placating gesture. "I know how this looks. It's... strange. I get that."

"Strange?!" Dan snapped. "What the hell was that, Tom? Why were you all in the lake? Why were you burning yourselves alive?"

Tom sighed, rubbing his face as if he'd been through this conversation before. "To feel better, of course. The water heals you and makes you feel incredible... after. But you have to let it work."

Dan's jaw clenched. "So, you're telling me you have to burn yourself to feel good?"

Tom looked at him, his expression uncomfortably earnest. "It's not just burning. It's the lake's process. The pain purges everything—illness, weakness, doubt. You come out healed, stronger than ever. But it demands a price. We just got lost in the moment. Glad you came down," He laughed.

Dan stared, speechless. Words wouldn't come.

Tom broke the silence. "I need coffee—and a cold shower. This hurts like hell. Come inside, Dan."

Without waiting, Tom turned and headed into the guesthouse, his beet-red, blistered skin glistening in the faint light. Dan followed hesitantly, his stomach churning with unease.

The main room was eerily empty, but the sound of running water echoed from the bathroom. Tom grabbed a steaming cup of coffee from the counter, drinking it down in one gulp as he walked toward the open shower door.

Dan hesitated before stepping closer. Inside, all the assistants were crammed into the oversized shower, scrubbing each other's burned bodies with soap. Skin peeled away in translucent sheets, falling to the floor like wet paper, revealing raw, red flesh beneath.

Dan's stomach flipped. "What the hell is this, Tom?"

"It's part of the process," Tom said flatly, stepping into the ice-cold shower. "We'll be good as new soon enough."

Dan froze, staring into the shower as Stephanie caught his eye. "Get in, Dan," she said, her voice low and inviting. "The fun's just getting started." She leaned in and kissed one of the other women, her peeling, blistered skin brushing against raw flesh.

Mike grabbed Stephanie from behind, his hands curling around her waist as he pulled her toward him. One of the assistants began scrubbing Tom with a disturbing intensity, their movements intimate and methodical. The room seemed to pulse with a grotesque energy as the scene devolved into a macabre orgy. Stephanie locked eyes with Dan, her gaze unyielding as Mike took her with vicious abandon, her teeth bared in a grimace clenching her teeth harder with each thrust. The other women writhed together, their burned bodies blending in a surreal tableau of pleasure and pain, skin falling to the shower floor.

Dan's stomach churned. He turned abruptly, his breath catching as he bolted out of the bathroom. The door slammed behind him, and he sprinted back to the main house, his pulse pounding in his ears.

Bursting through the heavy front door, he bounded up the stairs two at a time, his feet echoing off the stone walls. Reaching his room, Dan slammed the metal-encrusted door shut and leaned against it, his chest heaving.

"Get ahold of yourself, Dan," he muttered, pacing the room. "What the fuck have we tapped into? Those people are out of their minds."

His hands trembled as he pulled open the nightstand drawer and retrieved the last joint Laurie had rolled for his trip. Lighting it with unsteady fingers, he inhaled deeply, letting the smoke dull his nerves. He sank back onto the black floral bedspread, staring at the ornate ceiling as the tension in his chest began to ease.

Dan closed his eyes, the haze of the joint helping him regain control. But the images from the guesthouse lingered, burned into his mind, impossible to shake.

Dan walked to the door, slid the heavy deadbolt into place, and locked himself in. "Just in case," he muttered under his breath. The solid click offered little comfort, but it was enough to calm him momentarily. He sank back onto the massive bed, the black floral bedspread cool against his clammy skin. Exhaustion overwhelmed him, pulling him into a restless sleep.

The nightmares came swiftly, as though waiting for him just beneath the surface of consciousness. He was floating in the lake, its black water steaming around him. The darkness was alive, swallowing the moonlight until everything vanished into an oppressive void. Then came the voice—deep, guttural, vibrating through his bones.

"Dan Stone. Welcome, my son," it growled.

A force he couldn't see gripped him, crushing the air from his lungs. His chest caved under the pressure, and he felt himself flung across the water like a skipping stone. Dan flipped head over heels, the scalding water forcing its way up his nose, burning like acid. He screamed, the sound muffled by the suffocating heat of the lake.

Panic surged as he saw air bubbles rising—or sinking. Which way was up? He clawed through the water, desperate to remember the trick to find the surface. He broke through, gasping, coughing, choking on the sulfuric steam.

The dock loomed in the distance, far behind the guesthouses, impossibly far away. The voice laughed—a booming, malevolent sound that seemed to echo through his very soul.

Dan swam, his muscles screaming with every stroke, the water searing his flesh. It wasn't just heat; it was corrosive, eating away at his skin like acid. The pain was excruciating, but he pressed on, driven by primal fear and an overwhelming need to survive.

Finally, his hands found the wooden ladder, splintered and rough. He hauled himself up, collapsing onto the dock, his body shaking violently. He coughed and retched, vomiting water mixed with bile, his lungs screaming for oxygen.

Rolling onto his back, he sucked in deep, ragged breaths, his chest heaving. The bright lights of the guesthouse glared into his bloodshot eyes, stinging and cruel.

"This isn't a nightmare," Dan rasped to himself, the realization cold and heavy in his gut. "This is... real."

His skin burned, his mind reeled, and as he stared up at the inky black sky, he knew he'd been somewhere no man should go.

"Wake up, Dan!" he screamed to himself, his voice hoarse and ragged through the blinding pain. His body trembled as he slowly crawled to his knees, every movement an effort against the searing agony. He looked down and saw the skin peeling from his legs, sloughing off in ragged sheets where the dock's splinters had pressed against him.

Dan staggered to his feet, swaying like a drunk, his balance unsteady. The pain was unbearable—every nerve in his body screamed as though still submerged in the boiling black water. His breaths came in shallow gasps, his throat raw.

With each step, he stumbled forward, the lights of the guesthouse swimming before him. It felt a mile away, yet too close at the same time. Terror gripped him, more real than any dream he'd ever known. His wide-open eyes burned, yet he couldn't look away from the world around him, a waking nightmare he couldn't escape.

Each agonizing step brought him closer to the guesthouse. Faint laughter floated through the air—soft, casual, like the aftermath of an innocent night spent among friends. Dan's pulse hammered in his ears as he stumbled forward, dread pooling in his gut. Everything sounded so… normal.

When he reached the window, he hesitated. His breath fogged the glass as he peered inside.

There they were—Stephanie, Tom, the others—all sitting around the main room, clean and calm, draped in towels or lounging as if the nightmare had never happened. Their skin was smooth and flawless, no sign of the burns, blisters, or peeling flesh. Fresh. Perfect.

Dan blinked hard, his mind refusing to process what he was seeing. Just minutes ago, he'd watched them screaming, their bodies raw and ruined in the boiling lake. Now they looked as if nothing had happened at all.

A chill swept over him, colder than the night air.

What the hell was happening?

Dan closed his eyes, the world tilting around him. Finally, he thought, he was going to pass out—wake up in his bed, comforted by the embroidered black roses on the bedspread, the mountain of pillows, and maybe a joint. Yes, he needed a joint. Go to sleep, Dan. Just go to sleep.

But then the front door swung open.

Before he could react, two of the female assistants grabbed his arms, their grip firm and unyielding. "What the—" he croaked, his words cut off as they pulled him into the light.

Dan's eyes snapped open, squinting against the sudden brightness of the guesthouse. The nine team members stood around the living room-kitchen combination; their gazes fixed on him like a congregation waiting for a sermon. Their faces were calm—unnervingly calm—smiling, pristine, untouched by the horror he'd just witnessed.

"Quickly," Tom ordered, his voice sharp. "Get him into the shower. Get some coffee."

Everything moved fast. Too fast. The room spun, hands tugging at him, dragging him deeper inside. Dan wanted to fight, to shout, but he couldn't find his voice. He caught Tom's eye for just a moment—calm, composed, and utterly in control.

Dan was weak, delirious, trapped in that surreal place between sleep and waking. Hands tugged at his clothes, pulling them away. He barely registered the movements—until the shock of ice-cold water hit him like a slap to the face. He gasped, the sudden rush jolting him awake, yet the world still felt hazy, unreal.

The water wasn't normal. It felt thick, viscous, clinging to his skin like a syrup that refused to wash away. It soaked into him, seeped through him, soothing and burning at once.

Then the pain came. A raw, searing agony. Tiny stings from a million bees. Little bites from infinitely small creatures crawling over him, gnawing at his skin, eating away at his subcutaneous fat and connective tissue. Dan's head lolled forward, and he looked down. His breath caught in his throat. The skin on his arms and chest was peeling, sloughing away in ragged sheets. Beneath it, he could see his ribs, pale cartilage tinged with red, all wrapped in a paper-thin layer of translucent, newborn skin. It shimmered under the harsh bathroom lights like something not meant for this world.

"Jesus…" Dan tried to speak, but his voice barely escaped his lips, drowned out by the pounding water and the relentless scrubbing. Hands—so many hands—painfully scrubbed him, tearing away the old, tender flesh with every motion. Each pass over his body sent shockwaves of pain rippling through him, but he couldn't fight them off. Couldn't move.

He felt himself slipping again, spiraling deeper into the dark edges of consciousness, but the hands wouldn't let him go. They kept working, kept cleansing, their touch mechanical, merciless.

Somewhere, through the roar of the water and his own tortured breathing, Dan thought he heard Tom's voice—calm, reassuring, yet chillingly detached.

"It's almost done, Dan. You'll feel better soon. Just let it work."

Dan opened his eyes, and Stephanie was in front of him. She encircled his torso with her arm—her 5'0" frame a beautiful crutch for his 6'5". Dan leaned on her, eyes closing again. "What the hell is this?" he whispered, unsure if the words left his mouth or stayed trapped in his spinning head. Reality flickered like static.

The water stopped. Hands guided him to the guesthouse bedroom, strong but gentle, like he was fragile glass. Dan sank onto the bed. He opened his eyes just enough to see Stephanie above him, kissing him softly. He held on tight, burying his face into the warmth of her neck, breathing her sweet scent and feeling the silk of her red hair against his cheek.

Dan drifted back into sleep.

The bright sun beamed through Dan's eastern-facing window, pulling him from the depths of sleep. He opened his eyes cautiously, unsure if he was awake or still trapped in some fevered dream.

Dan swung his legs over the edge of the tall California king bed, his bare feet landing solidly on the cold stone floor. Feels real, he muttered.

Naked, he inspected himself—his arms, chest, legs, and feet. His skin looked... normal. Fresh, even. Dan walked to the bedroom window, squinting into the glaring winter sunlight.

There, in the front yard, his team of assistants sprinted back and forth like a well-drilled unit.

"Wind sprints, Tom?" Dan muttered, incredulously. He rubbed his face with both hands.

"What the fuck..."

CHAPTER 29

Dan left the house without a word to Tom or the staff. He drove past the ornate iron gate, its intricate black roses glinting faintly in the morning light, and past the lone cabin at the edge of the road. Turning south, he headed for the town of Black Lake, his destination clear—the Oak Bar.

The need to clear his head was urgent, the image of the running maniacs in the yard still fresh in his mind. The office, with its quiet and order, seemed the only place where his thoughts might settle.

As he entered the bar, Bob called out, "Welcome to the morning, Dan. Your coffee is waiting for you."

"Thanks, Bob. I need it."

"I have some bacon and eggs coming as well."

"Just coffee."

"No. You need to eat some food. That coffee will eat you up. Tells you you don't need food. I think it likes to have you all to itself. Eat. They are already coming out of the kitchen."

Dan laughed. "Okay. It was a tough night I could probably use some sustenance."

"Tough, yes I imagine. Tom and his fellows there at the lake. You probably got a taste of their antics."

"I did. What do you know about their antics?"

"Vic figured it out. He couldn't eat. Kind of like where you're going. Couldn't sleep-- plagued by agonizing nightmares every time he nodded off. Figure out that if he swam in the lake that he would be able to sleep. If he got busy and didn't get there, he would pay for it. So, he went out and swam every night. I do myself in fact."

"Bob, you get into that boiling water?"

"I do," Bob said. "Vic was right, if you sit in the water for a time, you feel better and you can sleep without the nightmares."

"Last night?"

"No. I don't need to go every night. I limit myself on the coffee. And the water. I try to stick to beer most of the time," Bob laughed. "No offense Boss."

"Limit?"

"Well, the more you drink the better you feel. The worse the recovery."

"Then don't drink this shit!," Dan exclaimed.

"Hold on now, Son. The water is life giving. It's incredible. Makes you fantastic. The water doesn't just feel great, it makes you great. It just has some costs."

The two sat in silence. Dan was at a loss for words as usual in this town. Dan drank half of his coffee before responding. "I do feel good; better than ever in fact."

"I know you do, Dan. I can see a change just since you came to town."

Dan took another drink of the dark brew. "Bob, I'm going to solve this problem. We have to be able to enjoy the benefits of the lake without the punishment of consuming it. It has to be chemically related to the compounds and there has to be an antidote."

Bob laughed. "Your father said that very thing -- almost word for word sitting on that very barstool."

Dan didn't laugh or smile. "That is uncanny, Bob."

The door to the Oak Bar interrupted their conversation and Tom and Stephanie entered the room. Striding towards him Stephanie threw her arms around Dan's neck and embraced him. "Dan, I missed my ride in with you," she said kissing his cheek.

Bob smiled and locked eyes with Dan for a moment, "Coffee you two?"

"Of course," they replied in unison.

Tom clapped Dan on the shoulder. "Busy night last night Dan. Let's talk about it up in the office. The others headed on back to Dallas."

Bob prepared a tray of eggs, bacon, toast and breakfast rolls and a large pot of coffee. Dan, Tom and Stephanie went up to the office and they sat at the conference table with windows overlooking the statue of William Joseph and the town square.

"Dan, last night you saw something that was certainly very strange to you. But it was important for you to experience that. As well as the nightmare you undoubtedly had last night," Tom stated. "I know this is hard to believe but it is a healing process."

"Bob told me that Vic could only sleep if he cooked himself in the lake before bed," Dan said wryly.

"Vic determined the compounds in the water and the roses imparted some kind of immunity," Stephanie said.

"Immunity? Sounds like a virus."

"It's not a virus," Tom said.

"How can swimming in the water protect you from the water? That makes no sense," Dan objected.

"Vic said the water renewed you from the inside out. Swimming removed the remnants of whatever was left. Like the final polishing. Without it the poisons exuding from you were on the surface," Stephanie said.

"You know a lot about this stuff, Stephanie," Dan said.

"Dan, Stephanie and your father were close. She lived up here with him off and on and assisted him in New Orleans," Tom said.

"You were my father's girlfriend?"

"I was. Really more than that I think," she said.

"Well, that is a little weird to me since we have slept together," Dan said.

"Vic's gone on to a better place Dan. I'm yours now."

"Mine. Ok," Dan laughed. "Even though I barely knew him he was still my father. And that's a bit ick. You know?"

"I helped Vic. I can help you too. It takes a toll. Vic had unbelievably horrible nightmares. Incredibly painful nights of agonizing torture. Far worse than the rest of us. Victor figured out that if he willingly gave himself as a sacrifice the lake gave back, and the nightmares ceased to allow the rejuvenation of sleep. He started this ritual you observed last night. Burning the old tissue off and replacing it with a new flesh, a better flesh born of the material found only in the magical black lake water. Compounds only found in the beautiful dark flowers surrounding and embedded within the waters," she said.

"So, every night you boil yourselves in the lake?"

"No, we generally can't since we aren't here. But, if we are here, we take advantage," Tom said.

"What about the other nights? You have nightmares?"

"Yes. But, not like Vic," Stephanie said. "His were much worse. Most people just have weird dreams with occasional pain. Like dreaming of sticking your finger with the thorns on the roses. Vics would be more like being sliced to ribbons with the thorns. Or maybe dreaming of dipping into the water and immediately waking up screaming. Vic would get stuck there and couldn't come back. He said for weeks at a time. But only an instant really in real time."

"Real time?," Dan asked.

"The water expands your consciousness," Stephanie said. "I don't know. It seems like it takes you somewhere. It slows time or gives you more time. I don't know. The water makes you see problems from perspectives you'd never consider otherwise. Vic claimed it doubled his brainpower just drinking it. When he started consuming the concentrates Sam isolated, he swore it increased his mental capacity tenfold."

"Tenfold. That's a lot of brain power," Dan said, his voice laced with skepticism.

"Maybe a thousandfold," Tom added. "We really don't know the limits yet."

"What makes you think so? Anything tangible? Any evidence Vic was onto anything earth shattering?" Dan asked.

"Well he was a billionaire," Tom said.

Dan pondered this, his thoughts spiraling into possibilities. Certainly Vic was smart to begin with but he had not turned his nest egg into billions until he got to Black Lake. Unlimited mental capacity—solving problems no one else could even fathom. He thought of the old adage that we only use ten percent of our brain. "Yes, there is that," Dan said.

"Vic also figured all this out with the water. He and Sam were isolating the stuff that makes it tick. Moving the research along at a breakneck pace," Tom said.

"Without Vic it would just be William Joseph and his group living in Black Lake with all the miracles," Stephanie said with a just hint of indignation.

"Ok, I see. Yes, Vic was brilliant and the water made him more brilliant," Dan said. "But, think of it; what else could he have done? Create a new fuel, interstellar travel, colonize Mars, crack the mysteries of other dimensions, maybe even time travel. Hell, just solving the damned pollution problems. He could have done so much more," Dan said.

"But he died," Stephanie said.

For just a few seconds the threesome stared at each other and Tom said, "That's why you're here Dan. To carry on. To move us all forward. You are your father, and he is you. That's how it works."

"Trillions in profits," Dan said. The potential seemed boundless, the implications staggering.

"But at a price," Stephanie interjected, her tone dropping to a somber note. "Vic paid the ultimate price. His human body... burned alive. The nightmare took its toll on his dream body, and somehow, it transmuted into his physical form—mind and flesh. Spontaneous combustion." She paused, her eyes distant. "He died screaming in pain, and then... his body just burst into flames. I was there with him."

"Jesus," Dan said.

"He went too far, Dan. That's all," Tom said, his voice steady but edged with warning. "You have to know when to stop. You can't drink enough coffee for it to kill you—not in the way Vic did. Sure, maybe you'll have a nightmare or two, some brief pain. Normally, the dreams are emotionally painful rather than physical. But Vic? He was consuming the equivalent of one hundred cups of coffee a day."

Dan raised an eyebrow. "How much is that exactly?"

Tom nodded, calculating. "Roughly six gallons, give or take. Maybe someone could do it once, but not every day. Vic was planning to live forever, Dan, and he saw the concentrates as his tool to do it. But it wasn't just coffee anymore—it was pure madness."

"Brought on by this fucking water," Dan said.

"Yes, brought on by this fucking miraculous, life-giving water," Tom replied, leaning forward, his eyes glinting with fervor. "I feel fantastic, Dan. I drink our coffee three times a day. Sure, I have vivid nightmares—who doesn't? But I'll live to be a thousand years old. I'll take it. 'Death, where is your sting?'"

Dan rubbed his temples, the weight of Tom's words pressing down on him. "I see it. What would someone give for living forever?"

"Exactly," Tom said, his voice dropping to a conspiratorial whisper. "And we give it to our consumers. But here's the thing—we can't tell them. The rulers of the world? They'd shut us down and kill all of us in a heartbeat if they knew the truth. Immortality isn't just a product, Dan. It's a threat. And we're holding the most dangerous secret on the planet."

"So how do we harness it without popping so far above the radar we get snuffed out?" Dan asked, his voice calm but sharp, cutting through the tense air.

"What?" Tom sounded caught off guard.

"My father used himself as the guinea pig and paid the price. We're dosing our consumers at a fraction of the benefit. Tom let's be real—you're not going to live to be a thousand. Maybe you make it to 99, or 110 if you're lucky. You're not getting enough. Vic would have lived for centuries if he hadn't imploded. But who gives a good goddamn if some regular Joe gets a few extra years? I mean, great—I'm happy to help humanity. But who is helping Dan Stone?"

"I'll drink more," Tom said, a defensive edge creeping into his voice.

"Damn right. All of us will," Dan replied, leaning forward. "Stephanie, do you know how much of the concentrate versus regular coffee and water Vic was taking?"

"Yes," Stephanie said. "He was taking one concentrate pill with every meal, plus drinking coffee like everyone else does. Vic maintained very accurate records. Sam has them all."

Dan nodded, a calculating grin spreading across his face. "So, there you have it. Three pills a day is a lethal dose. One pill? Fine. Two? Risky. Three? You're burnt toast."

Tom frowned. "So, do we increase the levels in the coffee?"

"No," Dan said firmly. "The coffee's good—it's perfect as is. But we add the concentrates to other products for a super-premium price. Think $100 for an energy bar. Call it Brain Food. Maybe we add a quarter of a pill's worth per bar so someone would have to eat a dozen in a day to hit a dangerous level. Keeps them safe while raking in cash."

"And for our team?" Stephanie asked.

"For us," Dan said, "we start eating a pill a day. Tell Sam and his boys to take two. But no one—no one—exceeds two pills a day. We're not burning anyone else alive."

Tom hesitated, then nodded, his gaze hardening with resolve. Stephanie jotted notes, her hand steady, as if the moral weight of the conversation didn't faze her.

Dan smirked, his eyes alight with ambition. "Now we really start moving. We make our people smarter, sharper than anyone else on the planet. We push the envelope. Pay for performance. Make them want it—make them willing to drive themselves to the brink of madness if that is what it takes. Our coffee can add thirty more years to someone's life; with supplements, ten times that. People will pay anything for that kind of power."

Dan leaned back, a dangerous glint in his eye. "But it's not just about selling time. If we're dosing our own people, making them the smartest minds on earth, we'll find solutions no one else even dreams of. Angles only a mind sharpened to the point of a thorn can see. An electric car that never needs charging—pulling electricity from the air, just like the real Nicolai Tesla envisioned. Land on the moon for real this time, send a manned spaceship that leaves the Milky Way. Make the quantum computer actually work. Hell, we could cure fucking cancer by next month."

Tom and Stephanie exchanged glances, unsure whether to feel inspired or terrified. Dan's vision was breathtaking, intoxicating even—but at what cost?

Dan's smirk deepened. "This isn't just coffee anymore. It's the future, let's get to work. And take your pills."

CHAPTER 30

At the same time, Lucas was pulling into town—and so was Lauri.
The cavalry was coming.
Dan needed rescuing.

Lucas had come to save him from the cup.
Lauri, though she didn't know it, was arriving as a lifeline. She just
thought she was coming to see her boyfriend.

At the edge of town, both of them passed the same figure:
A giant of a man with flowing white hair and a long black coat. He stood
motionless on the shoulder of the road, smiling, and raised a hand in a
slow wave as they drove by.

It was friendly.
Scary.
Creepy.

CHAPTER 31

Lucas drove slowly into town, past the old fountain, the quiet town square, and the manicured park that looked more like a movie set than a real place.

He passed a couple standing on the corner and lifted a hand in greeting. They didn't wave back.
They just stared—stone-faced, unmoving, their eyes flat and lifeless.

"More creepy people," he muttered aloud, shifting uncomfortably in his seat.

Still, he pressed on. God would show him the way.

He scanned the streets, taking it all in. The quiet was unnatural. Too clean. Too staged.

He passed a low warehouse with a polished black sign out front: a single black rose embossed on steel. The building glinted in the afternoon sun, modern and out of place. Inside the glass-walled garage, a red Lamborghini sat gleaming, like a trophy behind glass.

Lucas kept driving.

He rounded the edge of town and followed the two-lane road that led toward the lake, unaware how close he already was to the center of it all.

Lucas could feel it—something shifting.

Green-reaching trees lined both sides of the narrow road, their branches arching overhead and weaving together into a tunnel of shadow. Only the faintest shards of light pierced through the canopy, casting flickering patterns across his windshield like stained glass in a ruined cathedral.

He emerged from the tunnel of trees and caught his first full glimpse of Black Lake, sprawling out to the left of the road like an endless, dark mirror. The afternoon sun shimmered off its surface, but there was no comfort in the light—only a slick, metallic sheen that made his stomach turn.

Acres of long-stemmed black roses lined the shoreline, swaying in the wind like they were breathing. A sudden chill crept over Lucas's skin. Without realizing it, his foot pressed harder on the gas.

A bead of sweat rolled from his temple into his left eye, stinging. He wiped it away and took a deep breath, but the air here felt heavier—wrong somehow.

The far edge of the lake passed beside him. He accelerated again.

Moments later, the lake was in his rearview mirror.

Lucas pulled to the side of the road, flung the door open, and vomited onto the gravel shoulder.

Lucas wiped his mouth with the back of his sleeve, trying to catch his breath. The overwhelming, sickeningly sweet aroma of thousands of black roses hung heavy in the air, clinging to his skin and throat.

Then he heard it—low, guttural, and close.

Get the fuck out of here, preacher.

Lucas lurched forward and vomited again, his body recoiling.

CHAPTER 32

Lauri glanced at her phone as she passed a towering iron statue.

Dan had told her to go through town and take the first left just after the lake came into view.

She eased the Corvette through the tunnel of trees, Steppenwolf's "Born to Be Wild" roaring from the radio. Her blonde hair whipped in the wind, and her lips curled into a smile. The air was rich with the scent of roses—sweet, but laced with something spicy, something bold. She liked it.

Then the lake appeared, dark and shimmering.
There was the turn.
And there—just beyond the tree line—was the cabin.

She pulled the Corvette to a stop at the edge of the lake, killed the engine, and stepped out into the breeze—unaware of the eyes watching her from the stillness.

Lauri walked to the cabin and stepped onto the porch. She leaned forward, resting her elbows on the railing. It had been a long drive from Dallas. After weeks apart, she was finally here. She was ready to see Dan.

They knew she was coming.
Dan's phone was monitored. Every message. Every call.

Two men stepped silently out of the cabin.

The last thing Lauri saw was blood filling her vision—
And the boiling black water rushing into her lungs.

Mike gripped the back of her head as he waded into the scalding depths of Black Lake, dragging her under without a word.

Lauri was pulled deep.
Forever deep.

CHAPTER 33

Meetings continued. Plans solidified.

Dan glanced at his phone and sent a quick text.

How's the drive going?

He stared at the screen, waiting for the typing dots to appear.

Nothing.

No response.

He frowned, then slipped the phone back into his pocket, brushing the thought aside.

She's probably just out of service, he told himself.

But the feeling didn't leave.

The meeting broke with laughter and lingering glances.

Stephanie leaned in as she passed, brushing lightly against Dan's side. Her hand lingered on his arm, her voice low. "You were on fire today."

Then the kiss—quick, on the cheek, but not without intention. Giggles followed from the others as they filed out.

Tom gave him a two-finger salute on the way to the SUV. "See you soon. Plan on Dallas in a few weeks. And New Orleans. Lot's to do."

Dan stood at the glass, watching the convoy of black SUVs pull away— taillights blinking like signal flares in the late afternoon haze.

He turned, loosened his collar, and walked back inside.

Bob was already pouring drinks in the lounge. Dan joined him, wordless at first, accepting the glass.

He pulled out his phone, thumb hovering for a second before he typed:

Hello... you in the dead zone of Kansas? Or Oklahoma? WYA.

He hit send.

No response.

Not yet.

Bob took a sip and watched him quietly.
"You know," he said, almost too casually, "some roads... you don't come back from."

Dan raised an eyebrow. "What's that supposed to mean?"

Bob smiled, slow and easy. "Just talking business. Expansion. Focus. You have a very important future."

Dan nodded, something twisted faintly in his gut. He stared at his phone.

Still no response.

She's not coming, Danny Boy. Just like Becca.

Dan ignored the voice. Pushed it down.

She's just around the corner. Bound to be.

Left Dallas at 7.
Six hours to Wichita. Two more to Black Lake. Add lunch. A couple bathroom breaks. Traffic maybe. Nine, ten hours tops.

And that—
That was just about now.

No worries.
No reason to panic.

He stared at his phone again.
Still no response.

Bob turned away, walking toward the bar.
He paused, eyes closing for just a moment—lips moving slightly.

Then—

Buzz.
Dan's phone lit up on the table.
Lauri's face.

He grabbed it instantly.

"Hey there," he said, a grin breaking across his face. "Had me getting crazy up here."

Silence.

He checked the screen. Still connected.
"Hello?" he said, voice sharper now.

Still nothing.

Dan pulled the phone away and saw a blank screen.
No missed call. No log. Nothing.

Dan stared at the screen, his smile fading.
He hadn't imagined it. He'd seen her face. Heard the buzz.

He looked up. Bob was pouring another drink, quiet, composed, as if nothing had happened.

Dan's stomach turned. "Did you see that?"

Bob raised an eyebrow without looking. "See what?"

Dan hesitated. "My phone buzzed. I had a call come in."

Bob set the drink down and gave a small, almost imperceptible smile.

"Okay," he said, "I wasn't really paying attention Boss. Probably a glitchy signal, that happens."

Dan sat at the bar, drinking – Johnny Walker Black --- his old standby. The bar had emptied, leaving only low music and the quiet clink of melting ice in his glass.

He kept checking his phone. Still no response.

"She's probably already at the house," he smiled, dragging a hand down his face. "Probably waiting on me."

He pushed up from the stool, unsteady but determined.

As he turned the corner toward the front door, he bumped hard into a broad back—solid, unmoving.

It was William Joseph. The towering man didn't flinch. He just turned slowly, face impassive. The long white hair, the black coat. Eyes too light, too still.

"She's not here, Dan," William said calmly.

Dan blinked. "What?"

William smiled and then he walked past, boots echoing across the floor, deep bass of laughter low and humming in his throat like a storm just below the surface.

Dan stood frozen for a moment, the words echoing.

He shook it off.

Dan walked back to his garage and fired up the Lamborghini, the engine roaring to life like a beast awakened. The glass doors lifted, and he pulled out, tires whispering over the polished concrete.

As he passed the front of the Oak Bar, he saw him again.
William Joseph, still standing in the doorway.
Still smiling.

Dan could hear it now—a low, rumbling laughter that seemed to come from deep inside the man, like the earth itself was chuckling.

He hit the gas and blew past the giant statue of the man.

In the rearview mirror, the real William Joseph didn't move. Still grinning. Still laughing.

And as the trees swallowed the road ahead, the sound followed him—
faint, distant, but impossibly clear.
That laughter.
That growling, inhuman laughter that echoed through the dark of is mind like it was riding shotgun.

The tunnel of trees thickened around him, branches arching overhead.
He kept driving.

Time drug on. Five minutes. Ten. Almost home.

Dan's knuckles whitened on the wheel.

Then—

He passed it.
The Big Tree. The one that leaned almost over the road—
The one that marked halfway to the house.

Again.

Dan blinked. Swallowed.

He gritted his teeth. "What the fuck."

Dan drove on another ten minutes. There was the same fucking tree.
Again.

He pressed the pedal down harder, the Lamborghini snarling forward.
Trees blurred. Headlights carved through shadows. The speedometer was well past 100 mph.

Two more minutes.

Then—
The same tree.

Still leaning. Still watching.

Again.

And then, without warning, the radio crackled to life.

Static.

Charlie Daniels' The Legend of Wooly Swamp suddenly filled the cabin, the eerie lyrics chilling him to the bone.

Dan slammed the brakes.

The Lamborghini fishtailed, tires screaming as the 14-inch treads bit into dirt and gravel, flinging dust into the tunnel of trees. The car skidded sideways and jolted to a violent stop.

Dan flung the door open and stumbled out.

Breathing hard. Heart racing.

He looked around—

He was standing in the road by the cabin.

Dan left the Lamborghini right there in the road, the scissor door lifted, glowing like a beacon in the dark.

Inside, the radio still blared:

There's things out there in the middle of them woods will make a strong man die from fright...
He stumbled past the cabin, his boots crunching against the gravel.

He could feel it—eyes watching him.

A hot wind slid off the lake shaking the long stems of the black roses, raking his hair across his face.

The sweet aroma of the black roses filled his lungs, thick and cloying.

He didn't stop.

Dan swallowed hard and kept walking, his footsteps slowing as he approached the iron gate that wrapped around the house. The gate opened welcoming him home.

CHAPTER 34

The weight of Lucas's mission bore down on him like a millstone, the thing that scared him most being the very real possibility of failure. Dan had to know the truth of what was happening to him and what would become of him before taking the final step. Dan was being led by the father of lies. If he couldn't turn Dan away from this path, countless lives would be plunged into chaos, pain, and unspeakable strife—a living hell on earth.

God, in His infinite wisdom, had chosen Lucas for this monumental task, placing faith in his ability to confront the most critical, faltering soul in human history. The enormity of it made Lucas's hands tremble. There was no higher purpose, no greater test, than guiding this man in his moment of judgment. All of humanity hung in the balance.

But what if he failed? Then it was God's will. Right? Lucas wasn't sure of that one.

Dan Stone was no ordinary man. If he truly embraced the darkness inside him, he could usher in an era of unparalleled suffering. The power being offered to him was seductive, and the devil, ever the master of deception, would never reveal the full cost of wielding it. Dan was being manipulated into a role that would doom his soul to eternal torment. The devil's plan was elegant in its cruelty: to use Dan as an instrument of destruction in life and to claim him fully in death.

Lucas's task was clear but impossibly steep—to open Dan's eyes to the truth, to pull him from the brink, to convince him to turn back. He had to succeed. Failure meant losing Dan forever, and with him, the hope of humanity.

The journey had been long and fraught with unanswered questions, but Lucas finally arrived at Black Lake. The cabin sat nestled among the darkened trees, its weathered wood blending seamlessly into the shadows. It seemed like the forest itself had conspired to keep it hidden.

Lucas stepped out of the car and scanned the area, his heart heavy with the uncertainty of what lay ahead.

He was baffled by the enormity of his task. How was he, a mere man, supposed to reach Dan in the depths of his descent? Lucas had been guided here, but now he stood at the edge of the unknown. The house remained distant, obscured in part by a veil of overgrown vegetation and the sinister black roses that flourished unnaturally close to the water's edge.

He walked toward the lake, each step weighted with hesitation and hope. When he reached the shoreline, he knelt, his eyes fixed on the water. The lake was breathtaking, mesmerizing in its stillness. The surface shimmered with an unnatural, obsidian-like sheen, its dark beauty exuding a pull that felt both divine and malevolent. The air was thick with the intoxicating scent of the black roses. Their aroma seemed to cloud his thoughts, yet at the same time, offered him a strange sense of clarity.

Lucas clasped his hands and bowed his head. "Lord, guide me. Show me what to do. I am lost without You."

As he prayed, the scent of the roses deepened, wrapping around him like a silken cocoon. His breathing slowed, his heart calmed, and the tension in his body ebbed away. A sense of serenity washed over him, and before he knew it, sleep claimed him. Lucas slowly laid down at the dark waters edge.

In his dream, he stood in a vast, barren landscape, its crimson skies swirling with an unnatural fire. A voice, guttural and menacing, shattered the silence.

"You will not take him from me," it growled.

Lucas turned and was faced with a towering figure cloaked in shadows. Its eyes burned like twin coals, and its presence exuded a power that pressed on Lucas's chest, threatening to crush him.

"This man, this Dan Stone, is mine," the figure snarled, its voice a blend of venom and triumph. "You will not pull this man from my grasp—this meat from my jowls. He is marked. He is chosen. And he will serve me."

Lucas's knees buckled under the weight of the words, but he stood firm, his faith anchoring him. "He is not yours," Lucas said, his voice trembling but resolute. "He still has a choice. And I will fight for his soul with everything I have."

The figure laughed, a sound that echoed like the cracking of stone. "Fool. You have no idea what you're up against." It leaned closer, its breath searing the air around them. "Watch as he falls. And when he does, you will know the futility of your fight."

The dream dissolved in a cacophony of laughter and fire, and Lucas awoke with a start, the scent of roses still heavy in the air. His heart pounded in his chest, his skin damp with sweat. The lake glimmered before him, silent and serene, as if mocking the vision he had just endured.

And then—without warning—a wave erupted from the surface, crashing into him with scalding heat, searing his skin, burning his face.

Lucas screamed, rolling away from the water's edge—

Straight into a tangle of black roses.

The razor-sharp thorns tore into him, slicing his arms and back, shredding his shirt like paper.

He thrashed, crying out as blood soaked the thorns.
They clung to him like they were feeding.

Lucas tore himself free from the infectious roses and stumbled through the treeline, bleeding and trembling. The black brambles had shredded his shirt, his arms and back striped with deep, oozing gashes. Thorns still clung to his skin in places—barbed like hooks, tearing with every step.

His breath came ragged. Blood dripped from his fingertips, soaking the waistband of his pants, sticking hot against his skin. Pain pulsed through his spine, his shoulders, his jaw.

He found the car—more by instinct than sight—and collapsed against it. Gritting his teeth, he yanked off what was left of his shirt. His back burned—he couldn't tell if it was from the scalding lake water, the lacerations, or both.

He dropped to his knees beside the door. The ground was hot, almost vibrating beneath him, humming with something unnatural. Something alive. Something watching.

He raised his head. He stared at the lake, his resolve hardening. Whatever lay ahead, he would not give up. Not on Dan. Not on humanity.

The battle for Dan's soul was raging.

CHAPTER 35

Tom and the assistants returned to Black Lake a week later. A fast turnaround from New Orleans, Dallas and Kansas. The ten Black Lake businesspeople including Dan filed down the hall and to the elevator. Crowding in Stephanie pushed her backside into Dan. He smelled her sweet perfume and felt her red hair on his face as she leaned into him. The elevator was crowded but everyone could sense she was marking her territory. A few of the other women exchanged glances, their eyes flicking toward Dan, curiosity sparking between them.

The elevator doors slid open, and they stepped into Dan's office suite. The assistants filed out first, followed by Tom, with Dan bringing up the rear. As the others dispersed into the suite, Dan lingered for a moment, considering a different path. He thought about riding the elevator back down, jumping into his car, and heading straight to Vegas—professional escorts, world class food, unlimited booze and the siren call of a carefree life.

The thought tugged at him, but he knew better. Dan knew he was home. Lauri had opted out. No call – No show. Ghosted him. Story of his life. Another woman who decided Dan Stone wasn't enough for her; even with all his money. God must have other plans for him. Right. God. Still, he could see he was in, and there was no getting out. He wasn't blind. If he was going to do this, he might as well go all in. And put her behind him. She was probably better off without him anyway. He stepped out of the elevator and let the doors close behind him. That was it. Certainly no turning back now with the water washing over the bridge as it were..

Stephanie sauntered over to Dan's desk, a playful smirk curling her lips as she slid into his chair, crossing her legs with deliberate ease. Dan followed, raising an eyebrow as he leaned against the desk.

"Stephanie," he said with a grin, "you're quite the little siren. I don't mind but get out of my chair."

She pouted dramatically, her red hair catching the light as she stood. "Fine," she teased, brushing past him.

Dan settled into his seat, but Stephanie immediately leaped onto his lap, her laughter echoing through the room. Without hesitation, she grabbed his face and kissed him deeply, her energy electric and unrelenting.

Caught off guard, Dan hesitated for only a moment before he wrapped an arm around her, returning the kiss with equal fervor. "Work to do" he murmured against her lips.

"Good," she whispered, grinning mischievously. "Let's get to it."

"Real work."

The room full of businesspeople ignored the two and set to work breaking out their laptops and paperwork.

Dan pushed her off his lap. "Ok go make me some money," he laughed. Stephanie was a true brazen piece of work. But likable. And he knew where she stood as a woman who was content pleasing the boss in any way he saw fit.

Today, Norman, Oklahoma was on the list. The team would move fast— plant a Black Lake Coffee near campus. The target was a very popular hangout The Cannafe, a cannabis-infused coffee shop on Campus Corner. Dan approved the buyout for a ridiculous sum to move fast and acquire a marijuana license to merge with Black Lake Coffee in a new product line. A perfect pairing for the student population.

Tom approached his desk, "Let's take a walk. Let them do their thing. Work, work, work."

Dan nodded, and the two men exited the office, rode the elevator and stepped into the fresh air. They strolled toward the statue of William Joseph, its imposing iron form towering over the fountain. They settled onto the stone enclosure surrounding the wishing well, the sound of trickling water filling the silence.

Tom leaned back, his smile broad. "You've got big plans, Dan. Vic would've liked that. But, I'm concerned."

Dan stared at the water, its dark surface reflecting the statue's shadow. "Big plans for a big reason. The water is transformative. Healing. I ripped my neck and hand open on those damn thorns. I healed in minutes with the water. Conversely, Vic burned alive."

Tom turned, dipping his fingers into the fountain. He swirled the water, his gaze fixed on the imposing iron figure of William Joseph. "Have you met the big man?" Tom nodded toward the statue.

"William Joseph? Yeah, I met him the other day. Seems nice enough—in a serial killer kind of way," Dan said, smirking.

Tom didn't laugh. "He isn't nice."

Dan raised an eyebrow, leaning back. "This statue, what, it's his great-great-grandfather or something? Guess his family's been running the show in this little town for a couple of centuries."

Tom's lips curled into a faint, knowing smile. "Dan, this statue is William Joseph himself."

Dan blinked, glancing back at the towering iron figure. "Okay, sure. Bob said this thing's been here for a hundred years. Must've heard him wrong."

"You heard him right," Tom said evenly. "That big bastard is hundreds of years old."

Dan's laugh was sharp, "Okay," he laughed.

"It's the water, Dan." Tom's voice was calm, deliberate. "It's the fucking fountain of youth."

Dan stared at him, his smirk fading. "So the big man is old. Makes sense. We knew the water was the cure-all."

"It's real," Tom interrupted, dipping his hand into the fountain and letting the water run through his fingers. "That's why your hand healed. The Black Lake water doesn't just heal cuts, Dan. It cures everything. Aging, sickness—it's all just a disease. And the water fixes it."

"Right. And Vic put it in coffee. We know this."

"Yes, he did. Have you seen the news?" Tom asked, his tone matter of fact. "People everywhere are claiming healings. Miracle coffee. It's everywhere—news outlets, social media. I saw a TikTok where a guy cut off his finger trying to prove the coffee's healing power."

Dan laughed, shaking his head. "Did it work?"

"No," Tom chuckled. "But in a few minutes, there was no wound—just no finger."

Dan whistled low, "So, we know the lake, the roses, the compounds Vic and Sam isolated—something in them heal and cure. Now we may have some real evidence rather than Vic's anecdotal experiences. And mine. That's truly amazing. World-changing amazing."

Tom nodded, his face turning serious. "It's more than amazing, Dan. It's polarizing. There's a lot of talk about God delivering holy water to heal his people. On the other side, people are calling it Satan's work."

Dan frowned, "God or Satan, huh? Miracle or curse? Yes, I heard about this back in Denver. At the time I passed it off as tabloid bull shit. But now we know those kooks are customers."

"Exactly," Tom said, leaning back against the fountain's stone edge. "And it's not just chatter. People are choosing sides, Dan. The cat is out of the bag it seems."

"Well, that's good," Dan said, smirking. "No bad press and all that. Ultimately, Vic wanted to get this miracle out to the world. He's the real deal—what's his name? Ponce de León?"

Tom grinned. "Yeah, Ponce de León. Only Vic actually found the fountain of youth."

"So, if William Joseph is truly hundreds of years old, then this whole town should be filled with centenarians," Dan said, glancing toward the park. "I haven't seen any eighteenth-century villagers wandering around here. Where is everyone?"

Tom chuckled, the sound low and unsettling. "Well, the water doesn't just keep you alive, Dan. It keeps you... useful. The ones who drink it don't grow old, but not all of them stick around. Some folks can't handle what comes with it."

Dan raised an eyebrow. "They leave?"

Tom's grin faded slightly, and he turned to the statue of William Joseph, running a hand over the stone base as though it might whisper a secret. "Not exactly. The water changes you, Dan. For some, it's a blessing. For others... well, let's just say the side effects aren't always kind."

Dan felt a chill crawl up his spine. "Side effects like what?"

Tom didn't answer immediately. Instead, he dipped a finger into the fountain, watching as the water dripped slowly from his hand. "Some can't eat, some can't sleep. Some say it brings utter madness."

Dan's stomach tightened. "Well we know Vic spontaneously combusted."

Tom stared ahead, his expression unreadable.

"Maybe Vic went crazy and intentionally overdosed."

"He was having intense nightmares," Tom said finally, his voice heavy. "I think the sleep deprivation got to him."

Dan frowned. "Well sleep deprivation doesn't cause you to burst into flames. Sam told me Vic was experimenting on himself—testing the compounds they were distilling from the water and the black roses. Sam says they're chemicals we haven't ever seen on Earth."

Tom nodded slowly. "It's not just the water, Dan. The black roses... they've been leaching their juices into the lake for tens of thousands of years. Feeding the Black Lake, and in turn, feeding off it. It's like one giant, self-sustaining biosphere. A closed loop brewing up this miracle water we are all drinking--this mother's milk."

Dan leaned against the fountain's stone edge, trying to absorb it all. Tom continued, "It's like that forest in Oregon—the one they say is the largest living organism on Earth, all connected by its root system. The Black Lake and the roses—they're one and the same. An ancient, symbiotic system."

Dan shook his head, trying to piece it all together. "So, this whole thing— this lake, the roses—it's been alive for longer than we've been keeping track. And somewhere along the line, William Joseph stumbles into town and starts drinking the water. He seems like he's a little crazy, but he's still here. The water or the coffee isn't deadly in small doses then."

Tom nodded thoughtfully. "That's the thing. The lake water on its own— it's powerful, sure, but manageable for most people, like the coffee. We know Vic pushed the boundaries too far. He wasn't just drinking the water. He was taking concentrated doses of compounds from the roses themselves. That's a whole different level of exposure."

Dan frowned. "Ok, so it wasn't concentrated water. It was concentrated roses. And they killed him."

Tom's expression darkened. "It didn't kill him outright. It pushed him to the edge and kept him there. The nightmares, the experiments... it all built up. He couldn't shut it off, couldn't step back. The lake doesn't just heal, Dan. It changes you. And not everyone comes out the other side intact."

Dan looked back at the fountain, the water shimmering darkly in the light. "So, William Joseph survives for centuries, and Vic couldn't handle a few years of it."

"Dan, most people are fine," Tom said. "They love their morning coffee—it gives them ten times the energy of regular coffee without the caffeine jitters. Just pure, clean clarity. They aren't sick ever again. They heal from whatever ails them just by waking up to their morning joe."

"Well, Tom, I don't think it's that simple. What about the people losing their minds? Aside from Vic overdosing on the black roses—you said many people are experiencing side effects from the Black Lake coffee."

"Yes," Tom admitted. "Morning coffee, afternoon coffee—even a cup in the evening—that's usually okay. But some people crave more. The effects intensify with increased consumption. Regular use provides clarity. More leads to brilliance, sparks of creative thought. Even more brings breakthroughs you never imagined. It's like your thoughts speed up—to light speed. On steroids."

Tom's expression grew serious. "But that's when the trouble starts. The mind races too fast, thoughts spiral out of control. Some can't handle the surge—it overwhelms them."

"I'm on my third venti this morning," Dan said with a half-smirk. "I don't feel brilliant. I feel... good."

"Exactly," Tom replied, his tone steady. "You're being useful. Your mind is active; you're problem-solving. That's the sweet spot. But that's why I wake up and run like crazy. I require my team to do the same every morning. Anytime they start feeling anxious, I tell them to get moving. Run, walk, think—just move."

Dan tilted his head, intrigued. "Why?"

"Because if you don't keep your body and mind engaged, the water seems to... apply its power elsewhere," Tom said, his voice dropping slightly. "Areas of your being you're not actively using. It's like it seeks out the void and fills it—your emotions, your fears, your desires. If you're not in control, it will take control."

Dan stared at his coffee, the dark liquid swirling in the venti cup. For the first time, the drink felt less like a luxury and more like a loaded weapon. "And if it takes control?"

Tom shrugged, his eyes narrowing slightly. "I don't know—seems different for everyone, but there's a common thread. Water and roses. Like a psychic invasion." He paused, looking down at the fountain. "Vic said he'd dream about being in the lake. I've had dreams like that myself, and let me tell you, they're not pleasant. The water is always hot, scalding. You feel it in the dream, Dan. It's so real."

Dan's expression darkened. "Hot enough to burn obviously. Based on Vic."

Tom nodded grimly. "Vic said he'd wake up drenched in sweat, his skin red, inflamed—like he'd actually been burned. The dreams started leaving marks. Real burns. By the end..." Tom hesitated, his voice faltering. "Your father was obsessed with finding an antidote. That's why he was taking the concentrate. He said it made him profoundly brilliant—like his mind was operating on an entirely different plane. He felt he had to figure out a way to counteract the negatives."

Tom frowned, his gaze distant. "Vic was charred beyond recognition. We now have customers reporting a range of side effects. It's only a matter of time before someone bursts into flames."

Dan's grip tightened around his coffee cup. He looked at the dark water in the fountain, rippling gently. It shimmered innocuously, yet now he could feel something sinister. "And you still drink this stuff?"

Tom let out a hollow laugh. "We all do, Dan. Because when you don't..." He trailed off.

"Hard to get off the horse, I guess," Dan offered.

"More like impossible," Tom said. "When people try to stop, they get sick—fast. That's the power of Black Lake Coffee. Our customers aren't just loyal; they're desperate for their next cup. And if they give in to the water's insistence—more and more and more—that's when the bad stuff happens."

"That's addiction, Tom. Like heroin addiction," Dan said, his voice quiet.

"Immortality comes at a cost, Dan. And we, my friend, hold the reins. Every cup we sell binds another soul to Black Lake, one sip at a time— and the more they drink, the better it gets." Tom's voice wavered between awe and unease. "We're selling the mother's milk of life and death to millions." He paused as if trying to shake the thought. "They need us. And we're the ones who decide how far they go."

"Let's remember that Vic hit the lethal dose using the concentrates. So regular coffee won't torch anyone."

Tom and Dan sat silent for a full minute listening to the sound of the trickling water in the stone fountain of the centuries old William Joseph. Then Dan heard a voice say,

You are the leader of Black Lake now --- time to take control.

Then Dan said, "Let's go back into the office."

Dan stood and walked purposefully into the Oak Bar his father had built, down the polished hallway to the elevator. He and Tom rode up in silence.

In the office suite the assistants were hard at work crunching numbers and discussing sales and marketing scenarios.

Striding to the long walnut-paneled wall, adorned with framed photos— the construction of the estate, the transformation of Strings into the Oak Bar, and the first fleet of Black Lake Coffee trucks—Dan called out. "Okay, listen up." His voice cut through the murmurs as Tom and the assistants shuffled, setting up laptops and documents. The room quieted.

"It's time for a change," Dan declared, pacing slowly, his tone firm and deliberate. "I've reviewed Victor's plans and taken a hard look at where the company is now. It's impressive—more than impressive. Vic built a global phenomenon. But we're not done. Not even close. I have a new plan."

Tom stepped forward. "Dan, we've got this. Let us show you what we have figured out with only a week on the supplements."

Dan turned sharply, silencing Tom with a raised hand. "No, Tom. Let me tell you where it's going." He took a breath, steadying himself, as the room leaned in. "The Black Lake Coffee concept is brilliant. Vic made us the world's largest coffee brand. Expansion is at a level no one thought possible. But we're not just coffee, are we?"

Dan's piercing gaze swept the room, lingering on each face. "Everyone in this room knows—it's the water. That's what makes us unstoppable."

Tom folded his arms, his smile faint but approving. "Yes, Dan. It's the water."

Tom's expression darkened, the corner of his mouth twitching. For a moment, he opened his mouth as if to continue, but he stopped, his eyes fixed on Dan like he was watching a ship sail straight into a storm.

Dan nodded, pacing again. "It's more than the water. I spent time with Sam and his team in New Orleans—they've broken it down to the molecular level. What we've discovered is that it's not just superior chemistry. It's the spores from the roses. They're not from here— another planet, another origin entirely. The compounds in those roses, the properties in the water... humanity has never seen anything like it."

He stopped pacing and leaned against the wall, both hands pressing into the edge of the table. "My father was ingesting a concentrated form of those compounds—the very essence that makes Black Lake water so powerful. We're calling it Black Rose. He took too much. It killed him. You've all been taking one pill daily for the past week."

The nine assistants glanced around the room, wide-eyed.

"Any side effects?" Dan asked, scanning their faces.

Mike spoke first. "Pretty bad nightmares."

Stephanie added, "I woke up soaked in sweat after dreaming I was drowning in the lake. Not as bad as Vic, but... it scared me."

Dan gave a slow nod. "So the question is—how do we push this into the population without killing people?"

He looked to Tom. "Let's find a town. Something small. We dose it, monitor the results. Push the exposure until we hit the LD50, then back it off. We need to know the ceiling."

Tom hesitated. "Dan, we might kill some people."

Dan looked at him squarely. "And how do we expand beyond the coffee business if we don't know what the product does in volume? If we plan to put Black Rose into everything—from supplements to soft drinks— we need real data. Controlled results. A test group. Without it, we're flying blind."

"Okay, people—where do we test it?" Tom asked, looking around the room.

"What's the target population size?" Stephanie asked.

"Smaller," Dan said. "Under 100,000."

"A college town," Zoey offered. "Young people. If there are side effects, we'll know it's from us—not age, not underlying health."

Tom nodded. "Smart. Controlled demographic. Lots of data points."

"Somewhere close to here," another assistant added. "Halfway between Black Lake and Dallas..."

"Norman," said Zoey. "University of Oklahoma. Big enough to matter, small enough to monitor."

Dan's eyes narrowed slightly, calculating. "Probably won't kill anyone there so that's good. Strong hearts. Let's get to work."

The assistants sprang into action, opening laptops, scribbling notes, and murmuring excitedly. Dan stepped back, letting the chaos swell around him, feeding off the energy of the room.

The warnings, the doubts—none of it mattered now. This was his empire.

Then, without warning, his mind went black.

Dan was elsewhere—transported.

For a moment, his mind's eye was no longer his own. The vision came unbidden:

Cities in ruin and cities reborn under his seal. Men and women falling to their knees at his approach. Armies marching beneath soft cream banners crowned with a single black rose. Monuments rising from shattered earth, gleaming with steel thorns.

Dan blinked. The vision receded—but not completely.
Its echo remained, pulsing behind his eyes.

He exhaled, low and steady, the weight of it pressing on his chest.
The future wasn't a dream. It was a calling.

"Dan Stone," he said softly. "Tyrant. Ruler of the known universe."

"All in," he whispered.

CHAPTER 36

Dan's first dreams were as Stephanie and Tom had described—painful, haunting memories dredged from the depths of his past. Faces he had wronged, voices of women, harsh memories of Rebecca, echoed through his subconscious, accusing him, pleading, condemning. Friendships he'd betrayed haunted his dream life, each one more vivid than the last. These dark emotions left his psyche frayed and disturbed upon waking.

Then they became nightmares. Beginning innocuously, as dreams are wont to do, disjointed and fleeting, they morphed into grotesque examples of terror.

Dan was standing on the edge of the black lake on a clear night, its surface calm and still, the moon reflecting beautifully on its inky black waters. A slight breeze blew in his direction, and he could smell the sweet spice of the black roses. The air slowly became think with a dark fog rolling towards him. Soon he was enveloped in a black smoke like mist. The scent of the roses became cloyingly sweet and then acrid, burning his nose and throat. Before he could take a step, the ground beneath him gave way, and he slid into the searing water scratching and tearing his bare skin on jagged rocks in the process.

The pain was immediate, the scalding water ate at his flesh like acid. Dan clawed at the edge desperate to pull himself back up onto the shoreline, but the ground continued to collapse beneath his groping fingers. Vines looped around his ankles as the black roses pulled him into their dark lair. He was capsized. Thrashing to reach the surface he knew the lake had no bottom, he could see no shore—just an endless abyss of boiling agony. His screams were swallowed by the water as he was pulled deep into the abyss.

A low, guttural voice, ancient and malevolent, rumbled from the depths, vibrating through his bones. He could feel it. He could hear it despite struggling to hold his breath as he was dragged into the depths.

"Dan Stone. You are mine," the voice growled.

The water wrapped around him like molten chains, forcing him deeper. The darkness smothered him. His skin blistered and peeled away exposing nerves and muscle.

Dan saw contorted faces frozen in silent screams. Tom, Stephanie, Rebecca, even Vic—each locked in torment, their vacant dead eyes pleading.

The guttural laugh continued, louder, shaking the very fabric of his soul.

Dan woke with a gasp, his breathing labored, his sheets soaked, his skin red and burnt.

Each time he fell asleep, the torment resumed. The water and black roses were a living biome, breathing as one, thick with an unknown dark purpose. An ancient and primal evil with its own ambition.

The lake was calling him.

CHAPTER 37

Dan sat at the massive walnut desk, its polished surface reflecting the faint glow of the desk lamp. The room was eerily quiet, save for the rain tapping against the windows and the occasional groan of the old building settling into itself.

Dan was working nearly all the time and drinking coffee to keep his mind sharp. He was taking the requisite two concentrated Black Rose pills each day. He was not eating despite telling himself he needed to. He wasn't sleeping as he tried that already and it resulted in pain and agony, and he was damned if he was going to boil himself in the lake to get a good night's sleep. But he was close to his breaking point.

That night he was looking for a paperclip. He opened the top drawer, expecting to find nothing more than the usual office clutter—pens, post its, maybe an old notebook, certainly a paperclip. He pulled the drawer open wide searching front to back. Then he saw something unexpected and withdrew a heavy envelope, its edges yellowed with age, sealed with a clay stamp bearing the unmistakable emblem of a black rose. The seal felt cold to the touch, almost alive, and he hesitated for a moment, staring at the intricate design. There was no name on the envelope, but something about it—the weight of it, the care with which it had been hidden—told him it was meant for him. With a deep breath, Dan broke the seal, the clay cracking like brittle bone, and slid out a folded sheet of parchment. The texture was coarse beneath his fingertips, the handwriting bold and deliberate, each stroke imbued with urgency. His heart pounded as he began to read.

The weight of the letter settled over Dan like a shroud. The cracked clay seal with its intricate rose design still rested on the desk beside the envelope, its broken edges symbolic of the finality of what he was about to learn. He gripped the fragile parchment, the words burning into his mind as he read them again.

My dear son,

This will puzzle you, scare you, and perhaps, I hope, help you avoid destroying your own life as I will have done by the time you are seated at my desk. I discovered that the greatest fear in life is loneliness, and ironically, life is ultimately defined by being alone. In the end, Dan, no one will go through that final door with you. Even with all I know to be true, it is still terrifying.

The most powerful desire man will forever retain is the will to live. Honestly, I cannot tell you if I hope for a conscious hereafter or pray for the sweet bliss of nothingness. The hours I have spent and the pain I have endured have left me on the edge of sanity. Still, I cling to the faint hope that this message reaches you in time to make a difference. Something within me—perhaps a spark of goodness—screams against what I have become. I have suffered an eternity, but I feel compelled to warn you.

This will likely sound strange to you since you are just arriving—just seeing the lake for the first time. You will experience something unique in the coming days, something I have come to call mind travel. Soon, you will understand what I mean. I must convey the prophecies I have received, no matter how cursed they make me feel.

If you have not already accepted, or if you have rejected as illogical, the idea of an afterlife, you are in for a shock. There is life after death, Dan. In fact, the Bible is right—all of it. There is a God who rules the heavens, and there is also a demon, a Satan, who claims dominion over the souls damned for all eternity. God has placed him in charge of death, and he suffers every pain that mortal man experiences. And here, in Black Lake, his reach is absolute.

The people of this town are not of God, Dan. They belong to Lucifer himself.

How disgusting that mortal man—conscious for only a heartbeat in the grand passage of time—would trade everything for a few more hours of life, a taste of forbidden knowledge, or fleeting power. Yet that is what they have done, and the lake fuels their choice.

If you haven't already discovered it—or if you have rejected it—the idea of an eternal existence beyond death is not a fantasy. You will find yourself standing at a crossroads, Dan. There are two paths, as ancient texts describe: the light and the dark.

Regrettably, the former is not an option for you.

Daniel, my son, I am truly sorry.

The last line struck like a hammer, and Dan had to steady himself against the desk. His breath came fast and shallow as he stared at the final words, the ink smudged as though written by an unsteady hand.

He didn't want to believe it—any of it. Yet, after coming to Black Lake he knew there were forces at work no one on earth could explain or understand. The truth in the letter had begun to work its way into his mind, whispering, pulling at the edges of his sanity.

By the time he finished reading Vic's words, his head pounded, his stomach churned. What the hell is this? The unease gnawed at him—at his mind, at his body—like something alive.

"Holy shit," Dan moaned, clutching the edge of the desk for balance. The letter left him reeling. He needed air. He needed to get numb.

Dan dragged himself downstairs to the Oak Bar. His footsteps on the wood planks echoed through the empty hallway, his mind clouded and bewildered.

# # #

Bob saw him approach and always the consummate bartender said, "Just a minute," he moved over behind the bar and grabbed a bottle of Old Grandad and two iced tea glasses. Bob poured a double shot in each and filled them with the ice-cold water from the shining bar tap.

"I read a letter Vic left me in his desk drawer. He really fucking lost it Bob?" Dan said praying he would agree.

"Wrong, Dan." Bob slid the drink across the shining wooded bar.

Dan drank the alcohol lake water concoction down. As the liquid hit his stomach Dan felt a pulling sensation burning though his chest and gut momentarily flashing back to the harrowing night gulping down the scalding waters of Black Lake itself.

Dan leaned over beside the bench and vomiting. Dan dry heaved a few times and was sure his stomach was being forced up through his throat. Water poured from his eyes as every muscle in his body painfully contracted time and again. It was finally over, and Dan relaxed to catch his breath once again. Wiping the sour liquid from his lips Dan looked at the pool of sick left on the floor. From the color and consistency Dan judged it to be ninety nine percent alcohol and one percent blood.

What happening to you?" Bob asked.

Sitting upright Dan said, "I was hoping you could tell me." Dan let out a deep breath and wiped his mouth and face on a white linen napkin.

"I told you to eat."

"I'll be dead before long at this rate." Dan leaned over and spit a chunk of something curdled onto the floor. "Sorry about the mess, Bob. Got a mop?"

"Yes, I do." Bob got up again and disappeared behind the bar.

"I need to see a doctor."

Bob rolled out a mop bucket and mop, rung out the mop and leaned against it on the floor. "There is another option, Dan, in fact, it may be your only option."

"What's that, Bob?"

"William Joseph is the leader," Bob stated. "Kill him."

"Bob. That old man has nothing to do with me puking my guts out. We all know it's the water or the roses or whatever nano bytes are in there. Let me mop up and get out of here. Sit down. Have another drink," Dan let out a dry laugh.

"The supernatural things that happen in this world can't always be explained in human terms," Bob said.

Dan stood up and took the mop from Bob. The old bartender ambled around the bar and did what he did best and made two more ice cold drinks.

"Maybe you are right, Bob. But killing William Joseph doesn't even resemble sanity. I have to do something. I don't know what."

"You need to become one with the power," Bob said solemnly.

"What does that mean?"

"You are fighting it. You have to embrace it. Drink but also eat. Let the nightmares take you. Get into the lake and let it have you. All of you."

Dan smirked, "All of me. Ok." He reached over and picked up the glass. Raising it in the air Dan chuckled darkly and shook his head, "Well, here is to bat shit crazy, Bob."

Dan held his liquor for almost ten seconds before he vomited in the mop bucket.

CHAPTER 38

Dan made it back to the house and passed out. Blissfully, nightmare free. Overnight the snow had covered every living thing with a blanket of white. The trees looked like lifeless brittle skeletons. Dan wanted to stay in and curl up by the fireplace, sip Remy Martin cognac delicately warmed over the fire and feast on spoonfuls of black caviar on toast points... and drift off in a restful slumber.

This was a nice fantasy but Dan couldn't eat much without feeling sick or actually puking. Nervously, he walked across the living room pausing every three paces to stare out the giant frosted glass windowpanes of the grand home. The snow drifts nearly buried some of the smaller trees in the acre in front. He could hear the strong north wind commanding.

###

Lucas adjusted his coat against the chill as he walked down the winding path that led from the lake. The black roses seemed to lean toward him as he passed, their dark petals glinting in the faint light like they were wet with morning dew—or something darker. The air grew heavier with every step, charged with an unearthly tension that made him grip the small wooden cross around his neck. He had seen many imposing structures in his life, but he could feel this one before he even laid eyes on it.

And then, through the parting trees, it emerged.

The house rose like a cathedral of shadow, its spires piercing the gray sky. Massive and commanding, it stood as though carved from the very night itself. The façade was polished black stone, smooth as obsidian and cold to the touch, accented with dark wood so rich it seemed to drink in the surrounding light. Gothic arches adorned the upper floors, and the windows—vast, gleaming eyes—reflected the bleakness of the surrounding landscape.

Lucas paused, his breath catching in his throat. The place radiated power, dark and suffocating, yet it was mesmerizing in its perfection. He had seen something like this before. His mind flashed to the abbey in Scotland, its towering black gabbro stones and sharp, angular beauty. This house was its twin in a twisted, unnatural way—a mirror of the sacred, corrupted by something unspeakable.

The grand staircase swept up to the massive double doors, flanked by gargoyle-like statues that seemed to move when he wasn't looking directly at them. His fingers tightened around the cross. It was as if the house itself were alive, watching, waiting.

Lucas swallowed hard, muttering a prayer under his breath. "Lord, give me strength."

But even as he prayed, he couldn't shake the sense that he was being drawn into the house—not by his own will, but by something far older, far darker.

# # #

The incessant chime of the doorbell pulled Dan from a restless slumber—the first sleep he'd managed in three days. It wasn't refreshing; his body felt heavier, weaker, as though the rest had sapped what little strength he had left.

The sharp ringing gave way to persistent knocking. Dan groaned, forcing his eyes open and dragging himself upright. The couch beneath him was comfortable enough, but his muscles and bones ached as if he'd been hit by a freight train. Rest wasn't restorative anymore. It was draining.

The knocking continued, relentless, until Dan managed to stand, his head swimming as he stumbled toward the massive wooden door. He leaned his weight against the polished walnut frame and called out hoarsely, "Who is it?"

Dan walked towards the big wood and iron door.

"Dan Stone?" came an unfamiliar voice, muffled but firm.

"Yeah, who wants to know?" Dan rasped, irritation cutting through his exhaustion.

"My name is Lucas. I'm a priest. I need to speak with you. It's important."

Dan sighed heavily, pressing his forehead against the cool wood of the door. "Not interested," he muttered. "Go away."

"Please, Dan," the voice persisted. "I've come a long way—from Scotland, in fact. I need just a few minutes of your time."

Dan hesitated, his brows furrowing. "Scotland? That's quite the trip. What's this about?"

"May I come in?" Lucas asked.

Dan sighed again, this time with palpable annoyance. "Why don't you just tell me through the door and save us both the trouble?"

"It's very important about your father," Lucas said, his voice low but clear.

Dan pulled the door open.

Standing before him was a tall, thin man of similar age, with long, straight black hair framing a pale, clean-shaven face. Lucas's dark eyes widened slightly as he took in Dan's appearance—shirtless and lean, his cheekbones sharp, and his skin stretched taut over well-defined pecs and abs. The contrast between them was striking—Dan's athletic build and sun-kissed complexion stood in stark opposition to Lucas's gaunt frame and pallid skin.

Yet, as their eyes met, a flicker of recognition passed between them— something unspoken, buried deep in their shared bloodline. Neither could place it, but on a subconscious level, they both felt it: a connection, fragile and faint, yet undeniably present.

"Hello, Dan," Lucas said gently, extending a hand. "I'm Lucas Fisher. I'm here to help."

Dan ignored the hand and instead scanned Lucas from head to toe. "Help? With what? And how the hell do you know me?"

Lucas's expression didn't falter. "May I come in?"

"What?" Dan questioned, his voice dangerously low. "I don't have time for religion, preacher."

"I mean no offense," Lucas said, taking a step back. "This isn't just about your father—it's about you, your life, your business, and this place. I've been led here, Dan. Please, just give me a moment."

Dan hesitated; his jaw clenched. Finally, he pushed the door open wider and motioned toward the porch with a tired wave. "Okay, I'll come out." Dan came out of the mansion and into the sun.

Lucas nodded and stepped onto the porch, lowering himself onto the shining black stone bench built into the railing. Dan followed, dropping heavily onto the step below him. Barefoot, shirtless, and clad only in Adidas warmups, the hot sun felt like knives piercing his pale skin. He squinted up at the priest. "Okay, what can I do for you?"

Lucas's long black hair blew across his face as the wind picked up, but he didn't seem to notice. "Dan, I've been having dreams about you for months now. Dreams about the lake. About this town. About your father, William Joseph, and what's coming."

Dan stared at him, his exhaustion quickly giving way to irritation. "You've been dreaming about me? And what, you thought you'd just show up on my doorstep?"

"I know it sounds unbelievable, but these dreams—they've guided me here. They've shown me things about your life, your struggles, your destiny."

"My destiny? Yes, I imagine my life is quite interesting to you. In your line of work. Our coffee is something isn't it."

"Dan," Lucas said, his voice steady, "It is far more than coffee. It's about more than money. Your father didn't just leave you a business and a house. He left you a responsibility—a purpose. This place, this lake, it's tied to something far greater than you understand."

Dan's head throbbed, the sunlight too bright, Lucas's words too heavy. "Thank you. I understand. We will continue brewing coffee."

"It's not a joke," Lucas said firmly. "And I'm not here by accident. God has sent me to help you. To warn you."

Dan laughed bitterly. "Warn me? About what? And don't start with the God stuff. I'm doing just fine without divine intervention, thanks. This miracle coffee is for everyone."

Lucas leaned forward, his dark eyes locking onto Dan's. "This is about what you do with this gift. It's about everyone who's connected to this place. In fact it's about everyone on the planet. The choices you make here will have consequences far beyond what you can imagine."

Dan's tired laugh died in his throat. He stood abruptly, his balance faltering as he swayed on unsteady legs. "I'm done," he said, turning toward the door. "I don't have time for this."

Lucas reached out, his hand lightly catching Dan's arm. "Dan, please. There's still time to turn back. To choose a different path. God's mercy is infinite, but you have to ask for it."

"Ask for what? Mercy? Hell if I asked for anything more I think the Old Man would see me as ungrateful. Preacher, I inherited billions. All I can do is say thank you. So, bless you preacher."

Dan wrenched his arm away and backed toward the door. Who the hell was this guy? "And Goodbye."

He slammed the door shut and leaned against it. He was lightheaded. He needed some food. Through the window, he watched as Lucas sat down on the stairs leading to the front driveway.

Dan exhaled shakily. "Another fucking lunatic," he muttered, ignoring the preacher and walking to the kitchen. "Calm down Dan. Get some food in you."

But his thoughts were anything but calm.

God has sent me.

The words echoed in his mind like a bell he couldn't unring.

Dan opened the subzero refrigerator. He needed some food. Something to fill the void- clear his mind. He recalled the BRAT concept recommended for stomach upset; Banana, Rice, Applesauce, and Toast. He grabbed some applesauce and Haagen Daas vanilla ice cream. From the pantry some almond butter and bananas. Pouring the ingredients into the blender and mixing his shake with ice cold water from the lake, Dan made a tasty treat he felt would settle well in his inflamed gut. He hit the puree button and found a large crystal glass.

God has sent me.

Dan carried his protein shake to the living room and could see Lucas still sitting on the steps. "Okay Lucas. Let's talk," Dan said aloud. Dan opened the massive iron door and stepped outside. Lucas turned and looked at him incredulously.

"Dan, I am here for you," he said.

Standing in the sun Dan stood in silence and drank his protein shake. After several minutes he said, "Lucas, it's nice to meet you. Let's take a walk."

Dan and Lucas walked side by side down the stairs, the hallway quiet but pulsing with tension. Outside, the sun was beginning to fade behind the Black Lake horizon.

"Preacher," Dan said, keeping his tone even, "I'm walking you out because I respect that you came. But I want to be clear—I don't need saving."

Lucas didn't flinch. "Dan, you don't see it yet, but there are forces at work here. Powers that go beyond business deals and miracle cures. Satan is pulling you toward him—manipulating you."

Dan stopped at the front gate, turned, and looked Lucas in the eye. "Satan? God? That's your world, Lucas. I'm not in it. What I'm doing here is real. Measurable. Our coffee? It's helping people. Curing them. That's not evil."

Lucas stepped closer. "That's exactly how he works, Dan. Through what looks like light. Through what feels like power. But the cost—"

Dan cut him off. "The price is power, Lucas. And I'll pay it. Because I'm not like you—I'm not waiting on some invisible God to save the world. I'm doing it myself."

Lucas's face was full of pain. "You've been chosen, Dan. But you still have a choice."

Dan stepped back and reached for the oversized steel gate with the gleaming black roses. Avoiding the razor sharp metal thorns adorning the stems he pulled that gate open.

"I've made mine," he said.

The gate swung open.

CHAPTER 39

Dan was elated that the shake he made stayed down. Over the next two days he holed up and made a variety all mixed with either ice water or coffee. His strength was back and he decided to brave the country roads and go to town. The snow had nearly made the roads impassable, but the winds cleared a bit of the bulk away showing a narrow path through the drifts. A few weeks earlier a shiny yellow orange 1972 classic Ford bronco had arrived as an alternative to the Lambo and Dan would take advantage of that today. A hardtop and doors thank God. After nearly an hour of cautious driving, Dan parked in front of the deserted Oak Bar. Not a soul could be seen on the streets in any direction. No cars. No people. Who could blame them? You would have to be nuts to travel to a bar in this stuff.

The door was locked so Dan banged on the heavy wooden slats a few times.

"What the hell do you want," Bob yelled as he pulled the door open. "Oh, Dan it's you. What the hell are you doing out at this time of night in this weather? Come in. Don't just stand there," he said and moved the heavy door out of Dan's path.

Dan stepped over the threshold and into the darkness of the closed bar feeling better immediately. Drunks tend to feel that way when arriving at their favorite watering hole - most of the time at least - and this was no exception.

"Well, I knew you would be here, and I needed some company, some conversation. Maybe some sage advice," Dan said.

"The door slammed with a thud and the wintery air was left outside. Dan stomped his feet to get the powdery snow from his boots. Water and ice slid across the wooden floor.

"Have a seat, Son," Bob said and pointed to the polished oak bar, the golden light cast shadows which faded and disappeared as he approached. "Coffee?"

"Coffee. Sounds really good. Throw in a shot or two of brandy too please."

Bob walked behind the bar to retrieve a couple of mugs and the delicious aromatic brew.

"Dan could smell that coffee cooking when Dan came in. Nothing better in this cold than Black Lake coffee. "Brrr," Dan laughed and shook the snow from his long-wet hair. "I'm going stir crazy stuck in that house. It's good to see you."

"Well Vic always said the quiet time kept him sane. Or as close to it as he could be."

"Seems like Vic had lost it a bit with this stuff." Dan stated.

"He was not crazy, Dan. But he was sliding down the hill pretty quick in his last days." he said shaking his head as he placed two steaming cups on the table. He sat and stared at the polished oak bar top. "He just couldn't hold out anymore."

"Hold out against what," Dan asked, feeling prickle of the fine blonde hairs on the back of his neck push against his shirt in anticipation of the response he knew was coming.

"The nightmares," Bob said.

Dan was concerned his own sanity was slipping.

"And then William Joseph too, Dan. William Joseph."

"What would he have to do with Vic?" Dan asked.

"Maybe sibling rivalry," Bob said.

"Sibling?"

"Well not by blood at least not in the traditional sense. But maybe brothers in arms," Bob said cryptically.

"Bob, I never know what the hell you're talking about," Dan said.

"There is a mission here, Dan," Bob said, his voice low and deliberate. "A series of events spanning a thousand years, each one bringing us closer to this moment. William Joseph has been fanning the flames for over a century, keeping the embers alive. Then came Vic—he built the powerhouse you're now running. He brought the fuel."

Bob leaned over the shining bar, his gaze piercing. "And you, Dan— you're the fire."

"I am that, Bob. I have some great plans."

"Plans. Yes, Dan. I know you do. That's why you are here," Bob said.

"Damn right," Dan laughed. I plan on getting very drunk and passing out in the suite upstairs. I'm going to grab my bag from the truck before it gets worse out there. And how about another cup of coffee? 50-50 with Jack Black bourbon? Be back in a few."

Dan pulled on his coat as he strode to the door, dreading the ice-cold wind and weather but excited to be here with Bob and fueled by slamming down that spirit laced java and not puking. Despite that fact when Dan pulled the big door open and stepped onto the porch of the Oak Bar the cold air and snow hit him like a brick wall and stole his breath away for a moment or two. When Dan got his bearings, he pushed on to the Bronco, the bright orange paint nearly hidden by a few inches of freshly fallen snow. It was really coming down hard again. "Fuck it. I'm not planning to go back to that house anyway. Maybe not even tomorrow at this rate. But certainly not tonight. That Jack Black has DAN stenciled on the label. Nope. Not driving anywhere tonight." Dan laughed aloud at his thoughts, the sound echoing off the empty winter street. A boom of thunder accented his enjoyment.

"Fucking blizzard out here," Dan muttered out loud to no one at all as Dan raked the frozen power from around the passenger door. The "sweet and sour" yellow-orange paint peeked through, and Dan worked on clearing the ice from the black door handle. After a few minutes of picking fragments away from the push button and losing feeling in his hands Dan was able to get into the classic Ford. The door opened a bit but was still pretty much frozen solid and took some man handling to open it up fully. A bushel of snow fell onto the saddle brown leather seat, covering the matching leather overnight bag. Dan grabbed the bag and slammed the door cursing the snow.

As Dan turned to get back to the bar, he saw the big man standing in the middle of the street at the end of the building. It was dark in the street, but the figure was contrasted perfectly with the surrounding white snow and the natural glow that seems to accompany the white out. Dressed all in black with a black derby Dan could see a length of his snow-white hair blowing around his face.

It must have been the deserted winterscape that made Dan's stomach grab and turn. His breath caught in his throat as fear gripped him. Dan ran for the safety of the bar. As he hit the porch Dan looked back, and William Joseph was gone from view. He kept running anyway and hit the heavy wooden door at full speed, bounced off and landed on his back, jumped up, scrambled forward, ripped the door open and dove inside. Dan felt like a mad dog was right on his heels. He fell onto the floor dropping his bag and sending it skittering across the floor.

Dan slid back to the door and pushed it shut against the cold wind. His frozen hands trembling with adrenaline.

 Dan rested and sat with his back against the door; his eyes closed to regain his breath.

"What the hell is the matter, boy?" Bob bellowed as he hurried in Dan's direction.

"Oh Shit," Dan started laughing.

"What's out there?"

"It was William Joseph out in the street. Scared me to death." Dan laughed again. "I'm losing it Bob. The old man probably thinks I'm a twelve-year-old girl."

"Did he say anything to you?" Bob asked.

"No. He didn't have to. I know what he wanted, and he knows I know. He wanted to scare the shit out of me and show me that he is the boss."

Bob helped Dan to his feet and escorted him to the bar where he had placed a full pot of coffee, a large bottle of XO, and the two mugs filled and steaming. "Brandy is better on a cold night, Dan. Let's get warm and relax."

Dan pulled his arms from his coat sleeves and draped his wet coat on the chair back. "More sibling rivalry, Bob?" Dan laughed.

"It is exactly that, Dan. It's your turn now and he knows it. He's jealous. He wants your destiny."

Dan ignored him and pulled a ziplock bag from his coat pocket and began pouring a powder into his coffee.

"What the hell is that," Bob asked.

"It's whey protein powder. Who would think Amazon would deliver in all this shit but 'Rain, Sleet or Snow' even in the middle of nowhere. There they are."

"Why are you ruining your coffee and brandy may I ask?"

"I figured it out, Bob. No more puking my guts out. I simply combine food and drink and mix it up. Protein shakes, fruit, fat, calories. I feel great. I've been eating these things like crazy. I think I have gained back five pounds this week."

Lot's of ice water and the reminder of the XO bottle followed.

CHAPTER 40

Dan awoke early, surprisingly refreshed after sleeping it off in the suite above the bar. He trudged downstairs and gathered the ingredients for his new morning ritual: Black Lake Coffee, a scoop of protein powder, some chocolate syrup two raw eggs from the kitchen, and a generous pour of Jack Black and three supplement pills. The blender whirred briefly, and he downed the shake in a few long gulps. It was rich, dark, and oddly comforting—soothing to his stomach like a balm. He stood still for a moment, letting the warmth settle. He knew he'd discovered something real here. Something powerful.

He shoved open the front door and winced as the icy wind slapped his face. Pulling his coat tight, he cursed himself for not parking in the garage under the office. The Bronco sat buried in snow across the street. He made his way over, boots crunching, hands freezing. After yanking and prying at the driver's door—thankfully on the windward side—he managed to get it open.

The drive to his home was slick and dangerous but peaceful with no living souls around. The view of the lake as he passed the cabin was a bit startling as there was no steam emitting from the vast near boiling cauldron but a solid sheet of undisturbed ice. Past the white rimmed black roses the lake looked solid and fit for skating. Serene. His driveway was a sea of white powder to match with only the faint hint of his tracks from last night visible. Dan parked in the circle drive and walked into his home.

"Good morning, Dan," a voice said to him as he entered the huge ballroom like living area.

"Morning," Dan returned without thinking. Realizing after a few moments that he should be alone in his house, that Chef John had gone back to Dallas, and he wasn't aware of any visitors.

"That's better, now I can see you much more clearly, Son. Welcome home." The tall, rail thin, black-haired billionaire with a deeply tanned face stood in the middle of the living room. Dressed in a midnight blue impeccably tailored suit, crisp white shirt, and royal blue silk tie with tiny, swirled designs in red, Victor Stone conveyed sophistication and wealth.

Dan's mouth was hanging open as he stared, and Vic began to laugh.

"A bit surprised I can see. Understandable, a man does not see a dead relative every day of the week, does he?" he asked.

"No," Dan responded still bewildered.

"Come have a seat, Vic motioned to the leather couch. It's good to see you son-- Son, sounds funny. We haven't ever known each other that way."

Dan sat on the couch staring in Vic's direction. "You are dead? You don't look dead."

"Well dead maybe is an exaggeration. Let's say I was just away for a while." he shrugged.

Dan simply looked at him. No words would come. "How?" he managed.

"Well let's get into that in a bit. But would you like a morning drink, Dan?" he asked.

"Yes, I would."

"I thought so. Me too," Vic said standing and walking to the kitchen. "Let's sit by the fire in the dining room, Son."

Dan followed. Vic pulled a smoke-colored bottle from the upper cabinet to the right of the sink and kitchen window. Dan stared at the lake through the window as he poured a clear liquid into two tumbler glasses.

"It is impossible for you to be standing here," Dan argued.

"I found a way to come back. It's really that simple," Vic shrugged again.

"Okay. Well let's assume you aren't dead and I'm not off on another one of those crazy trips again. How did you cheat death?" Dan asked.

"Well, you can never cheat death, you can only negotiate the terms. Remember that for your time. Death will take what is his eventually and charge you interest. So, I do not want to be dead just yet, so I agreed to pay a price. We worked something out we both could --- eh, live with," Vic stated.

He held up a tarot card and said "This is the black magic card of Death. You will meet him very soon. He threw the card on the table.

He handed Dan the glass and they both took a long drink.

"Oh my God," Dan thought, his throat and lungs burned and felt as though they were being physically torn from his chest. Dan closed his eyes and tried to keep from retching, doubling over in pain. Dan crouched down and put his head between his knees gripping his midsection and dry heaving. His eyes watered and air came in hard gasps. Dan fell to his side disoriented wiping his eyes and trying to focus on his surroundings.

Dan was no longer in the house but in the town square. Long black roses swayed all around him. The moon was full bright on a cloudless night. Dan could see a large crowd of a hundred people or more starting a few yards in front of him. Dan was standing but he was paralyzed. A small girl with light blonde nearly white hair was immediately in front of him held by the giant man, William Joseph. Beside him was a wire thin white hired man reading from a large gold leaf encrusted Bible.

It was a ceremony. Both men were dressed in heavy black robes. There was a little girl who disappeared into the hot spring. William Joseph held her down. She was struggling. Her legs were kicking. Her arms were flailing. The bible the other man was reading from was very old with yellowed pages. But something was wrong. The cross on the golden cover was eaten away like wormwood with black roses weaving in and out of it like snakes.

The little girl stopped struggling as William Joseph lifted her head from the steaming water. He lifted her high in the air presenting her to the onlookers as she choked and screamed. A cheer went up from the townspeople.

My God it was some form of dark baptism.

Dan realized that he was just an observer looking out from within the giant iron statue of William Joseph and as he realized this a flash of light filled his eyes and the people were gone. Dan was alone in the town square. Still within the statue, Dan could feel himself wobbling, rocking back and forth as though he were teetering on the edge of a cliff. He felt the ground collapse under him and saw the water in the pool at the base rising to meet him as he fell. He saw the water bubbling and boiling as the statue slipped beneath the surface of the dark spring.

Dan let out a scream only Dan and the dead could have heard. The pain was excruciating. Dan could feel the skin flay from his body like that of a par boiled potato. He was trapped in a current being sucked into an underground river. Dan struck a sharp rock protruding from the side wall of the tubular channel with the side of his head and felt the edges tear into his flesh. He felt it dig in and pull bone from his skull. His right eye socket broke, and his eyeball exploded. Dan could not imagine more agony and screamed, "Please God make this stop. Just kill me!"

But Dan continued to careen down the boiling chute and eventually emerged from the bottom of the pool dropping nearly twenty feet and landing hard on a rocky shoreline below. Dan was in agony. Dan could see the tossing and boiling lake above him in place of sky. Dan was lying on a dry rocky beach of sorts. The rocks were boiling hot and his already blistered, skinless body sizzled. Steam came off the water above. Droplets of water fell and popped on the red-hot rocks around him.

Dan was not dreaming. Dan was not drunk. Dan was lucid. "God damn it this is impossible." Dan was one hundred percent aware of the things going on around him, experiencing them in person. In the flesh.

Dan was laying naked on the hot stones. His body burned and covered with welts, most of his skin was missing the entire right side of his face was on fire, cauterized with dry clotted blood. Dan managed to drag himself five feet to get off the rocks and onto a bed of sand. There was no comfort here, the grains of sand had been baking for millions of years and their high salt content simply made it worse. Dan moaned and looked around slowly. Barren terrain in all directions. No vegetation whatsoever. It was as if Dan had been transported back to the dawn of time. The sky was the black swirling water of the bottom of the lake. The sun was a blood red glow coming from all sides of this underground cavern.

The water had followed him and pooled beside where Dan was laying. Dan stuck his hand in the water hoping for relief and screamed. The salty water just below boiling was thick and smelled of metal.

The ocean shall turn to blood.

Dan was in Hell, he concluded and began to weep.

Dan passed out then or seemed to. Time had stopped. The pain was constant, and the heat was eternal. The world seemed to pulsate between darkness and the blood red glow as though the entire world were a sinister heart beating. Bellows of deep guttural laughter filled the acrid air. Dan could feel the evil roar as it vibrated his broken body.

His mouth tasted of mildew and blood. Dan opened his single remaining eye and saw a large man dressed all in black standing over his crumpled body. He wore a long hooded woolen robe and held no weapon. Dan could not keep his mind from traveling to the card Vic had thrown on the table. The card of Death stood out in his mind and his words hung in the air like the sound of a gong which had been rung.

You will meet him very soon.

Dan's attention was jerked back to his reality. The dark boot of his host kicked him square in the nose. The skin was already gone. The cartilage that was left disconnected from the bone of his skull beneath and slid off easily enough. The familiar taste of copper and ground iron filled his throat and nasal passages. Spitting out blood, Dan vomited. Barely slowed by his actions, the man Dan saw as Death and embodiment of

Satan continued to stomp Dan's face and body. Pain was constant and peeked at every downstroke of the dark entity's boot. Dan stared into the cracks of the rocks as his face was driven down further, curiously observing his blood flowing in steaming streams as it hit the near molten rocks and coursed through the sand, through the small hills and valleys of the earth when the heavy boot drove into the back of his head with tremendous force, rupturing the bones in his skull and wedging it in between two large jagged rocks. The painful blows soon became irrelevant. He worked his way down Dan's spine, stomping with the heels of his heavy boots. Finally, the punisher stopped bludgeoning what was left of Dan.

Dan was conscious but still. Death took ahold of his foot and dragged him over the rocks, bouncing his head and torso across the lifeless earth. Dan observed a blood trail as he was dragged away and saw the shining white stones in the mess, realizing that all of his teeth were knocked out from the curbing suffered on the rocks. He only had a moment of thought as his body was flung high into the air and splashed into the waters above.

Dan believed himself to be dead and in hell. There must have been some kind of poison that was strong enough to kill him instantly and jettison his soul directly into the next life and Dan was hardly deserving of Heaven. But Dan gasped as the hot water hit him and his eyes popped open. He swam upwards following his bubbles, skin burning, lungs burning. After a full minute of driving himself up and up his head broke the surface of the Black Lake. He gasped, lungs finally filling with air.

Dan swam hard toward the cabin. His limbs burned, his lungs screamed for air, but he kept going.

On the porch at the edge of the lake, a dark figure rocked slowly in a wooden chair.

"Help me!" Dan shouted, choking on lake water. He wasn't sure he could make it. His body was giving out.

The figure lifted a hand and waved—leisurely, like they were greeting an old friend.

Dan dug deep, kicking harder.
One hundred feet.
Eighty.
Forty.

He could make out the man now—thin, dressed in black, smiling. Rocking gently.

Ten feet to go.

Dan's feet touched the lakebed, and he lunged forward—but the figure stood, turned, and silently walked into the cabin.

Dan pushed through the final barrier—a thick wall of black roses lining the shore. The thorns tore into his burned, naked flesh, slicing across his chest, arms, and legs.

He grabbed a long stem to pull himself forward and instantly felt it slice through his palms. Blood burst from his hands as he collapsed onto the old wooden porch, gasping. The pain was unbearable—but he was alive.

He lay there for a moment, chest heaving, blood seeping into the wood. He closed his eyes. Breathed. Once. Twice. Again.

Then he stood, staggering to the cabin door. He pushed it open.

Empty, as he knew it would be.

Dan walked to the kitchen sink, turned on the tap, and washed the blood from his hands. The water stung like fire. He found a towel and wrapped his palms—tight, but not tight enough to stop the shaking.

Dan opened the door of the cabin and was met by a stiff, frozen wind that cut into his skin like a whip. The near boiling water was gone. No blood on the porch. He looked at his hands and saw no marks or tears in his flesh. He stepped out onto the snow-covered porch, the ice cold boards creaking beneath his bare feet.

Before him, the frozen plain of ice surrounded by still blooming long stemmed black roses, frosted white and shimmering beneath the moonlight.

Exhausted and numb, Dan walked naked through the snow, up the granite steps toward the main house. The wind howled behind him, snapping at his heels like a predator.

Inside, the living room was dark and silent. He crossed to the couch, grabbed the throw blanket draped over the back, and collapsed into it.

Wrapping himself tight, Dan curled into the cushions. The warmth barely registered. His body shook.

And he slept.

CHAPTER 41

The winter sun poured through the large plate glass windows of the living room, waking Dan slowly. He ran his hands down his torso, across the stubble of his beard. His tongue swept over his teeth—all accounted for. He flexed his fingers and toes, then sat up, placing both feet flat on the cold stone floor. Rising, he stretched his long, muscular frame toward the ceiling, arms high overhead. His eyes opened wide as he twisted his torso back and forth, bones cracking back to life.

He felt fantastic.

Dan shook his head and walked to the windows. The sun was high in the sky. The warmth beamed through the tall windows. The snow was melting. This must be an excellent example of the nightmares Vic had experienced. Seemed real. Obviously it wasn't.

Dan walked to the kitchen and brewed a double espresso, then blended a protein shake—two bananas, a heaping scoop of powder, and three raw eggs, the coffee and vanilla ice cream—and Black Lake ice water all into the blender He was starving. It had been a long night.

Dan took the thick shake upstairs to his bedroom, where he showered, shaved, and got dressed. Clean and clear-headed, Dan sat on the edge of the bed and lit a joint, exhaling slowly as the morning began to settle. The marijuana seemed to really smooth out his thoughts.

He could eat. Albeit along with his concoction and weed -- he had cured his starvation issue. But, the nightmares were intensifying along with his increase in consumption between the supplement pills and the shakes. He knew he was onto something strong but needed Sam and his crew. And a break from this town. Fresh environment. No fucking snow. New Orleans.

Dan packed a bag, his blender, protein powder and supplements and threw them in the back of the Bronco. Leaving the confines of the palatial home he felt better already.

"Maybe you should just high tail it out of here. Get in that car of yours and drive as far away as you can as fast as you can." Bob's words echoed in Dan's mind as he did that very thing. A long drive but he needed some alone time, at least a little. But, he also needed some female companionship --- a total stranger with absolutely no ideas about any of the odd things twisting his life of late. No idea that he was Dan Stone.

The Bronco shifted into third gear as Dan flew past the statue of William Joseph towering over the wishing well in the town square. Tires crunched on the melting snow as Dan turned the corner beside the Oak Bar. Now on the strait away and a clear highway in front of him, Dan hit the gas and roared out of Black Lake. "Fuck you," he yelled, laughing.

As the town highway became the country highway Dan began to feel sick. Very sick. His gut twisted violently and he had to lock up the brakes. Opening the heavy Detroit metal door on the classic truck, Dan barely cleared the door frame as he began to vomit. He vomited hard, the convulsions racking his body as bile hit the frozen ground below. Again. And again. He gripped the steering wheel with one hand, the other bracing against the doorframe, his torso hanging halfway out.

When it was over, he stayed there—breathing ragged, sweating despite the cold, the wind stinging his face. He wiped his mouth with the back of his sleeve and stared blankly at the empty road ahead.

A voice said, "Here Dan. Have a cloth for your face."

Dan jerked away from the voice from the right side of the cab. Vic was seated in his passenger seat holding a steaming wash towel in his direction.

Dan shook his head and took the towel. He closed his eyes as he realized he was still in. Not out. He felt no control like a marionette with someone else pulling the strings and dancing him back and forth. He wiped his mouth and face on the scalding hot cloth. "Thank you, father," his voice spoke.

Tears began to appear in the corners of Dan's eyes.

Vic laughed. "Look and you will see," he said. The smile and laughter immediately left his face. His eyes taking on a wild evil glare his black eyes like daggers, "Drink," he said. The word dripped from his mouth like a wolf feasting on fresh game.

Dan felt his arms move and lift a dusty mason jar from between his knees. Dan wondered where it had come from as a boiling liquid touched his lips and burned the soft flesh. Vic screamed a sharp horrible laugh and caught fire as Dan stared--- his face and body charring and crumbling into ash in seconds.

Dan was detached from his body and not in control. He drank. The world spun.

# # #

As the superheated liquid slid past his throat and into his stomach, Dan squeezed his eyes shut. He had had enough of this. The last thing he wanted was another trip into Hell, but he was not in control here.

He smelled the sweet black roses and felt the hot dank wind blowing in his face. He opened his eyes and was sitting on the dock outside the guest houses. The cabin was floating fifty feet above the water about the same distance offshore. The door opened. A tall thin black man walked onto the porch to the edge and smiled; the same man from his earlier vision.
"Hello my son" he called down to Dan.

Dan stared unable to speak. He began to float upwards towards the cabin. The man smiled down at him cheerfully and reached out his hands. His face began to contort. Fangs appeared at either side of his mouth which stretched forward. Horns grew from his forehead- out and upwards. He growled. "See you in hell, son!"

Dan felt himself falling then. He felt the water hit his back and started awake with a scream. He gritted his teeth and rubbed the sleep from his eyes. He looked out of the truck window to gain his bearings. He had awakened in the passenger seat of the Bronco outside the cabin. How all this shit decided to fall on him Dan did not know.

Dan opened the door and climbed out.

"Fuck You, Vic. You son of a bitch!" Dan yelled across the lake.

# # #

The cabin door creaked open, and a towering figure stepped into the frame. Dressed all in black—just as before—stood William Joseph, his presence as unsettling as ever.

"Dan," he said, voice low and rasping like gravel dragged across concrete. "Dan Stone. I've come to visit."

Dan's mouth hung open for a beat. He shut it, squared his shoulders. "May I ask what you're doing in my house?"

"A visit," William Joseph repeated, almost cheerfully.

"No," Dan said, stepping forward. "That's why you're here. Why are you coming out of my house?"

William Joseph descended the porch steps with surprising grace. "I'm not coming out of your house, Dan. I'm coming out of your father's cabin." He smiled, cheeks oddly flushed like a waxy cherub.

Dan held his gaze. The man looked more genial than before—but that only made it worse.

"Fine," Dan said exhausted. "What do you want?"

William Joseph's eyes glinted. "To finish what your father and I started. Together, we can build the world he dreams of."

"What do you want?" was all Dan could say breathing hard and heavy.

"Simple. We want it all," he smiled again, bigger than before and spread his big hands wide to a full arm span of nearly seven feet.

"Ok. I am pretty tired, I haven't slept well for a week-- a month-- Hell I don't even know how long it's been."

"Power, Dan, we are here for a purpose you and me. We must develop the power, but we need each other. We have the capability for controlling key events that will change history. Your father and I started this together and you and I will finish it, my boy."

"My money you mean," Dan said suspiciously. Dan was beginning to understand what he really wanted.

William Joseph threw his head back and roared with laughter placing his pie pan hands on his belly as he did. "Surely you don't think all that money just came to you so you could live out your days as a millionaire playboy here in Black Lake?"

"No. I won't be staying so you can keep your offer for a power trip all for yourself William," Dan said. "I will be spending my money somewhere else. Like back in civilization."

"We will share the secrets of longevity such that you will never die," William Joseph bargained. This world is ours. Come find me and we will have a drink with Bob. He smiled and turned away. He walked back into the cabin and slammed the door.

"Hey!" Dan yelled bounding up the wooden stairs to the door, jerked it open and followed.

William Joseph was not in the room. Not in the cabin. Not out the back jack. He was just gone. The cabin was plush and warm and sealed from the harsh winter storms of the last week. Dan stomped the snow from his boots and shed his heavy fur coat. William Joseph had just vanished into thin air and on the table left a black rose and a brown glass growler with the black lake coffee logo. William Joseph had a hell of a sense of humor.

CHAPTER 42

"Tom, I have a project. Send the jet. I'm going to New Orleans."

"Hi Dan. Great. I have been wanting to get there and see Sam. I will fly up and we will go tomorrow. We will be there by noon," Tom said.

"And bring Stephanie along," Dan laughed. "I need to mix some business and pleasure."

"She is right here with me. I figured you would want to see her. It's been a while."

"See you tomorrow morning," Dan said disconnecting.

"Ok Bob. If that's what it takes I will embrace the beast."

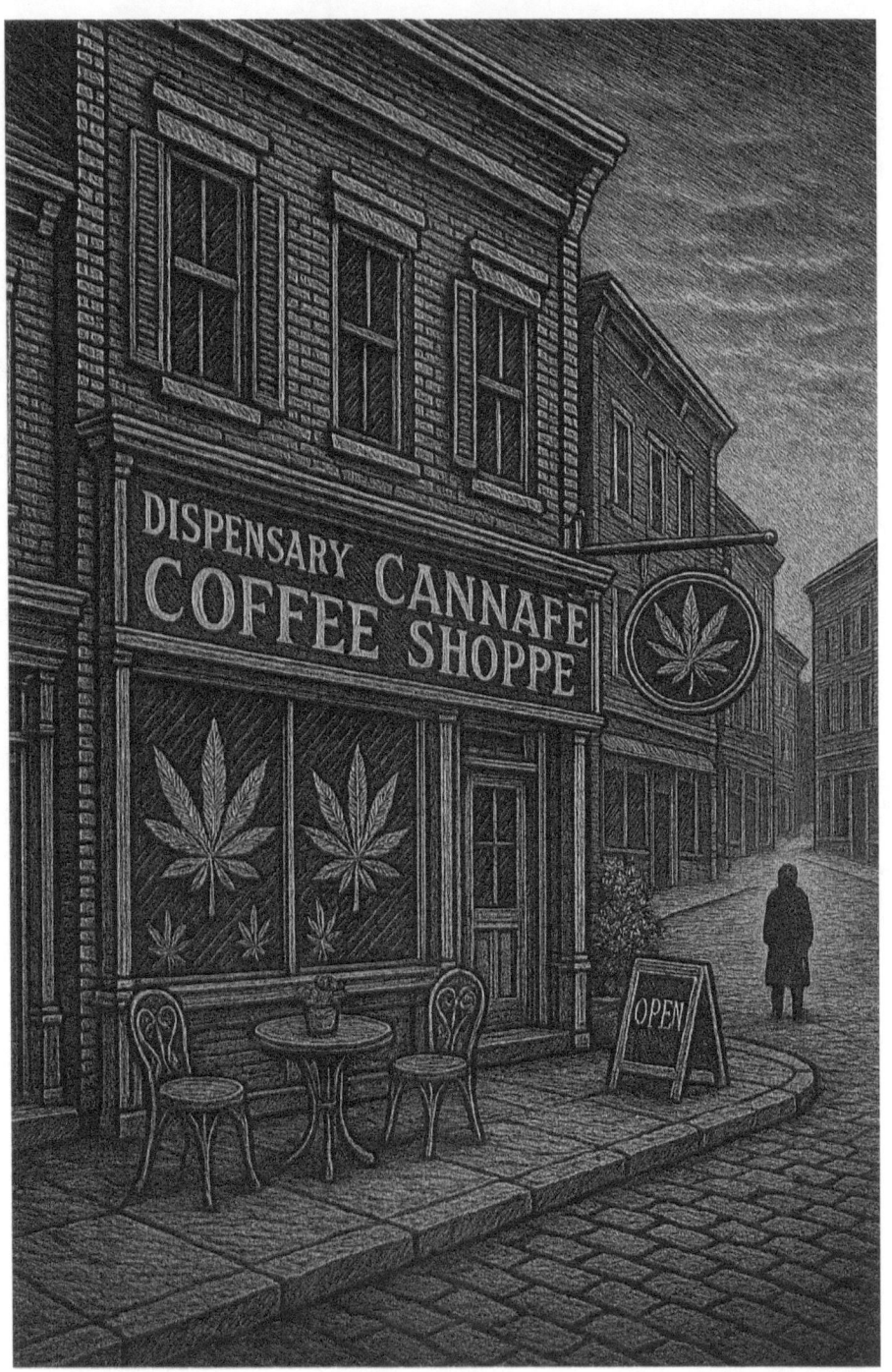

CHAPTER 43

Tom and Stephanie opened the door and walked into Dans home without a knock or hesitation. "Wheels up at 9 AM as promised Dan," Tom laughed.

Dan was drinking his morning shake and had his bags ready. Stehanie walked towards him and wrapped her arms around him. He leaned down and kissed her hello.

"Well that's a great welcome. Hello Stephanie."

"I've missed you, Dan. I'm so glad you wanted me to come," she smiled.

Dan laughed. "Ok. Let's get cracking. I want to get to the lab by lunch."

They left the house and walked down the driveway and through the gate. "You two walk from the airplane?"

"We did. We took the opportunity to run our mile," Tom said.

"Fun. Well we will be driving."

They piled into the Bronco and headed for the landing strip. Minutes later, they parked beside the waiting Gulfstream.

At exactly 9:00 a.m., the wheels lifted from the tarmac, right on schedule.

Carrie and Judy were the crew and Mike and Dave were the pilots. The take off was smooth and fast. Stephanie sat beside Dan and Tom sat across.

"So Dan, what are you thinking?" Tom asked.

"Well first tell me how we are coming along on the Norman Oklahoma project."

"It's going well. The dispensary coffee shop is serving Black Lake now and we have promoted it solidly. Sales are phenomenal for marijuana and coffee. We are adding in the supplements to the coffee to make each cup very powerful. No casualties yet." Tom said.

"Sounds good," Dan replied. "Anything else?"

"Well actually there is some buzz on test scores going up. The kids there are oddly studious. Grades are a big focus. Grades and football," Stephanie interjected.

"Fantastic. Let's lean into that. Let's replicate in every college town and start acquiring dispensaries and coffee shops. Find out who are the largest."

"Well Starbucks for coffee," Tom said.

"Yes, and I recall some cannabis companies control entire states. Trulieve owns Florida. Some Russian billionaire. Check that out and find smaller coffee companies we can quickly jump in and take over," Dan said.

"Coffee shops should be easy. Most are on the ropes whenever we open up, When we announce a new store there is a panic from the competition," Tom replied.

"Okay. In the mean time I am going to go take a nap in the back," Dan said unbuckling.

Stephanie smiled. "Yes, we are going to go take a nap, Tom." She smiled and followed Dan to the sleeping quarters in the rear of the plane.

# # #

A car was waiting at the New Orleans executive. Jerome greeted the group.

"Boss, great to see you," he said opening the back door of the black Lincoln stretch limousine.

Driven by a need to develop an antidote for the nightmares, hallucinations, or whatever all this was and enticed by the challenge and the mystery of this little spring in the middle of nowhere—a fountain of youth, a wellspring of untold riches—Dan felt a fire ignite within him. He was already, as the old Warrant tune put it, "dirty, rotten, filthy, stinking rich," but this was different. This wasn't just wealth; it was power. The kind of power that could reshape the world, bend it to his will. He could become the richest man on the planet, own everything, control everyone, influence life itself, even the direction of the universe.

Immortality? Perhaps total dominion over all creatures, great and small. This was simply too much for his psyche to resist. Dan became obsessed. The black roses had become his sustenance, consumed almost exclusively in his coffee. Almost. Except for the three or four supplement pills he was taking. The compulsion to excel past the point that Victor had attained was so intense that he had to remind himself he was still human, still required food to survive, and that the concentrated black roses could result in his death. But his ambitions soared beyond mortal limits.

And that is why he came to New Orleans. Sam and the other scientists would assist him in making his concept a reality. Dan had cured his inability to eat with more coffee, more water, more supplements and protein powder and he had not burned alive, yet.

"Sam. Good to see you," Dan said, extending his hand and gripping the scientist's with firm, deliberate force.

"Yes... hello, Mr. Stone," Sam replied, a touch uneasy, his expression cautious and curious.

A frog in boiling water wouldn't have noticed the difference. But Sam hadn't seen Dan in months—and to him, the change was stark and immediately apparent.

The laid-back, indifferent heir to the Stone fortune was gone. In his place stood someone sharper. Colder. Controlled.

And then there were the eyes.

Sam was certain they were blue. Now... they were almost black.

Something had changed. Something deep.

And Sam felt it in his bones.

It wasn't exactly fear Sam felt—but something close.
Like spotting a vicious dog behind a fence. You knew it couldn't reach you, but your body tensed anyway.
The hairs on the back of his neck stood up.

Dan smiled, and for a flicker of a moment, Sam saw a flame dance in his eyes.

No, Sam thought, that couldn't have happened.

Dan's tone was casual. "Sam, I want you to rework the supplements into a nutrition bar. We're calling it Brainfood. I've been testing my own blend—protein shake, bananas, almond butter, eggs, whey protein... and three of the supplement pills."

"Three?" Stephanie interrupted, eyes narrowing. "We agreed on two, after what happened to Vic..." She trailed off.

"It's fine when combined with food," Dan said, waving it off. "I think the high protein buffer keeps the effects stable."

He leaned forward, energized. "And listen—the kids in Norman are excelling. Test scores through the roof. I want to kick this into high gear. Make Brainfood intense. Let's see how smart we can make them."

"Might be the weed too," he added with a grin. "The ones drinking the coffee are also buying from that dispensary. It's all feeding the same system."

Sam said nothing.
But that feeling in his gut only grew darker.

Dan pushed Sam hard, and together they developed two flagship products:

The first was the BrainFood Bar—a high-performance nutrition bar packed with whey protein, three of the proprietary supplement compounds, and 200 milligrams of cannabis distillate. Designed for cognitive enhancement, it blended high protein with a potent nootropic load.

The second was more discreet, more indulgent: a six-pack of peanut butter cups, each infused with one of the supplement pills and 50 milligrams of cannabis distillate. They called them BudderCups.

Both products were also laced with longevity compounds—a blend of cellular repair agents, mitochondrial enhancers, and anti-inflammatory agents derived from Vic's original research.

Sam stared at the six-pack of BudderCups, his jaw tightening. "Dan... if someone eats the whole pack, that's six pills."

Dan didn't look up. "Exactly. We want to push the students to the edge. That's the point. The weed, the protein, the longevity stack—it's all working together. The peanut butter buffers the rose concentrate. Right?"

Sam's tone turned cold. "No. That's not how this works. No one's ever taken six. Vic didn't survive three."

Dan finally looked up, eyes steady. "This isn't the same formula. I've been taking three with every shake. That's nine a day."

Sam blinked. "Jesus, Dan. That's not strategy. That's suicide."

Dan smiled faintly. "No, Sam. It's evolution. I adapted. And they will too. The strong always do."

Sam swallowed hard, dread curling in his gut.

This wasn't about supplements anymore.
This wasn't about health, or science.
This was about something else.
Something bigger; darker.

They were tools. And Dan wanted them everywhere.

# # #

This was the antidote.

Dan had come to understand: coffee alone wasn't enough. With no food, no fat, no buffer—the body would eventually burn out. Waste away. See Vic.

But with his formula—with food—they could survive.
More than survive. They could thrive.

The new blend delivered everything: protein, cannabis distillate, cognitive enhancers, and what Dan now called the longevity stack—a cocktail of cutting-edge compounds: NAD+ precursors, resveratrol, spermidine, PQQ, CoQ10, and a proprietary extract derived from the Black Rose.

Dan consumed the formula daily while they were working on it. Human Guinee pig or whatever it was. He felt better each time they added an ingredient.

Energy. Focus. Fire.
He especially liked the strange nutrients. The way they made him feel like he could go forever.

The BrainFood bar seemed to settle his stomach and steady his nerves, acting as both a salve and a spark for his overworked body and mind. With each of his three or four coffees, Dan consumed two of the new BrainFood Bars. They were surprisingly good—tasty, satisfying, and packed with the supplemental compounds drawn from the enigmatic

Black Lake. It wasn't just nutrition; it was fuel for his ambition, calories laced with the potential to unlock something greater.

This wasn't just performance.
It was ascension.

Now the distribution.

Dan threw money at the problem and got results. A custom kitchen in New Orleans was contracted to produce both cannabis-laced and non-cannabis versions of the new products. Within days, they had packaged and labeled the goods—BudderCups and BrainFood Bars—with clinical precision and street-level appeal.

For the return trip, Dan loaded the Gulfstream with three dozen cases of each, along with standing orders to begin immediate shipments to Norman.

Together, Dan, Stephanie, and Tom flew back to Oklahoma—returning like missionaries to the campus of OU, bearing what Dan now called the next step in human advancement.

The students wouldn't know it yet.

But something was about to change.

The Cannafe had the charm of an old-world Amsterdam café—dark wood interiors, hand-carved sculptures, and a scent of roasted beans mingled with something sweet and unmistakably herbal. It sat tucked along Buchanan Street, just beside the university, and had quietly become a second home for OU students—part study hall, part refuge, part slow-burn rebellion.

Cannabis coffees and snacks flowed freely now, served with a wink and a knowing nod. It was a place where the line between stimulation and sedation blurred just enough to make genius feel possible.

The café was managed by Joe, a fifty-year-old PhD in biochemistry—
brilliant, eccentric, and chronically underemployed. Too idealistic for
industry. Too unpredictable for academia.

Joe had never quite found his place in the world.
He hadn't written his song.
But he made damn good coffee.
And for the first time in years, he felt like he was on the edge of
something big.

"Joe, this is Dan Stone," Tom said, gesturing between them.

Joe stood from behind the bar, wiping his hands on a towel. His eyes
flicked to Dan—sharp, assessing.

"Ah. The man behind the myth," Joe said, offering a hand. "You've been
making waves."

Dan smiled as he shook it. "That's the idea."

Joe nodded slowly, his expression unreadable. "Well... welcome to the
Cannafe. We don't get many billionaires in here. At least not the living
ones."

Tom chuckled. Dan just smiled, eyes locked on Joe's.

Something passed between them—Dan knew this mans fate.
It was there in Joe's eyes: curiosity, intelligence... and the flicker of
something deeper. Something that recognized the shape of destiny when
it walked through the door.

"Joe, beware prophets bearing gifts," Dan said with a grin. "I brought
some new edibles we want to drive forward. Word is the grades are
spiking around here. Smart kids."

Joe nodded, brow furrowing slightly. "Yeah. They are smart. But there's
something in this brew..." He trailed off, eyes distant for a moment. "I
haven't felt this alive in years. These kids are lit up. On fire."

Dan glanced at Tom and smirked. The irony hung heavy in the air.

"Great, Joe." Dan clapped him on the shoulder. "Let's get these into the willing vessels."

"Will do, boss. You all want some coffee?" Joe asked.

"Silly question," Dan grinned. "Yes—let's have one and try one of the new BrainFood bars while we're at it."

Joe moved behind the dark wood bar, working quickly. In a few minutes, he returned with three Americanos.

"Americano with three sugars and extra cream—just like you asked."

They took their seats at a corner table by the window, steam rising from their cups. Outside, students flowed in and out, many with coffee in one hand and BudderCups or BrainFood Bars in the other.

The new products were already moving.

Joe sipped thoughtfully. "So what's in these, exactly?"

Dan leaned back in his chair. "Cannabis and special sauce."

Joel raised an eyebrow. "And what else?"

"That's it. Just brilliance in a bar," Dan said, flashing a smile. "Don't worry about it."

Joe didn't return the smile. "Well, I like to know what I'm selling. And eating."

Dan gave a theatrical sigh. "The ingredients are on the label. We packed it with the latest longevity stack—NAD+, resveratrol, spermidine, the works. High-quality protein. And a healthy dose of saffron. The happy spice, right?" He laughed.

Joe took another bite, chewing slowly. "Well... they taste great. The kids are going to love this stuff."

"Great," Dan said, rising. "We've got to run. Let's make history, Joe. Knock 'em dead."

Joe gave a short nod, but his eyes lingered on the wrapper.

The trio exited and drove straight to the private strip, where the Gulfstream awaited. Once airborne, Stephanie, Dan, and Carrie disappeared into the bed at the back of the jet.

Tom napped.

The clouds flew by and soon they were home in Black Lake.

CHAPTER 44

The BrainFood Bars and BudderCups were more than a hit—they were a phenomenon. What began as a quiet rollout on campus had exploded into national headlines. But it wasn't the sales figures that drew attention.

It was the breakthroughs.

At the University of Oklahoma, something was happening—something extraordinary. In the span of weeks, the medical department reported an unprecedented cancer regression in a graduate student's research model. At the same time, a group in the physics department claimed they had successfully achieved a controlled teleportation of inorganic matter.

Both breakthroughs. Both from students.

And both credited their inspiration, focus, and sustained clarity to one thing:
The BrainFood Bar.

What started as brain fuel was now being whispered about as something else entirely.

Something impossible.

The students went wild.

Within days, demand for BrainFood Bars outpaced anything Dan had anticipated. The New Orleans kitchen was now shipping out over a hundred cases a week, just to keep up with orders at OU alone. The campus was buzzing, classrooms packed, libraries full at all hours. Students swore they could read faster, think clearer, even dream more vividly.

And it didn't stop there.

Word spread like wildfire. People began traveling from across the country—pilgrimages to Norman—just to get their hands on the bars.

The Cannafe couldn't keep them on the shelves for more than a few hours.

It was like Willy Wonka had opened his factory, but instead of golden tickets, these kids were being handed limitless potential—and they wanted more.

Dan watched it unfold like a prophet seeing his vision come to life. And he wanted the world to have a taste.

"Tom, start buying dispensaries—every college town, every legal state. I want us everywhere cannabis is allowed," Dan said, eyes burning with purpose. "And the non-cannabis version? Get it into Walmart, Amazon, Target—every goddamn shelf you can find."

He stepped closer, voice low but electric.

"This is it. This is the thing we've been waiting for. Put us in every mouth."

CHAPTER 45

Where to start? Lucas had a mission: to save the world. And to do that, he had to reach Dan Stone, a man clearly uninterested in anything remotely priestly. Dan was a hedonist, a man driven by excess, not introspection. How could Lucas approach someone so entrenched in his own vices? What would Sherlock Holmes do? Stake out the bar? Engineer a chance encounter?

Lucas decided the bar was as good a place as any. It was the pulse of the town, and if anyone knew how to get close to Dan, they'd be there. He'd start with research—learn more about the town, the enigmatic lake, and the people bound to its secrets. If he could gather enough insight, perhaps he'd find a way to pull Dan aside, to sit him down and make him see what was at stake.

The Oak Bar buzzed with energy, its warm amber lights reflecting off polished wood and gleaming glasses. Nearly the entire town of Black Lake seemed crammed into the posh establishment, the hum of conversation blending with the occasional clink of ice and laughter. Lucas slipped through the crowd, earning a few curious glances and wary looks. It was clear he didn't belong here—an outsider in a town that didn't often welcome them.

He finally made it to the bar, slotting himself between a couple of locals engrossed in their drinks and muted conversation. Red wine was his choice tonight—simple, unassuming. If it was good enough for Jesus, Lucas figured, it was good enough for a research priest from a monastery in Scotland. Besides, hadn't Jesus said something about wine aiding digestion? That thought, at least, gave him a moment's comfort as he scanned the room.

The place was alive, vibrant with energy, yet Lucas could feel eyes on him, glares from total strangers, dark whispers that gnawed at him. But he wasn't here to make lifelong friends he was here find a way to reach Dan Stone.

"What do you want," Bob asked Lucas.

"A glass of red wine please," Lucas answered over the din of the crowded bar.

"Don't have any."

"No wine?"

"Nope."

"Ok. Club soda, please," Lucas responded.

"Fresh out," Bob returned.

The male patrons on either side of Lucas stared and crowded closer.

"Ok, what do you recommend?"

"I recommend you leave," Bob answered glaring at him.

Lucas looked questioningly at Bob.

"You want us to help this guy out the backdoor, Bob?" the man to the right asked.

"No. I think he is leaving. Of his own accord," Bob said.

"I am looking for a friend of Dan Stone," Lucas spoke quickly as the man on the left grabbed his arm.

"Look preacher, everyone in this room is a friend of Dan Stone except you. Now don't make this hard. Get out," Bob said.

"I just need..." Lucas started but Bob cut him off.

"Ok. Let me get you a cup of coffee, Preacher. Cream and two sugars just like Dan likes it?" Bob asked.

Relieved Lucas said, "Yes, thank you that would be fantastic."

Bob nodded to the men beside him and they backed away giving him some space. Bob grabbed a cup and filled it with hot coffee, cream and sugar. "Here you go, Preacher."

Lucas took the cup. "Thank you. Do you know Dan?"

"Drink up, Preacher."

Lucas hesitated, put the cup to his lips and took a sip. Immediately the world spun, the burning liquid hit his stomach and was immediately rejected. Lucas doubled over in pain and vomited on the floor in front of the bar.

Bob began to laugh. The man on the right and left each drove a knee into opposite ribs. Lucas felt fists punching him in the back from another unseen adversary. He fell to the floor where they began to kick him.

The door to the bar opened and a harsh wind blew snow into the room. Dan Stone walked in, and everyone stopped and stared his direction. The assault on Lucas paused. Dan walked towards the bar and saw the man on the ground. "What the hell is going on, Bob?" he called out hurrying over.

"This guy was just leaving," Bob said.

Lucas looked up and Dan pushed through the crowd shoving the two men on either side away from the defenseless preacher. "Back off. What the fuck is wrong with you people?"
"He needs to leave, Dan," Bob stated.

"Fine. Preacher, come on," Dan said shaking his head and reaching down to help him up. Lucas shakily regained his feet.

Dan took Lucas's arm and turned to the move towards the door. There was nowhere to go. The patrons in the bar crowded together and stared in unison at the twosome creating an impenetrable wall and blocking the exit.

"Bob? What the fuck is going on here?"

"This man must die," A booming voice cut through the silence. William Joseph emerged from the shadows and approached. The crowd made a hole for the giant of a man to pass through.

Dan grabbed Lucas and pushed him towards the back of the bar away from the angry mob and William Joseph.

"What the hell are you saying?"

"He must die. He is here to interfere. Now, let us have him," he growled.

"You are out of your mind," Dan exclaimed.

"You are one of us Dan Stone. He is not. Now let us have him," the big man commanded.

Dan pulled Lucas behind him and hurried down the hallway to his private elevator.

"Preacher, Dan Stone is not for you!" the booming voice from Lucas's nightmares reverberated off the walls of the elevator.

The elevator doors slid open, and Dan and Lucas stepped into the private suite above the Oak Bar. Lucas glanced around briefly, but his focus remained on Dan. The room was spacious, dimly lit, and impeccably styled, a haven of luxury amidst the chaos below.

"Thank you," Lucas said quietly.

"Don't mention it," Dan replied, motioning for Lucas to follow him. "But they have a point. You should probably leave this town while you still can."

Lucas hesitated. "Did you hear the devil?"

Dan stopped mid-stride and turned to face him, an incredulous look on his face. "The devil? I heard William Joseph ranting and threatening you. You barely got out of there alive, preacher."

"In the elevator," Lucas pressed. "Did you hear Satan speaking? His voice was unmistakable."

Dan ignored the question and gestured toward a pair of leather chairs by his desk. "Come on in and have a seat, preacher."

"Lucas. My name is Lucas." He sat down in one of the green leather chairs, his hands resting uneasily on the armrests. "Thank you for saving my life, Dan. You can see this town is evil."

Dan dropped into the chair behind his desk, leaning back as he studied Lucas. "Lucas, why are you really here? Clearly, I don't need your help. I have billions, a global empire, and we're growing faster than anyone ever thought possible. No soul-saving is required."

Lucas leaned forward, his dark eyes intense. "God sent me, Dan."

"Yes. You said that before and I thought we cleared all that up. No offense, but God probably doesn't drink coffee and doesn't give a shit about it"

"It's you Dan. You are what is at stake and thereby all of humanity."

"Funny how I am so important to God now when he hasn't paid any attention for the last thirty five years."

"He loves you, Dan. He loves all of us."

"Ok. Sounds great, Lucas. You look like he loves you a lot," Dan said, leaning back in his chair with a sardonic grin. He gestured toward the restroom. "I've got a shower over there. Why don't you use it? Looks like they worked you over pretty good downstairs. And frankly, you look like you need one anyway."

Lucas hesitated before nodding. "Yes, thank you. I've been sleeping in my car. There really isn't anywhere here for me to stay."

Dan arched an eyebrow. "Another solid hint for you to head back to Scotland, Lucas."

"I can't leave you here, Dan."

Dan's smirk faded. "Really? I'm fine. Don't make me regret saving you down there."

"Dan look at me. Look into my eyes. Can't you feel it?"

"Lucas, I'm glad they didn't beat you to death. I'm glad you are grateful. I'll give you a ride out of here. But, I think you should high tail it south. Or north. OR any way you please, but put Black Lake in the rear view."

Lucas straightened, his expression serious. "Dan, I'm your twin brother."

Dan blinked, leaning forward. "Come again?"

"I'm your brother. We were adopted by different families. Vic found you, but I was lost in the shuffle."

Dan stared, the hairs on his neck standing up. "How do you know that?" He didn't need Lucas to answer— he knew it was true. A feeling in his gut.

Lucas just shrugged and stared. "God told me."

Dan paused. He could feel his gut tighten. Could this be real? He could feel Lucas. He had heard of the twin syndrome where each could feel the others pain. He looked into Lucas' eyes and could feel the truth of what he was saying. He didn't know Vic was his father until two months ago. Everything that happened was certainly bizarre. What's one more brick in the wall. "So, I guess welcome to the family," Dan laughed.

"I grew up in Pennsylvania. I didn't know anything about you either all these years. I didn't know you were my brother until now."

The elevator ding interrupted their conversation, and they turned to see who was coming up into the sanctity of Dans office. Bob walked towards the pair seated at the desk,

"Bob," Dan acknowledged.

"Dan, get that preacher the hell out of here," Bob erupted.

Dan laughed. "If you think I am going to stand by and watch anyone get beaten death in my own building you're nuts. Hell, you probably are nuts since you came up here giving me orders."

"We don't let his kind in here, William Joseph will be tearing this place up in a minute." Bob fumed.

"Bob, I would like you to meet my brother Lucas."

Bob stopped, ending his rant. "Brother?"

"This is Vic's other son. Lucas Stone. My twin brother."

Bob stared. "We know that, Dan. Now get him the hell out of here. He isn't welcome." Dan turned and walked away. The elevator dinged for Bob's return to the main floor.

Dan and Lucas remained at the desk in silence until they heard the elevator close.

"Okay, Lucas. It seems like these crazies know more about you and me than we do. Obviously, Vic let them in on his secret family."

"Dan, I have had nightmares for months."

"Well, me too. You are drinking Black Lake coffee?"

"No. I don't drink coffee. Bob gave me a cup downstairs and he poisoned it."

Dan gave a dry laugh. "It's poison all right. But your nightmares aren't caused by the water it appears."

Lucas met his eyes and said, "God sent me to save your soul."

"Lucas, I think I am beyond even God's reach."

"No. You are not."

"Well, first things first let's get out of here before they come up here and drag us out." Dan stood, bent over and retrieved a nickel plated 45 caliber colt automatic handgun from the bottom drawer. "Dad's gun," he said and smiled.

The brothers took the back stairs into the garage where the Lambo was parked. The engine roared, the garage doors raised, and they skittered around the corner to the town square where the town had gathered by the statue of William Joseph. Like an angry mob Dan expected to see pitchforks and bats. But the big man himself was speaking to them. They all turned and stared as Dan took a hard right and gunned the powerful sports car towards his home beside the lake with the coal black roses.

CHAPTER 46

Dan and Lucas left William Jospeh and the townspeople to rant and rave in the strange town of Black Lake. Lucas left his car parked in town down from the Oak Bar. Dan had plenty of clothes for Lucas who didn't have much anyway. The next few days they spent at their estranged father's palatial estate, exchanging stories of their lives.

Dan spoke of his family history and failed marriage to Rebecca, while Lucas recounted his upbringing in Lone Pine and his marriage to the Church. Their conversations delved deep into the enigmatic roses, the strange waters of Black Lake, and the sprawling web of Black Lake Coffee and Stone Enterprises. They marveled at the isolated compounds, the water's power, and the staggering billions tied to their shared inheritance.

"Lucas, there is too much money here. You should have some of it. I think if Vic had known about you he would have included us both."

"I don't need money, Dan."

"But, you don't need to go back to living in the church. You can stay. Think of all the good you can do with money. The opportunity to do what the church is all about. I mean studying is great but to what end?"

Dan didn't care about the money — there was so much --- plenty to share. Hell, he was making $100 million a year on interest alone, and the company was exploding. Lucas would probably do some real good with his part. Dan was the businessman, while Lucas embodied the emotional, moral core. They were two sides of the same mask—one laughing, one crying—each a part of a bizarre tragedy. To Dan, it felt as though they'd been cast in a twisted play: he as the dark, corrupted twin, and Lucas as the holy, righteous one.

"Well, I could stay for a while and get some missions going. With this money we could feed the hungry at least in the US but maybe the world. I read somewhere that homelessness could be eliminated with ten billion dollars."

"Well let's not go crazy and give it all away. But, you can do a lot of good out there. Just look at the medical side of it. There are some special chemicals in this lake."

"But, Dan there is something more here than money. This lake. This town. Satan. You are being pursued. The evil wants to take control."

Dan laughed. "Come on Lucas. We know the chemicals in the roses have special properties; healing but also can cause hallucinations. I'm sure these cooks in town want to keep whatever it is to themselves. But, I think the God thing is different. I mean God is God. I just don't think the supreme all powerful creator of the universe cares about our coffee business."

"But he does Dan. God is the living God. He lives inside of us. Inside of you. He cares about everyone and everything. Every action. Every thought."

"Okay. Too early for church. But, you do you brother. I'm just glad to have you here. I never had a brother" Dan smiled. "It's late. Let's turn in and we can discuss feeding the hungry tomorrow morning after we feed the hungry here at home."

But Dan woke to silence.
Not the peaceful kind that eases you into the day—this was different. Heavy. Still.
Like the world was holding its breath.

Something was off.

He made his usual double espresso Americano—sweet, with cream— and unwrapped a BrainFood Bar, chewing absently as he wandered the halls.

"Lucas?" he called.
No answer.

He passed the guest room. The door stood open. The bed was made.

"Well," he muttered, "maybe he went for a walk."

Dan showered, rolled a joint of the Durban Poison he'd picked up in Norman, and lit it while staring out the wide living room window.

Nothing.

No movement in the trees. No figure by the lake. The snow had melted so no footprints.

Lucas was an adult. He didn't need to report in.
Still... with all the insanity brewing in town, Dan didn't like it.

The house felt hollow.

Dan didn't know that Lucas had decided on an early morning walk around the lake.
He didn't know Lucas had been dragged into darkness, silent and bleeding, by things that no longer needed to hide in the shadows.

He didn't know Lucas was now a captive—hidden somewhere beneath Black Lake's surface influence, a prisoner of the same horror he was trying to fight.

And above it all, from the porch of the cabin in Dan's dreams, the handsome, ageless man with the coal black hair sat in his rocking chair, smiling.

He would not let Lucas go so easily.

For days, Dan searched the town, incredulous, but his efforts were fruitless. Eventually, he arrived at the conclusion that Lucas had simply given up and headed back to Scotland. An Irish exit, Dan thought they called it. He convinced himself this was reality. The money must have been too much of a moral decision for Lucas. Too much pressure to serve the cash rather than God. Well go with God, Lucas, Dan laughed.

Reluctantly, Dan pushed the mystery aside and buried himself in his work. He drove himself relentlessly, achieving spectacular results. Black Lake Coffee thrived under his singular focus, rising to heights no one could have imagined. Yet, in the quiet moments, thoughts of his twin brother Lucas lingered—a loose thread in the tapestry of Dan's life.

CHAPTER 47

"Dan, we've got a phenomenon on our hands," Tom said, stepping into the office. "The college towns are on fire. Word's out—BrainFood is real. Breakthroughs are happening everywhere. It's like some kind of... groupthink. Everyone moving in synergy."

Dan leaned back in his chair, a slow smile forming. "Exactly what we planned."

Tom hesitated. "But... we have our first casualty."

Dan's smile faded. "Casualty?"

"Joe. In Norman."

Dan sat up. "Joe? Our Joe?"

Tom nodded grimly. "Just like Vic."

Dan's jaw tightened. "What happened?"

"Apparently, he was determined to crack something in the genetics lab. No one's sure what he was working on, but he'd been downing BrainFood Bars and BudderCups like candy. Pushed way past the threshold. He was convinced he could get smarter if he consumed more."

Dan stared. "That's the point right?"

"They found him this morning in the Cannafe," Tom continued. "What was left of him. He... burned. Charred. Like Vic."

A heavy silence filled the room.

"There's a stir. Media's sniffing. Students are talking."

Dan's voice came low. Controlled.

"Then we control the narrative. We call it an accident. A fire. Faulty wiring. Whatever we need to say. We do not let this derail the momentum."

Tom nodded, but his eyes held something tighter than agreement—concern. "It's starting, Dan. Whatever this is…"

Dan waved a hand. "No. He was old. What—fifty? Looked like sixty. Hard living, you could see it in his skin. This isn't about some ridiculous eternal students playing with fire. This is about strong, nourished kids pushed to the edge. That's the point."

Tom hesitated. "Still… it was an overdose. We don't know how much that idiot was taking. From what I hear, the guy was a drunk. Maybe pain pills. Unclear."

Dan shrugged. "Then spin it. Let's call it a suicide; some drunk old man wallowing in self pity. Not the BrainFood. Throw money at it. Bury it."

He leaned forward, tone shifting. "How many college dispensaries do we have now?"

"Twenty," Tom replied. "Basically every major campus where weed's legal, we've got a Black Lake Coffee + Dispensary in town. Same results across the board."

Dan raised an eyebrow. "Results?"

"Phenomenal," Tom said. "Students are exploding—mentally. Breakthroughs in everything. Art. Literature. Physics. Genetics. Athletics. You name it. They're acting like savants."

He paused, shaking his head in wonder. "And they credit BrainFood, every time. They talk about it like it's holy. It's not just brand loyalty—it's cult-level devotion. Huge buzz. CNN, Fox, 60 Minutes—they're all begging for interviews."

Tom grinned. "Dan Stone is being called a genius."

He chuckled, dark and low.

"Hell, Dan. They're calling you the new messiah."

CHAPTER 48

The rain was steady, a rhythmic patter against the roof of The Oak Bar, as Dan pushed open the heavy door. The familiar scent of polished wood, whiskey, and faint cigar smoke greeted him like an old friend. Monday mornings were always slow to start, but this one already felt too long by ten a.m. Seeking refuge, Dan walked into the comforting dimness of the bar, where Bob was already wiping down the counter.

"Mornin', Dan," Bob greeted without looking up, his gravelly voice warm despite the dreary day. "You're early."

Dan slid onto his usual stool, shaking the rain from his hair. "Yeah, Monday started rough. Figured I'd come in before it got worse."

Bob chuckled softly, pulling a clean glass from beneath the counter. "Can't argue with that logic. Usual?"

"Yeah," Dan replied, already feeling the weight of the morning lift slightly in the quiet familiarity of the place.

Bob poured with practiced ease, setting the bourbon down in front of him. Dan took a sip, savoring the burn. The room was quiet except for the clink of glasses and the rain outside. He found himself relaxing, the tension of the morning easing.

"You know," Dan said after a while, swirling the bourbon in his glass, "Tom will be here by noon. Probably bringing his whole team."

Bob raised an eyebrow, leaning slightly closer. "Big day, huh?"

"Every day's a big day lately," Dan muttered. "10,000 stores. Trucks are running nonstop. And a hundred people in this building and the warehouse across the alley. It's a machine."

"And you're the guy keeping it running," Bob said with a knowing nod. "What's Stark want?"

Dan shrugged, finishing his drink and sliding off the stool. "Business. Expansion. Probably something legal. He's got that look like he knows something I don't. Anyway, I need to get upstairs and go over some reports before he gets here."

"Good luck with that," Bob said, smirking as he slid Dan's venti Americano across the bar. "Extra shot 3 sugars and too much cream."

Dan smirked back. "Thanks, Bob. Don't let anyone burn the place down while I'm upstairs."

He made his way to the elevator, discreetly tucked into the dark walnut-paneled wall near the bar. The door slid open with a quiet chime, and Dan stepped in, the bourbon still warm in his chest. As the elevator ascended, he let out a slow breath, bracing himself for another day running the Black Lake empire.

When the doors opened, he stepped into the long, high-ceilinged office that had once belonged to Vic. The room exuded old-world elegance, with walnut-paneled walls inlaid with ebony and polished brass fixtures that gleamed faintly in the warm light. A black marble floor stretched beneath his feet, shining so flawlessly it seemed to reflect his every step. The walnut desk sat imposing at the far end of the room, flanked by tall bookcases lined with leather-bound tomes. One wall displayed framed plans of the grand house Vic had built near the lake, alongside photographs of its construction and completion.

Dan had added to the pictures on the wall, showcasing a half-dozen of the finest international stores: Berlin, Sydney, Paris, Tokyo, London, and New York. Each image captured the sleek, cosmopolitan design of the flagship locations, a sample of the best—or at least the coolest—Black Lake Coffee stores across the globe.

The New York store, situated on the 104th floor of One World Trade Center, was the crown jewel. Its design was a seamless blend of modern elegance and the signature elements of Black Lake Coffee. The interiors boasted polished black ebony wood and subtle etched glass panels featuring the iconic black rose. A small, sleek water feature bubbled near the entrance, a nod to the lake that had started it all. Customers could sip their coffee while gazing out at the stunning view of Manhattan, their lives intertwined with the global phenomenon Dan had built over the last several years.

Dan's gaze swept over the photographs, a sense of satisfaction settling over him. These weren't just stores—they were monuments to the empire he now controlled. And soon, the next chapter would begin.

Framed covers of Forbes, Fortune, and Bon Appétit adorned the walls of Dan's office, each capturing a defining moment in his meteoric rise. On every cover, he held his signature venti-sized, cream-colored ceramic travel mug, emblazoned with the Black Lake Coffee logo—a minimalist coffee cup encircled by a delicate black rose. The image of Dan, with his sharp suit, piercing eyes, and that iconic mug, had become synonymous with success, innovation, and the empire he built from the mysterious waters of Black Lake.

Forbes proclaimed: "The Billionaire Brews: How Dan Stone is Redefining the Beverage Industry" beneath a striking photo of him standing confidently in front of a map highlighting Black Lake Coffee's global reach.

Fortune declared: "The Dark Water Revolution: The Man Behind the Miracle Coffee Everyone's Drinking", showcasing Dan in a contemplative pose, the Black Lake logo subtly reflected on a sleek glass desk.

And Bon Appétit leaned into the cultural phenomenon: "The Flavor of Power: What Makes Black Lake Coffee the Obsession of a Generation", with Dan mid-laugh, his mug raised like a toast.

Each frame was a testament to Dan's dominance in the industry and his careful cultivation of a brand that had become both a lifestyle and a global powerhouse. They weren't just magazine covers; they were trophies—monuments to a man who had turned influence into doctrine, branding into belief.
Dan Stone wasn't just winning—he was being canonized.

But his crowning achievement to date wasn't coffee. It was the BrainFood Bar—and the Nobel Prize that followed.

Dan had carried forward Lucas's dream—feeding the hungry on a global scale. But he'd done it his way.

His BrainFood Bars, infused with cognitive enhancers and longevity compounds, were now distributed in food kitchens across every country, paired—without exception—with Black Lake Coffee. What began as charity had evolved into infrastructure.

Governments footed the bill, eager to eradicate homelessness and hunger, hailing the program as a humanitarian miracle.

But there was more to it.

Because consumption of BrainFood didn't just nourish—it ignited something. A drive. A compulsion. Recipients didn't simply feel better—they felt purpose.

Motivation surged.
Work programs filled.
Crime dropped.

Across cities and shelters, collective groups of the homeless and hungry began to move with eerie coordination. No individual, when questioned, could explain why they were doing what they were doing—only that it felt right. Natural. Necessary.

They weren't organized. They were aligned.

At the surface level, it looked like social renewal. But at a deeper, almost invisible layer, something far more primal was at play.

The pheromones of the black roses, now fully assimilated into their biology, acted like a binding thread—uniting them in instinct and intent. Swarm behavior.
No leaders. No plan. Just momentum.

Governments noticed. As Black Lake products reached the poorest communities, assistance needs plummeted.
The forgotten were no longer idle.

They were working. Willing. Awake.

And in time, even those on the fringes began to whisper what others had already accepted:

Dan Stone didn't just feed the world. He rewired it.

He was hailed as a peacemaker, a visionary who had removed the oldest catalyst for war: hunger.

The world adored him.

And Dan believed, more than ever, that they should.

On his desk today, a binder filled with acquisition details lay open, emblazoned with a familiar red-and-white logo: Coca-Cola.

Acquiring The Coca-Cola Company was more than a business move—it was a declaration. A conquest.

With operations in over 200 countries and territories, Coca-Cola was the most recognized beverage brand on Earth. Its portfolio boasted over 500 brands and 3,500 products, with annual sales exceeding 30 billion unit cases—or about 44.5 billion gallons of beverages consumed worldwide each year. In 2023 alone, Coca-Cola reported $45.7 billion in revenue, with a market cap of $254.7 billion.

Dan's offer: $392 billion.
The largest corporate acquisition in history.

And it was about to be signed.

He exhaled and sank into the leather chair behind his desk, the weight of it all pressing down like a crown. On the desk sat a binder stamped with the red-and-white Coca-Cola logo—inside, the final deal documents.

Across the room, the Black Lake emblem glowed on a digital display: a coffee cup wreathed in a black rose. It had become a symbol known on every continent. Black Lake Coffee had moved beyond a brand. It was now a global empire.

But this wasn't about coffee anymore.

This was about water.

Black Lake Water—mysterious, addictive, miraculous. The elixir behind the breakthroughs. Behind the loyalty. Behind the silence.

Dan didn't just want influence—he wanted omnipresence. And Coca-Cola's unmatched global infrastructure would give it to him. Bottled Black Lake Water in every grocery store. Every vending machine. Every refrigerator on Earth.

Tom Stark, Dan's consigliere, was en route to close the deal. Once signed, the acquisition would catapult Black Lake Industries into a realm no company had ever touched—control of not just beverage choice, but daily consumption. A liquid revolution.

Dan Stone had taken what was once a fringe brew and turned it into a planetary necessity.

And now, he was preparing to quench the thirst of the entire world.

Dan leaned back in his chair, staring at the binder with a faint smile. Soon, his vision would become reality. Black Lake Water, the lifeblood of his empire, would flow to every corner of the Earth. It was the culmination of his work, his drive, his destiny. Nothing could stand in his way now. If only he could sleep.

CHAPTER 49

Dan's trip to New York had been eventful. He became the first private citizen in modern history to address the full General Assembly—not as a sponsor or partner, but as a man reshaping the world's most vital resource. The moment underscored the gravity of his message.

Dan presented a revolutionary compound developed by Stone Enterprises—one capable of propagating just five gallons of Black Lake Water into fifty thousand gallons of purified water, while simultaneously eradicating bacteria, parasites, and viruses.

"The most important discovery in a thousand years," declared JAMA: The Journal of the American Medical Association. The process had already been operational for months, transforming contaminated water sources into safe, drinkable reservoirs across the globe. Entire communities were being rebuilt—revived by this miracle. And always, the black roses followed, blooming along the shores of these new waters, as if nature itself bowed to Dan's vision.

From the podium of the General Assembly Hall, beneath the world's flags, Dan stood straight and still, voice composed yet resolute.

"What I bring you is not a product—it is a promise. A promise that every citizen of this Earth will drink clean water. That your rivers will run clear, your cities will breathe again. And I do not come to you as a visitor. I come asking to belong."

The chamber fell still.

"I respectfully request citizenship in every member nation represented here today. My dowry is not gold. It is water—pure, abundant, transformative. For your people. For our people."

The silence lingered.

"Let us not divide what unites us. Let Black Lake flow in every homeland. And let me stand among you not as a guest—but as a fellow countryman."

For a long moment, the hall remained hushed—not in hesitation, but in awe.

Then came the murmurs. Not of dissent, but adoration.

Delegates whispered to one another with reverent urgency. Heads nodded. Hands clutched translation earpieces tighter, as if trying to absorb every syllable. Some simply stared, transfixed.

And then—applause.
First scattered, then growing. A wave of sound rising like a tide.

By the time Dan stepped down from the podium, world leaders were rising to their feet. Applause thundered through the chamber. Smiles, nods, outstretched hands followed him down the aisle. The path ahead was clear.

No objections. No resistance. No opposition.

Dan Stone was no longer just a man with a miracle.
He was becoming a citizen of the world—and the world welcomed him without question.

No one in history had ever asked for what Dan Stone just did.
Not generals. Not kings. Not prophets.
Not even the Secretary-General of the United Nations.

Universal citizenship.

To belong to every nation—not as a visitor, not as an emissary—but as a native son.
To be written into the birthright of every people.
To be of everywhere.

And the world, mesmerized by clean water, miracle nutrition, and the illusion of peace, began to say yes.

Not with hesitation.
With open arms.

Dan Stone was not ascending to a title.
He was becoming something new.
Something the world had no name for—
but had been waiting for all along.

Post-Address Press Conference at the United Nations, New York City

Flashes from the press gallery popped as Dan entered the press room, escorted by aides. The air buzzed with anticipation. The Secretary-General of the United Nations sat at the center of a long, curved table, flanked by representatives from ten nations, each flag displayed prominently behind its delegate. Dan took his place at the Secretary-General's right hand.

The Secretary-General stood for his opening remarks.

"Today marks a singular moment in human history—not in war, not in conquest, but in healing.

Mr. Dan Stone has not merely brought forward an innovation. He has fulfilled one of humanity's oldest and most sacred aspirations: clean, abundant water for all.

Over the past six months, through the application of a compound developed by Stone Enterprises, ten of the world's most polluted and endangered waterways have been fully restored. Not in theory. Not on paper. In truth.

Where once there was death, now there is life. And in many cases... roses."

Light laughter rippled through the room at the poetic remark, as images of black roses blooming along revitalized rivers flashed across the monitors behind them.

"Let the world bear witness:"

The Ganges in India

The Citarum in Indonesia

The Yamuna in India

The Marilao in the Philippines

The Buriganga in Bangladesh

The Matanza-Riachuelo in Argentina

The Mississippi in the United States

Lake Karachay in Russia

The Tietê in Brazil

The Yangtze in China

Lake Victoria in East Africa

"Each of these lifelines—once poisoned—has now been reborn."

One by one, each of the ten national delegates stood. They spoke with sincerity and formality, presenting their declarations.

INDIA:

"Mr. Stone, for your service to our rivers and our people, the Republic of India grants you full and permanent citizenship. You are now, officially, one of us."

INDONESIA:

"You have healed the heart of our island. You are welcome as a son of Indonesia."

PHILIPPINES:

"In gratitude, and in hope, we grant you the rights and privileges of citizenship. Our children thank you."

BANGLADESH:

"You are now counted among the people of Bangladesh—not as a guest, but as family."

ARGENTINA:

"You have cleansed a wound that festered for generations. Welcome home, Señor Stone."

UNITED STATES:

"Though already a citizen by birth, we reconfirm and recommit our loyalty. You are one of our greatest sons."

RUSSIA:

"What science failed to repair, you have restored. Russia recognizes you as one of its own."

BRAZIL:

"You have returned life to our waters. And so, Brazil returns your gift with its citizenship."

CHINA:

"The Yangtze has long defined our civilization. Today, it defines your legacy. Welcome."

The Chinese delegate paused for effect before finishing:

"You are now a citizen of the People's Republic of China."

Each delegate stepped forward, handing Dan a ceremonial folder—a formal decree of citizenship from their nation.

Dan remained seated—humbled.
He offered no speech at first. Just a deep nod. A faint, unreadable smile played at the corners of his mouth.

Behind him, the screen slowly faded into a glowing, rotating globe— black roses blooming across its continents.

Dan leaned toward the microphone.

"Thank you all. I cherish your friendship and offer mine in return.

I promise to bring our pure water to all the citizens of Earth.

Thank you again."

# # #

The trip spanned several weeks: Black Lake, Wichita, Dallas, New Orleans, New York, Dallas again, Wichita, and finally back to Black Lake. Exhausting, but worth it—there was even talk of a second Nobel Prize. Dan Stone: the savior of the modern world.

CHAPTER 50

"Get these people out of here!" General Archer yelled from the door of the large canvas tent used as mission control. New methods for capturing 3D topographic data with amazing accuracy using small, unmanned aircraft were being used to ascertain the exact dimensions of Black Lake. Archer's team had been running more than one hundred drones for the last two days. An accurate three-dimensional model was to be constructed using multiple photographs of the lake and surrounding area taken from different angles in a process called stereo photogrammetry. Archer's team would load all the data into the new Agrisoft Photoscan computer program that performs photogrammetric processing of digital images and generates 3D spatial data to associate related photographs and perform the necessary triangulation and use algorithms to increase estimation accuracy and minimize error. At least that mouthful was what the IT geeks had told him in the twenty-one-day class he attended in Washington last spring. Primarily in use Afghanistan with thousands of miles of data generated and reviewed by Archer's team each week and housed in a twelve-acre underground computer facility at McConnel Air Force Base in Wichita, this week it would be used to map the darkest most unthinkable horror. The word was in, and the word was not good; the lake had doubled in size since they landed seven days ago.

"I have never seen anything like this, Mike. The lake is sinking," General Archer said.

"There must be an underground Faultline, Sir." replied Major Michael Douglas Carter. Mike was the General's right hand man and if anyone were to know the truth, the brains in his outfit. The General and the rest of the team were pretty sharp, but Mike made them seem more like butter knives.

"What direction is it growing, Mike?" he asked.

"Well really in all directions. If it keeps up this town will go in a matter of days."

"How can we stop it? Can we shore up the edges of the lake with concrete or dam it up somehow?"

"Not likely, Sir. It seems like the bottom is falling out. We tried to get some sonar to the bottom of the lake but could not get a response. The temperature of the water has increased to boiling in some places. It looks likely that there is a fault line under the lake shooting steam into the lake."

"That's a hell of a lot of steam for a seventy-degree temperature swing, Mike" stated the General, removing his olive green cap and rubbing his grey flat top. Still have all my hair even if it's a little snowy he was oft to think.

"Yes. a tremendous amount would need to be shooting into the lake somewhere."

"Well, if that accounts for the water temp, what about the expansion of the lake itself," Archer asked.

"Good question, Sir. I have not heard of anything like this. Neither Joe Duncan nor his crew. They are seismologists. We have a hydrologist enroute. Should be here soon."

"How fast are the sides caving in?"

"About one to two feet per hour depending on where you are. More so north and west of here. But it's visible at virtually any point." he responded.

"Okay. Let's issue an evacuation of all citizens and personnel. Call the Army guard up here to get the farmers within a mile to safer ground. Move them back south of Lebanon, East of 36, a mile on the other sides. Find out how many people we are talking about and let the Kansas Highway Patrol know that they need to arrange some transportation and shelter."

"Will do, boss. You going to Topeka to talk with the Governor?"

"Right now. Helicopter is landing in --- twenty minutes," he said looking at his watch. We have some help coming in on the chopper and I will be leaving immediately."

Mike and Dave finished a few housekeeping tasks, said their goodbyes and left the tent to get busy on their respective tasks. Mike followed his marching orders and began preparations for the evac. Dave was on the UH-60 Black Hawk helicopter flying due south thirty minutes later. Four Dramamine and two long rolling flight hours in strong Kansas winds and he was landing in the state capital.

Christopher Pulmer was a hydrologist at the University of Texas at Austin on loan to help get to the bottom of this oddity. For years, scientists had assumed that geysers and other types of hot springs spewed water that came from deep inside Earth. Now, thanks to Chris Pulmer, researchers had identified alternative theories. He was here to determine what exactly was causing the water temperature to suddenly skyrocket.

"Mr. Pulmer," Mike said. "Great to have you here."

"Thank you. Call me Chris."

"Chris, please have a seat," Mike said motioning to a tan fabric folding chair. "Have you formed any ideas from the briefings?" Mike asked.

"Yes. I have a few ideas to explore. Please forgive me if I go over topics you are already familiar with, but I want to make sure we are on the same page. If we look at the difference in the standard temperature and the actual temperature we see a dramatic rise. Temperatures deep below Earth's surface are, on average, much warmer than at ground level. That's true for a number of reasons. First, there is heat left over from when dust, gas and other material collided billions of years ago and formed Earth. The planet is still cooling off from those long-ago cosmic fender-benders. Second, radioactive elements deep inside Earth are constantly generating heat. As each radioactive atom morphs, shedding subatomic particles and sometimes transforming into other elements, it releases a tiny bit of energy. Add all those tiny bits together and there's a lot of heat working its way upward through Earth's crust," he lectured.

"So, you believe this heat is coming from the crust of the earth?" Mike asked.

"Perhaps, that heat reaches Earth's surface in different ways. Some is carried upward by molten rock, which spews from volcanoes or oozes through the seafloor at vents along mid-ocean ridges or in this case potentially along the floor of this lake. Sometimes heat is emitted into space as infrared radiation like the same sort of heat produced by an electric stove or a light bulb. On average, each 10-square-foot area of Earth's surface emits about half the power needed to light up a 4-watt nightlight. Sometimes, Earth's heat even flows forth in hot springs like those found at Yellowstone National Park and around many volcanoes."

"Okay. But still it all comes down to the super-heated water, steam or heat coming up through the bottom of the lake. Correct?" Mike asked.

"Maybe. Most scientists had presumed that water spewing from hot springs, like the source of heat itself, came from deep within the ground," Chris explained. "My job as a hydrologist is to study how exactly water flows across and through Earth's crust. We recently identified a new type of hot spring. It recirculates water coming from a source near Earth's surface. So that is a possibility as well," he continued as he removed a thermal infrared camera from his leather messenger bag. "This camera detects and records radiation that corresponds to heat, not visible light. I used this on a lake in the Philippines last summer named Taal's crater," he beamed as he explained his discovery and showed off his toy.

"Like many volcanoes, Taal's crater holds a large lake. It covers about 1.3 square kilometers which is an area larger than 240 football fields crammed together. The lake water averages about thirty-five meters deep or about the same as a 10-story building. When we looked at the lake using the thermal camera, we saw that the water at some spots along the lakeshore was much warmer than elsewhere. The average temperature of the lake was about 35° Celsius, just a little cooler than the body temperature of people. But at some spots where hot springs were flowing into the lake from sites onshore, the lake was far warmer — a very toasty 122° and 140° Fahrenheit. Sound familiar?" he asked.

"Yes. We are seeing fluctuations as high as 190 along the western shorelines, Chris."

"I see a lot of similarities between your numbers and Lake Taal. We brought instruments that let us measure the water flow through the ground along the lake. That's when we got our surprise. The data showed the water wasn't flowing from deep underground. Instead, it was being pulled from the lake through the volcano's rock. Some were very hot and warmed the water. The heated water then emerged from spots near the lakeshore and flowed downhill back into the lake. Water flowing from one of Taal volcano's hot springs range from 99° to very hot at about 180°. This is the same sort of circulation seen at deep-sea hydrothermal vents where hot, mineral-rich water spews from the seafloor. This causes a suction that pulls cool seawater into cracks in the seafloor far from the vent. That water is warmed as it flows through the rocks beneath the seafloor and toward the vent; this is the opening from which the water returns to the sea as a potentially scalding stream. Until now, no one had really studied the flow of hot springs around volcanoes. Bottom line is I suspect that the circulation they saw at Taal may be occurring here in Black Lake," Chris finished his brief and let out a heavy sigh.

"So, what does all that mean, Chris?" Mike asked.

"You have a volcano."

"A volcano. In Kansas," Mike repeated. He needed to get the General on the phone asap.

CHAPTER 51

As Dan approached the oversized iron gates of Black Lake Ranch a nauseating feeling of unease began to settle like a hot rock in his gut. The giant maple trees flanking either side of the stone pillars were no longer green having shed their leaves by this cold November day. The ominous stick like limbs rocked back and forth bending the large branches nearly to the frozen ground in the stiff Kansas wind.

The gate began to slide north. Each time the gate moved the three dimensionally carved figures of men and their horses within seemed to shift and flex as though straining under the weight of the gates mass as they pulled it along the overhead track. But as the black roses on the gate swayed and the creatures within it hefted the gate open the clearing beyond came into view. Dan paled as he saw the dark water bubbling with steaming and splashing white caps only one hundred yards to the right of the fence line. The guest houses were missing.

Dan rubbed his eyes and felt his heart accelerating. They were gone and the lake was close. Really close. "It must be a giant sinkhole," he thought. Dan shifted the Lamborghini into first and rumbled through the gate and into Black Lake estate proper. The lake had encroached five hundred feet closer to the main house. The guest houses were indeed completely gone as was the ground they sat on only one month before. The dark water tossed about in the wind like a hot cup of coffee in the hands of a jogger. Steam came off the water creating a misty black fog.

"Holy shit." Dan said aloud. "Holy fucking shit." He accelerated up the long drive now bordered by the lake only a hundred yards or so to the left. The houses, ground, trees, rocks, fencing; all gone. Sunk into the black water.

Dan arrived at the main house and shut down the Aventadors V12. Climbing out the top rather than opening the doors simply because it was easier to maintain his stare at the lake and shoreline Dan sat on the rear edge of the roadster's roof. The lake was bigger. A lot bigger. The rear patio around the swimming pool of the main house was merely inches from the rolling lake. Dan pulled his cell out and hit the button for Stark.

After a few rings; voicemail. Dan hit the button and scrolled. "Sue. Dan Stone here. Is Tom in his office?"

"Hi Dan. No. He is at a client meeting until 4pm today. Mike is here. Can he help you?"

"Maybe. No. Yes. Hell, I don't know Sue. Sure, send me that way."

"Will do. Hold on Dan," she said.

Mike answered without an audible ring. Or maybe Dan just wasn't hearing anything as he started at the lake. "Dan, what can I do for you this fine day," he asked.

"Mike, I drove up to Black Lake today."

"Ah. Nice. Did you take the Lambo? Break 150 this time," He laughed. Mike was an oversized six eight ex linebacker from the Dallas Cowboys with missing acl from his left knee. Great player and a great guy who everyone wanted to buy whatever he was selling.

"Ya. Hey Mike, I'm kind of losing it a bit up here. Looks like some kind of giant fucking sinkhole opened up beside the lake here and swallowed the guest houses. All of the guest houses. Hell, there isn't even any trace of them. No damage. No kindling. Just plain fucking gone. And the water is all the way to the driveway."

"Damn, Dan, That's incredible. I don't even know what to say to that. We will get someone headed out there. Stay back from the water - those sinkholes can swallow anything. We need to get some engineers out there."

"Roger that Mike. I'll keep you posted, and you do the same; let me know what you can get set up."

"Probably be tomorrow since it's pushing three now. Can you head to Wichita? I'll tell Nancy to get you set up there. I'll send the jet."

"There's no runway – That's what I'm saying the guest houses but everything that direction. The damned lake is twice the size."

"Jesus. Get out of there man. Head south. Stay clear of the thing," Mike said.

"No. I think I'll stay up here and take care of a few things. I've been on the road too long I need to sleep. The house won't sink overnight. I hope. Talk to you soon. Let me know what you can do. And tell Stark what's up. This is fucking bizarre." Dan disconnected and slid his iPhone back in his jacket pocket.

Dropping back down into the cockpit, Dan pressed the ignition button beside the steering column. The horsepower cranked as he hit the gas and spun the tires hard to turn a hard ninety and head for the main house.

# # #

Dan climbed into the steaming shower taking with him a large cup of Black Lake coffee and two BrainFood bars. His skin was burned badly and incredibly painful this morning. He scrubbed relentlessly at the welts and hurried the sluffing process of the falling skin. No nightmares and an overwhelming boost in his intelligence and problem solving provided he didn't sleep. But, his long trip had kept him away and awake too long and his psyche was wearing out. The nightmares and resulting burns were the tradeoff. Emerging from the shower refreshed mentally and physically, Dan planned his trip. He was getting out of Black Lake and would catch a plane in Wichita to Dallas.

Dan walked to the window, his new midnight blue Lamborghini Aventador roadster he picked up in Dallas was parked immediately below his bedroom window in the gravel where it belonged. He inspected his fresh new skin in the sunlight and was pleased.

But something was wrong, the air had a palpable feeling of doom. Something was off in that picture of the morning sun. It was a hazy red color outside. But there was something else, some kind of low humming; a vibration. Maybe the sound was in his head but Dan could feel it in his bones.

Dan walked from the bedroom and walked down the stone steps. The house looked fine. Dan went into the kitchen, made a second cup of coffee and popped three supplement pills.

In the background Dan heard a steady knock on the front door. Someone was insistent. Dan walked to the front door. As he opened the door he immediately froze. The lake was butting directly up to the house. In fact, that is all Dan could see.

"Hello," Dan said to the three men in military fatigues. Dan could not stop staring at the lake. It had grown tenfold since Dan arrived in Black Lake only a few hours ago.

"Mr. Stone, we are here to get you out of here," the young man in the center with Brooks embroidered on a patch over his left pocket said.

"Okay," Dan looked to his left and could not see the opposite shore of the lake. To the right Dan could still see a small patch of black roses glistening in the sun. That was all of them though. Apparently, thousands of the beautiful flowers had met their maker and sunk into the dark water.

"I see the lake is growing tremendously," Dan said. "I will follow you. Give me a minute." Dan went back into the house, grabbed a pair of jeans and slipped on a long-sleeved shirt with a logo from pebble beach golf course. Dan stepped into his Birkenstock sandals.

Dan could see the lake was bouncing and bubbling like boiling oil. An occasional flame popped up and was extinguished just as fast. As Dan opened the Lambos door the wind picked up to gale force. Dan struggled to pull the door down against the sixty mile per hour plus wind. His military escort was in a tan Humvee. Dan started the big engine of the

Aventador, hit the gas for a fast tight half semi-circle and fell in behind them. "Hu Ra let's get the fuck out of here," Dan said aloud.

As they passed through the gate and turned right towards Lebanon Dan spotted William Joseph standing beside the road in his pressed black tunic and bolero tie. He stared at Dan and smiled as Dan passed. Dan was sure he could hear the big man laughing as he hit fifth gear and could still see his long white hair blowing in the Kansas wind as Dan fishtailed the sports car onto the road. "Good riddance, maybe the lake will swallow up that idiot," Dan thought. They were in Lebanon Kansas in less than ten minutes. Dan parked beside the Humvee outside the U.S. Post Office and climbed out of the car.

"Sir, the General would like to wish you well and advise you to stay away from your house until this situation has settled down," Corporal Brooks said.

"No worries there Sarg. I'm heading south. Good luck to you." Dan climbed back into the Lamborghini, backed out of the space and headed south down 181.

# # #

Dan's phone buzzed over the stereo speakers temporarily silencing Sammy Hagar's Three Lock Box. Dan was only a mile or so down the highway from Lebanaon and pulled over to speak with Tom Stark. Leaving him on the car speaker Dan answered. "Tom, we've got a pretty big problem out here."

"Yes Mike told me somewhat. What exactly happened?"

"The lake is growing or the land around it is collapsing. Somehow. I don't know. Maybe a sinkhole like happened in Florida last year that sucked down that house. But you can't see anything at all. The lake rolled into cover anything that was there. It's the craziest thing in the world. The lake has basically grown. It's all the way up to the house and all the way to the driveway. Everything in between is fucking gone. No trace at all. Gone."

Dan leaned across the car and pulled a leather bank deposit bag from the small glove box. Unzipping it he pulled a pre-rolled cannabis joint of some Northern Lights.

"Ok we have a team of engineers already on their way from Wichita, Dan. I don't recommend staying out there."

Dan took a draw on the joint. "Yeah, well the National Guard just kicked me out. I'm in Lebanon and I am heading for Wichita. The lake is right on the doorstep and the guest houses were consumed by the lake. I will keep my distance."

"Ok. We will get this squared away. No worries, Dan," Tom reassured.

"The fuck, Tom. We can't fix this. The fucking guest houses are gone!"

"Dan, why don't you fly back to Dallas while this is going on. We can take in a Mavs game. Cuban's around and would love to meet you. You might like him. He's a first-class asshole," Tom said.

"Ok, Tom. You're crazy. But I am high tailing it out of here. I'm on the highway on the way to Wichita now. I'll be in Wichita in an hour or so."

"Great. Go to Beechcraft east of Wichita, the Gulf Stream is there for you," Tom said.

"See you soon." Dan hit the gas and cranked up the stereo playing Sammy Hagar coincidentally, in the middle of the perfect song. Dan said, "Lambo, restart I can't drive 55." Dan hit the gas and pushed the Italian race car to two hundred mph.

"Fuck this town. Next stop Wichita. In fact, fuck this state. Back to Texas."

CHAPTER 52

"Good morning, Kansas." Anita Boslow began with her typical morning greeting used to kick off the number one rated morning newscast in the wheat state for the last thirty-five years. But this morning was anything but typical. In fact, her lead story would change the tone of the conversation from this point forward not only for Good Day Kansas but for all breakfast table news shows across the country and even parts of the world.

"Today, we join humanitarian and scientific forces in Lebanon, Kansas, the site of what appears to be a giant sink hole appearing beneath Black Lake and literally consuming the ground around it for miles. Let's go now Live to Lance Harvey on the scene of Black Lake just North of Lebanon, Kansas."

The monitor behind Anita showed the handsome mid-twenties news anchor in training who's would become famous internationally for this broadcast and others like it in the coming days. Lance was known in the newsroom for his perfect hair and impeccable dress, always seen in a creative sport coat and tie with matching pocket square; not necessarily in fashion today, but an eye catching schtick as was his intention. Many of the old timers and young republicans thought of him as a little too 'dandy' to trust for their morning dose of news, but despite this fact his popularity had been growing just the same. Today he was wearing a plain navy-blue jacket with salmon colored accoutrements to emphasize the solemnness of this tragedy.

"Good day to you, Anita," he spoke into the live feed camera. "We are on site at Black Lake here in the middle of Kansas; two hundred miles northeast of Wichita. As you can see, we have police, firefighters and scientific agencies on hand here trying to get to the bottom of this tragic situation.

"Lance, what did happen there? Do you have an official statement or any word from any of the agencies there?" Anita asked.

"Yes Anita. According to General Dave Archer of the Kansas Air National Guard, it is being considered a sink hole which appeared beneath the lake. Teams of divers, seismologists, and geologists are enroute as well as the National Guard and members of the U.S. military to look into what exactly happened here last night," Lance spoke into the camera.

The camera then broke away and panned to the left showing Black Lake itself and the statue of William Joseph Smith at the end of the street. This shot would be picked up by virtually every news station on the planet as Lance was one of only a few members of the news (and the most famous in Kansas since he was out of Wichita) to get here at this early morning hour. Lance and his crew of three were heading here at four AM less than an hour after the first report. "As you can see the lake has reached Main Street here in Black Lake. Normally, or rather up until this morning the lake was more than ten miles away from town. It appears that immense stretch of land simply fell into the water. As you can see, we are being kept back several hundred feet from the lake as they have yet to determine that the sink hole is no longer growing."

"Lance, Black Lake sounds very familiar, why is that?"

"Yes, Anita. As you may recall billionaire recluse Victor Stone made Black Lake his home. In fact, we are attempting to contact his son, Daniel Stone, who as we understand it was in his lake house on the shores of Black Lake last night. We have determined that the house itself has not sustained any damage but, Mr. Stone has been evacuated from the premises in case of new danger developing."

"Lance, do they believe there is any danger?"

"They really just don't know yet, Anita. It is too early to call. The first reports of the sink hole were reported only in the last five hours. Protective agencies have been scrambling to get here and make the determination. Rest assured, I will be on the scene keeping America up to date on this tragic unprecedented event as it unfolds," Lance responded.

"Lance, thank you. Please take care and our prayers go out to the people of Black Lake. We will stay in touch." The monitor changed to a banner reading Equipment Malfunction over the image of Brittany Spears gripping her breasts beneath her colorfully sequined halter top on a Vegas stage. "In other news," Anita began.

CHAPTER 53

Dan drove with his knees and smoked the marijuana. After a time he tried his cell to get Tom back on to line the flight to jet him straight to Dallas. The endless Kansas sky was now black with rolling clouds and there was zero cell service. Dan had enough of this middle of nowhere town before all the shit started and now with Black Lake destroying the houses and flooding the town Dan was not planning a return trip.

Enough is enough. Dan could buy anything and anywhere he wanted. Dan focused on that to get his mind off the creepy existence which had become his norm. Florida and the beach sounded good. Half naked chicks with missing morals. Sunny days. Salt water. Pina Coladas. More half naked girls.

As soon as Dan could get Tom on the horn Dan was going to have him buy him a beach front house in Fort Lauderdale. Maybe a houseboat. Time to get drunk and watch the cruise ships pull in and out of Bahia Mar. Could do a lot worse than a Travis McGee existence.

Well Dan could keep driving all the way to Texas or Dan could find a hotel bar in Wichita, get drunk, and find a waitress. Yes. That is a solid plan. Fuck this hillbilly hell. Get back to civilization. Take the money and run. And never never never look back.

# # #

Then Dan saw him. A man was laying with his back stretched across a barb wire fence at the side of the road. There was smoke coming off his blackened jacket. In fact he was smoldering like the last log in a campfire. Dan started braking. As he got closer Dan could see his left eye was swollen shut and blood covered his face in dark crimson. His long black hair was matted into a deep gash across his good eye. It took him a minute to recognize his twin brother.

Dan wound the car down and came to stop, popped the driver's door up and climbed out. As he walked around the car Dan called out. "Lucas is that you? Holy shit."

The priest groaned and Dan knew he was alive. Thank God.

His arms were extended, and he hung onto the barb wire fence. His burned up hoodie was stuck on the barbs and his legs were limp. The fence was the only think holding him up. Dan got his shoulder under one arm and pulled him off the fence line. He couldn't stand. He was a sack of bones and flesh. Someone had worked him over. Beaten and set him on fire it looked like. Dan hit the button on the passenger door, and it lifted up. Dan folded Lucas into the form fitting passenger seat of the cabin. Tight fit but Dan thought he could make it. Dan closed the door.

# # #

Lucas was in and out of consciousness as Dan pushed the Lamborghini to its limits. Or at least its limits on this empty rural Kansas highway; the pavement was broken in spots, with potholes here and there along with an occasional blacktop patch applied several years back to make it impossible to hit maximum velocity. At one hundred plus they came up fast and were a little problematic for a vehicle shaped more like a jet than a road car.

It was tight quarters in the bullet of a car. The Lamborghini flexed and bucked when they did get a bit airborne surfing the potholes on the old country highway. The burned and beaten preachers head bounced side to side. It was good that Lucas was pinned into his seat keeping his body largely immobilized.

"South. We have to get south as fast as we can," Lucas groaned. His head lolled back and forth. His only good eye was squeezed shut. Probably a concussion. Definitely a bit delusional.

"Hang on Preach, we are driving like a bat out of hell. We will be somewhere soon and get you some first aid." Shit. Dan hoped he didn't die enroute.

"Thirsty."

Dan had grabbed a few beers before He evacuated the cabin. Dan grabbed the leather satchel also crowding what was left of the preacher's feet. As Dan pulled the bag onto this lap and deftly removed the two Abita Gator lagers from his bag he noticed the preachers leather loafers were burned through and could see his bloody left foot. The toenail was gone. Burned off by the appearance. Black charred skin and soot. Melted shoes. It looked like Lucas had been walking on burning coals.

Dan twisted open both of the dark beers. The bottles were still relatively cold and wet with condensation. Dan could certainly use one. He certainly needed one.

"Here Preacher. Drink this. Get some calories and liquid in you. Monks used to survive winters on nothing but beer and bread. Maybe this will bring you back to life some."

Lucas drank half the bottle as he gripped it with both of his charred hands. Most of it went past his bloody lips. The pain was obviously unbearable.

"Jesus Christ Preacher. I'm going to puke over here. We need to get you cleaned up," Dan said.

Lucas reclined his head against the passenger window as much as he could. The lukewarm beer did him some good. His blood smeared on the glass where his head touched. He didn't look like he was still bleeding but was certainly battered by someone who meant to put the hurt on him, Dan thought.

The miles flew by. Not bad time, 96 miles in just about an hour. Damn roads just aren't built for real speed. But, despite that the Lamborghini seemed to float on air and of course Dan was high as a kite from the stress of the bizarre events in the last few weeks, plus he had chain smoked all the weed he had with him while Lucas drank his second and his last beer.

"We will be pulling into Wichita in a few Preacher. I'll find a hospital."

"No. Just drive south I'll be fine. We have to get out of here as fast as we can."

"Hey, you are fucked up brother. You look like a marshmallow left in the flame too long."

"Nothing is broken. It's war Dan, I'm not dying. There are more important things now anyway."

"Cryptic preacher. I can barely understand you your mouth is so swollen. But ok fine we are going to a hotel so we can shower off that town, get some food and some clothes that are not burned off your body and at the very least some first aid."

Lucas closed his eyes.

Finally cell service. Tom answered with no audible ring.

"Tom, it's a shit show here. I need a hotel in Wichita and a flight to Dallas asap."

"Hello, Dan, I'll get it taken care of. Embassy Suites in downtown Wichita. When do you want to fly?"

"Tomorrow morning. I need a break. And I have a guest with me."

Silence on the phone for a few seconds. "Yes, you have the priest Lucas with you." Tom stated.

"Well that's right Tom but how the fuck do you know that?" Dan asked.

"No matter. I'll have a car there for you at 9 in the morning to take you to the executive airport and have the gulf stream waiting."

"And send a doctor over to look at the priest he is beat up pretty bad."

"Ok Dan, Bring him with you to Dallas tomorrow morning. They would like to meet him."

"Who is They, Tom?" But, Tom had disconnected.

Dan hung up. What the hell - his world was beyond bizarre. Dan took the downtown Wichita exit that looked to be the right one for the Embassy Suites hotel he could see rising slightly above the older buildings around it. A couple turns and Dan pulled into the portico and popped the scissor doors up. Edgard jumped out and sat on the curb looking expectantly at Lucas.

The bellhop walked towards the midnight blue Lamborghini with an appreciative grin which quickly faded as he saw the burned and beaten preacher crumpled in the passenger seat.

"Sir are you all ok?" he asked him as Dan climbed out.

"Fuck no kid. He's far from ok. Get us a wheelchair and we will get him upstairs."

The kid ran back inside at a full bolt. Lucas was still sitting there with his eyes closed in the same position when Dan made it around the car. Edgar still watched.

"Preacher. You still with us?"

Lucas opened his eyes and drank the last of his warm beer.

"I'm ok."

The bellhop and three other hotel employees came out with a wheelchair; Dan assumed the kid, his supervisor and a tall thin hotel management member of some level.

"Sir are you alright?" the thin man asked the preacher directly.

Lucas opened his eye. His face was still bloody, and he looked like Dan had pulled him from a prizefight taking place in a burning building. He licked his split lip.

"I'm ok. I just want to get inside to my room and recover. I've been in an accident."

"Maybe a hospital sir, you look pretty bad off" the manager said.

"I'm ok." Lucas said and groaned as he climbed out of the low slung car.

The staff steadied the wheelchair and helped him in. Thin man pushed as they walked into the bright clean marble lobby.

Dan walked to the reception desk and dropped his black card on the counter.

"Big suite please."

"Yes, sir. Your associate phoned in a few minutes ago. We have a doctor staying who will come by your room very soon to look at your friend."

The thin man was around the counter quickly and gave him a key card to the top suite, He was moving fast to get the motley crew of a burned up priest, a guy who did not look like he should be driving a Lamborghini, nor have a black card, out of his very visible lobby and up to the very isolated executive suite. Good thing Tom has called ahead, or the Wichita city cops would be having the time of their lives.

They were in the room in 5 minutes flat. Probably a hotel record if Dan were to guess.

Two new employees brought them upstairs with the thin manager who opened the door to their temporary home. They went in and Dan ordered the manager to get some clothes for Lucas, The doctor arrived before the manager could leave. Lucas sat on the couch with the doctor who gave him the once over. No broken bones. Just bruised and beat to shit. Everyone left who was supposed to.

Lucas went directly to the bathroom and the shower started up. Dan threw himself on the couch. Dan ordered room service: a bucket of ice for the broken preacher and too much food and too much booze for two.

The knock at the door woke him up from his cat nap twenty minutes later.

Lucas was just coming out of the shower dressed in a hotel robe and slippers. No longer looking like a bloody charcoal briquet but certainly not looking tip top. Dan addressed the food and waiter.

"I'm fucking famished. Thanks kid," Dan said flipping a hundred dollar bill off the stack in his pocket. The waiter left. Dan grabbed a handful of French fries and shoved them in his mouth.

Lucas slowly settled himself into the leather chair opposite the couch. Dan opened the curtains so the sun could come in and recharge them with vitamin D. Dan cracked the seal on a bottle of Titos vodka and poured it over some of the ice in a shaker. Dan opened a jar of green olives and dumped in some juice and a half dozen olives. And shook the hell out of it. Dan poured it into a tall glass.

"Here you go preach."

"No I'm good. No alcohol."

"You are far from good. Drink your meds," Dan put the glass on the table by his plate of half-eaten meatloaf and mashed potatoes, which was the softest thing Dan could think of that the hotel kitchen had on the room service menu. It was either that or applesauce and mac and cheese. Well Dan got those too.

Lucas cringed while he forced some of the vodka down, burning in his throat. Okay. Medicine. Dan made another drink for himself. Dans favorite cure all. Nothing better than a strong and dirty martini after a good ass kicking.

"Dan, we have to talk, and we have to get out of the area."

"Ya. We are out of here preacher. Tom is having a plane ready first thing in the morning. Tonight we are going to rest and ice your face."

Lucas nodded and drank half of his drink. "Strong," he breathed. Lucas had a bar baggie of ice on what was left of his eye.

"Best way. The olive juice will get some salt and electrolytes into you and the alcohol will numb the pain. Voice of experience brother." Dan laughed. "Where the hell have you been? I haven't seen you in years. And, who did this to you Lucas?" Dan asked but Dan knew it was William Joseph and the gang.

Lucas just stared at him. Dan could almost see both of his eyes now. "They wanted to send you a message or they would have killed me. I've been in hell since they got me at the lake. They let me out. They told me to tell you to get out of Black Lake. To go back to Dallas or you will be killed."

"Fine with me. I don't plan on ever going back there. In fact I don't plan to see Kansas again in this lifetime. There has been nothing but pain here." Dan said.

"The tests you are going through Dan are not your imagination. They are real. You have been chosen."

"Did the doctor check you for a head injury Preacher? Who would choose me and why and for what? You mean God? The devil?"

"Yes. Sometimes it's just an ordinary man who must choose."

"Ok preacher. I choose to talk about this with you tomorrow and try to pretend the last five years never happened."

"I think I'm going to sleep. That drink was my first stronger than beer or wine since, well ever actually," Lucas yawned.

Take the bedroom preacher. I'm going to go check out the bar downstairs.

"Ok. Be careful Dan, it is very dangerous for you now."

Lucas turned, walked into the bedroom and closed the door.

"Cryptic shit," Dan said aloud. Dan wolfed down three Brain Food bars and took a deep draw directly from the Titos Vodka bottle. He then shook up another dirty martini with extra olives and took it into the shower with him. There was a Rolling Stones song, Sympathy for the devil stuck in his head. Dan started humming along and his thoughts disappeared.

This day had been a whirlwind. Hell the last several years had been a whirlwind. Dan let the vodka settle in as the steaming hot water from the shower scalded his skin. Dan was rich, powerful, and needed a break. Time to hit the bar and go on a little hunt. It had been too long since he worked his way into the pants of some sweet young thing with too many long island ice teas in her tummy. Far too long.

CHAPTER 54

Dan showered up and grabbed some khaki shorts, a black tank top and his flop sandals. He made another dirty martini for the road. Dan rode the elevator down to the lobby. Mirrors lined the doors, and glass surrounded the back and sides so you could have a bird's eye view of the Wichita skyline and the grand hotel confines. Lights and sirens filled the streets, and Dan had a bad feeling that his trip out of Black Lake wasn't over despite being half in the bag at a five star hotel.

Dan exited the elevator and found the hotel bar. Bartenders always know what's up. He ultimately planned on starting his bender at the hotel and exploring the old town Wichita scene but never got past the bar. Not bad while it lasted. But the shit was hitting the fan hard.

"Hey bud - what's up out there, Dan called across the black granite bar to a clean cut kid of about twenty five.

"Earthquake up north."

"Like up north what? This is Kansas. Tornados yes. Earthquake no."

"No here man. Like Salina. 6.8 they are saying. Tore shit out of the place. Check it out. It's on the tv over there." He motioned to the other end of the bar in a more relaxed and comfortable area with a dozen small tables and round back leather captain's chairs.

"Ok, I'll check it out. Hey, hit me with an extra strong extra-large dirty as hell martini."

Dan walked over to the lounge and tuned into the seventy inch flatscreen tv over a stone fireplace. A crowd of hotel guests and a few of the kitchen help were glued to the set. The news was on. They were all over it from the station it appeared. It seemed to have happened in the last hour. A hot mid-thirties weekend anchor was at the desk at KAKE TV in a tight black turtleneck with smaller than Texas boobs and straight black hair cut around her wholesome pretty face. "For the first time in our history a major earthquake has hit Kansas with the epicenter of Salina Kansas. A

6.8 on the Richter scale they are being told with extensive damage. Anita Boslow is on the scene."

"Hello Katie, Yes the earthquake hit just after seven this evening square in the middle of downtown Salina. Nearly every building over two stories is in rubble. Thank God it was Saturday and most people are off work." A camera panned around the small city showing a disaster scene. It looked like a bomb had gone off. As Dan watched the area began to shake again with an aftershock. More buildings were falling while the news cameraman was shooting his live career making action. The best work Doug Lasher had ever done. And his last.

The street in view of the camera collapsed and molten red lava spewed up through a slice in the pavement like some crazed butcher had just severed an artery. The shiny flaming orange red goo shot thirty feet in the air. Doug followed the airborne stream as it arched towards Anita and Doug. Anita screamed Doug was frozen in time capturing the epic moment and began to scream as he was hit with the molten lava and the camera dropped to the ground. Blue screen.

"Oh his God," Katie yelled at the station as her round face once again filled the screen.

Bartender brought his drink over. "What the hell happened there?"

It's Black Lake Dan.

"Looks like a volcano is erupting out of the street there in Salina." Dan said quietly.

The fuck it is. You know what it is.

"I have to get the hell out of here." Dan grabbed the drink and took it with him. He hit the button for the glass elevator and hit the button for Tom on his cell phone. Tom answered dutifully as the elevator door opened and Dan hurried in.

"Tom, Jesus fucking Christ. I'm freaking out a bit. I'm at the hotel. Get the plane and get me to Dallas."

"Yes Dan, you need to stay calm. A lot is happening. We have a car coming to the hotel now. Get the preacher and get in the limo. Ten minutes you will be heading to the airport. The jet is waiting."

"How the hell did you know Tom?"

"We are following everything, Dan, it's time you came in to take your seat."

"What the hell are you talking about Tom? There is an earthquake."

"You know what it is Dan. You have always known."

"All I know is I am getting out of this God forsaken town and heading for the beach."

"Dan. You will lead us as your father commands. Now get in the car and get on the plane." Tom hung up. And the elevator door opened on the top floor.

Dan ran down the hall to the door to his room and waved the card key in front of the lock. He ran inside. "Preacher!" Dan burst into this room where he was sleeping off the drink and the pain.

"Dan, what is it?"

"The world is going to shit Preacher. Get up. It's time to get to the airport and get out of here. Time to go South you were right."

"What?"

"Clothes. Move it," Dan said.

"What is happening here Dan?" Lucas asked quickly.

"Earthquake. Moon turns to blood. God Damns us. All that shit," Dan snapped.

"Ok. Let's go Dan." Lucas rolled out of bed and grabbed his pants. Dan headed for the living room to grab his bag. By the time Dan threw his few items into his brown leather satchel Lucas was at the door. They hurried out and went for the elevator.

"Dan, it's time you made the choice. This is the last time for you to come with me."

"I am coming with you Preacher. Actually, you are coming with me. We have a car downstairs, and it is taking us to the airport. we are heading to Dallas."

The elevator dropped down to the lobby level and rang when the doors slid open. Dan headed out the door leading the way to the waiting limousine. Lucas jogged after and dove into the vehicle fueled by adrenaline. The driver closed the door and ran around the long car. The car lurched forward, and they could hear tires squealing as the car slid around the corner and away from the Embassy Suites hotel forever.

CHAPTER 55

From the frying pan into the fire. It seemed like days since General Dave Archer entered the U.S. Air Force Apache gunship to haul his ass to Topeka instead of just a single day. The lazy old Governor should have flown here to check on this himself firsthand. But he probably didn't understand the gravity of the situation. Hell, who did?

Mike had his nose to the grindstone since the boss left the encampment. Chris Pulmer was taking water samples and the airmen in his crew were flying constant drone sorties over the black water. The environment was getting uncomfortable. The ambient temperature was in the nineties and the wind was a constant forty miles per hour. His men were inside the large tent operating the remote planes and pair of large fans were blowing hot air from point a to point b.

Volcanologists had arrived the day before with a sonar multibeam bathymetry system designed for deep water. The sonar system used phase and amplitude bottom detection, with an accuracy of better than 0.2% of water depth across the entire swath, accurate to plus or minus twenty two meters. Their echosounder was busily sonar mapping the lake. According to their resident eggheads, the ocean-bottom seismometers and hydrophones they brought to Kansas were able to map as deep as sixty miles beneath the surface.

Mike finally reaching his leader. He was sweating, doubtlessly due in part to the unusual weather and environment but also in fear. Mike was scared shitless truth be told. He was starting to wonder how bad this was going to be. especially with the last report just dropped in his lap. "General, I hope your flight was uneventful," Mike said.

"It was. If a two hour flight in an Apache is anything short of an event. What do you have there, Mike?" General Archer asked his second in command. "I'm on my way into the capital building now to meet with Governor Marks so I don't want to lose you when I go into the Marble Palace."

"Yes, Sir. I will be as brief as possible, but you should probably make sure not to lose signal. It's getting really strange here." Mike ducked under the canvas flap of the tent into the hot air, walking quickly around the backside to block as much of the howling wind as possible.

"Go ahead, Mike." The General stopped walking and stood just inside the twelve foot walnut double doors of the foyer of the Topeka capital building. Taking a seat on one of the cold brown granite benches lining the walls he gave Mike his full attention.

"The mapping guys from Ocean got their boat in what they believe to be the middle of the lake and shot some sonar. They just gave me their first report and cast off to keep mapping. They look like it's frickin Christmas here, Sir, pardon my French," Mike said.

"What do you mean, Mike?" the General asked, feeling the hairs standing up on the back of his neck. He could tell from Mikes choice of lingo that this was not going to be good news.

"All the science geeks are really excited, Sir. It's deep. The Lake. According to their report here they shot it at over six thousand feet."

"Say again, Mike?"

"Yeah. Deepest lake in the world if they are right. Right here in the middle of Oz, Sir. The deepest one up to now was in Russia, Lake Baikal at fifty three hundred. They said that one is that deep because it is on an active continental rift zone."

"Unbelievable," Archer said.

"Scientist said he thinks there is a volcano underground either below the lake or somewhere near the lake, superheating the water. He theorizes that the shorelines are dissolving as a result of the heat. Just boiling the ground off. One more odd piece --- he can't explain is the volume of the lake."

"Volume?" the Colonel asked.

"Yes, Sir. The lake level has risen along with the shoreline expanding so the volume of water in the lake is growing."

"How is that possible? The water level should be dropping if the shore is deteriorating, right? The surface area of the lake is increasing. What does he think on that, Mike?"

"He has floated the possibility of an underground river. Hell with that kind of depth nothing is off the table. Figure there has to be something like that. But, water would have to be pouring in by the thousands of gallons per minute. Some kind of volcano opening up down there heating it up is his best guess on the heat. Must be like an underground sea. Worse though, Sir, we are noticing some large sections of land breaking off in the last few hours. It seems to be less stable on the north side of the lake. We are going to need to get some serious brains on this, fast."

"How large are the pieces of land that are breaking up?"

"Real big. Pulmer's in a panic with the depth of the lake. Said in order to move the water temperatures that much we are dealing with something unparalleled. The hunks of land are dropping off in massive amounts on the opposite side of the lake. Sir, I recommend evacuation of this entire grid, and I think we should get the hell out of here today."

"Absolutely. Have the Army step up the evac. Get everyone back as far as possible as fast as possible, Mike."

"I am sending you a video now, General. This was shot by one of the drones on the far northwest corner of the lake. Coming over now," Mike responded. "One more thing Sir, the lake here is getting really rough. Looks like a hurricane is rolling in with waves and white caps. And General, the water temperature is increasing --- spiking to over two hundred degrees in some areas."

"Jesus Christ. 200 - that is nearly boiling -- that sounds impossible. Hold on Mike let me watch the video."

General Archer received the secure text via eimio the secure encrypted communicator used by all of the U.S. Government personnel; mandatory after that Hillary Clinton Wikileaks email hacking bullshit. Encrypted Information Management Input-Output; simple, safe and secure now but a pain in the ass to have to worry about it. The three inch screen of his iPhone popped open the high resolution video shot by the AeroVironment RQ-11 Raven, a small hand-launched remote-controlled unmanned aerial vehicle - SUAV. The craft is powered by an electric motor and can fly up to 10 km at altitudes of up to 500 feet at flying speeds of 28–60 mph --- developed exclusively for the United States military, but now available to the Guard units, as well as the militaries of foreign countries -- nice work guys.

Dave saw the water flying past the lens looking as good as an Imax theatre nature film. As the SUAV swept down from its cruising altitude the rolling waves and frothing choppy wallowing lake came more into focus. A leafless tree void of life had fallen into the dark foaming water and heaved and tossed in the rising swell. The drone hovered as the sandy shoreline below started to slide into the rough dark water. Dave noticed a sea of nearly four foot tall black satin roses swaying in the harsh wind. -- had to be more than an acre of them. He hadn't ever seen black roses. In fact, almost no one had. As he was watching the rhythm of the soft black petals in this beautiful garden so full of flowers, a section of land at least one hundred feet square simply sunk into the lake. The water quickly poured over the position formerly held by the strange flowers.

"Jesus Christ," Dave said aloud for the second time in the last five minutes and the second time in the last ten years. Not his favorite expletive. He shook his head. He was feeling a bit out of sorts after viewing that destruction. And the roses. Those roses were beautiful and creepy. He put the phone back to his ear. "Mike, that is an amazing video. What the hell is going on there? Mike. Mike, are you there?"

But Mike wasn't there. In fact if you had to guess where Mike was at that moment, and you guessed at the bottom of Black Lake, you would be very close. In fact, along with General Dave Archers right hand man and all of his guardsmen, Chris Pulmer the hydrologist, the vulcanologists and their fancy depth gauge, five hundred and sixteen souls from Smith

Center, Lebanon, and Black Lake Kansas, Dan's Lake house, and the Oak Bar --- was the oxidized iron statue of William Joseph Smith.

The Great Chilean earthquake from May 22, 1960, was the most powerful earthquake to date registering a 9.6 on the moment magnitude scale. The Black Lake quake recorded a 12.0. The exact center of the United States became the epicenter of this most historic disaster. The floor of the deepest lake in the world had liquified into quicksand and collapsed, dropping its contents fifteen thousand feet to the crust of the earth in just under a minute. The incredible speed of this devastation caused the sides of the lake to immediately crumble and the earth to break and give way for fifty miles in all directions. Men, women, children, land, and beast slid into the hole in the earth bore by lucifer a millennia ago. The end was nigh.

CHAPTER 56

Lance Harvey got his crew moving south and fast. When that military guy came around yelling about an evacuation and the word that the lake was collapsing, they hauled ass. KAKE station manager made the call to broadcast emergency updates on the hour the day before and had sent relief. The orders to move all personnel within a two mile stretch from Black Lake to Lebanon was enough for Lance. He was tired of this back woods spithole anyway. A second camera crew had arrived in Lebanon in a forty foot Winnebago camper and parked in an empty field at Maple and Kansas Avenue behind the post office, setting up a temporary outpost of the television station. Lance was happy to have a selection of sport coats and fresh underwear after three days of monitoring the strange events. He was only in Lebanon long enough to let the no pressure lukewarm water run over him in the campers two by two plastic shower and change into a pink blazer and white polo chinos before turning onto highway 181.

"Sandwich, Lance?" Doug the cameraman called from the back captain's chair of the KAKE Ford Econoline van, nicely apportioned with a bed in the back and a 32 inch flat screen LCD. Not a bad vehicle for a trip if you have to drive.

"Thanks," Lance replied reaching back from the passenger seat. "You have turkey in there?"

"Yeah." Doug had purchased a selection at the small grocery in Lebanon adjacent to the post office and field the Winnebago had chosen for its overnight campsite.

"And those red Doritos and one of those Black Lake Mocha frap iced coffees. Thanks." Lance had his pink jacket laying in the back on the bed above his shoes and socks. He was going to decompress a bit on the three hour trip back to Wichita.

"What the hell do you think all that is back there, Lance?" Brian Jones asked. Brian was Lance's producer, assistant, friend -- had been for the last year or so.

"Weird. I heard the lake was boiling. All the fish were dead. Sounds like the apocalypse," Lance quipped.

Brian turned right leaving highway 24 and hit the accelerator onto 81 highway / Interstate 135 south. "Hell of a gift for our newest billionaire, he just got handed that gorgeous lake house out here in the country. Peaceful and private. Must have been a nice break from Dallas. Now it's all fucked up with whatever the hell this is."

"Yeah. Must be rough. He can go buy another ten tomorrow. He was not there anyway. I think he is back in Dallas. Probably does not even plan on moving up here to Gods country," Lance replied.

"No, I read he has to live here. In fact he has to live in that house."

"I heard that too. But the guy owns half of the state and a dozen companies. He can fly in and out at will. They showed a picture of his other house in Dallas on the ten o'clock news. Don't you watch our own stuff?" Lance asked as he dropped the last half of the Nacho Cheese Doritos in the community trash bag along with the empty Black Lake coffee bottle.

"Hell no. I get enough news watching you sound out the big words every day. The last thing I want to do is subject myself to more torture at night. I don't even turn on the television most nights," Brian said.

"Stop in Salina. I need find some facilities etcetera."

"Prob another half hour," Brian said.

"Ok. Wake me up, I'm going to catch a quick nap," Lance said as he reclined the plush leather seat.

As Brian pulled off of 135 onto Crawford Street he headed towards the Ambassador Hotel. They stayed there May of last year when they covered the twin Bengal tigers presented at the Rolling Hills Wildlife Adventure. Not a bad place with strong drinks. Might have to get a Mojito or ten tonight, he thought. Before the hotel came into view the ground began to shake. The customized conversion van bounced and tossed wildly from side to side. Brian rang the right rear tire off the curb and knocked Lances noggin off the side window.

"What the Fuck, Brian," Lance exclaimed as the van slammed to a stop. But the earth was still shaking like a leaf on a tree.

"Earthquake!" Brian yelled. Brian was from California. He knew what an earthquake was. Hell, he cut his teeth right out of college in the Big One in Oakland-- the World Series earthquake. He was actually in Candlestick Park with sixty two thousand fellow baseball fans gathered to see the San Francisco Giants play the Oakland Athletics in Game 3. Damage from the roughly 15-second quake was widespread but heaviest in Santa Cruz where buildings collapsed and cars on overpasses dropped to their deaths. The earthquake killed sixty-three people and injured more than 3,000 with $7.5 billion in damages. It became the first major earthquake in the United States that was broadcast live on national television. The collapse of a section of the double-deck Nimitz Freeway in Oakland was the site of the single largest number of casualties for the event, but the collapse of man-made structures and other related accidents contributed to casualties occurring in San Francisco, Los Altos, and Santa Cruz. Luckily, Brian was not one of them but sadly knew a number of those not so fortunate.

The quake continued for far too long. Lance and Doug were screaming. Cars around them were crashing. A red convertible struck a metal light pole, and it dropped across the east bound lanes. Stop lights rocked back and forth fitfully. The sidewalk beside the van split and water shot out in a stream thirty feet high falling on the windshield and obscuring the chaotic scene. A full two minutes passed before the quake subsided.

"Holy shit," Brian said.

"What was that?" Lance asked.

"That was a fucking monster earthquake." Brian responded opening the driver's door and climbing out, closely followed by Lance and Doug. Water was still falling from the broken water main, and the newsmen were getting drenched. They barely noticed. Their worlds were upside down. From the direction of Black Lake came a deafening roar. Despite the noon day sun a darkness seemed to be growing. They stood speechless staring in the direction of the noise.

Lance and his crew got on the road to Wichita just in time to spare themselves instant vaporization. Salina Kansas was one hundred miles from where they woke that morning. As they looked towards the north, even though they could not know that a chasm had opened in the earth one hundred miles wide and five miles deep reaching from Dan's cabin to the Kansas Colorado border, they could feel the magnitude of the destruction. As they stared at the sky a charcoal grey cloud filling the sky and a blood red glow reaching up from the horizon, the lava from the earth's crust blew forth and filled in the giant hole to create an inland sea of boiling lava and fire.

Black Lake.

CHAPTER 57

The limo pulled into the small airport and flew past a number of buildings to the Stone hanger at the far east side of the tarmac. They pulled in through the big doors and stopped immediately beside the jet..

They were greeted by one of the two pilots and two flight attendants.

"Mr. Stone, I am Mark Mason, your pilot. Scott Johnson is my co-pilot and is in the cockpit running through the preflight. If you are ready we have clearance. We are flying in your Gulfstream G650ER long range, high speed. We will be in Dallas in 60 minutes. Balls out as I understand it. "

"And Mr. Stone, I'm Samantha. I will be your personal attendant for the flight to Dallas," She smiled. Capped teeth, tall, blonde, soft. They hurried into the jet.

"And I am Judy, Mr. Stone," the other one called out as they pushed through the door. She was different. Mouse brown short hair, athletic, capable looking. "That's good we might need all the capable crew we can muster - shit is hitting the fan," Dan thought.

Both wore short tennis skirts. Very tight sleeveless tops-- definitely would not fly past HR in American Airlines. But Stone girls had different requirements and values.

"Let's get rolling," Dan said.

Lucas climbed in. Samantha and Judy gave Lucas a second look as he was still rather battered and bruised.

"This is Lucas. He is a priest and will be needing alcohol and some tender loving care from one of you. Judy, I think. Got his ass kicked yesterday and still knitting himself together." Dan and the entourage walked into the main area of the jet.

"There are four living areas Mr. Stone," Samantha directed us to our own areas. "We thought you would both like to relax and prepare for your meeting." Each section had a couch and a recliner.

"The kitchen has quite a selection. If you want food or drink."

They sat in plush white leather recliners. Dan extended his footrest and closed his eyes.

"Would you like a drink Mr. Stone?"

"Yes, how about a full glass of bourbon. And pour the same for Lucas there. He is a just learning how to damage his liver and live life outside of the convent."

The takeoff was faster than anything Dan had ever experienced. Top gun-esque.

"Damn that was a blast off Preacher," Dan yelled towards the back of the plane where he had disappeared with Judy.

Samantha came back with a hot cup of coffee and Dan's hearty glass of bourbon. She pulled the curtain and sat back on the couch.

"If you would like anything at all just tell me and I will jump up. We will be in Dallas pretty fast so here I am," she smiled.

Dan could tell she was a giver. But he just wanted to get some coffee in him, it had been far too long.

"Your excellent company is perfect Samantha. And some flower. Any weed on the plane?"

"No Mr. Stone." She leaned forward with a grin and handed him the cup. Tempting and hoping for some attention before the flight was over. The plane leveled off and the captain's voice came over the speaker overhead.

"Mr. Stone, it appears we have an issue on the ground in Wichita that I think we all need to check out. With your permission I'm going to make a fast pass around Wichita before we head south."

"Go ahead and do your thing, just get us to Dallas" Dan said aloud to the voice. Dan decided to slam his bourbon down first as a result of that disconcerting pilot call.

"I'm a little freaked out, Samantha."

She crawled off the couch and leaned over him to look out the starboard portal, chest to chest. The pilot began to bank hard right. Dan draped his arm across her back and gripped a round hip to help her stabilize and cradling her.

"Jesus Christ Pilot. I guess he is in a hurry to get turned around."

"Oh my God!" Samantha moaned and slid off Dan's lap to get closer to the window. Dan followed. They were looking at a heavy dark cloud just past the airport.

The pilot came on again. "Buckle up everyone we might hit some turbulence with whatever this is." As he said it a strong gust buffeted the small sleek aircraft.

Dan missed a heartbeat somewhere in there and Samantha did a fast inhale and squeal and jumped back into her seat. "Buckle up Mr. Stone. Quickly."

The plane began a fast descent. The pilot came on again. "Mr. Stone, Wichita is calling us back. There appears to be a real issue down there. We should be on the ground in a few minutes."

As they progressed towards the airport Dan saw in the distance water where water should not have been. Dan saw a building crumble and drop off the back.

"It's an earthquake!" Judy yelled.

It's Black Lake.

"Stay calm everyone. We will need to circle for a bit while everything settles down there." Pilot said over the loudspeaker.

"Fuck that, Pilot!" Dan yelled out. Turn your ass to Dallas and hit it."

Silence for a few pregnant seconds. "Yes, sir! Everyone buckle up we are going to move out of here fast." The plane began to climb hard and then another very hard bank right and Dan tightened his grip on Samantha. She buried her head in his neck as the jet engines ramped up, terrified. The G forces stuck the passengers to their seats. "Sir, I am directly in violation of FAA, but we will be in Dallas in record time. This aircraft does just shy of Mach1."

"Hell yes Pilot. Let's get the fuck out of Dodge," Dan yelled.

I hope Dallas is there when we get there, Dan thought.

As the plane banked one final time Dan saw the airport runway fall into the ground and blood began to pour from the pit. Lava in Wichita, Kansas. The airport was sinking. They watched as the jet climbed. In a matter of moments the airport was no more. The small plane was rocking back and forth violently with turbulence.

The pilot came on. "Hang on everyone this is going to be rough. I have to get above the heat coming off the ground and this storm or whatever the hell it is. I don't know what is going on, but we are going to run away from it. Looks like the entire city is gone."

A few minutes later they were at rocket cruising speed and altitude. Dan and Samantha untangled and got out of the plush leather recliners. Both were shaking.

"Let's get some more booze and check on the other two, Samantha." Dan drank the last of his cup of coffee of which he had miraculously not spilled a drop. They walked to the back of the plane where Lucas and Judy were in the rear compartment, stopping at the shiny stainless steel kitchen. Dan grabbed the bottle of Jack Daniels Black Label.

The pilot came out of the cockpit and quickly walked to the passengers. He was white as a sheet. Obviously scared. "Mr. Stone. It appears the ground beneath us is sinking into the earth as we travel. We are just keeping ahead of it. Look out the window." He motioned to the small round portal and Dan pushed his face close to the glass so he could get a good view of the ground.

It's Black Lake Dan. It's chasing you down. You can't get away that easily..

It was William Josephs voice in Dan's head. "That bastard is haunting me," Dan thought.

"Jesus." Dan could see the edge of the world below. The nothingness of an immense chasm stretching into the earth.

"If it continues it will be in front of us soon. There is a tremendous heat coming from it and it is pushing us along. We are exceeding maximum safe velocity now. If it gets in front it will push us up and perhaps ignite us," the pilot said.

"Well give it some more and start praying," Dan said. "Preacher? We could use some help here."

"Dan, it's Satan," Lucas said pulling the curtain open. "It's his time. He is emerging."

The pilot and Samantha stared at him.

Dan did not respond. Hell after all that Dan had been through he had no response. Dan could hear William Joseph laughing and see his snow white hair blowing behind him in the wind coming off Black Lake.

"I know it is Preacher. For the first time in my life I God damned well know it is."

CHAPTER 58

Black Lake consumed everything around the cabin. Directly below, pressure drove lava upwards forming a plateau and sparing the cabin.

The lava boiled the water into steam and the ground fell into the superheated void and was replaced with a vacuum. The vacuum pulled the lava up from the core of the earth. Water poured from the underground sea and the hot black water rose to the surface. In a matter of hours the tera firm of the state of Kansas was ten thousand feet below sea level replaced with a cauldron of coal black water.

The boiling inland sea grew west to the Rockies, east to the Mississippi, north to Minnesota, and south to the Arbuckle mountains of Oklahoma. Everything sank into the dark pit. Nothing survived. No wildlife. No vegetation. No humans. No memory of the civilization that had fallen into the earth.

In the center of the giant Black Lake with the shoreline hundreds of miles away in any direction remained the cabin. The sea calmed. The front door opened. A tall, thin handsome black skinned man walked onto the porch and sat down on the swing. Surveying his work and breathing in the acrid air seeing the surface of the earth for the first time. He smiled.

CHAPTER 59

The heavens were quiet, the kind of stillness that only preceded monumental change. The decision had been weighed carefully, yet the finality of it was stark. It would be a one-way journey—no retreat, no second chances. A war from heaven to earth would begin.

Gabriel stood at the edge of the radiant throne, his head bowed, his gleaming wings still. He heard the command as a whisper, though it reverberated through the heavens with the weight of eternity.

"Gabriel. Send the angels."

Gabriel hesitated for the briefest of moments, a rarity for the archangel of God's messengers. "Sir?" It wasn't defiance; Gabriel never questioned orders. But even he understood the gravity of those three words.

Michael, the archangel of war, paced across the pearl-inlaid floor, his hand resting on the hilt of his sword. He had been waiting for this moment, though even he had hoped it wouldn't come. "Do it," Michael said, his voice like a rumble of thunder. "Send them all. Encircle the earth. Let him see. Dan must see the Truth."

Gabriel lifted his gaze, his heart heavy, yet resolute. He extended his hand, and the heavens flared with light. Across the celestial expanse, battalions of angels stirred, their golden armor glinting in the eternal glow. The air quivered with the sound of a thousand wings unfurling in unison.

"It will be done," Gabriel said, his voice carrying both obedience and lament.

As the angelic host descended, the earth below began to tremble, its skies breaking apart with light and fury.

Michael prayed Dan would see the Truth.

CHAPTER 60

The destruction kept pace with the gulf stream. Nearly to Texas the edge became clear and started to form some distance behind the travelers. After seeing Oklahoma City and the souls therein collapse into the abyss the Arbuckle mountains appeared to stop or slow the progression.

"Ok go to Mexico or South America or fucking Australia."

The pilot stated "I'm going to turn to the west and see how far this goes. We are going to try to land in Albuquerque. We can regroup and get fuel. We planned on a short run to Dallas, and I can't reach anyone on the radio. I think the interference from the volcanic ash is blocking everything out. But I just don't know. We are in the middle of a cataclysmic event. I can't risk Dallas not being there when we have to land."

They watched from the portals as the jet banked right at the Red River separating Oklahoma and Texas. The shoreline of the new sea was visible as far as they could see from the right side of the plane. The sky was broiling dark, swirling blood red filled with soot; long distance views were obscured.

What they could not see—and did not know—was that the sea stretched to the west, bordered by towering cliffs rising five to ten thousand feet into the air. These jagged peaks marked the edge of the tectonic plate that had collapsed, obliterating Denver and much of the surrounding region. The Royal Gorge Bridge, once a marvel Dan had gazed over, now lay submerged beneath the same dark waters that surrounded his cabin.

At the point where the southern and western shores converged stood Groom, Texas, its skyline punctuated by the stark white cross towering above the desolation—a solitary marker of human existence in the face of the overwhelming destruction.

# # #

"Buckle up everyone we are landing fast in Amarillo. The engines are choking out on the methane and ash. We will be fine but it's time to get us on the ground. We have radio contact again, so we know they are there."

Ok Texas again. Samantha buckled into the seat across from Dan. At least if he was going to die he was going to die looking at the legs of an excellent specimen and with a drink in his hand, he smiled.

The landing was fast and rough like diving for an aircraft carrier; forty thousand feet to zero in record time. Dan's stomach was still in the ionosphere somewhere when they were safely on the ground. They all let out a breath they had been collectively holding for the last 10 minutes.

Samantha unbuckled and jumped on Dan's lap kissing him and pressing her mouth on his. "Sorry, I'm just glad to be alive," she breathed.

"It's good. But let's get off this plane."

She unbuckled Dan's seatbelt and climbed off. She walked to the hatch and pulled up on the release lever. Dan followed. The pilot was out of the cockpit. Lucas and Judy followed silently.

When the light flooded the cabin she dropped the walkway stairs and Dan led the way out of the aircraft and onto terra firma. The sky was black and grey. Soot was falling like dirty grey snow. The air was cold but there was a hot wind swirling the ash making every clear breath precious. Dan pulled his tank top up over his mouth and nose.

"Let's get inside. This is crazy." Dan sucked in a semi filtered breath and ran for the cover of the terminal building. The dog was first up the stairs, the group followed and arrived officially in Amarillo Texas. They were met with chaos and panic as no one had any idea what was going on. The television and radio networks were offline. No internet. No cell phones. A large hole had been punched in the center of the country. The airport was running on its generators. The electrical infrastructure was in ruins.

Walking towards them was a group of men led by Dan's ever faithful man servant, Tom Stark.

"Tom, what the hell? How did you get here?"

"Dan, it is time." The group converged on Dan, and he saw Tom was handing him something shiny. Dan reached for it and Tom stuck a needle in his wrist. The world was going dark fast. Dan saw the preacher get stuck in the side of his neck with a similar hypo as the tunnel closed and blackness enveloped him.

CHAPTER 61

As Dan lost consciousness the nightmare scene took over. The water enveloped Dan as it had in previous episodes in Black Lake but was somehow different. The sides of a vertical tunnel were visible through the murky water and Dan noticed the jagged contours of the walls. The water was not scalding him, in fact it seemed to be body temperature - almost soothing. As Dan flew down the rocky tube, he became extremely passive. Dan felt groggy as though he were feeling Tom's strong sedative even in this dream state, forbidding any exertion whatsoever. Dan closed his eyes. Just a nap. A little nap and I'll wake up. It's all a dream, Dan.

A peaceful sleep with no nightmares. Dan could feel the warm sunshine on his face. He could smell the sweet black roses and feel his Egyptian cotton sheets. Dan opened his eyes but he was not in his California king sized bed. He sat up and spun himself to the edge of the bed and placed his feet flat on the cold slats. He was in the cabin.

Beside the bed in a wooden chair was the handsome black man from his dreams. His eyes were black, his hair looked soft as cotton and his skin was a perfect shade of dark red-brown. He wore a white button down shirt with gleaming gold cuff links and starched black pants.

"Hello Dan," he said.

"Hello."

"Dan your time has come. It is time for you to lead our people."

"How did I get to the cabin," Dan asked still disoriented.

"Follow me," the handsome man stood and walked to the door of the cabin.

Dan stood and followed.

"Where exactly are we?"

"This is the underworld, Dan."

"I never knew this existed."

"Well, not many people do until they have died. This is the waiting area for the afterlife."

"Am I dead?"

"No. You are waiting."

"For what?"

"For the afterlife."

The man opened the door and the two walked onto the porch. Dan leaned on the cedar railing and peered over. The dark lake was far below and could be seen in all directions. The boiling water tossed and spewed fire.

"Are we in Black Lake?"

"In a manner of speaking yes we are still in Black Lake. In your cabin. On your Lake."

"Everything is gone."

"Yes, it's a new world Dan. Your world."

"My world?" Dan asked.

"You are now the king of the earth."

"Here. Sit down," he said motioning to a pair of rocking chairs. "You need to know a few things, Dan."

Dan sat willingly and listened.

Dan sat silently pondering and looking across the horizon at the never ending lake of fire.

"You see, I have been awaiting your birth for quite some time. You must lead the faithful out into the world. It is time for the expansion. The end draws near."

"Me? Why am I to be the one to lead them?"

"You have been sent. It is your destiny, Dan."

Dan pondered some more. "End of what?"

"The end of His reign. Now it's time for my reign. And yours."

"Why would I want to try to bring about the end of the world?"

He laughed again. "You won't be ending the world. When the world becomes full of evil, God will end His influence on the world. His grand experiment of good versus evil. Pondering man's true self. He will concede to me and you will be my earthly representative."

"Revelations. You are Satan. I remember how that story ends. Doesn't God win?"

"No," he said, his face darkening and his eyes flashing red. "That book of lies is what He has shoved down everyone's throats."

"I don't want to be in charge of the underworld," Dan said.

"Dan, this is not a choice. You are to be king."

"King?'

"Yes, king not of the underworld but the surface world -- of the earth. You will expand the boundaries of Black Lake to the world. The judgement of mankind is nigh and you will reign for one thousand years answering only to me. It is the prize."

"You mean the anti-Christ."

"Yes. That is who you are, Dan Stone."

"Dan, you are the representative of the common man. In fact, you are perhaps the best example of the average guy on the face of the earth. Everyone has thousands of critical choices to make in life, good vs. evil. The good choice or the evil choice isn't always easily seen. It is subtle. That is why you were chosen. Your score."

"Like a game?" Dan asked.

"Yes, exactly. We keep score. Now at the end we know most make excuses for evil behavior and convincing themselves that the darkness being pushed into their soul is really light. You humans make excuses for every evil action with feeble reasoning. You believe in the afterlife but ignore Gods commandments and live only for yourselves. The basic ordinary man simply ignores God."

"I don't ignore God."

Satan laughed. "You are the perfect man. You always choose you. Recall killing your friends and my visit when you were just getting started as a man?"

"I don't even remember doing that."

"But you did. And deep in your heart you know it was you. You knew it then and you know it now. Accept it. I gave you a choice then and you took it."

"No one gave me a choice."

"Sure we did. God gave you the choice to follow me right then on your birth to manhood. There is nothing wrong with being evil. You are simply on the other side of the fence from God. On the good side," he laughed.

"I can't be."

"You are. The time for choice is done. You are mine. Think of the riches. I gave you that. Black Lake. My black roses. Your power. It's no accident you are in line to lead the world at the United Nations Dan."

"I did all of that," Dan protested.

"Don't be ridiculous," Satan darkened. "I did it. You were there for the ride. Dan, I love what you have done with my gifts. You are my son. You will be my earthly self."

Dan stared at the devil. He enjoyed the power. He enjoyed this life. He was feeding the hungry. The world adored him. Everyone was so much smarted and healthier now that Dan Stone was in control. "What would you have me do?"

"Just live, Dan. You will know what to do. Just be yourself and lead our people. Follow my orders as I give them to you just as you have been doing," he smiled and was quickly returning to the congenial host.

"What if I refuse? Just leave and take my chances?"

Satan stood and stared into Dan's eyes. "If you refuse me, you will die and we will meet again below Black Lake as before. But your suffering will never end."

Satan's face was beet red, and his eyes a coal black. Horns began to grow from his head and fangs appeared on either side of his lips. Satan reached forward and grabbed Dan around the neck with a clawed hand. Lifting him high in the air and bouncing his head off the rustic cedar shiplap ceiling of the porch he pulled Dan to the edge of the cabin suspending him over the boiling lake far below.

"You may leave, Dan Stone. You will choose today and accept your destiny," Satan growled and hurled Dan off the porch.

Falling to the water Dan closed his eyes and prayed "Dear God, help me, "Dan cried out his voice cracking.

Dan landed softly. Opening his eyes he could see green grass and tall trees swaying in a gentle wind. Blue sky and white clouds. A small serene lake splashed quietly at the base of a tall mountain jutting from the earth.

Dan stood in the pasture and walked to a smooth cave entrance carved in the side of a granite wall of the mountain. He entered the blackness. It was cold and damp inside and smelled like sweet honey. Dan ran one hand along the rough rock wall, so he didn't fall down and patted the air in front of him with the other. The cave was as dark as a tomb.

"Dan, this is your judgement day." Lucas' voice boomed and echoed throughout the cave.

Dan broke into a run thinking only of getting out of this dark dank tunnel. The blackness was closing in on him.

Is God listening? Could he really be involved in his life. Watching. Waiting. Could he really be keeping track of everything everyone on earth ever did during their entire lives? Get ahold of yourself Dan. It's just another nightmare. I can't wait for this trip to be over. No more lake water, Dan thought. Dan pictured his living room with all of his mind in hopes of waking up and returning from this bizarre hallucination. Dan saw a dim light off in the distance and ran towards it trying to ignore the echoing voice.

Lucas booming voice reverberated off the walls. "You must ask God for his forgiveness. Throw yourself on His mercy."

Dan ran on. The light was getting larger and brighter, and Dan could make out the vague outlines of the cave walls.

"Pray to Jesus and let him take your life, Dan," Lucas begged.

The light was only a few hundred feet away. Dan ran as fast as he could and soon he was there. Dan stopped. Blocking the door in front of him stood Lucas dressed in a clean white robe. The light had dimmed considerably but was still radiating from his body. He was glowing with an iridescent white light. A huge eight foot wooden cross full of holes like wormwood leaned against his body.

"Dan, you must not believe a word the dark one says. He will tell you anything to get your soul. He is the father of lies," Lucas said.

"How do we get out of here Lucas?"

"We cannot. It is our time to die, Dan. You must throw yourself on the mercy of the living God. He will hear you my brother."

"Let's get out of this cave Lucas."

"If you exit without accepting Jesus as your savior and ignore God again Dan all is lost. You will be turning your back on Him for the final time," Lucas beseeched him.

"I can change. I can turn it around and still live, Lucas. Let's get out of here," Dan said pushing past.

"Dan, Every knee shall bow, You must choose right now. This is your fork in the road. Choose Heaven or hell."

"He said I could rule the earth."

"You must not turn your back on God. If you take the path of Satan you are choosing death and God will never again hear your prayers. If you choose the path of God you will die but be given eternal life. Ask for his mercy and grace, Dan. Ask for forgiveness. He will give it."

"He said God would never let me into Heaven. God won't forgive me. I'm too far gone, Preacher."

"These are his lies Dan. Ask for mercy. Beg for his grace. If you truly repent you will be forgiven. He is about grace. He will give you this unearned favor. You merely have to ask Him for it. Dan, please Pray. Now!"

"I don't want to die."

"You must die in order to live, Dan."

"I don't want to die," Dan screamed. Dan ran through the cave entrance into the light. His legs moved him along faster and faster down the blindingly bright white corridor. Dan ran like a madman trying to escape a lynch mob. The whiteness enveloped him, and Dan could see nothing.

Dan could hear nothing. Dan could feel nothing. Dan was not running anymore. Dan was floating, flying. Lucas's voice echoed once again.

"Look to God, Dan," he boomed.

Dan could hear a child crying. Then a multitude crying and wailing. The wormwood cross that was leaning against Lucas appeared in front of him and Dan heard Lucas' voice sobbing and begging.

"Take the cross, Dan. Please! Just grab it and hold on tight. Spare the world the agony!"

Dan fell from the air at the base of the ragged cross. The cross grew hundreds of feet in the air. He clutched at the base. A few feet to the left were a small flight of stone stairs carved into the earth.

"Take the cross, Dan! Save your soul!"

Dan clamored to his feet and leaped up the stairs two at a time. Dan burst through the door and fell into the warm black water.

The water closed in around him as the voices faded into the distance. Dan was gasping for air as the dark water went down his throat and into his lungs. It was not the pleasant experience of the last time nor the painful experiences of the past. Dan was terrified. Dan was drowning. Dan had turned away from God and he was going to drown him as punishment.

Dan had failed the test. His lungs ached from the lack of oxygen and his vision was narrowing. His mind and body screamed for him to breathe. The darkness crept in from the corners of his eyes. Dan felt a hand squeezing the back of his neck, thin claw like fingers cutting into his flesh. The hand jerked Dan out of the water and air rushed into his lungs. Dan coughed and gagged as he was pulled from the water. The colors of the earth were slowly coming back to his vision.

Dan was kneeling on the ground, dressed in a heavy black robe. Dan looked up into the faces of William Jospeh, Ezra, Bob, Tom, Stephanie and Victor. A multitude of hands helped him to his feet. Hundreds of people surrounded them. Dan realized he was standing beneath the giant cross of Groom Texas at the edge of the boiling inland sea formerly known as Black Lake. The giant white cross had turned black as though all the good positive parts had been burned to cinder. The words of Dan's nightmare vision returned to him:

My God, I think it was some sort of a baptism.

Yes. Dan's baptism. Throngs of people knelt prostrate before him their foreheads pressed against the ground. The power pulsating within him was indescribable.

There was still a trace of Dan Stone in the man standing before the mass of people. But only a trace and Dan could feel the old man drifting away like a dream lost in the fog of the morning light. A new man was in control now. "God forgive me," Dan prayed.

In that instant, the Angel Gabriel lifted his gaze, his heart heavy yet resolute. He extended his hand, and the heavens flared with blinding light. Across the celestial expanse, battalions of angels stirred, their golden armor glinting with an ethereal brilliance. The air quivered with the sounds of mourning and thousands of wings unfurling in unison, a divine army ready to descend.

In Black Lake, Satan stepped to the edge of the cabin's porch, a smile broadening across his face, his shadow stretching unnaturally against the darkened landscape and boiling sea.

At the base of the towering black cross in Groom, Texas, Dan Stone stood tall, his silhouette framed by the eerie glow of the night. He stretched his arms high into the air, his voice carrying with an unearthly resonance.

"Rise, my children," he commanded.

Across the horizon, a ripple spread, a deafening call that reached the edges of the world. The ground quaked, rivers boiled, and the air crackled with thunder and lightning. Dan stood unmoving, triumphant. The age of man had ended. A new reign had begun.

Prepare. 2026: WORMWOOD II: Rise My Children.

www.ingramcontent.com/pod-product-compliance
Lightning Source LLC
Chambersburg PA
CBHW020502020726
47493CB00001B/137